Gwendolyn Fader
January 30, 1999
Thank You God!

MURDER IN THE SMOKEHOUSE

MURDER
IN THE
SMOKEHOUSE

Amy Myers

St. Martin's Press ⋈ New York

Library of Congress Cataloging-in-Publication Data

Myers, Amy.
    Murder in the smokehouse : an Auguste Didier
whodunit / Amy Myers.
        p.   cm.
    ISBN 0-312-15598-0
    I. Title.
PR6063.Y38M872   1997
823'.914—dc21   97-12327
                                                  CIP

First published in Great Britain by Headline Book
Publishing, a division of Hodder Headline PLC

First U.S. Edition: August 1997

10   9   8   7   6   5   4   3   2   1

For Marion and Ned
with love and thanks

AUTHOR'S NOTE

I owe an enormous debt to my friends Ned and Marion Binks who were not only the means of my getting to know and love Settle and Yorkshire but uncomplainingly traipsed through rain and snow in search of a suitable location for Tabor Hall. The geography of Malham has been slightly adapted to accommodate it.

The title for this novel sprang from a visit to Levens Hall in Lancashire when I saw their delightful smokehouse for the noxious weed, and I am grateful to Levens Heritage for permission to borrow their usage of this word. Levens Hall has no other resemblance to the Tabor Hall of this novel, nor does Priscilla Tabor's smokehouse resemble theirs.

Dot Lumley my agent and Jane Morpeth my editor have as usual been the rocks of expertise and judgement on which I have depended and I am most grateful to them.

PROLOGUE

Deepest black is a great leveller. Only the curious shape inflicted by the newly fashionable straight-fronted corsets at first distinguished the guests. Closer inspection might have revealed a difference in the fit of the gentlemen's deep-black velvet court attire and mere cloth morning suits, and between their ladies' black crepe and humbler silk. But then no one, after the finest fourteen-course luncheon the Marlborough House kitchens and cellars could provide, was greatly interested in closer inspection. This was, after all, a wedding.

'Ah, Auguste.'

If Auguste Didier had needed confirmation that the dizzy experience he had just undergone was fact, His Majesty King Edward VII's greeting, somewhat overhearty, would have supplied it. It was not every day that a commoner, a chef at that, married into even the outer purlieus of the royal family.

'Your Majesty?' Auguste bowed.

The King relaxed. The fellow still knew his place. Uneasily he recalled how he had been forced to regal compromise in their first conflict. After he had generously granted permission to Tatiana to wed the fellow, he had naturally expected them to wait a few years until the court should be out of mourning for Mama. It had politely been made clear to him that waiting was not on this cook's menu. Auguste had

1

compromised with a wedding in July, shortly before deepest mourning changed to half-mourning, whether His Majesty liked it or not. He didn't, actually. A Black Wedding meant no dancing, and, since the wedding breakfast would have to be held at Marlborough House, that meant no Alice Keppel or any other form of light relief.

Moreover, although His Majesty was aware that this chef had rendered him sterling service in the past, and not just in the form of perfectly cooked mutton chops, his royal spurs had yet to be won. He had no intention of awarding them at this time. He smiled benignly at his newly acquired remote relation.

'Excellent sermon, eh?'

Auguste could remember little of the proceedings in St James's Palace, save arriving in the Presence Chamber and being shown the initials of Henry VIII and Anne Boleyn by a compassionate flunkey, hoping to divert him after seeing his white face. Auguste had merely meditated on whether Anne's unkind fate on marrying into the royal family might yet be his own for his temerity in marrying in the very chapel in which the late Queen and her beloved Albert had wed. The rest was a blur.

'I don't remember, sir,' he bravely confessed.

The King roared. 'Quite understandable,' he beamed, relieved that after all Auguste might be human as well as a chef.

Emboldened, Auguste plunged into folly. 'I understand we shall be meeting at Tabor Hall in September, sir.'

His Majesty frowned. Unfortunately for Auguste, Tabor Hall conjured up unpleasant thoughts.

'Quite a change, eh? You won't be cooking this time, or ever again,' he barked.

Auguste blinked. Did he hear aright?

'Not now,' the King pointed out, surprised that it was necessary to do so. 'It wouldn't do.'

Auguste met his monarch's eye squarely. 'I can't promise that, sir.'

His Majesty's face darkened. Then he remembered this was a wedding, and time to be jovial. He noticed that inspector fellow from Scotland Yard whom Auguste had insisted on inviting and it jogged his memory.

'No more murder then. Understood?'

Here Auguste was in full agreement. He nodded. 'Perfectly, sir.'

Chapter One

Country house visiting had many drawbacks, Auguste reflected crossly, as he fidgeted outside Settle railway station. One of them was the Midland railway. Two changes of train and the necessity of superintending thirty items of luggage had rendered the whole idea of Yorkshire even more depressing. It was dismal, cold and wet and the grey stone around them did little to help.

Nor did the sight of Tatiana's glowing face as her tall figure, clad in the dark purple zibeline that mourning etiquette now graciously permitted, strode to the pile of trunks and miraculously brought order to chaos.

'*Alors*, Auguste, you look like the bridegroom whose wine was turned into water.'

'Obviously he lived in Yorkshire,' Auguste retorted, as a large raindrop evaded hat and ulster and slid triumphantly down his neck.

'Don't you like rain?' Tatiana asked surprised, as she looked round with interest at this new territory which bore little resemblance to her native Paris.

'No. Nor do I like *guns*,' Auguste told her back succinctly, as she whirled round to remove a hat box from over-close proximity to the oysters. Their presence indicated that the Tabor Hall staff had other missions in Settle besides the conveyance of the Didiers. 'And I *do* like cooking. The life of a gentleman, it seems,

5

forbids me to do what I like and orders me to do the other.'

'It is only for four days,' Tatiana told him regretfully, as at last he was able to hand her into the Tabor carriage. 'Four days *here*.' Her eyes lit up with the enthusiasm of a Cortez surveying the Pacific.

An eternity! Auguste reflected on the prospect ahead. Friday 27 to Monday 30 September to be spent at Tabor Hall, which was hidden somewhere in those wild dark hills outlined menacingly against the overcast sky. The gathering was to celebrate the engagement of the Honourable Miss Victoria Tabor to Tatiana's cousin, Alexander Tully-Rich. Tatiana seemed to be related to most of the Almanack de Gotha. The invitation had sounded so innocuous when Tatiana had first told him of it. Foreboding had struck on learning that the King would be present, for Auguste was only too aware that this visit could be a trial of his suitability for the honour of being termed a gentleman. A master chef, albeit one who had been trained by Monsieur Escoffier himself, could naturally not have automatic entrée to such exalted status. Not in England.

He reflected with some satisfaction on his victory in the Battle of the Kitchen with His Majesty – or, if he were honest, a draw. Subtly he had reminded His Majesty of the ortolans braised in Armagnac, of the *poularde Derby* and the numerous other gastronomic treats he had prepared for him in the past. The King had shrewdly taken the point. Auguste might continue to cook for charity, he might superintend banquets in the homes of friends, and he *must* cook when the King was to be present. He could do, he gathered, whatever he bally well liked when abroad, and safely out of His Britannic Majesty's realms.

It wasn't much, but it was something.

'I could say I want you by my side,' Tatiana said hopefully, 'then you would not have to shoot.'

'That is no excuse,' Auguste said hollowly. 'No English gentleman would remain with his wife in preference to shooting.'

'You are only a half-English gentleman,' Tatiana reminded him. 'Very well, consider the game pies you will produce.'

Auguste preferred not to. True, Brillat Savarin had declared that the pheasant was an enigma whose glories could only be appreciated by the truly trained palate, but he had too many memories of Stockbery Towers' game larders overflowing with hung birds and the inevitable trail of pheasant *à la financière*, pheasant pie, pheasant soup, pheasant *à la Marena*, pheasant galantine, godiveaux of fillets of pheasant, and every other way of honouring pheasant until his dreams were full of gloating birds running amok around his beloved kitchens and procreating in his larders.

His reluctance to join the inevitable shooting party at Tabor Hall stemmed from baser emotions, however. His previous experience of shooting had been confined to the occasional *lapin* on the hillsides of his native Provence, a training that did not qualify him to stand in a line of Lord Tabor's best guns. A sudden happy recollection that the pheasant season did not open till 1 October was promptly succeeded by the less happy thought that partridges, hares, rabbits and waterfowl might prove acceptable targets for the Tabor party while limbering up for the great day.

'I could say Mr Marx disapproved of shooting,' Tatiana offered, struck by sudden inspiration.

Auguste failed to share her enthusiasm. Karl Marx was Tatiana's latest excursion in attempting to discover new worlds that had been closed to her as a Russian princess in Paris.

7

'Did he?'

'No, but the Tabors will not know that.'

He managed a laugh. 'I will say my devotion to His Majesty's cuisine demands my presence all day.'

'Does it?'

'No, but the Tabors will not know that.'

Good humour restored, he took his wife's hand in his, thus abandoning any pretension to the status of English gentleman for a while longer as the carriage at last pulled away.

'*Mon brave*, this is adventure, is it not?' his wife said happily, as the carriage jolted down the station approach, and soon turned into what was obviously the main street, crowded by gaily dressed townsfolk. Auguste caught a glimpse of a fair in progress in the distance, and suddenly that seemed the most desirable place on earth to be. But the carriage turned and the horses were led up a steep lane between the limestone houses and shops of Over Settle. The lane narrowed, leaving civilisation behind. His doom was upon him.

'Nothing will go wrong, George. How can it?' stated Priscilla, Lady Tabor, with her usual conviction. 'I have organised everything for His Majesty's visit.' She implied – with reason – that it would take a daring god of mischance indeed to presume to counter her arrangements. Her purple silk rustled approvingly on her Junoesque figure.

'Do remember this wasn't my idea, Mother,' Victoria put in brightly. An engagement party bound by stuffy royal etiquette – and, worse, in black in deference to the King's state of mourning for his mother, and his sister, not to mention a recently assassinated President McKinley – was far from the halcyon day of wine and roses she and Alexander had blissfully imagined.

Lady Tabor turned on her daughter. 'Most young

ladies would be overwhelmed at the privilege of His Majesty's presence at their betrothal reception, Victoria.'

'So long as Alexander is there, why should I care?'

'Your mother's right, Victoria,' interposed Lord Tabor, nervously, one eye on his wife.

'Oh, George, don't be such a namby pamby.' His mother Miriam was as usual bent on annoying her daughter-in-law. 'Victoria's quite right. Love is more than coronets. Or is that kind hearts? I can never remember.'

Whichever it was, Priscilla Tabor stiffened. She was aware she was on shaky ground, being one of the many American heiresses who had come to find love in England provided it were suitably encased in title, if not diamonds. The main salon at Tabor Hall might not boast the domed ceiling and painted Laguerre murals of Marlborough House, but Priscilla Tabor had done her best in presenting five hundred years of Tabor history in tapestry, aged oils and watercolours to guests sufficiently hard of hearing to have escaped her conversational lectures on the subject.

'I have worked extremely hard, Victoria,' she informed her daughter reproachfully, 'in order to crown your social position.'

'And yours, Ma.' Alfred, lounging on a chesterfield, was all for leaping on any passing bandwagons, providing he was reasonably sure of their not overturning and trapping him beneath.

'Mother, it's taken three months to redecorate and refurbish the entire west wing for the King's visit. All for two nights,' her daughter pointed out as impatiently as she dared. 'What should we have done if the Queen had decided to come too?'

'I should have used a paler shade of pink,' her mother replied seriously. No one laughed. Not at Priscilla.

'After all,' Victoria pressed on, 'the King can only sleep in one bed.'

'That's not quite accurate, my dear,' her grandmother said innocently. 'Priscilla has invited Mrs Janes at His Majesty's request.'

'We have to accommodate his equerries, aides de camp, secretaries,' Priscilla said loudly to regain control. 'Also his ushers, an Extra Gentleman usher, and I believe Gold Stick. And two bodyguards,' she added dismissively, 'for his personal security. Not that they will be needed—'

'At least we don't have to lodge his kitchen staff,' Victoria broke in, confident of aiming straight for her mother's silk-clad Achilles heel. 'Not with Mr Didier coming.'

Auguste was Priscilla's major social problem. This was not, after all, her native America. How did one treat a member of the royal family who properly belonged to the servant class? Moreover one who refused to play down this fact and insisted on flaunting it before all of them by demanding to cook for His Majesty, apparently with the latter's blessing. 'We are fortunate Breckles took it in good part.'

'Breckles only took it in good part because he thinks he can snap any cook from beastly old London in two over his knee if need be. He's looking forward to it,' Victoria pointed out gleefully.

'Nonsense.' Priscilla firmly refused to acknowledge the possibility of trouble below stairs when all concerned were required to pull their weight for the good of the Tabors. 'There's nothing to worry about. Don't you agree, Laura?' She looked for support from her sister-in-law, who had been placidly reading throughout the skirmish.

'She's mooning over a letter from Roughneck Robert. He's rushing back to see her, now he's a household name, to claim her hand. Poor old Olly, eh?' Alfred said loftily.

Laura hastily put the letter aside. 'You are wrong, as it happens, Alfred. It is not from Mr Mariot. It is from Mr Carstairs, telling me he's driving over with Alexander today instead of arriving tomorrow.'

'Really, Laura.' Priscilla was outraged. 'You might consider the maids.'

'Oliver would not dare to seduce them under your roof, Priscilla,' Miriam reassured her.

'Mother!' Laura said warningly, as Priscilla's formidable bosom swelled.

'No need to bother with the maids with Aunt Gertie around,' put in Alfred provocatively.

'Silence.' The tone in his mother's voice stopped him instantly. Couldn't go too far with the mater. Not while she controlled the purse strings, and he required them to open rather too frequently of late.

'She's deuced attractive,' said George incautiously of his brother's new wife.

'As a chorus girl, doubtless she had need to be,' said Priscilla. 'Now she has succeeded in marrying Cyril, she requires other qualities.'

'Such as?' Victoria asked.

'She has no knowledge of *petit point*.'

'Deplorable,' agreed Laura.

Priscilla looked at her suspiciously, but could perceive nothing in her sister-in-law's shocked face of which she could complain. She swept on to deliver her broadside.

'Furthermore, I hear Cyril permits her to take a smoke.'

There was a hushed silence now. Victoria broke it, rushing in with the temerity of one shortly to escape the parental nest. 'So there'll be a high old time in the smokehouse. Or are you going to relax

11

the rules for His Majesty, Mama?'

The verdict was delayed by a loud explosion outside. 'By jingo, what's that?' George demanded angrily. 'An infernal machine?'

Victoria ran to the window and looked down upon the drive beneath. 'Not infernal, Papa. It's darling, darling Alexander's. And sweet Mr Carstairs is with him, Aunt Laura.'

She rushed out and down the staircase, colliding with Richey the butler in the doorway. Speeding ahead of him down the steps, she threw herself into her beloved's arms, as he leapt from the motorcar.

'Oh, now we can start having fun,' she cried.

Greatly to her surprise, Alexander disengaged himself gently. 'Darling, I have to see your mother. Immediately.'

Victoria looked at him, and alarm shot through her. What *now*? What could be wrong? He looked far more worried than an imminent meeting with Mother would warrant. Fun was obviously going to be a little delayed.

So this was Yorkshire. Steep stony hillsides, softly curved crests melting into one another as gently as mounds of beaten egg whites, and everywhere grass and sheep. Obligingly the rain stopped and a weak sun shone, as the Tabor carriage lurched over the moors. Sheep scattered reluctantly from the path, annoyed at being interrupted in their contemplation of eternity. The occasional shepherd stared at the carriage with a frank curious interest before he returned to the real business of life: sheep. The moorland glowed with the changing colours of bracken, yet as the carriage turned further into the remote fells, Auguste shivered, remembering they were not far from Brontë country. How easy to believe now in the elemental passions of Catherine and Heathcliff.

This was as far from Provence or London as it was possible to imagine, an alien countryside, whose people seemed of a different race. He reminded himself firmly that on Monday evening he and Tatiana would be back in their new home in Queen Anne's Gate surrounded by the comforting noisy bustle of London. Back where safety lay.

Safety? Auguste laughed at himself. He was to be living in luxury at a country house in which His Majesty the King was also a guest. What could be safer than that?

At last, having left a small village and inviting inn behind them, the horses turned on to a rough track across a narrow river, then followed the track with hills rising steeply on one side. Auguste could just see ahead of them, wedged between steep hillsides, the grey shape of a large house. Was it an omen that the bright streams now flowing fast on both sides of them were busy scurrying in the opposite direction – away from Tabor Hall?

'*Alors, mon amour*,' Tatiana cried excitedly. 'The die is cast.'

An unfortunate choice of word, as it turned out.

His Majesty Edward VII gazed moodily out of the window of the royal train, trying not to think of ordeal by Priscilla Tabor. It was too bad. Weeks with Alexandra's parents in Denmark, and now that he was free to go to Balmoral he had to stop in Yorkshire en route.

Had not the late Baron Tabor done him some service when he was Prince of Wales, in extricating him from an entanglement of more interest to the young lady than to himself, it was doubtful whether the Tabors would ever have reached the social eminence to which they had been catapulted in the last twenty-five years.

The then Prince had developed a liking for Tabor's son, George, the present baron who was five years his junior, chiefly because he was a fair shot; but even her striking good looks had failed to kindle a similar emotion for his wife. When a daughter was born to the pair, he had agreed to be the girl's godfather for the sake of old times, not foreseeing that this promise would eventually come home to roost in the form of occasional but obligatory attendance at family celebrations.

One of these was this Friday to Sunday. Alexandra had flatly refused to come, choosing to go straight to Balmoral. Only the prospect of Beatrice Janes awaiting him as one of the guests cheered him. And even the rewards that that brought forth never seemed quite as satisfying nowadays. *Poularde Derby* had more to offer on the whole. He remembered that Auguste Didier would be cooking for him at Tabor Hall, and cheered up a little. At least deepest mourning didn't affect the menu.

'I wish we'd never invited him,' moaned Priscilla, staring calamity in the face.

'He is married to my cousin,' Alexander pointed out, somewhat reproachfully, 'and since my parents could not be present, I wanted Tatiana to be here.' Priscilla was aware she had put a foot wrong, but Priscilla's foot once planted was hard to retrieve.

'I have no intention of having a murder at Tabor Hall,' Priscilla glared around at her family as though they were responsible for this serpent in her carefully constructed Arcadia.

'We could tell them the whole thing's off,' George offered almost hopefully.

'Too late! The carriages have arrived.' There was a note of positive relish in his mother's voice. At seventy-

14

nine years of age, she had to take her enjoyment where she could.

Was this one of Mr Wagner's Valkyries awaiting them, Auguste thought wildly, as he handed Tatiana down from the carriage and prepared to be hurled into the arena to be torn apart by Society's lions. He cautiously advanced beside the easy stride of his wife, trying not to peer at the house in order to guess where the kitchens might be. This was not an easy task in this huge grey three-storeyed mansion with its massive pillared portico.

He was right. She *was* a Valkyrie, judging by the wide-brimmed grey hat with two coiled white horns – he caught himself, plumes of course. That, together with today's new shape of bosom thrust forward and posterior bouncing ostentatiously backwards, and Brünnhilde herself stood before him, albeit a somewhat mature version.

Resisting the temptation to step nobly forward, smite himself on the chest and sing out: Here am I, Siegfried, Auguste bowed to his hostess.

'Welcome to Tabor Hall, your Highness. Mr Didier. I trust you'll enjoy your stay.' Priscilla's gracious charm enveloped him but failed to reassure.

'Oh, pray do not call me Highness, I am Madame Didier,' Tatiana assured her earnestly. 'I do not approve of titles – *my* title,' she amended hastily.

Priscilla paused, then decided to dismiss this as Russian eccentricity.

'I say, you haven't become an anarchist, have you, cousin?' Alexander demanded with interest.

'A Marxist,' Tatiana told him amiably.

A bewildering array of Tabors were introduced to them, an ordeal Auguste survived efficiently by imagining them as guests ordering at his restaurant:

15

the nondescript man with pale eyes and thinning fair hair, was their host, Lord Tabor (mustard sauce and devilled kidneys); a middle-aged woman in dove grey with a calm face and intelligent eyes, his unmarried sister, Laura (the much undervalued boiled sole). The owlish and spotty youth with a dashing waistcoat which paid mere lip service to complimentary mourning, was the Tabor son and heir, Alfred (caviare and grouse), and a younger and plumper replica of Lord Tabor, his brother, Cyril (pheasant and hare). His much younger wife, Gertie (champagne and oysters) was an attractive girl, who looked as nervous as he felt. He warmed to Alexander, who had a distinct family resemblance to Tatiana. He and the blonde-haired Victoria, whose exuberance conquered the dullness of the lavender dress complimentary mourning demanded of her, made a striking couple (strawberries and orange).

'Would you like a walk up Willy's Brow?' Victoria asked him brightly. 'We could go now.'

Auguste gazed at her, completely at a loss. Was this some aristocratic term for a staircase? He was saved by his host — if saved was the right word. 'No! I'm giving Didier a turn round the gun room right away.'

Gun room? Willy's Brow? Auguste's spirits sank. He had always thought guests went to their room, bathed, changed and in due course descended for social intercourse.

'I will come too,' Tatiana announced briskly.

'What a splendid idea, George,' his wife boomed enthusiastically. She ignored Tatiana's offer. 'Afterwards Alfred can take Mr Didier to inspect the kitchens.'

Auguste was taken aback. Eager as he was for the latter experience, a few minutes' respite, if merely to attend the calls of nature, would have been welcome. Then his last line of retreat was cut off.

16

'I will take care of Pr – Madame Didier.' Lady Tabor looked at Tatiana much as Mr Bram Stoker's vampire might have eyed his choicest victim.

'I too would like to see the kitchens.' Tatiana might be a match for vampires, but not for her hostess.

'Tea, I think,' pronounced Priscilla with a quiet smile, 'dear Mrs Didier.'

'Then after dinner you can tell us all about your murders,' Victoria announced brightly to Auguste.

'Steady on, Vicky,' drawled Alfred.

Was it his imagination, Auguste wondered, or did Priscilla suddenly look pale? With the recent assassination of President McKinley and the presence of the King here, perhaps murder was as unwelcome a word to his hostess as it was to him.

Victoria failed to take her brother's hint. 'But murder is what you're famous for, isn't it, Mr Didier? You must tell us everything, or since His Majesty will not be dining with us this evening, perhaps you would prefer to wait until tomorrow? I am sure he would be most interested too.'

Auguste was only too well aware that His Majesty would most certainly not be interested, but was not proof against Victoria. '*Enchanté*,' he replied warmly. How could he explain that, gifted though he might be in the ways of detection, it was his culinary skills of which he was truly proud. He was already planning a ten-volume work recording the best of his cuisine. *Dining à la mode de Didier*. It would be his legacy to the world.

'Perhaps tonight might be the better,' Laura said lightly. 'It would be a most absorbing communal entertainment this evening.'

Her family nodded fervently. Was there not something just a little strange here? Auguste was not over-modest, but how could he be of such interest to

17

them? Or did they think he might run off with the family silver if left alone for one moment?

'Nonsense,' he told himself, feeling the familiar warmth of his wife's arm as they entered the house. He was seeing oddities that did not exist. The problem was simply that he was for the first time on the other side of the green baize door at a country house gathering.

'Of course it is nonsense,' hissed Tatiana indignantly, since he had spoken aloud. 'I do not want tea. I am tired of tea, Russian, China, Lemon, my Lord Grey's tisanes—'

'Not tisanes,' August broke in, slightly shocked. 'Camomile, for example, or mint—' But he was talking to air. Lady Tabor had borne away her prey.

Auguste suffered ordeal by gun room patiently, in view of the fact it offered the facilities he now urgently required. Moreover the lure of the kitchen was irresistible. He would not, since the King was dining on the train this evening, be cooking until tomorrow but to savour the smell of the kitchens, to enter a new kingdom – his spirits rose as he anticipated his first glimpse of Paradise again after having taken voluntary exile.

The door to the main kitchen stood open. He and Alfred were being escorted there, as was only right and proper, by Mr Richey, the butler, who was highly disapproving of this flouting of the rules dividing upstairs from downstairs. Richey neatly side-stepped as they approached the door, leaving Alfred in the vanguard, and Alfred stopped on the threshold so abruptly that Auguste cannoned into him. All he was aware of was a huge white-clad figure with arms like ham bones, legs like tree trunks, and a face like thunder.

'Naw.' Entry was barred.

18

'I say, Breckles,' Alfred spluttered.

'I say naw. Tomorrow.'

The king of the kitchen had spoken, and this was his realm. Auguste recognised his place immediately.

'Certainly, Mr Breckles,' he said briskly. 'I quite understand.'

The eye fell on him slowly and consideringly. Its owner grinned as he sized up his opponent. 'Tomorrow,' he repeated almost lovingly and slammed the door shut in their faces.

It was a bad start. Not invited to tea upstairs, not wanted to cook downstairs. There was no comfort to follow. When he eventually reached his room behind the impassive broad back of the housekeeper, Tatiana was not there. Balm was sadly lacking in Gilead.

His wife reappeared only thirty minutes before dinner, by which time Auguste was torn between indignation and nervous anticipation, having forgotten whether the imminent arrival of His Majesty meant donning full mourning or complimentary mourning and what, for a man, the difference was anyway.

'Where have you been?' he was appalled to hear himself asking somewhat querulously.

To his amazement, she rushed straight past him. Where were the kisses, the explanations, the loving words? 'Where is Katya?' was all she threw at him.

'You said Mr Marx disapproved of maids. You did not bring her,' Auguste announced with some pleasure.

'Perhaps Mr Marx has not tried to do up his own corsets or style his own hair.' Through the dressing-room door Auguste watched fascinated as clothes flew in all directions, and then answered the summons to stand in for the absent Katya. At any other time he would have relished the task. Now there were questions to be answered.

'Where have you been?'

19

'Tea,' she replied tersely, as he struggled with hooks. 'You said you did not like tea.'

'We have been discussing rats.'

'Pardon, chérie?' His fingers paused.

Tatiana patted her long dark coiled hair complacently. 'For myself I do not need them. I have thick enough hair already. Rats are pads for ladies' coiffures. Perhaps Mr Marx—'

'I am not interested in Mr Marx.'

'He has much to teach us,' she said sincerely. 'The proletariat have nothing to lose but their chains.'

'I have no chains and—'

'Chains of love, *mon amour.*'

The last hook gave way, she turned and wound her arms round his neck and he quite forgot to enquire further as to the reason for her absence.

The Tabors were as solidly embedded in Yorkshire as the grey stones of their country seat. In mediaeval days when the great lords of the north battled out their enmities and feuds throughout the Wars of the Roses, the Tabors, following the lead of their neighbours, the famous Cliffords of Skipton Castle, had been unwise enough to back a loser by supporting the Lancastrian Henry VI. Tabor, like Clifford the Butcher, had marched to Towton Field, and, unlike Clifford, had survived. As the lord merely of a small manor, this was not treated as a major catastrophe by the incoming Yorkists. While all around his neighbours were fast shedding heads or estates or both, the Tabors managed to retain their modest manor, yet were not so unwise as to favour the Yorkists so ostentatiously as to attract the suspicious eye of Henry VII when he came to the throne and united white and red roses. They continued to avoid undue involvement in politics or religious wars and quietly devoted themselves to the expansion and enrichment of their estates; elevation to the lowest grade of the peerage in due course suited them well. Life would have proceeded thus undisturbed into the twentieth century save for the unexpected rise in the Tabors' social standing.

Unfortunately, August discovered on the Saturday morning, the kitchens had not followed a similar upward path in development. They appeared, to his startled eye, little changed since the original mediaeval manor house had boasted its central fire and vent in the roof: cast iron ovens, smoking chamber over the fireplace, a mechanical spit . . . True, there appeared to be one or two relatively modern improvements, a kitchener or two, a Niçoise mixer, an iron digester – even, he brightened slightly, a refrigerator.

With all their disadvantages, however, the kitchens were a haven of refuge, firstly from the shoot, and secondly from the world of upstairs life. Friday evening had not been quite the ordeal he feared since the King had arrived late. There had been no jolting over the fells for His Majesty, Auguste noted. The royal train had stopped specially at the hamlet of Bell Busk only a mile or two away. Saturday too had begun well. Tatiana had been particularly attentive to him, refusing to leave him until he was delivered into the custody of Mr Richey to be escorted to the kitchens again.

His spirits rose at the prospect before him. He was a Jupiter returned to Olympus, a Pluto to his Underworld. Unfortunately the latter was guarded by an unprepossessing Cerberus in the stalwart shape of the Tabors' chef, William Breckles.

'How do you do?' Auguste greeted him politely.

'Growthead,' was the only distinct word Auguste could make out in reply, and he didn't know what it meant.

'I am honoured to be working with you,' he ventured

21

in what he hoped was a winning manner. He won nothing, as he made a detailed tour round the kitchen to check preparations so far, a difficult task since pots were defended as strongly as Skipton Castle under siege, by pastry cook, meat chef, vegetable chef, sauce chef and colleagues.

'His Majesty's mutton chop?' Auguste's practised eye detected the omission from the table set aside for the King's dishes.

A grunt.

'Stracklin,' Breckles threw at him, grinning at his daring and winning approving looks from his private army. 'Oz nobbut want nobbut yan t'eat.'

'The chop,' Auguste said firmly.

Breckles folded his arms. 'Ez slape ez a greasy pole.'

Auguste lost patience. '*Messieurs*,' he said, squaring up to the enemy, 'in France we show politeness to visitors.'

A look of amazement passed among the troops, then a beam lit Mr Breckles' broad face, followed by a bellow of approbation. 'From France, are you?' he said in perfectly understandable English, if heavily accented. 'We thought you was a daft outcomer from London.'

Breckles then volunteered a tour of the larders, which in Yorkshire involved various rituals hitherto unknown to Auguste. Hares were hung ready for roasting for the servants' dinner. Only young leverets would adorn the Tabors' table. How much the upper classes missed through stubborn prejudice. Properly cooked, mature hare was a feast. Pig's carcasses dripped blood collected for something called Black Pudding. This was a dish he must investigate. A pudding with blood? Evidence of successful shoots earlier in the week filled several larders to overflowing. A working relationship had been established between himself and Breckles, and harmony reigned in the kitchen.

'The garnish for the mutton chop? *Epinards au fleuron?*'

Breckles looked doubtful. 'Gardener's come and gone.'

Auguste's heart sank. There was no help for it; if he had missed the daily visit, the mountain would have to visit Mahomet, or, rather, his garden. Spinach he must have.

He left the kitchen, and set off into the grounds in the direction Breckles had indicated. He had not gone far before to his astonishment he saw Lady Tabor hurrying towards him. Had she discovered he was avoiding the shoot, and come to march him off, he wondered nervously. 'His Majesty's chop,' he managed to say, smiling weakly.

'What?' Priscilla gazed at him blankly, then summoned up her best hostess manner. 'I regret you are too late for the shoot, Mr Didier. If only I had known—'

'The kitchen,' he began feebly.

'Of course, Mr Didier. Let me show you.' Brünnhilde's arm firmly claimed her Siegfried, and then swept on. 'Tell me, how are the Yorks?'

'They are cured, I am told.'

'Splendid,' said Lady Tabor heartily.

'I saw them hanging in the larder only this morning.'

Lady Tabor gazed at him blankly. 'Such delightful people,' she pressed on regardless.

Too late, Auguste remembered his new neighbours at Queen Anne's Gate, and blushed at confusing them with the rather more interesting York hams he had seen about to be smoked with oak sawdust.

'Lady Tabor, I must return to the vegetable garden,' he told her firmly.

'I adore the vegetable garden,' she replied equally firmly. 'I shall accompany you.'

'But—' Aghast, he glanced at the delicate T-bar suede shoes that had clearly had no intention of leaving the carpeted floors of Tabor Hall that morning. Was this some testament to his own masculine attractions? He had heard of such women of course, but somehow he could not imagine Lady Tabor pinning him down in passion amid the Brussel sprouts. 'Mud, Lady Tabor.'

She followed his look, and smiled benignly. 'In that case, Mr Didier, you may escort me back to the morning room.'

Bemused, he found himself listening to an earnest monologue on the fourth and fifth Barons, as he walked beside his hostess back to the garden entrance of the house. He felt like Alice in Wonderland with the leaden weight of the duchess on his arm, and was relieved when they reached the house. Freedom was at hand. Or so he thought.

In the entrance hall Laura was descending the staircase.

'Ah, Laura,' carolled his hostess. 'I doubt if Mr Didier has yet seen the library.' One female arm was replaced by another, he was forced to submit to ordeal by library, before he could successfully plead that his presence was needed elsewhere. He breathed a sigh of gratitude to be reunited with his working table, and decided to abandon the spinach. It was just possible the King would not starve. *Capon à la Régence*, the ortolans cooked in Armagnac, the sweetbreads *à la financière*, black game *à la royale, poussin à la Richelieu, gigot de chevreuil, soufflé de cailles, rognons au Xérès, gratin d'homard*, roast quails – and of course the mutton chop. Yes, that should be sufficient. Then the savouries, most dear to His Majesty. And the oysters ready for his private supper.

He was just adjusting the position of a truffle, when there was a scream. It was outside, but was promptly

24

followed by a kitchenmaid rushing in through the door. He forgot the truffle, and hurried to her to calm her distress, one arm slipping naturally round her; then he remembered his married status, but still kept the arm in place.

'What is the matter, *chérie*?' he asked. The kitchen staff crowded round her as she gasped out a torrent of words that were incomprehensible to him.

"Tis a crawing hen,' Breckles informed him tersely. 'Hickity O, pickity O, pompolorum jig,' he added soberly to himself. Whatever was amiss, Auguste decided, it was a Yorkshire matter and nothing to do with a foreigner. He would tactfully slip away. Breckles caught his arm before he could do so.

'A crawing hen brings ill luck on the house.'

Chapter Two

All superstition of course, Auguste told himself. Nevertheless he remembered how often la Mère Bouchier's prophecies of dire happenings had been fulfilled in his native Cannes, and was not inclined to scoff at a Yorkshire hen. He walked through the baize door dividing 'Them' from 'Us' (whichever 'Us' he was at the moment). Immediately Victoria Tabor stepped smartly out from the gun room and offered to accompany him wherever he might be going. Perhaps this was some rule of northern hospitality he had not yet grasped, he thought, beginning to find this love of his company distinctly unnerving. Bidding Victoria farewell, he opened the door of their room with some relief, expecting Tatiana to be present. She wasn't.

Even her appearance a few minutes later did not restore good humour this time. He was convinced that something was going on in which he was not involved. 'Where have you been, *ma mie*?' he enquired, trying to convey that the answer was not of great interest to him.

'Taking tea,' Tatiana replied quickly. 'I understand now why English ladies, even those from America like Lady Tabor, take tea. It is so they can burst out of their armour and wear teagowns.'

Auguste eyed her suspiciously. It was true it was teatime, but surely more than tea and whalebone was going on here. A lover? At this wild thought he laughed at himself. He was being foolish.

"Course, they don't approve of me.'

'How could they not?' asked Auguste sincerely. 'You are the former Miss Gertie Gum, the ornament of the Galaxy Girls chorus line.' He had been charmed to make this discovery the previous evening, courtesy of Alfred.

Gertie giggled. 'You were the restaurant chef, weren't you? Before I was there, that must have been.'

Auguste thought back to those days of '94, only seven years ago but like a different lifetime. Then he looked at Tatiana and regretted not a single change. (Or very few.) Gertie's reign in the chorus line had been brief, so Alfred had told him, before she succumbed to the blandishments of the Honourable Cyril who, faced with the meltingly beautiful and innocent face of Miss Gum, had found himself strangely unable to offer the lure he had intended and proffered marriage instead – which had resulted in the entire satisfaction of both participants, if not of Priscilla Tabor.

Drawn by fellow feeling, Auguste had gravitated to her side under the sparkling chandeliers of the salon as the company, dressed in deepest mourning, awaited the arrival of His Majesty for dinner. This was promptly at seven, unusually early for His Majesty who favoured dining at nine, but his easy-going nature let Priscilla have her way. One usually did. Priscilla had strict views on the Sabbath and the desirability of early retiring. So did His Majesty when Mrs Beatrice Janes was unaccompanied by her husband, but unfortunately the King had been disgruntled to find he was very much with her on this occasion. He liked old Harold, but expected him to do the decent thing and stay at home. Harold was, Tatiana had confided to Auguste in bed last night, anxious to remind His Majesty of his existence, with the first November Birthday Honours List in mind, and was either oblivious or ignorant of other factors.

'Lady Tabor has given them adjoining rooms,' she whispered, 'and is making sure Harold has a lot to drink, otherwise the King will not be amused.'

There were some benefits, Auguste had thought, highly diverted, to Tatiana's tea-parties. She learned the most intriguing pieces of gossip. Cyril, he was told, was thought to be over-susceptible by his sister-in-law. His first wife having died, he had spent several years searching enthusiastically for replacements, most of them temporary. There had been a lady called Alice, with a peppery father in the Indian Army, for example. It always fell to George Tabor to extricate his gullible brother, but he had failed to act in time over Gertie. Priscilla had not forgiven him.

'There's only one has any time for me in this house, and that's her Ladyship,' Gertie confided to Auguste, who was appreciative of her entrancing bosom, none the worse for its black lace covering, pressed right up against him. She had daringly broken the rules of mourning by flaunting a white rose, he noticed, when only pearls were permissible. Full marks to Gertie for courage. His Majesty was unlikely to object, but Priscilla . . .

'Our hostess?' Auguste asked startled, since he thought the Valkyrie sadly lacking in rapport with Gertie. He glanced round to see where Tatiana was, just in case she might be watching. She was not; she was chatting to a pink-faced footman. Much as he approved of this democratic behaviour, he doubted if Priscilla Tabor would be so impressed.

Gertie giggled. 'No, Miriam, the Dowager. Haven't you met her? I'll introduce you. Mother to Cyril, Laura

29

and old George and the scourge of Priscilla's life. She lives here in the north wing.'

The Dowager Baroness Tabor was a diminutive figure, but the first thing to strike Auguste were her eyes, clear, blue and remarkably lively for her years. So was her pink and white complexion, complemented by white hair, and she had a grace of quick movement that made Priscilla seem a battleship to her graceful sloop, a Chelsea bun to her *petits fours*.

'Ah, Mr Didier, what fun to have a chef in the family. For you will be in the family, will you not, once Alexander marries Victoria? Now you must tell me about Paris. So clever to marry a Parisienne.'

'Only to be compared with an English rose such as you, *madame*.' Auguste bowed and began to relax at such humanity.

'Mother!' Priscilla bore down on them in full black sail, or rather silk swathed in crepe. 'His Majesty approaches.'

Meekly, the Dowager Lady Tabor, winking at Auguste, followed in the majestic wake of her daughter-in-law.

A hush fell as His Majesty King Edward VII arrived for dinner, definitely out of sorts. He had come to the conclusion that even Beatrice's presence did not compensate for Priscilla Tabor. Marmoreal thighs and majestic bosoms were all very well, but even the largest and most majestic lost their appeal when their owner behaved like an over-forceful sheepdog.

August found himself, to his pleasure, seated next to Gertie, albeit well below the salt. He congratulated himself that so far he, the proletariat, had committed no major solecisms, provided one did not count failing to notice the layout of the house so that when he led Mrs Janes down the stairs for dinner yesterday evening, he had offered that effusive lady the wrong arm and found himself crushed against the wall by her protruding corseted rear.

Tatiana had been placed sufficiently far from the King not to irritate him by any disconcerting observations on Mr Karl Marx, but near enough not to insult a minor Romanov, as she was. His Majesty sat in state at one end of the table with Beatrice on one side and Priscilla on the other. He did not look particularly happy. Only Victoria and Alexander, allowed to sit next to each other, floated blissfully in their private dream of happiness.

'Madame will take the consommé,' Auguste instructed the footman firmly, earning a grateful glance from Gertie. At Romano's she had never been forced to choose, since every infatuated admirer simply ordered the best for her. Speed of supply and dispatch was essential at this end of the table, Auguste knew, as otherwise there was a danger of His Majesty finishing before they had begun. Etiquette demanded that the whole company lay down their knives and forks as soon as the King did. If in a good mood he ate slowly. Today, however, it was clear speedy eating would be necessary, especially as there were ten extra guests invited just for the evening. Auguste began to worry about His Majesty's menu once more. He had been forced to yield the final garnishing of truffles on the silver plates bearing the King's favourite *côtelettes de bécassines à la Souvaroff,* cutlets of boned snipe and foie gras with Madeira sauce. It had been an agonising parting.

The consommé *à la princesse* was a success, he decided cautiously, though some might say there was slightly too much tarragon. He watched the charade as Tabor footmen handed dishes solemnly to the King's own footmen who waited on him, then handed the dishes back. Almost like mediaeval food-tasters,

Auguste thought, pondering the possibilities of poison being inserted into the King's food, then remembering all too vividly an occasion in his past when it might so easily have been. Hastily he turned his attention to Oliver Carstairs, a tall man in his forties with a lazy charm and interesting face. He had not spoken to him at length last night, and was not sure of his role here. He decided he would find out.

At much the same time, His Majesty turned thankfully from Priscilla to Beatrice. Now for some entertaining conversation, which by etiquette he must initiate. 'Fellow should be hung by the thumbs,' he informed her. 'He shot one of the Sandringham gold pheasants.'

The Honourable Cyril recalled his social obligations and stopped studying his pretty little kitten across the table; he belatedly registered the word gold and decided to contribute.

'Market's getting difficult, so they say, sir.'

'What market?' the King asked, nonplussed.

'Gold market.'

'Gold will never lose its value,' pontificated Harold Janes. He was, he wished everyone to know, an authority on this subject.

'What with the war in South Africa . . .' Cyril's voice trailed off miserably.

'I hear the unions are flexing their muscles in Colorado too,' Carstairs rescued him.

'Didn't your brother have something to do with gold out in Colorado, Priscilla?' enquired Miriam innocently.

Priscilla glared at her. Oscar was not a subject she wished to discuss, and dear Mother-in-Law was well aware of the fact.

'Pheasants,' emphasised the King loudly, annoyed at this tangent. '*Pheasants*.'

'Was it a good bag this morning, Your Majesty?'

ventured Didier, bravely coming to the aid of the party.

'Splendid,' he roared cordially, glad that Didier was taking life seriously – without, he noted approvingly, losing his old skills at cooking. That chop had gone down very nicely, as also the *soufflé de cailles*, not to mention several other dishes. 'Few dozen ducks as well as partridge.'

In this spirit of goodwill towards all, even Priscilla, the rest of the dinner proceeded tranquilly.

'Shall we adjourn, gentlemen?' George cleared his throat as the last rustle of black taffetas and silks returned to the drawing room just before eight. Oddly, Auguste noticed, George was definitely avoiding the eye of his monarch.

Auguste had looked forward to the moment when, relaxing in an old armchair watching others play billiards, he might light up a cigar, drink a brandy – surely the essence of the small pleasures of being a gentleman, though, true, not ones he had expected to indulge in so early in the evening. It was greatly to his surprise that he found himself being almost frog-marched behind the monarch, not towards the billiard room but into the dark cold night air. Here Lord Tabor and his monarch climbed into a trap, leaving himself, Cyril, Alfred, Alex, Harold Janes, and Oliver Carstairs on the steps.

'*Monsieur*,' Auguste asked, puzzled, addressing his companion as they set off at a spanking pace into the murky blackness. 'Where are we going?'

'To the smokehouse,' declared Oliver cheerfully.

'But is the smoking room not where the billiards are?'

'Good heavens, no,' Alexander told him blithely. 'Not at Tabor Hall.' He glanced at Auguste's bewildered face. 'You'll get used to it,' he assured him. 'My revered mother-in-law-to-be doesn't care for tobacco smoke, you see. She has this quaint idea it ruins furniture, tapestries, paintings and health. And while she doesn't mind about health too much, she does mind about the Tabor heritage.'

'But it is not her own heritage,' Auguste hissed to Oliver, hoping Alfred was out of earshot.

'No zealot like the convert. She guards each blob of paint more fiercely than George, Laura, Cyril and Miriam put together! Now Miriam *is,* or rather *was,* a hostess. Couldn't care less what was done in the house provided her guests enjoyed it, but Priscilla is a different matter.'

'Blasted walkies,' Auguste heard Janes mutter to himself in front. 'Must think we're bulldogs.'

'But most hostesses simply have a room in the house appointed for smoking. Why not here?' Auguste shivered as, hemmed in by dark hillsides, they joined a path lit by oil-lamps leading to a wood.

'This smokehouse is Lady Tabor's very own invention,' Alexander told him. 'As it's so far away from the house, she argues that it's a test of resolve to go to her smokehouse after dark.'

'But for the King surely—' Auguste said, horrified, seeing an ever-longer path unwinding before him.

'Priscilla wouldn't change her mind for George Washington, let alone the King of England,' her brother-in-law told him with less than his usual joviality. 'You note she does provide a trap for him, but the rest of us can jolly well walk. There it is now.' He pointed to a building that seemed to arise before their eyes at the edge of the wood.

Through the half-open door as they approached Auguste was aware of the King and his host already puffing contently on cigars, but it was the outside of the building that riveted his attention. Perhaps to ram home the undesirability of the noxious weed, Lady Tabor had selected a most unusual smoking room. Jealous of a neighbour who boasted a peel tower in his garden, a Tabor of the 18th century had decided to go one better (in his view) and erect a Gothic folly of tumbling towers, sharp pinnacles, and castellated roofs.

On her arrival at Tabor Hall, Cyril explained, Priscilla had decreed this gloomy monstrosity would make a most admirable smokehouse. She would brook no argument, and George wisely put up none. Instead, secure in the knowledge that his high-principled lady would never compromise her integrity by setting foot inside, he had adorned the smokehouse with the kind of paintings usually only hung in the back rooms of gentlemen's clubs, a collection he had much pleasure in updating from time to time. Thus the Alma Tadema 'Psyche' over the mantelpiece had been replaced with a distinctly more erotic Sickert nude of the type usually only exported to Paris, and by a variety of Parisian art of lesser distinction in which garters and stockings were the only concession to haute couture.

Faced with this unexpected entertainment the King seemed somewhat dazed, as Auguste entered, but no doubt reflecting that he was used to such exoticisms in Paris, he was politely congratulating his friend on his choice of artistic adornment, and accepting his second brandy.

Equally slightly taken aback by his surroundings, Auguste accepted a cigar from Alexander, whose Russian and English ancestry were both clearly visible in his dark romantic good looks.

'Like it?' he asked Auguste, grinning. 'Victoria thinks it's wonderful.'

'Most original.' Auguste cleared his throat, desperately trying to think of polite conversation in the face (or in some cases rear) of so many flaunted ladies who were anything but polite. Standing by the mantelpiece, he was unable to avoid close study of the Sickert, which showed a lady on a bed, bursting from her armour all too efficiently. Uncertain of his company, he passed a remark to Oliver on the glories of the dead duck on the mantelpiece so charmingly carved in wood. Oliver chuckled, and he relaxed. 'I gather you are an old friend of the family?'

'Not so old. Late forties,' Oliver informed him, handing Auguste a glass. 'I'm a regular visitor every six months. I only come here to propose to Laura. She never accepts. Perhaps luckily so.'

'Luckily?'

'It would affect my career, Didier.'

'And that is?' Auguste brightened, now he knew he was in the company of a fellow member of the working proletariat.

'I'm a professional bachelor. I'm invited to Society occasions to make up numbers, make amusing conversation – and at Tabor Hall to propose to Laura of course.'

'Why does she refuse? Does she not love you?'

'Apparently not.'

'Waiting for that ne'er-do-well to roll home,' grunted George, overhearing. 'Fellow wasn't a gentleman.'

'Not in your sense of the word, no,' Oliver agreed, good-humouredly. 'But after all, when Adam delved and Eve span, who was then the gentleman?'

George tried to make sense of this, failed, and dismissed it. 'Only one sense of the word. Fellow either is or he isn't and nothing can be done about it.' George's eye suddenly fell on Auguste and he realised to his horror that he had been guilty of the ultimate ungentlemanliness of making a guest uncomfortable. 'Seen this one, have you?' he asked, to make amends. He swung back a folded panel to reveal a fetching study of an otherwise naked lady looking winsomely through her plump black-stockinged legs.

'Er—' Auguste gulped, reflecting that there were some advantages after all in the restraining armour of the less artistically pleasing portions of a lady's anatomy. 'No, I haven't had the pleasure.'

Alfred sniggered. 'Rather like our Beatrice, isn't she?'

Auguste looked aghast, noticing the King in earnest conversation with the lady's husband, who was much of the King's own build, despite his being twenty years younger. Harold Janes looked as exciting as a vegetable marrow – and yet, Auguste reflected, the marrow was a much neglected vegetable.

'Surprised old Bertie hasn't noticed the resemblance,' Alfred continued, with uncalled-for familiarity in referring to his monarch.

'Isn't it time we rejoined the ladies?' His father had clearly decided the conversation had gone far enough. Alfred might be twenty-one but he had not yet reached the years of discretion. The young folk of today were far too precocious. 'Carstairs, keep an eye on Didier, will you?'

'Did you attend Ascot this season, Mr Didier?'

'I regret not.'

'Ah, Goodwood?'

'We were on our honeymoon.'

No excuse apparently. 'Henley?'

'I regret not.'

All conversation ceased.

It seemed exceedingly strange to be dancing not in the servants' hall, graciously offering to dance with scullerymaids terrified of offending their god, the chef, but to be circling with over one hundred and sixty-eight solid pounds of aristocratic kid-gloved hostess in

37

your arms, fully aware that one was being judged as to one's suitability for Society. The stiffly corseted back did not give an inch. Duty was merely being done in dancing with all one's guests. Even ex-cooks.

The engagement of Victoria and Alexander had duly been announced by a nervous George. His Majesty had then indicated that dancing to the three-piece band that coincidentally happened to be present would not be an affront to his state of mourning, and Priscilla Tabor was congratulating herself that all had passed off excellently. She smiled beneficently on the cook, and swept away, the black feathers adorning her coiffure nodding their approval of her charitable deed.

It was with relief that Auguste took Tatiana in his arms. Gloomy black crepe did little to dampen the fires of curiosity in Tatiana's eyes.

'What is it like, this smokehouse?' she hissed.

'Not proper for princesses.'

The eyes gleamed. 'I am no longer a princess, so I can go there.'

'Certainly not.'

'Why not?'

'The adornments are not meant for ladies.'

'There are pots in the cupboards, you mean?'

'No,' he hissed.

'What then?'

'The pictures.'

'Oh. I *must* go. I once met Monsieur Toulouse Lautrec. Such interesting drawings.'

'These are not of the same quality.'

'One must experience everything. Where else can I have a smoke?'

He almost lost his footing. '*Quoi?*' he asked faintly.

'I wanted to find out what it was like, so I asked John for a cigarette. Then I tried a cigar.'

A few judicial words would be spoken to footman

John on his return to Queen Anne's Gate, Auguste decided. True, his relations with the staff had not so far been easy. The very first week the cook had given notice, on account of Auguste's interference in matters which were none of his concern. After the third cook had left, even Auguste was forced to admit that it might have something to do with him. Hurt, he had pondered the matter, and discussed it with Tatiana. There was no problem. *She* would cook, she blandly informed her husband. Blinis, for instance. And dumplings. He shuddered, and promptly came to a working arrangement with the fourth cook, whereby Auguste might have the run of the kitchen on the cook's day off.

'Oh, Mr Didier, so romantic. It's like King Cophetua and the Beggarmaid, only the other way round, to see you and the princess together.'

'Quite,' said Auguste shortly, regretting his invitation to Beatrice Janes to dance, and eyeing Carstairs enviously as he took Gertie on to the floor. Gertie no longer wore the white rose, he noted sadly. Authority, in the form of Priscilla, had intervened.

Dizzy after wine and the effects of smoke, assaulted by Mrs Janes' high-pitched giggle that inevitably followed one of her conversational sallies, he yielded her gratefully to the arms of her portly husband, only to find himself accosted by the Dowager Lady Tabor, resplendent in black lace over silk. 'Do take pity on me, Monsieur Didier. I have not danced with a Frenchman since the fall of the Third Republic.' Whether a Strauss waltz was the best choice to make her reacquaintance with this experience was doubtful, but her energy seemed greater than his.

'You're still with us, I'm glad to see, Mr Didier.'

Uncertain he had heard aright, he gave a non-committal answer.

'I thought you might be dead by now.'

He could *not* have heard aright. He had definitely had one brandy too many. 'What did you say?' he asked faintly.

Miriam Tabor smiled at him. 'I said I thought you might be in bed by now. You mustn't mind an old lady like me. But I'm going to bed anyway.'

'But the King, my lady, he has not yet retired,' Auguste blurted out, mindful of protocol.

'Phooey. He won't be wanting to take me with him, will he?' Miriam enquired, unanswerably, but quashing all Auguste's doubts as to her sanity.

In the event the King retired shortly afterwards, either in pursuit of an early night or after having reached an understanding with Mrs Janes. Black skirts swept the floor in deep curtseys. He was hardly out of earshot before Priscilla Tabor called for the carriages of those guests not staying in the house.

'Withdrawing time, gentlemen, is eleven-thirty.'

Oliver groaned. 'Amazing how George lets her get away with it. I think he's frightened of her. Like Wellington.'

'*Boeuf Wellington?*' Auguste asked, still befuddled.

Oliver laughed. 'The Iron Duke himself. Remember what he said when the troops arrived to fight in the Peninsula? "I don't know what effect they may have upon the enemy, but, by God they terrify me!"' He contemplated Priscilla for a moment. 'The curfew isn't for billiards. It's intended for the smokehouse. She locks the doors of the Hall at eleven-thirty, so that the smokehouse has to be vacated by eleven-fifteen at the latest. At eleven twenty-five the path lights are extinguished. Her excuse is the need to prepare for the Sabbath.'

'Does everyone obey?' Auguste asked amazed.

Oliver regarded him kindly. 'Take a close look at

her, Auguste. Would you gainsay Priscilla? She counts every damn man of them, kings, dukes or maharajahs, and locks the front and garden doors herself. Promptly. Fortunately, she doesn't realise that the staff exist and have their own means of exit. Richey has to lock the smokehouse and put out the lights, after all. One can always get in and out of the kitchens.'

Auguste looked round blearily for his wife but she was nowhere to be seen. She must already have retired. Just one quick game would do no harm, surely, now he was a gentleman. He joined Oliver in the billiard room, and only the chiming of the loud stable clock reminded him of the lateness of the hour. Even so, it was twelve-thirty before he staggered somewhat drunkenly to his room.

He was rather more drunk than he realised for he noticed nothing odd; he vigorously cleaned his teeth several times, and only as he approached the bed did he realise that Tatiana was not in it. He contemplated various courses of action, and decided there was only one, dressed as he now was. He would sit up in bed and wait for her. He was just a little hurt, even in his bemused state. This was the first time, such was her enthusiasm for her newly married status, that he had sat in bed alone. He read a page of Zola upside down, his eyes closed . . .

'Wake up! Wake up!'

He felt sick, he was being swung from side to side. Was he in a boat? If so, it was on some unknown nightmarish sea. A sea that would not be calm. 'Auguste, *chéri*, wake up!'

His eyes opened, the room swam round him. Into slow focus came the face of his wife, leaning over him, her eyes full of terror in the light of the candle she was holding. He tried to force himself awake. 'What is wrong? And why—?' His eyes went to her dress. She was still in her black evening gown with a cloak around her shoulders.

'There is a body in the smokehouse. Darling, you must come, please.'

He shut his eyes thankfully again. For a moment he thought she'd said . . .

'Wake *up*.' Reluctantly he opened them once more.

'A body? Someone is drunk?' Confused by dreams, it did not occur to him to question his wife as to how she came to be discovering drunken gentlemen in smokehouses.

'No, Auguste. *Dead,*' she told him quietly. This was one new experience she did not relish.

Save for his wife's obviously confident belief that he was well competent to remove such horrors as dead bodies from smokehouses, he would still have thought this part of his nightmare.

'An accident? A joke?' he asked without hope, seeing any chance of nestling down beneath these inviting bedclothes with an equally inviting wife vanishing rapidly.

'No, Auguste. It is a *real* body.'

At last he believed her. 'No,' he shouted firmly. 'No more dead bodies.'

Then he heard the real fear in her voice. 'Please, *daragoy*. Someone must do something and I told Alexander it must be you.'

She began to drag Auguste out of bed. He contemplated the thought of going in his nightwear across that murky blackness to investigate a body, and decided against it. He lit the oil lamp and clamber- ed into clothes. Should he wear deep mourning, he thought, still slightly confused. No, because doubtless, he told himself, this was some mistake. Men did not die in smokehouses. They got drunk in smokehouses, they were sick in smokehouses, they fell asleep in smokehouses. They did not die there.

Five minutes later, he followed Tatiana down the main staircase and towards the kitchens. So she knew, he noted automatically, that this was the only exit after Lady Tabor had supervised the locking of the doors.

In William Breckles' prized domain, Alexander was sitting slumped at a table, as scrubbed and empty as if it had never seen the passing of a hundred sumptuous dishes that day. For once, however, Auguste had little interest in the trappings of his art.

'What are you doing here?' he asked wearily as Alexander leapt up. 'And why—?'

'Please. Later, Auguste. That is not important. We must go. Quickly,' Tatiana said, tugging at his arm.

He looked at her. He hardened his heart. If he had to look at a dead body – though he was still sure this was some hoax – he must forget this was his wife for the moment.

'How did you discover it? When?'

Alexander shrugged, looking at Tatiana.

'I wanted a smoke,' she said quickly. 'Because of Priscilla, we had to go to the smokehouse.'

'The path lights were out. Why bother?'

'There are house rules. There are lanterns,' she said, her cheeks pink.

'It's also a house rule not to smoke after eleven-thirty.'

Tatiana stared at him and did not reply.

'You're wasting time, Auguste. Let's go,' Alexander said quietly. 'I didn't want her to call you in the first place.'

Auguste swelled with anger. And why not? He was her husband, he was a detective, and he was *here*. Moreover it was three-thirty in the morning, on a cold

September night. Convinced in righteous anger that there was some foolish mistake, he seized the lantern at Alexander's side, and marched out in silence. They followed him, picking their way in the dim light along the track to the smokehouse, avoiding the slugs relishing the dark damp air.

He ran up the steps and paused, anger gone now, senses sharp – just in case, *in case* they were right and this was violent death.

'Was this door unlocked when you came here?'

'Yes.' Alexander's flat monosyllable came out of the darkness behind him.

Auguste flung open the door to an oil-lit room, quite sure there would be nothing there save the artistic ladies guarding their beat.

He was wrong. On the floor was an undoubtedly dead body. A gentleman in full evening dress lay sprawled on his face, a pistol at his side and the reddish-brown stain of drying blood on the carpet.

Chapter Three

Auguste stood up, bracing himself for what was to come. He had done all he could without touching the body, but that was little. A thousand terrors raced through his mind, fear hammered somewhere at the pit of his stomach. He looked at Tatiana and Alexander, who had remained at the doorway as if distancing themselves from responsibility now Auguste was there.

'Did either of you move him?' he asked more sharply than he had intended.

'No,' answered Alexander evenly.

'So you don't know who it is?'

'No,' replied Tatiana, perhaps a little too quickly, or was his imagination over active, reason blurred by the unreality of night?

A man in a dress suit, middle-aged by his substantial build, the hint of a dark beard – Auguste instructed the panic that was still rolling in waves inside him to be still. The general impression of the body was not that of *him*, was it? He could not be sure.

'You think it is His Majesty, Auguste? Surely his Special Branch bodyguards would be here by now?' Tatiana said practically.

The man in him wanted such reassurance, the detective in him knew better. 'Alexander, please fetch Lord Tabor and send for the police.' As her cousin's footsteps first walked, then pounded along the path, Tatiana was the first to speak.

'Is it suicide?'

'I do not know.' Auguste forced himself to look again at the sprawled body and the gun at its side just beyond the outstretched hand. One saw such pictures in the *Strand Magazine* so often it was hard to believe it could have actually happened like that. Soon the police would arrive, the King's two bodyguards also perhaps, and his own part would be over. Only his worry about Tatiana stood in the way of the relief this thought brought.

'Tatiana, what were you really doing here? The police will discover and I must know first.'

'I have told you.' Her indignant face was pale in the shadows cast by the oil lamps. It seemed to him her voice was strained, or was that too the effect of night? 'I wanted a smoke.'

'It was *three o'clock*.'

'We Russians keep late hours. Alexander and I had much to say to one another.' Her voice rose. 'Do you think *I* shot him? Or Alexander?'

Tatiana had put voice to his fear: murder. Suppose the police thought so too?

'Of course not,' he shouted.

'Then why these questions?'

'Because they will be asked by others.'

Memories surged into his mind of the murders at Plums, Stockbery Towers, and the Galaxy. Was he supersensitive to witnesses who were not telling all they knew? And was one of them now his own wife?

It took twenty minutes of strained silence before there came the sound of footsteps, and Tatiana opened the door to Lord Tabor, accompanied by, Auguste was depressed to see, Priscilla. She wasted no time, he noted, in idle curiosity over the artistic attractions of the smokehouse, but went immediately to the corpse.

'Who is it?' she demanded.

46

'I do not know, your Ladyship,' Auguste replied steadily. 'We cannot touch the body until the police arrive, and at the moment—' He broke off, gesturing towards all that could be seen of the bloodied ruin of a face.

'Suicide,' said George disgustedly. 'What a time to choose, eh?'

Auguste did not answer, if answer were required. Did his host refer merely to the lateness of the hour or the inconvenience of such an event during a royal visit? And still he could not be sure that the corpse was not that of the King. Perhaps the same fear consumed Priscilla, for she said to him peremptorily:

'Turn it over.'

Taken aback, Auguste told her firmly: 'Impossible.'

'Turn it *over*,' Priscilla demanded again. 'Do you expect me to do it myself? George, you do it.'

'We should wait for the police,' Tatiana supported Auguste, seeing his appalled face. 'If it should be His Majesty—'

'It is not,' Priscilla interrupted scornfully. 'His Majesty would not commit suicide. Not here. Turn it over, George.'

Nothing short of physical force could prevent it. Auguste's usual authority in such situations had met its match in Priscilla Tabor. But at least he would mark the original position of the body. Quickly, he took matches from the Vesta cases provided on the mantelpiece, while Priscilla impatiently watched.

Then George knelt by the body, gingerly rolling it over. Auguste gagged at the repulsive sight, and Tatiana uttered a choked sound of distress. The man had shot himself full through the eye, half obliterating his face and spattering shirt front, waistcoat and tie with blood, as well as the carpet. Enough of the face

47

remained to bring Auguste some relief. It was not that of the King.

George broke the silence. 'Who the devil is it?'

'I have no idea, George.' His wife's flat voice was as unemotional as if such annoyances were a regular feature of life in Yorkshire. 'I have never seen him before. He is nothing to do with Tabor Hall.'

'But he is clad in full evening dress, even to black mourning tie and waistcoat,' Auguste pointed out, flabbergasted. He had fully expected it to be Harold or Cyril.

'I repeat, Mr Didier,' Priscilla's voice grew cold, 'he is a complete stranger to us, and why he should have found it necessary to come here to shoot himself I have not the slightest idea. I suggest now, Mrs Didier, you accompany us back to the Hall where I presume we must await the arrival of the police. Such as they are. You will remain here, Mr Didier.'

Tatiana obeyed without a word.

Auguste kept an uneasy vigil, his brain struggling to make sense of the night's events. Suppose the police thought this man had committed suicide because Tatiana had had a tryst with him here? And even worse, suppose it were not suicide? The cold hand of terror fastened on his shoulder once more. Alexander would testify that there had been no assignation of course. But suppose he had lied? Why should he? asserted reason. Because Tatiana had asked her cousin for help, came needling suspicion. No, she would have come to him, her husband. Or might she have feared to do so because of his association with the police?

Should he try to blot out any signs of her presence? No, he knew too well that that was the path to disaster.

Auguste glanced round at his claustrophobic surroundings: the semi-nude ladies seemed to be leering down at the unpleasant sight in their midst. His eyes followed their gaze. This wasn't the King. This man had a definite look of one used to the outdoors; his hands were tanned as though he had lived in sunnier climes than England. His hair was sleekly oiled. He wasn't wearing gloves; that was strange if he were a dinner guest. He looked around. The gloves were on the arm of that leather armchair. Now why would he have taken them off?

Too late he was aware his detective instincts were once more being aroused. Why me? an inner voice yelled at him, aggrieved. Why should he, Auguste Didier, be singled out by fate to cope with these horrors?

He still didn't like the position of that gun. Didn't the scene look just a little posed? He forced himself to examine his fear: suppose it were murder? Suppose this stranger (assuming the Tabors were not lying) had come to meet someone here. Who?

There was but one way to prove to the police it was not Tatiana: he must find out the truth himself. His heart sank, but he forced himself methodically to absorb every detail of the room, every bloodstain, every sign of occupation, worried not least at what a thankfully live King would say when awoken at breakfast-time to the news that once again Auguste Didier and a corpse were together on the premises.

Forty minutes later, Alexander reappeared, now accompanied by three representatives of the Yorkshire police force, and inevitably George and Priscilla Tabor, though without Tatiana, Auguste was relieved to see, and without the King's bodyguards. Clearly Priscilla was hoping this could all be cleared up before breakfast while His Majesty peacefully slept on. He doubted this very much. One of the policemen was the constable who had been guarding the main entrance to the Tabor Hall estate and was torn between indignation

49

that his profile had not hitherto been higher in this event and apprehension as to whether or not he could have been expected to prevent it. The second was a small terrier of a man with intelligent darting eyes, and the third a silent bulldog sergeant of huge stature who hovered protectively over his superior.

The constable gravitated to Auguste's side, apparently hopeful of making an immediate arrest.

'This is Mr Auguste Didier,' Alexander informed the police. 'I called him when I found the body.' Slightly to Auguste's indignation, this made no impact on the terrier, Inspector Cobbold. 'He is a guest in the house and a detective.' Auguste was torn between modest pride and awareness that this was hardly a trump card in his hand when faced with unknown professional competition.

'Special Branch?' Cobbold's tones were noncommittal, and fortunately less heavily accented than he had expected, yet he looked as shrewd a Yorkshireman as Auguste had yet met.

'No.' How could he convey he was a highly reluctant amateur detective? 'But I am known to Scotland Yard,' Auguste compromised.

Cobbold stared at him without commenting on this. 'On His Majesty's Staff?'

'No. I am related by marriage.' Auguste saw a wall of noncommunication rapidly nearing completion between himself and Cobbold.

The inspector did not comment. Instead: 'No one recognises him, that right?' A jerk of the head at the corpse.

'We do not.' Priscilla Tabor decided to make her presence felt. 'One of our guests may do so.'

'Including His Majesty?' Cobbold asked, obviously not one to be daunted, Auguste noticed admiringly.

'It is highly unlikely that a friend of His Majesty

would come here to shoot himself,' Priscilla came back witheringly.

'If it *was* suicide,' Auguste incautiously commented.

'Any reason why not?' Auguste's opinion of Inspector Cobbold shot up. Any man who could take such a fly in the soup so calmly won his appreciation.

'There was something strange about the position of the gun to the body when originally found,' he began.

'Originally?' Cobbold picked up instantly.

'The body was moved.'

'Why?'

Priscilla turned the Gorgon's stare upon him. 'I would remind you that President McKinley of America has just been assassinated. Suppose such a catastrophe had occurred to His Majesty?'

'Didn't occur to you to go to find out?' The Gorgon's gaze failed to turn Cobbold to stone.

'No,' Priscilla replied icily.

'What was strange then?' Cobbold turned on Auguste.

'I have put these matches to mark the original position. It seemed too neat, too close, for the gun to have fallen like that.'

Cobbold considered this. 'Murder, eh? No one passed PC Walters here. Not this fellow, nor anyone else. What other entrances are there?'

'One giving access to the woods, leading to the Malham and Gordale lane, another giving on to the fells at the back.' George came into his own. 'The fellow could have scrambled over the drystone walls, I suppose.'

'Not in that suit,' said Cobbold dismissively.

Auguste's respect grew. The black suit was unmarked.

'Otherwise, it would have to be someone in the house.'

'This is quite outrageous,' Priscilla intervened. 'It is a simple case of suicide.'

'Or one of the other guests this evening, who left after the dinner,' Auguste suggested, ignoring her.

'Mr Didier!' his hostess said furiously. 'I fear you forget your position.'

'There is no position, Lady Tabor,' Auguste responded firmly, 'where death is concerned. Only truth.'

'They all went,' Walter put in, full of importance. Then as everyone looked at him, he blushed. 'I counted them. Four carriages, ten people. They was on a list that London detective gave me.'

'Well done,' Cobbold said briefly. 'Suicide most probably.' The terrier features bore a sudden smile for Lady Tabor. A smile without warmth. He leaned forward and gingerly picked up the gun – by its barrel, Auguste noted with interest. 'Do you recognise this, sir?'

'Of course, my dear fellow,' said George Tabor, irritated. 'It's a Webley, Mark II service revolver. The butt has no pawl.'

'Do you possess one?'

'Of course. Kept in the gun room.'

'Is it there now?'

'How the devil do I know?'

Cobbold dropped the gun into a paper bag. 'As I say, probably suicide, sir. No need to worry.' But his eyes were more intent on the corpse, Auguste observed, than in reassuring Lord Tabor. So he did think it was murder, and if so Tatiana's role in finding the body would come under scrutiny. There was some mystery there which she was not prepared to tell him about – and time was running out. What to do? Suddenly he knew.

'If I might make a suggestion,' he ventured, apparently offhandedly. 'Since His Majesty is present,

I wonder if Chief Inspector Rose of Scotland Yard should be consulted. He is used to dealing with His Majesty and murder—' Even in his anxiety he thought how ridiculous this sounded, as if His Majesty were a Jack the Ripper in his private moments.

He was greeted by silence. Auguste was not yet used to the Yorkshire economy of words, or its pace of contemplation.

'Aye,' said Cobbold at last.

In Highbury, Chief Inspector Egbert Rose had long since laid aside the cares of the day, which this Saturday had involved shopping with Edith first at Mr Pinpole's, then the Maypole Dairy, then Gamages in search of some nice toy soldiers for Edith's younger sister's oldest. Highbury Saturdays were not devoted to partridge shooting, though they might be rounded off with a pleasant pipe or a drink in the local public house. However, this evening had seen a rare culinary triumph on Edith's part. Inspired by the presence of their new neighbours at dinner she had ventured to produce a creditable imitation of Mrs Marshall's Creole Cutlets. Hitherto Rose had privately been of the opinion that Edith and Mr Pinpole the butcher were in a conspiracy to pervert the course of English justice by producing meat so tough that the resulting indigestion could be guaranteed to disturb his thought processes for days on end.

Dreaming of Auguste's version of the same dish in which he had once indulged at Plum's Club for Gentlemen, Egbert slept peacefully until the sharp ring of the telephone split his dream asunder. How come these operators were all so blasted cheerful at five-thirty in the morning? His ill-temper was only slightly abated by the sound of Auguste's somewhat hesitant voice.

'Yorkshire?' Rose grunted. 'Out of my area,' and prepared to hang up the receiver.

'But, Egbert, the King—'

The worst two words in the English language so far as Chief Inspector Rose was concerned. 'You don't mean to say you've dragged him in again.'

An indignant squawk from the other end forced a reluctant grin even to Rose's face. 'Now let's get this straight. You've got a dead body. Shot. Not an accident. Probably suicide.'

A short silence, then, 'Possibly.'

Rose swore under his breath.

'You will come, Egbert?' Auguste asked, alarmed. 'You may speak to Inspector Cobbold if you wish—'

Rose had once made a trip to Scarborough – and what he had seen of Yorkshire convinced him that London was not only homelier, but warmer. Upstairs Edith would be hunched up under the warm bedclothes pretending to sleep but agog to know what was happening. He mentally weighed Yorkshire against the displeasure of King Edward VII as conveyed through the upper hierarchy of the Yard. 'Yes.'

At nine o'clock Auguste staggered down the ornate curved staircase after a mere two hours' sleep. When he had returned to their room, Tatiana, it had appeared, was asleep. This morning when he awoke – if awoke was the word – she was already dressing with the help of one of the Tabor housemaids. He could not avoid the unworthy suspicion that the girl had been summoned as a deterrent to any discussion of the night's events.

'Good morning, *daragoy*,' she called.

At the sound of her familiar greeting, doubts vanished and he went across to kiss her.

'Egbert is coming,' he told her in relief. Tatiana liked Egbert and Edith. Edith had been full of apprehension at the thought of a real princess visiting her home, especially as to what refreshment might be offered. Auguste had assured her that Tatiana was a great devotee of the recipes of Mrs Marshall, as was he himself; guilt at his duplicity had been assuaged by Edith's look of pleasure. Tatiana had entered the house, promptly seen in it the epitome of all Mr Marx would approve, even the china Toby jugs, and suffered Edith's cooking in the interests of a new-found-land. They got on splendidly thereafter.

So why the sudden chill in Tatiana's face at the mention of Egbert's imminent arrival?

Slowly Auguste went downstairs for breakfast. From the ecstasy of newly wedded bliss, he seemed to have been pitchforked into nightmare. Where was the safe world of yesterday, if even Egbert's arrival was overcast by mystery?

To his great surprise, nearly all the party save, of course, His Majesty, was present at breakfast including the Dowager. News of the night's events must have spread. Even Beatrice Janes was present, and thus it was highly possible that His Majesty already knew what had happened – or very shortly would.

The ramifications of this were firmly relegated to the back of his mind as he decided that his *estomac* could not contemplate them simultaneously with an assault by kidney or kedgeree (particularly not Mr Breckles' less than authentic version). A *café noir* on the other hand might well galvanise his mind into action. There was a silence as he entered. Then:

'Good morning, Mr Didier. I hear you are turning detective again,' Miriam greeted him gaily. 'I hope your tales to us on Friday evening did not inspire last night's events.'

'Really, Mother,' Priscilla said reprovingly. 'I have explained to you it is a case of suicide, not murder.' It was a brave attempt at re-establishing control after a night not so much broken as shattered.

'I heard Mr Didier was very clever when the Galaxy chorus girls were getting strangled one after the other. He got on ever so well with them, you see,' volunteered Gertie brightly, reaching for an apple and remembering she had forgotten the way Cyril had told her to peel it.

Auguste was no proof against such flattery, particularly from Gertie, and bowed his head in appreciation towards her, only to find Tatiana had entered and was gazing at him in obvious amusement. Her smile died as he rose to his feet to greet her.

'Oh, Princess,' cried Beatrice excitedly, anxious to hear what the horse's mouth had to say after what had obviously, Auguste now realised, been the subject of much discussion before he entered. 'Alexander tells us you wanted a *smoke* when you discovered that poor man last night.' If a princess could take a smoke, the twentieth century looked promising for women.

'Yes,' replied Tatiana gravely. 'Life is a voyage of discovery, do you not agree, Mrs Janes?'

'Oh, quite,' Beatrice readily did so, though her own voyages rarely took her beyond Bond Street. 'And do you approve, Mr Didier?' she added meekly.

'As a newly married man, I find everything my wife does is naturally perfect,' he murmured diplomatically, wondering how his wife's conduct could be the topic of discussion, when a dead body had been discovered only a few hours ago. Or was his arrival at breakfast the signal to cease speculation on that subject?

'It does not matter. I shall not take another smoke,' Tatiana said dismissively.

'I am much relieved,' Priscilla told her graciously. Obviously her Ladyship had recovered from the shock of what Tatiana must have disclosed to her during the night, Auguste reflected. The greater shock of the corpse had outweighed even Tatiana's grievous sin.

'Will you be accompanying us this morning, Mr Didier?' Laura's quiet voice asked.

'To church?'

'To see the body,' Oliver told him cheerfully. 'It's been carted off to Settle hospital mortuary in view of His Majesty's presence here, at the request of his detectives. Those of us who didn't take part in the night's proceedings are invited along to see if we can recognise him.'

'It is iniquitous,' Priscilla burst out. 'It is unfortunate enough that this deluded man chose our smokehouse for his despicable act, without our guests being put to inconvenience.'

'*All* your guests, your Ladyship?' enquired Auguste delicately.

'Not of course His Majesty,' retorted Priscilla, shocked.

'Yet who more likely to get murdered here than he?' Victoria pointed out, helping herself to another buttered muffin.

A little shriek from Beatrice. 'Oh, Miss Tabor, the very thought of it. Do you think he'll come back?'

'Who?' asked her husband.

'His Majesty's assassin.'

'Mrs Janes!' Priscilla's anguished voice rang out. 'I fear you have misunderstood.'

Cyril failed to take note of the warning conveyed in his sister-in-law's tone. 'Was it one of the Special Branch Johnnies that shot him?'

'Cyril!' Priscilla broke in desperately. 'I fear you are forgetting it was suicide.'

'Why should the King's assassin commit suicide?' asked Gertie, puzzled, oblivious of storm clouds since she lived amongst them most of the time.

'He didn't, kitten,' Cyril assured her.

'You mean it was murder?' asked Miriam brightly.

'It was not murder. It was suicide!' Lady Priscilla shouted, rising to her feet. 'Will you *all* please understand? It was *suicide!*'

But why, Auguste wondered, was she so certain?

His Majesty was seated at a small writing table in his salon as Auguste, bowing deeply, was ushered with Tatiana into the presence. There was a distinct lack of rapport between husband and wife. The air crackled with the tense politeness of a marital no man's land. An equerry had been sent to summon them, and Auguste had welcomed the opportunity to attempt to put matters in their true perspective to His Majesty. It was not going to be easy. Nobody hoped more than himself that Priscilla Tabor was right in her conviction; but there were too many unexplained loose threads for him to have any confidence that this was the case. And one loose thread was Tatiana.

'Ah, Tati,' was His Majesty's affectionate greeting, rising to kiss her before turning his attention to her husband. 'Now, Didier, what's all this about a suicide?' There was little affection for Auguste in his tone.

'It's most regrettable, Your Majesty, but—'

'I know that. Who is it?'

'No one so far recognises him, sir.'

The King frowned. 'Unusual, isn't it? I gather he was dressed.'

'Yes, sir.' Auguste correctly interpreted this and mentally congratulated himself it was a small sign that he had not yet been cast totally outside the pale of the royal family.

'No fear it might be anything other than suicide?' the King barked.

Auguste steeled himself. 'It is not beyond the bounds of possibility, sir.'

The King regarded him suspiciously. 'Don't let him go making a murder out of this, Tati, will you?'

'I'm afraid he's sent for Chief Inspector Rose, Bertie,' Tatiana told him.

Afraid? Auguste picked up on the word with some disquiet.

'In that case I'll leave.' His Majesty could be a man of quick decision.

'But it is possible he was a potential assassin, sir,' Auguste said in alarm. 'Dressing in formal clothes could have averted suspicion from him if he were spotted.'

'If he was,' the King pointed out pragmatically, 'the poor fellow clearly thought better of his plans. But –' driven to new heights of detection, ' – if it was murder, it's rather a coincidence that he was killed himself before he could make his attempt on me. My bodyguards deny all knowledge of him, so I've nothing to do with the matter.'

'Perhaps not, sir.'

The King looked at him. He expected more co-operation from Didier. 'I'll leave,' repeated His Britannic Majesty. '*Now.*' Even sweet little Beatrice was but poor temptation where scandal might lurk.

Sweet little Beatrice was not at that moment living up to her lover's idealised picture of her. She was pouting in displeasure.

'I don't want to come.'

'You have to,' her husband informed her curtly. 'It would look most odd.'

'*He* needs me.'

'*He* will have to manage without you. Besides, I've no doubt he had you last night.'

'Harold!' Beatrice was unable to believe she was hearing aright. Such crudeness from her own husband.

'Are you out of your mind?' He must be. Such things were never alluded to in polite society.

'You weren't in your room at one o'clock.'

'Yes, I was.'

'No, you weren't.'

'How do you know?'

'I went to see.'

'And where else did you go?' Sweetness had indeed turned acid. 'Not for a smoke, did you?'

Harold stared at her, and changed tack. 'I don't mind His Majesty,' he said heavily. 'After all, he's a friend of mine. It's the others.'

'Others?' asked Beatrice slowly. This was far worse than she had feared.

'That fellow in the smokehouse,' Harold said pleadingly. 'He wasn't one, was he?'

Terror shot through Beatrice, all the sharper for being so unexpected. 'What did he look like?' she whispered.

'About my age. Beard. Dark hair—' He stopped as she looked at him aghast.

'How do you know, Harold? Oh, Puppikins, what have you *done*?'

'It was the Tabors,' he gabbled. 'The Tabors told me. Truly, Pussikins.'

'Where are you going, Auguste?' Tatiana asked in surprise, seeing him don his ulster.

'To Settle.'

'But you have seen the body.'

'I need to be present.' He could not explain that he was impatient for news, since she had denied there was any need for concern. If by any chance Cobbold had now identified the corpse, he might be able to rid his mind of the still-nagging suspicion that Tatiana might know more than she was saying

60

about the events of the night.

'I will come in the carriage with you.'

He could not stop himself as tension burst out. 'This great desire for my company did not prevent you from absenting yourself from our bed last night.'

'So you try to stop me from seeing my own cousin? Are you jealous of Alexander? You wish to cage me up like a poor little bird?'

She did not look in the least like a poor little bird, more like an uncaged tiger.

Two could lose their tempers, especially after virtually no sleep.

'If you will creep around like a housemaid—' Auguste shouted.

'Huh! You know all about housemaids creeping around, eh? Creeping into your bed.'

'That is not so!' He was outraged.

'Oh, Mr Auguste,' she mimicked. 'You're so handsome, so clever.'

'And if I am?' he retorted, then broke off aghast. 'Tatiana, we are *quarrelling*.' Never, never had he imagined such a thing could happen.

Her eyes flashed. 'Naturally. We are married.'

He was bereft of words. He left the room in silent dignity, only to find her following him, though not with any sign of contrition. The air was icy between them as they reached the carriages. He turned to escort her to a carriage, only to see her staring in rapture at Alexander. For a moment, he was about to erupt in fury, then he realised it wasn't Alexander that held her attention. It was his motorcar.

Forbidden by her father to ride in such contraptions, she was consequently as drawn to them as to Mr Marx, and to this one, it appeared, in particular.

Alexander, seeing her bemused expression, swept her a deep bow. 'Would you care to accompany me, dearest cousin? Victoria has been commanded to ride in the family carriage.'

'I would.' All trace of the tigress was gone, as she climbed with alacrity into the undoubtedly graceful green two-seater. It chugged into life and juddered along the Tabor drive. Auguste's own carriage, shared with Mr Richey, the butler, a footman and the King's aide-de-camp, the first two commanded by Cobbold to attend in case they recognised a visitor to the Hall, followed in its wake. A definite smirk had crossed Richey's face as Auguste climbed in, as if confirming some private opinion of his own. Auguste gritted his teeth and proceeded to ask questions about visitors to the Hall. They could hardly not tell him. He was a guest, and whether they liked it or not, a gentleman.

It was with great satisfaction that, as their carriage turned to climb the hill out of the nearby village of Kirkby Malham, Auguste saw a stationary motorcar. De Dion Boutons, it appeared, found the incline too great and would have to take the lower much longer road. He did not wave.

At Settle Tatiana greeted her husband with enthusiasm as though motorcars oiled all troubled waters.

'Just think,' she informed him, 'the front axles are separate from the drive shaft. Isn't that exciting?'

'What does it mean?'

'I don't know,' she admitted, and Auguste meanly laughed. 'But I'm going to find out,' she added under her breath as he walked off to greet Cobbold at the Settle mortuary.

'Is it really necessary for the ladies to have to undergo this ordeal?' Harold Janes demanded ponderously of the inspector.

'Yes, sir. We still have no identification.'

'It's quite outrageous.' What he really considered

62

outrageous, Auguste suspected, was Beatrice bewailing the fact that she had wanted to stay behind with His Majesty.

Auguste watched the group's varying reactions as they inspected the corpse, which now awaited the arrival of Chief Inspector Rose before undergoing post mortem examination. Laura showed no emotion at all, her mother Miriam, who had insisted on attending, looked merely curious. Victoria was the most visibly affected, clutching Alexander's hand for moral support. Harold Janes registered annoyance, Oliver looked shaken, Gertie refused to look, burying her head in Cyril's shoulder. Cyril was more concerned with Kitten than with the corpse.

'I'm so sorry, Inspector,' Miriam informed him graciously. 'I wish we could have identified him for you. But I'm afraid not one of us knows who he was.'

At the very moment that King Edward VII, congratulating himself on a lucky escape, was enjoying a hearty luncheon of oysters, truffled mutton chops, and *soufflé de chocolat* on the royal train, which had soared triumphantly over the spectacular viaducts of the Ribblesdale Valley line on its way to Scotland, Chief Inspector Egbert Rose was enjoying a rather less grand luncheon of tripe and onions on the Great Northern railway to Leeds. His train was dutifully chugging rather than soaring. Its cook must know Edith, he thought sourly and unusually disloyally, not to mention Mr Pinpole; he chewed his way on through the tripe with the determination of a Stanley in search of Livingstone.

Luncheon at Tabor Hall, while by no means comparable with Rose's tripe, also fell short of the standards which His Majesty was now enjoying. Haute cuisine was not Mr Breckles' forte, Auguste decided.

This *blanquette* resembled English blancmange in its blandness, instead of achieving a subtle blending of flavours. Yet Breckles possessed all the characteristics of a good chef. Auguste considered this conundrum. Perhaps he would request the honour of being allowed further access to his host's kitchens. After all, he thought glumly, the remainder of their stay could well be longer than intended. Gone were his expectations of being home in time for Cook's Day Off on Tuesday. Queen Anne's Gate seemed a depressingly long way away. Yes, he would certainly seek to widen Mr Breckles' range. And, after all, if the corpse did prove to have been murdered, where better to seek accurate information on Tabor Hall's inmates than in its servants' hall?

He jumped as his host addressed him. 'The poor fellow was obviously here to visit another house and picked the wrong one.'

'Could he have been here to visit one of your servants or anyone living on the estate?' Auguste asked.

'He was a gentleman, Mr Didier,' Priscilla pointed out, her tone suggesting no gentleman would have asked such a question.

George looked up from his *blanquette*. 'I say, that's it, by Jove! He must have been visiting someone else. The lodgekeeper, or the gamekeeper.'

'Nonsense,' his mother pointed out. 'The tailcoat was far too good.'

Her daughter-in-law overruled her. 'I believe George is correct. I trust you will direct your enquiries in that direction, Mr Didier.'

'Mother has a point,' Cyril said suddenly. 'The cut of those trousers wasn't half bad. Trifle old-fashioned, but then he wasn't exactly a chick, was he? Someone's hand-me-downs, maybe,' he finished lamely, as there was a silence. The invitation to remember the terrible

64

sight of the corpse resulted in several sets of cutlery being hastily laid on plates.

'Please don't start talking about that poor man again,' Victoria begged. 'This has been the most horrid party ever. Alexander and I have our engagement celebrated in deep mourning, and now we have the death to follow it.'

Beatrice giggled, and Priscilla made a rare mistake. 'I see nothing amusing in my daughter's ill-timed remarks, Mrs Janes.'

The merry giggle was cut short, as Beatrice took in that she, intimate friend of His Majesty, was being reproved. Large tears formed in her eyes, and without a word she rose to her feet. 'We shall leave,' her husband hastily informed the company, picking up the unspoken message. 'We are not welcome here.' With a regretful eye on the Stilton, he held back his wife's chair for her to make a sweeping exit.

Tatiana took pity on Priscilla's dilemma. Public retreat was impossible for her, yet social ruin stared her in the face: not only had the King left early, but now his favourite was threatening to follow suit. 'Please do stay, Mrs Janes. I was so relying on you to explain to me about London society – and the latest fashions. As you are one of the leaders of London society, I had hoped for guidance.'

Auguste, not for the first time, admired his wife's social quickwittedness. Tatiana had no interest in fashions whatsoever.

Beatrice paused, turned, and graciously resumed her seat. Tatiana was after all a relation (of some sort) to His Majesty. *And* a princess, even if a somewhat unusual one, who chose to go to smokehouses in the middle of the night.

Tatiana, true to her word, bore Beatrice away after

luncheon, her arm firmly clasped in hers. They made an incongruous couple, Auguste thought: Tatiana tall, slender and firm of stride; Beatrice short, plump and definitely a trotter. He began to walk into the library to while away the time until Egbert should arrive.

'Ah, Didier!' Auguste's heart sank. Was he still to be allowed no peace for reflection? 'Fancy a game of billiards?' His host approached him eagerly.

'In fact, I—'

'Good, good,' George said heartily, shepherding him towards the billiard room. He probably didn't know where the library was, Auguste thought sourly. 'What do you make of this rum business, eh?' George asked him anxiously, having put a cue in his hand as if to prevent escape. 'Getting to the bottom of it, are you?'

'Not yet, sir.'

'George,' his host said enthusiastically. 'Call me George.'

'I'm honoured.'

'Deuced odd, corpse turning up in our smokehouse like that. Had a foreign look about him, didn't you think?'

'A touch of the sun, certainly. Not from Yorkshire.'

George laughed immoderately at this feeble witticism. 'Know who I thought it was at first?' he said a little nervously. 'That fellow Mariot.'

'Who?'

'Laura's chap. Can't be, of course. She'd have recognised him, though he left all of twenty years ago. Just a stupid fancy of mine.'

'When you say "left"—' Auguste began.

'Wanted to marry her. As Priscilla said at the time, she'd be wanting to marry the cook next.'

'Some people do,' said Auguste drily.

Belatedly George realised he had blundered. 'Things

66

were different then, of course,' he added hastily. 'People are more broadminded now.'

Auguste hadn't noticed.

'Anyway,' George continued hastily, 'Priscilla made her see it wouldn't do. He saw it himself, to do him justice. He had no money. No prospects. A sort of bookish navvy. Archaeologists they call them.'

'Not *Robert* Mariot?' Auguste asked astounded. 'Not Mariot of the later excavations at Troy? And now Babylon?'

'Heard of him, have you?'

'Yes,' said Auguste simply. 'Most people have.' He was thinking rapidly. It would not be too difficult to get a photograph of Robert Mariot. Just to be sure . . .

With some difficulty he extricated himself from billiards on the plea that he needed to speak to Tatiana. George, it seemed, was only too happy to come with him to the salon. It appeared he needed a word with Beatrice. Beatrice was, however, alone in the Blue Salon, deep in the *Illustrated London News* – the fashion column.

'The Princess has gone to the village. On foot,' Beatrice added, somewhat perplexed at this unusual activity. 'She wished me to go as well, but my shoes—' She looked at the white satin slippers, as Auguste speedily eluded his host's 'Perhaps I'll come—'

He was alone at last. For a few moments only. Hurrying down the steps behind him, came Alfred Tabor.

'Ah, Didier.'

Auguste turned. 'Alfred,' he said somewhat coldly, 'if you are intending to accompany me, please do not concern yourself. I am quite able to find my own way.'

'No bother,' announced Alfred cheerily. 'Noblesse oblige and all that.'

'Very well. We'll go this way.' Meanly, Auguste set

off on the path to Malham most certain of providing mud and puddles. Alfred was shaken but undeterred.

'What do you think are the odds it was murder, Didier?' he began eagerly.

'Your mother seems certain it is suicide,' Auguste reminded him.

'She would be, wouldn't she?'

For one startled moment Auguste wondered if young Alfred were suggesting his mother had stooped to murder.

'She's afraid it's her skeleton in the closet.'

'Skeleton?' asked Auguste with undisguised fascination.

'Uncle Oscar, her brother. He hasn't been heard of since the Cripple Creek Gold Rush in Colorado. The mater and her folks come from Philadelphia, but Oscar went to the bad. Grandfather threw him out without a dollar, so he went hunting for a few on his own. He turned up here about twelve years ago on the scrounge. Father was afraid he'd come to stay, but off he went and we heard he'd gone to Cripple Creek. He sent us a photograph. You can have a look at it. It's on the wall in the back corridor to the servants' quarters. He's holding up a lump of rock, grinning like a Cheshire Cat.'

'So he made good?'

'Oscar couldn't keep a fortune if he stored it in Fort Knox. Someday he'd come back, that's what Father always said.'

'But your parents would have recognised him.'

'Who's to say they didn't?' Alfred winked.

'Why am I accompanied everywhere like an English cod by parsley sauce?' Auguste demanded of his wife as she leant over the small stone bridge to admire the swift-flowing Malham beck. His voice rose sharply, to the great interest of two urchins playing with an iron hoop, and several worthies of Malham village on their way to the Buck Inn. Only with Tatiana in view had he shaken off the obnoxious Alfred.

'They like you, Auguste. And why not? So do I,' his wife told him fondly, putting her arm round him.

He was not to be so easily beguiled. After all, she had shown few signs of liking him earlier that day. 'It is more than that. I think it is to do with your visit to the smokehouse.'

She sighed. 'Tell me, chéri, again. Do you think I am a murderer?'

'Non!'

'Do you think I have a lover?'

'Non!'

'And if I had an assignation, would I have it in the smokehouse when His Majesty is nearby? *And* my husband?'

'Non.'

'Then let us forget this foolishness.'

'I cannot,' he said sadly.

'Detection is in your blood, is it not? You hear the hunting horn and feel you must follow the chase.'

Did he? Surely only in cooking, not detection? Cooking was a majestic exploration of uncharted seas in which ingredients fitted together by an artist formed a perfect recipe. Wasn't detection like that too? Its ingredients were culled from many quarters; would they fit, or would they remain obstinately refusing to combine like tomato in risotto, sage with lamb. Yet when detective flavours married, when instinct told him the last piece of the puzzle was safely slotted home, that was like cooking. And certainly in the back of his mind some memory of an article he had read was stirring . . .

'Perhaps just a little,' he admitted, won over.

69

'Do you think the corpse was murdered?'

'I am afraid it is possible. *Chérie*, did you move the body? I must know before I see Egbert.'

'Alexander did. I agreed.'

'You lied to me.' His heart sank.

'It was necessary.'

'Why?'

'I can only tell you that it has nothing to do with that poor man in the smokehouse.'

'He was a stranger to you?'

'Yes.'

He wanted to sing, to shout in relief. 'And were the lights on the path lit when you went there?'

'No.'

'And in the smokehouse?'

'No. We lit them.'

'Was the door locked?'

'No. Though we had taken the spare key from the kitchen, of course. They have one in order to stock up the wine supply and refreshments,' she explained.

Was there a slight pause before she answered? A shade too much helpful explanation? Of course not. Relief bathed him with its soothing powers. He told her so.

'Good. Now I wish to purchase potted trout. I am told it is good here. And it is useful. Mr Marx says that nothing is worthwhile unless it is useful.'

'I'm relieved Mr Marx considers food useful,' Auguste remarked laughing.

'I am not sure he would approve of the *truffles* that accompanied the mutton chops you served on Saturday evening.'

Auguste leapt on this philosophical point, perhaps in order to forget that the clouds were not completely lifted between himself and Tatiana. In marriage he had embarked upon a voyage of discovery, during

70

which hidden rocks might yet tear the craft from underneath.

He was beginning to know this road rather well, Auguste thought later that afternoon as the carriage jolted its way across Scosthrop Moor, past fells on which bears and rhinoceros had once grazed in prehistoric times, and on down into Settle once more. The ride was conducive to quiet contemplation of facts. Why, for instance, was Priscilla Tabor quite so vehement that it was a suicide? He played with the idea of one of the Tabors as a murderer, and dismissed it, rather reluctantly so far as Priscilla herself was concerned. No Tabor in their right mind would choose the day of the King's visit to commit murder. One of the guests, now. Suppose Priscilla suspected one of them? She would go to any lengths to minimise scandal . . . Yet the carriages and occupants had all been counted out by the constable at the gate before the Hall had been locked up for the night.

When he reached the New Street police station, conveniently set next to the Court House, he found Egbert Rose already on good terms with Cobbold. Not perhaps surprising, he reflected. There was something similar about their faces, albeit Rose resembled a bloodhound more than a terrier, but their eyes had the same alert, wary look.

'Hah,' Rose announced, well pleased at seeing Auguste and coming to greet him. 'Never thought to see Auguste the country squire.'

Auguste followed the direction of his glance to the mud on his elegantly polished country brown boots. 'There has been much to do today.'

'Seeing His Majesty off, no doubt?' Rose said resignedly.

Auguste nodded. It was not the first time that His Majesty had removed himself from an unfortunate situation with all the dexterity of a lady from a box in one of Maskelyne and Cooke's magical devices.

'Right, I'm ready for Tabor Hall.' Rose paused.

Auguste picked up the unspoken question. 'You will be lodged there.'

'That's decent of them.'

'Not really,' Auguste replied honestly. 'I suspect it was preferable to your inspiring local gossip if you took rooms in one of the Malham inns.'

'So I'll be in with the lampboy, will I?'

'Not at all. I persuaded Lady Tabor that the royal wing would do very nicely for you, since it is now vacated.'

'The King's bed?' asked Rose, highly diverted.

'That of a junior equerry.'

Rose grunted. 'Why should a stranger go to that smokehouse to shoot himself?'

Auguste had heard that question too frequently today. 'I suspect he did not.' Auguste glanced at Cobbold, who seemed about to object to his presence.

'Remains to be seen whether the Coroner's enquiry agrees with you. Cobbold does.'

'No powder tattooing. Suggests he was shot at a distance greater than about fifteen or sixteen inches,' Cobbold pointed out.

A fact he must have registered in the smokehouse, Auguste thought ruefully, and had had no intention of passing on to Auguste.

'Pockets,' Cobbold said tersely to Rose, and tipped out the contents of an envelope on the table. One handkerchief, unmarked. Box of matches, a key.

'No money,' Auguste pointed out.

'Not unusual for house guests,' Rose countered.

'But he wasn't a house guest. So he had to get to

72

Tabor Hall somehow. He would probably have needed money.'

'Must have sprouted wings,' Cobbold told them. 'We've got thirteen constables here and not one of them has been able to turn up anything. Neither the Golden Lion nor the Ashfield Hotel claims to have had a guest of that description. Nor the Victoria at Kirkby Malham nor the Buck or Lister Arms at Malham. And not the Temperance Hotels either. He doesn't seem to have come by train, or omnibus, or even carrier. If he leapt on a stolen horse, we'd have found the horse. I'm spreading the enquiries wider into the dales, but so far it looks as if he could only have come in a suitcase. Strangers stand out round here like currants in a Yorkshire pudding.'

'What about His Majesty?' asked Auguste hesitantly. 'It might have been an assassin.'

'As soon as we have photographs developed, I'll send a man up to Balmoral to see if the King or his entourage recognise our corpse,' Cobbold said dourly. 'That aide-de-camp he left behind is as much help as clogs to a mermaid.'

'If I know His Majesty,' Rose ruminated, 'we'll have every blasted equerry, plus Silver Stick, Gold Stick, and the Lord Great Chamberlain, demanding to know of the Yard whether this matter's been cleared up.'

'Then we'd best start by finding out who he is – and quickly,' Cobbold said practically. He turned to the clothes again. 'Good quality gloves – assuming they're his. Tailcoat, label inside pocket, badly stained with blood that's soaked through. Maker, somebody in Paris. Looks like Noire or Poire.'

'I have not heard of him,' Auguste observed, coming into his own. 'Yet it is good quality, if worn.' He looked at a shiny patch on one elbow and sniffed gently. 'Not new. Someone has tried to renovate this with ammonia

73

– see where the cloth is slightly brown?'

'Black tie and waistcoat. Both badly stained. No label on them but the tie is good-quality silk, wouldn't you say?'

Cobbold permitted himself a grin. 'This is Yorkshire, Inspector Rose. Nowt but good wool here.'

'High-collared piqué dress shirt. Again, good quality. Label – Amelia Pegg, New York. No laundry mark. Far travelled, our bloke,' Rose commented. 'What else?'

'White wool combinations. Nothing unusual there for a man of his age. No corsets,' Cobbold continued. 'Silk braces, suspenders, socks and old-fashioned black boots. No maker's name – it's worn off. That seems out of keeping.'

'No front braces in the trousers either,' said Auguste thoughtfully. 'Our man buys good clothes and keeps them regardless of fashion.'

'Only recently back from abroad perhaps,' Rose suggested.

'Back?' repeated Auguste, his recent conversation about Robert Mariot and Uncle Oscar coming to mind. 'But we do not know he started from Yorkshire. He could have been a foreigner.'

Cobbold looked taken aback, as if a nameless corpse to identify in Yorkshire was bad enough. Opening up the horizons to encompass other countries was far worse.

'Gun's British,' Rose pointed out, looking at the offending article. 'That's a Webley, ain't it?'

'Taken from the gun room, so Lord Tabor tells me,' Cobbold replied.

'And where is that?'

'Inside the house, near the garden entrance door.'

'That probably rules out suicide, then. Been touched by human hand, has it?' asked Rose casually.

'Only the hand that pulled the trigger,' Cobbold

answered, 'and maybe someone on the scene before I got here.' A pause. 'It's this new fingerprint business you're thinking of?'

Auguste froze in horror, not at the implication as regards himself, but instantly the thought came to him: had Tatiana touched it?

Rose nodded. 'Central Fingerprint Branch. Might as well give them some practice. I'll get a man up with the equipment.'

'I sent for some earlier this year, Chief Inspector.'

Rose gave him a friendly nod. 'Good. Let's check it, together with anything else we can turn up from this smokehouse.'

'What I don't understand, sir,' Cobbold spoke directly to Rose, 'is what the King's representative is doing here?'

Auguste stiffened. Him?

'Monsieur Didier?' Rose asked in glee. 'He's a cook, aren't you, Auguste?'

'I have had the honour to assist Inspector Rose in a humble capacity,' Auguste glared at Egbert, 'on several of his cases. One or two of those have concerned the King, of whom my wife is a relation. A cousin three times removed.'

'Now you're concerned with who removed the owner of this lot.' Rose bundled up the clothes again.

Egbert Rose looked out unimpressed at the fells and limestone crags on the way to Tabor Hall. He was, Auguste knew, a town man. Egbert liked people, buildings, alleyways, all the million and one secrets of mankind, not bubbling becks, saxifrage and fern-covered hillsides and bored-looking sheep. Rose's 'nose', famous in the Yard for its intuition, didn't work so quickly in the country – it merely felt cold. But the smokehouse forced even him into interest as he took in its pinnacles and towers rising into the grey late-afternoon sky. He insisted on visiting it before the Hall. 'You don't mean to tell me everyone has to tramp all the way from the house just for a smoke?'

'Even the King,' Auguste assured him. 'It is Lady Tabor's strictest rule.'

'It sounds a family whose bosom I wouldn't care to be in,' commented Egbert sourly. He liked a pipe from time to time.

'You won't know how apt that is until you see Priscilla Tabor's.'

Rose had enough bosoms to contend with in the smokehouse. 'Not, I take it, Lady Tabor's choice,' he commented disapprovingly. He tried to banish from his mind an irreverent picture of Edith in black garters with roses and nothing else.

'No, her visit last night – or rather, early this morning, was her first—' Auguste said, belatedly remembering his surprise at her lack of curiosity in her husband's choice of art.

Egbert studied his surroundings. 'You know, Auguste, things are changing in my world. Not at the Yard, or in England, but on the Continent they are way ahead of us. Forensic science is taught there at universities, here it's a dirty word. But it will come, just like fingerprinting has come now that Edward Henry's arrived at the Yard. I told you he'd set up a fingerprint branch in July, didn't I? Sooner or later, we'll get to the point when this room would be able to explain the whole crime to us. Even who did it, most like. Hairs, fibres, fingerprints, bloodstains—'

Blood – that was it, Auguste remembered with relief. 'I read an article about how analysis of bloodstains might be able to help in murder investigations.'

'That's right. In Germany. That Mad Carpenter of Rügen case. Heard about it? They're hoping to disprove his story that the blood on him wasn't human but an animal's. And that'll be just the start.'

'However good the stove, the cook is more important, Egbert.'

'Try telling the Yard that,' Egbert said sourly. 'Now, where was the body lying – and the gun?'

Trying to ignore his squeamishness, Auguste pointed out the marks he had made with spent matches, and those the police had added. 'Lie down and show me.' Gulping, Auguste obediently huddled into position.

'And you were the first to see the body? How was that?'

The moment he had dreaded. Egbert after all must know this from Cobbold. 'No. I was summoned.'

'Who by?'

'Alexander Tully-Rich, now engaged to the Tabors' daughter, and—' He plunged. 'Tatiana.'

'You said you got there at three-thirty. Did she see a light from the bedroom window?'

'No, she had come from the smokehouse.'

'Why?' the inexorable voice continued.

'She and Alexander wished to have a smoke,' shouted Auguste, red in the face, cornered.

Rose said no more, which alarmed Auguste more than the questions. Try as he might, that first sight of the corpse on the floor was imprinted on his memory. Sprawled on its face and the gun conveniently by the right hand, a gun he believed had been placed, not fallen. And a body he now knew had been moved before he got there. What would Egbert make of it? He relaxed, as Rose changed the subject. 'The doctor estimated he died between eleven-thirty and two. We'll know more later. Were you all still up then?'

'I was playing billiards with Oliver Carstairs till half-past twelve,' Auguste replied stiffly. 'I believe most people had retired. I thought my wife had, but I was wrong. She was with her cousin.' He made it sound the most natural thing in the world for a newly married woman. 'I heard nothing, but the smokehouse is a long way from the house.'

'A gun makes a fair noise in a quiet night.'

'So does the stable clock,' said Auguste eagerly, glad to be on neutral ground. 'And its striking twelve might cover the sound.'

'Lucky for a murderer.'

'Or planned.'

'A suicide wouldn't care.'

They regarded each other for a moment, well pleased at the familiar dovetailing of thought processes.

'Did he force his way in here?'

'The door is not kept locked.'

'Raining, was it, that evening?'

'No, but the day before it had been. Why?'

Rose glanced at the soles of his brown boots. 'The chap's boots were clean.'

A pause, as Auguste puzzled over this, but could find no explanation.

Rose heaved himself from the armchair. 'No hat. No overcoat. No mud. Cobbold said he came in a suitcase, didn't he? Looks as if he's right.'

How ridiculous was convention, thought Auguste indignantly. The famous Chief Inspector Rose of the Yard slept in a servant's room, albeit a superior one. He, Auguste Didier, a chef (albeit a maître), slept in a guest bedroom because he was now dubbed a gentleman – not because of anything he had achieved, but because he was married to Tatiana. This evening, however, he intended to rebel.

Since the household was no longer in deep mourning because of the King's presence, Tatiana had decided she might now switch to complimentary mourning.

78

When he had asked whether Mr Marx endorsed such slavish adherence to capitalist etiquette, she had replied to the effect that Mr Marx was not necessarily always right. A hopeful sign. The white dress made her look delightful, and the lavender muff and hat suited her, but he was aware there was still a barrier between them.

This evening Tatiana was to join the family and guests at the local church of St Michael at Kirkby Malham. He, Auguste, had other plans. He crept down to the kitchens, with a delightful sense of sin. He had heard it was Breckles' night off and thus supper would be both monotonous and cold. He, Auguste Didier, would improve the situation on both counts. Unfortunately he had been misinformed.

Opening the kitchen door nonchalantly, as if completely by chance, he ran straight into Mr Breckles himself whom he found holding an unfortunate pantry boy aloft by his collar, accusing him of the crime of mislaying the blood for the black pudding. The crime was a heinous one since the pudding could only be made with the blood of a pig killed while the moon was on the wane. Mr Breckles dropped the boy with a thud, and greeted Auguste triumphantly. 'Did I not tell you a crawing hen brings ill-hap upon the hoos?'

Nevertheless, it was clear from his friendliness that the kitchen staff had accepted as their due all the compliments that had descended from upstairs and, in the way of the world, had forgotten not only their former animosity but also any part Auguste may have played in their glory.

It appeared nothing would be too much trouble when Auguste stated he wished merely to prepare a small repast for Chief Inspector Rose. He had in mind a light *truite aux amandes* followed by *purée* of partridges and *crème brûlée*. Anxious to help, Breckles had different suggestions. He was eager to show the London policeman (who despite his native birthplace must be all right if he was vouched for by Auguste) that Yorkshire too was the home of fine cooking. What precisely? Auguste asked doubtfully, venturing to point out that roast beef and Yorkshire pudding were not exactly unknown south of Doncaster.

'Claggy toffee pudding,' announced Breckles.

Claggy, it transpired on cautious enquiry, meant sticky.

Rose's pernickety stomach and a pudding of that name did not seem destined to agree, but Auguste decided not to mention this. A brawny hand clapped him approvingly on his back, as he murmured that claggy toffee pudding would be an undoubted treat for Inspector Rose and agreed that if it were to appear on the Tabors' dinner menu he himself could scarcely resist the opportunity to taste it.

The resulting thump nearly sent him tumbling headfirst into the consommé. "Od rabbits, man, they eat nowt from Yorkshire in t'Hall.'

'That is a pity,' said Auguste diplomatically. 'The cuisine of the region is often the most interesting. I must try it. But first,' he said firmly, 'I require thyme for the partridge.'

'Plenty,' said Breckles, beaming. 'Two hours.'

Auguste disentangled this after a moment. 'You have a herb garden?'

Breckles proudly declared he had, and Auguste set forth towards the walled vegetable garden in which it was contained, pleased at the renewed opportunity to compare North with South. The vegetable garden lay some hundred yards away, tucked between the main drive, the Gordale beck and the rising slopes of infertile fells, which stretched far out up into the dusk. In London, he thought wistfully, it would already be

80

quite dark; up West, the streets ablaze with lights, filled with hansom cabs, motorcars, omnibuses, bejewelled women and cloaked gentlemen; in the East End, people would be packed into public houses and music halls, full of warmth and humanity . . . Here there was solitude, silence and a vast awe-inspiring stillness.

He opened the gate to the walled garden, to see it full of the mysterious shapes of apple trees, stunted from the wind despite the protective wall, and the familiar satisfying sight and smells of growing produce. In the semi-dusk he had to hunt for the thyme. At last he found it and bent down to pick a bunch. His mission achieved, he straightened up to return to the kitchen. Wasn't that parsley? That too would be helpful—

Quickly he bent down again. The crack of a gunshot rang out, just as he felt the sharp pain. He spun around to hear the gate clanging shut, automatically clasping a hand to his ear while expecting to see blood dripping from his chest. There was none – only a throbbing pain whose whereabouts he could not identify. Bewilderment fought with irrational anger, propelling him into action. He ran towards the gate, then turned to the left where he could hear his assailant crashing through bracken, obviously making for the wood and then perhaps the fells beyond.

It did not occur to Auguste that it was rather foolish to run towards a man with a gun who had evil intentions towards him. Pain and the twilight made him slower, however, while his assailant seemed to grow speedier. Beyond him he saw a dark grey shape emerge from the trees, rapidly climbing the steep fell. It remained silhouetted against the skyline on the rough moorland for a moment, looking down at him. Then, running sure-footed despite cloak and hat, it disappeared from view over the brow.

He was dreaming, he must be. No one would want to shoot *him*, Auguste Didier. But when he glanced at his hand, he saw blood-red. Experimentally he touched his ear. It was sticky. Blood was no dream. So neither was the misty figure now visible again, sauntering far away upon a moorland track. A figure that, as he strained to watch in the gloom, turned to give a mocking salute.

Chapter Four

William Breckles was a man of few words. He took one look at Auguste, and shepherded him through the fastnesses of below-stairs Tabor Hall to the sanctum that Auguste knew well from his days at Stockbery Towers – the housekeeper's room. The plump face of Mrs Breckles showed consternation as she saw the blood.

'That Mr Alfred take you for a duck, did 'ee?' she enquired scathingly, as she examined the damage. ''Tiz only a graze on the lug-end. Thou's ez strong ez an onion.'

Gratifying though this reassurance was, once he had translated it, it was not the sympathy for his smarting ear that Auguste wished to hear. As if reading his thoughts, the housekeeper rose to her feet in a rustle of bombazine. 'Come wi' me, honey.' He followed her into the sacred precincts of her still room and the suffering ear was soon bandaged against the world, whilst a potion of indeterminate origin, said to guard against witches, soothed the pain.

'Did tha bring bullet?' she enquired inexplicably. 'My granny did say if thee do tend cause, the harm be right in no time.'

'Thy granny were an au'd Mother Stebbins of a witch,' muttered Breckles. 'This is a gentleman from *France*, woman. Across water.'

'Witches get everywhere,' rejoined his wife, 'and if

you'd any sense, William, tha'd pay proper respect.'

Auguste was only too eager to pay proper respect. He was well acquainted with the charms, potions and beliefs of the wise women of Provence. One ignored them at one's peril. In his pain, he had forgotten the bullet, but he'd certainly go back to search for it. But not to hand to Mrs Breckles.

'Not one of his Lordship's guns, was it? Not on Sunday?' Breckles asked.

'No. Nor a poacher.'

'Not a Malham man, I'll be bound. One of them outcomers, thee'll find,' the housekeeper commented darkly. By which it transpired she meant someone not from Yorkshire.

'Have you seen any strangers?' asked Auguste sharply. He was likely to get more sense this side of the green baize door than the other.

'Sergeant asked us that,' Mrs Breckles informed him. 'That poor man in the smokehouse, you're thinking of. Told him nobbut the usual, tramps and travellers. 'Tis harvest time. Plenty of work for them that knows sheep, and coming up to pheasant season, tha gets beaters coming for work. We don't get gentlemen though. Mr Richey would know about gentlemen to see the family.'

Of course Richey would know. The butler was at the top of the servants' hierarchical pyramid, the all-important power, the contact between the upper world and the lower one. However, Auguste already knew from Richey that no strangers had called for the family that Saturday or even that Friday. How could they, indeed, with police vetting every vehicle and footstep through the gates? But then, if it were murder, the corpse of a gentleman did not necessarily imply his assailant was also a gentleman. Moreover, gentleman or tramp at the end of the gun, his own ear hurt just the same.

He re-examined an earlier theory. Could the dead man have been an anarchist, spying out the land to kill the King? Perhaps he had secreted himself in the smokehouse ready to make an attempt and been surprised before he could do so, perhaps killed by one of the King's own staff? Auguste found himself back with the same obstacle. There would be no reason for the detectives not to admit it if that had been the case.

''Tis that crawing hen,' Breckles stated gloomily.

'It may craw again, my friend,' Auguste warned him soberly.

Yorkshire eye met outcomer's. 'Aye.'

Egbert Rose was seated by the fire in his rooms, a contented expression on his face. He barely glanced up as Auguste entered.

Auguste had dined with the upper servants, partly to glean any information he could and partly to avoid the Tabors and their guests until he had had the chance to talk to Egbert. To his surprise, he had found these Yorkshire people the least talkative Englishmen he had come across. And now, unfortunately, even Egbert appeared to be having some difficulty keeping his eyes open. 'The long train journey, no doubt,' Auguste thought sympathetically. Then he noticed that the pudding dish was empty, as was the cream jug.

'Splendid recipe that, Auguste,' Rose shook himself awake. 'Your best yet for me.'

'Four eggs, lots of cream, even more sugar – very *rich*,' commented Auguste meanly. Had he slaved over trout, not to mention a *purée* of partridges and *crème brûlée*, only to be beaten by a *claggy toffee pudding*?

Fully awake at the dreaded word 'rich', Rose

instantly saw the bandage. 'What's wrong?' he asked sharply.

'It seems our corpse was definitely murdered, and our murderer is still near us. He meant to do more than graze my ear.'

'In the *house*?'

'No. In the grounds. He ran off over the moors, so I don't know whether he came from the house or not.'

'I'll let Cobbold know,' Rose said grimly.

'He could be miles away by now. Or he could be biding his time to return to the house.' This was an unwelcome thought. Alexander? Alfred? Oliver? Harold? His host? Imagination ran riot. The vegetable garden – Lady Tabor . . .

'Are you sure it was you he was after?'

Auguste tried to put aside emotion: fear, anger, confusion, the unreality of that twilight chase; and bring reason to his aid. 'It was growing dark, and I was picking herbs. The first suggests he could have made a mistake, the second does not – unless his target was intended to be one of the servants. Since it would be strange to have two unconnected murderers wandering the grounds, the probability is that he knew it was me,' Auguste concluded somewhat glumly.

'Then he must think you know something, Auguste. Anything you haven't told me?'

'No,' replied Auguste quickly. Too quickly.

'You were alone in that smokehouse for some time. Sure nothing odd struck you?'

'No.' Auguste tried to feign surprise. Unsuccessfully.

'Tatiana and her cousin were the first to discover the body. Did they move it?' Rose pounced.

'Lord Tabor moved it.'

'So Cobbold told me.' Rose did not comment on Auguste's red face. 'You let him?'

'I could not stop him. Lady Tabor insisted.'

'Did she indeed.'

'It might have been the King!' Auguste shouted, goaded.

'Very right and proper, I'm sure.'

'You have met Lady Tabor.' It had been a brief encounter between Egbert and Priscilla. There had been no instant rapport. 'You understand why I could do nothing.'

'Oh, I understand a lot of things.' Rose closed his eyes again peacefully. Auguste was dismissed.

For once Auguste was glad to find Tatiana absent when he returned to their room. He went into the dressing room to look at his bandaged ear. He studied it in the mirror; it looked like a frill on a mutton cutlet. Had he been mistaken for someone else? If so, whom? He studied his reflection critically. He was still slim for his years – no need for 'Dr Grey's Fat Reducing Pills' yet. Little was changed from when he had first come to England at the age of thirty to transform the cuisine of Stockbery Towers, and command the adoration of all his staff. He thought of dear Ethel . . .

There was a laugh behind him. 'Don Giovanni, I presume.'

He spun round indignantly, and Tatiana saw the bandage. Even as she framed the question, he said with dignity: 'I have been shot.'

'Shot?' Her face was very pale.

'In the vegetable garden,' he amplified, aware how funny this sounded. Tatiana did not laugh.

'Who did it?' she demanded.

'A man, but I did not recognise who it was.'

'This must *stop*,' she said firmly, walking to the window, as though even now his would-be murderer might be waiting beneath. 'You must leave it to me.'

'You?' he repeated in astonishment. 'I will not allow you to become involved.'

'But I *will* allow it.' A flash of imperious black eyes reminded Auguste that he had married a Romanov, albeit remote.

'*I* shall solve this murder,' he told her firmly. 'I must hold the clue to it otherwise why should I be attacked?'

'If only it were that easy,' she said to herself, staring out over the fells.

'Darling, it must have been terrible for you to find that poor dead man.' Victoria stroked Alexander's noble brow as he lay with his head comfortably positioned in her lap on a chaise longue in the Gold Salon.

'Not very pleasant,' he agreed lazily.

'And at this time. *Our* time.'

'We have lots more to come.'

'Not like this,' Victoria cried dramatically. 'We are on the threshold of our golden life, passing through the arch to enter our paradise.'

'I hope it's not wide enough for your mother.'

His fiancée giggled, then she grew sober. 'Alexander, it *is* coincidence, isn't it?' she asked.

'What?'

'Your going so late to the smokehouse and finding that corpse.'

'Are you suggesting I did it?' Alexander asked. There was no expression in his voice. Then he said more lightly, 'Who do you think I am? Edwin Booth?'

'You and Tatiana might have thought he was someone else.'

Alexander promptly sat up. 'Look here, Victoria, this is serious. You won't mention that bright theory to the police, will you?'

'Of course not.' She looked rather frightened.

'Vicky darling, you truly didn't recognise him, did you?'

'No!' She flushed. 'I only took a peep at him in that

beastly mortuary, but I'm sure I don't know him.'

He sighed. 'I wasn't going to mention this because I'm sure you couldn't hurt anyone, but in the smokehouse I found this.' He fished in his jacket pocket and produced a small silver comb with a familiar monogrammed handle.

'Someone must have taken it there by mistake. It's an old one I threw away,' Victoria told him coolly. Then less coolly: 'Anyway, it was suicide, *suicide*. You know it was.'

'Just now you thought Tatiana and I shot him,' Alexander said slowly.

'I didn't, I didn't. You're *stupid*.' It occurred to Alexander for the first time that in thirty years or so Victoria might look uncommonly like her mother.

'Laura, you're worrying over something, aren't you?' Oliver found her in the library. Ostensibly she was searching for night-time reading matter; in fact he found her staring into space.

'You are quite wrong, Oliver.'

'It's Mariot, isn't it?'

'What is?'

Oliver continued doggedly. 'You were expecting to see him, weren't you? He was coming back again to ask you to marry him.'

'Who told you that? It's nonsense.' Laura reflected. 'And what if he is? It's of no interest to you.'

'Oddly enough, it is.'

'A friendly eye?' she enquired caustically.

'Perhaps.'

'You must preserve your professional bachelordom carefully.'

'Sarcasm is not like you, Laura,' he replied gravely. 'After all, what are you so worried about if that corpse isn't Mariot?'

'Because—' she broke off.

He stared at her. 'You don't think *I* did it, do you?' he asked indignantly. 'Jealous lover and all that? Not my style.'

'There was nothing to *do*,' she told him quietly. 'It was suicide. Wasn't it, Oliver?'

Cobbold had evidently arrived at Tabor Hall early on the Monday morning. Refreshed by eleven hours' sleep and a light breakfast of kidneys and mushrooms on toast, followed by a visit to the vegetable garden, Auguste found Egbert already deep in conversation with him, over a silver pot of Tabor Hall coffee. This peaceful scene did not suggest intense activity in the search for the would-be murderer of Auguste Didier.

'Ah, Auguste. How's the ear?'

'I still have it, thank you. I am not Van Gogh.' The tartness of his reply was ignored by his friend. 'Have you discovered anything yet?'

'Still making enquiries,' Cobbold said uncommunicatively.

Making enquiries! The phrase Rose used when he believed investigations would be fruitless. Auguste fumed. If he were to survive it seemed he must indeed employ his own detective talents to the full.

Especially since there seemed little call for his culinary skills, at least from Egbert.

'Not much doubt about it being murder, Auguste. Have a look at this.' He showed him two sheets of paper with splodges of black, and more importantly one set of ten fingerprints.

Auguste forgot his grievance in his interest. He knew that taking fingerprints from the finger, dead or alive, was simple. The more difficult and still experimental stage was to take them from objects.

'Don't get too excited, Auguste. The set of ten are

90

the dead man's. They're not on the gun. All we've managed to get from that is one thumbprint, and it's not the corpse's. Not much to go on. But at least it proves it's not suicide.'

'And that's your proof of murder?' Auguste tried to sound rational. If Tatiana had touched the gun, who would believe she had not used it? No, he was imagining horrors that had no basis. 'It is true a corpse who had committed suicide could not return to shoot me, but is your evidence strong enough?'

'We don't know that your shooting was anything to do with the corpse,' Cobbold pointed out.

'I have not had enough time to upset anyone sufficiently in Yorkshire to make them wish to murder me, Inspector Cobbold.'

Cobbold said nothing and Auguste stiffened. Could it be Cobbold did not believe he had been shot at, and that he might be under suspicion of murder himself? If so, Cobbold was doomed to disappointment. 'May I show you this?' he said politely. It was the bullet, which had rewarded an hour's careful search by revealing itself in the grinning turnip face of the scarecrow.

Cobbold simply nodded.

As if conscious of his lack of sympathy, Rose observed: 'Doesn't tell us much, does it? We know it can't have been the Webley and even if the laboratory boys could sweep through his Lordship's gun room and tell us it came from the third gun on the right, where would that get us? Have a look at this instead.' He handed Auguste the post mortem report.

Auguste was always squeamish about physical details and in view of his own narrow escape from having to undergo a similar report, even more so today. 'Time of death between eleven-forty-five and one a.m. . . . Mature man in his late fifties,' he summed up, skipping through as quickly as he could. 'Physically fit, used to outdoor life.'

'Odd, ain't it? And look at these fingerprints again.' Rose pointed. 'See how distinct the ridges are? Those fingers have been doing some hard work. You find the same ridges in farmers.'

'Our man was a hunter perhaps.'

Rose, who knew well what he was about, grinned. 'You're right. I always said you were a marvel. But look.' He pointed to where the ridges at one point disappeared. 'You know what caused that?'

Auguste shook his head.

'Callosities. Ridges get covered up by toughened skin, wart-type things. No, I'd say our friend was used to wielding a spade.'

'Which might fit in with his sunburned appearance.' Auguste's mind ranged rapidly over the possibilities, until he firmly restrained it. 'The guests, including myself and my wife, are due to return home today,' he mentioned provocatively, torn between the hope of seeing his own home again, a desire to follow his twitching nose as far as his detective instincts were concerned, and a nagging knowledge that some mystery still remained where Tatiana was concerned.

'There'll be no going home till after the Coroner's Enquiry on Friday.' Rose paused, 'And anyway, I'd be glad of your comments. Might be very helpful, as in the past. You've got the entrée we haven't – upstairs *and* downstairs.'

Auguste glowed, even as he noted a quick glance between Rose and Cobbold as though this were confirmation of something they had discussed. Change of station for him and rank for Egbert had made no difference and how foolish of him it had been to feel it might be otherwise. The fact that Rose had chosen the words 'comments' and not 'assistance' did not register.

'Now tell me more about these Tabors and how the guests fit in. This Mr and Mrs Harold Janes, for instance.'

'Mr Janes is a rich stockbroker in the City of London and a close friend to the King.' Auguste paused. 'It is said that his wife is even closer.'

Rose looked mildly disapproving. He had never quite got used to the thought that royalty and aristocracy might act otherwise in private than as represented in the pages of the *Illustrated London News*. 'What about Oliver Carstairs?'

'In his forties and a friend of the Honourable Laura Tabor, Lord Tabor's sister. A bachelor. He played billiards with me until just before twelve-thirty on Saturday evening.'

'Did you see this bachelor to bed?'

'Egbert?' Auguste was startled till he saw the point of the dry comment. 'No, but—'

'Then he could have popped out to the smokehouse quite easily.'

'Yes, but—'

'Then there's you and your good lady,' Rose swept all demurs aside, 'and that completes the guests.'

'Yes and no – The Honourable Cyril Tabor and his wife are visiting. Cyril is Lord Tabor's younger brother who lives in Harrogate. Gertrude is his second wife, and she used to be at the Galaxy.' Auguste paused. 'She is as dainty as a *chanterelle*.'

'Have lots of conversations about the old days, do you?' Rose asked drily.

'Not all the old days,' replied Auguste stiffly. Since dear Gertie was a friend of Tatiana's, he did not wish to dwell on the details of his friendship with her years ago at the Galaxy. 'And Mr Tully-Rich, he too is a guest,' Auguste continued hastily. 'My wife's cousin.'

'Ah yes, I'll need a word with that young man.'

Auguste reflected uneasily on what that word might be.

'And the rest of the family?'

'Miss Laura is about forty-eight or nine, the youngest of the three. She was once, and may still be, in love with the archaeologist Robert Mariot, who was considered not worthy of her hand. There is a suggestion he might be coming back to ask her to marry him.'

'Which would give Mr Carstairs a motive if he'd any ideas about marrying Miss Tabor.'

'He proposes only because he knows she will refuse him.'

Rose chortled. 'That would sound good in a breach of promise suit. Next?'

'Victoria Tabor, who is a delightful, spirited young lady.'

'Like her mother?'

'Not yet.' Auguste shuddered.

'And the Dowager Lady Tabor?'

'His lordship's mother. She is charming and lively, although nearly eighty.'

'Young Alfred?'

'Still busy growing up,' said Auguste as kindly as he could. 'He thinks the corpse might be that of Lady Tabor's black sheep brother Oscar.'

'And why should Uncle Oscar turn up murdered in the smokehouse?'

'I think Alfred was following the family line that it was suicide, and implying his mother was deliberately disowning him because of the disgrace. It would certainly explain Lady Tabor's insistence on the point. There is a photograph of him in the house. I went to look at it, but as he is sporting a large hat, a beard, and a moustache, it is hard to tell. It could have been the corpse.'

'I'll take a look. What about Lord Tabor?'

Auguste considered. 'Who notices who stands in the shadow of the Great Pyramid?' he asked poetically. What was George Tabor like? Apparently ineffectual, in constant deference to his wife, yet an excellent shot and a friend of the King's. The King did not take friendship lightly and apparently this one meant so much to him he was prepared to tolerate Priscilla for two days. There must be more to George than he'd thought.

'At noon,' Rose observed, 'there's no shadow. Perhaps murder will have the same effect.'

'And so we come to the Baroness Tabor,' Auguste said.

There was no need for any of them to comment. They had all met her. 'Is she capable of murder, would you say?'

'If her family or standing were threatened, perhaps,' Auguste said doubtfully.

'That could be said of a large number of people. Would you say that until this happened, it was a perfectly normal houseparty?'

Auguste hesitated. How could he say yes, while he still could not define quite what had seemed abnormal on his arrival? 'I think so,' he hedged.

'But then a corpse appears by accident, and afterwards someone decides to shoot you – just as a result of the nothing you'd seen in the smokehouse.'

'Yes – no—'

'Not very normal, is it?'

Auguste went in search of Tatiana to inform her that Egbert wished to see all the family and guests in the Grand Salon shortly. On passing through the entrance hall, however, he came across a slight hitch to Rose's plans. Harold and Beatrice Janes were obviously about to depart, judging by the succession of hat boxes passing him in the careful hands of footmen and ladies' maids. Beatrice always kept personal vigil over this task. Hats to be admired by the King required the most respectful attention, for he had an observant eye for items of apparel he had seen on previous occasions, and had no hesitation in rebuking the culprit. Once even Beatrice had committed the solecism of wearing her lily leaf green appliquéd with cream lace twice. It had taken all her powers of charm to overcome this setback. Today, however, her face was sullen, and hats seemed of no interest whatsoever to her. Whatever charm Tatiana had worked yesterday had worn off by today. Her host and hostess, also present, did not look happy.

Feeling as welcome as a sliver of shell in a crab soufflé, Auguste walked up to them. 'I am told Scotland Yard would like us all to remain until after the Coroner's enquiry,' he said, trying to look concerned. 'With your permission of course, Lady Tabor,' he added rather belatedly.

Beatrice clutched her husband's arm and squealed at him appealingly.

'Nonsense,' her husband told Auguste gruffly. 'We've nothing to do with this unfortunate affair. I told that Cobbold man so. We're going.'

'Quite right too,' declared George Tabor, realising belatedly this was hardly hospitable. 'Not that I wouldn't welcome another shoot. After all, the pheasant season starts tomorrow. I was thinking of asking the Duke of Devonshire if I could join him. Or there's Ingleborough Hall. Good shooting there.'

'No,' cried Beatrice. 'I must leave. I positively must.'

Lady Tabor's eye fell consideringly on her. It had not escaped her notice that Beatrice's white fur three-quarter length coat over a dark grey skirt could be said to be complimentary mourning. Beatrice might therefore be planning a quick visit to Scotland, to the Balmoral area. She had no wish for His Majesty to know the royal wing was now occupied by Scotland Yard. 'I do *feel*,' she leant towards Beatrice to lend weight to her feelings, 'we must be seen to set an example and assist the police. After all, that is what His Majesty would expect, is it not?'

It was news to Beatrice if so, but Priscilla Tabor's obvious disapproval of her flight, plus her husband's discussions with his host as to how many pheasants might be lurking in the Duke of Devonshire's woods were too much for her. Harold had said they should stick it out, or it would not look good for him. Reluctantly she turned back into Tabor Hall, and the long line of footmen and ladies' maids, bearing suitcases, trunks and hatboxes, snaked back in her wake.

'You must speak to Cyril immediately,' Priscilla decreed, having bearded her husband in his study, where, baulked of shooting, he had repaired to read the *Sporting Times*.

'Dash it, Priscilla, is it wise? Aren't you going a bit far?' he asked weakly.

'It is most certainly wise. This is a time for family unity. Cyril is part of the family. He must be told what we know.'

'But not Gertie, I take it?'

'Gertrude is a simple-minded child. She cannot be trusted. I realise he is your brother, George. Discuss it with him and I shall then ensure that Cyril is in no danger.'

'I suppose you are right.'

'Of course I am right,' replied Priscilla simply, surprised that there could be any doubt about it. 'Do it, *now*, before this person from Scotland Yard emerges.

He will, no doubt, wish to speak to us about this *suicide*.' Her eyes met her husband's. 'Speak to Cyril.' It was an order.

Egberg Rose looked like a gun eyeing up his pheasants. Which target would he choose first? Auguste wondered. At first, Rose himself appeared to be the target, as he sat in the uncomfortable Louis XV walnut armchair allotted to him in the Tabor Hall salon.

'Murder?' Priscilla Tabor queried formidably. Her royal blue costume proclaimed that mourning was over. 'It is obvious the unfortunate man committed suicide.'

'His arms weren't long enough to shoot himself from a distance of three to four feet, your Ladyship,' Rose retorted gravely, Titan clashing with Titan. 'Nor would he have bothered to take off his gloves.'

'Unless you were present, Inspector, I fail to see how you can be sure. I am told Mr Conan Doyle is excellent at resolving such puzzles.'

'Mr Richey tells me he locked the smokehouse as usual that night, Lady Tabor, yet the door was unlocked when the body was found. He tells me that you have a key, that he has one, and that there is also a key kept by the kitchen door.'

Of course. How could he have missed that? Auguste wondered. Was his preoccupation with Tatiana clouding reason?

'What is your point, Chief Inspector? The dead man had to get in.'

'Then what happened to the key if it was suicide, Lady Tabor? It wasn't found in the door or inside.'

There was a dead silence. It was broken by Miriam, transparently happy to see her daughter-in-law vanquished. 'You are right, Chief Inspector, I'm sure. After all,' she announced brightly, 'this is an excellent

98

shire for murder. Look at Richard II, poor man, done to death at Pontefract. And there was Lady Elfrida Tabor, who murdered her companion in 1632 in a fit of rage. Not that I'd ever do that to you, Savage.' She smiled graciously at her companion-cum-maid, an elderly woman who sat protectively by her side, looking somewhat incongruous in the black, not of mourning, but of everyday service. 'And there was the saddler of Bantry, hanged on the evidence that he'd left his glass of beer untouched. Though now I come to think, he was merely a robber. Perhaps that is what your poor corpse was, Chief Inspector?'

Rose coughed, in order to stifle a laugh. 'Possibly, your Ladyship.'

Priscilla came back into the fight. 'I would suggest, if I may, that instead of paying attention to my mother-in-law's wild imaginings, you concentrate your efforts on discovering who this unfortunate man was.'

'Rest assured I shall, your Ladyship,' Rose came back instantly. 'For someone in Tabor Hall knows.'

'Do you have so-called evidence for this outrageous statement?' Priscilla asked coldly.

'Our man had no hat, no coat, no gloves, no obvious means of getting here. Either the murderer took the garments away with him, or the victim was staying somewhere very near indeed. So far we've not been able to discover where. It wasn't here, it wasn't with your closest neighbours. Nor did your lodgekeeper, gamekeeper, or any of your staff recognise him. The implication is that this was an arranged meeting, and a murder carefully planned. So what I'd like to do now is to reconstruct a picture of what exactly was going on in the Hall after His Majesty retired. I understand that was at about eleven-fifteen.'

'Carriages were then called immediately for those of our guests not staying in the Hall,' Priscilla informed

99

him. 'My husband and I then retired at about eleven forty-five after our remaining houseguests left the ballroom.'

'I left about eleven-thirty, but went to see my mother before retiring,' Laura volunteered.

'Did you, dear?' asked Miriam vaguely. 'I don't recall.'

Laura sighed. 'You know very well I came, Mother.'

'That's right, Miss Laura. You did,' Savage's deep rough voice confirmed unemotionally.

'Then I left to retire to bed. I had dismissed my maid earlier.' Laura smiled slightly. 'Do you therefore suspect me of slipping out to the smokehouse to murder this poor man?'

'What time did you leave Lady Tabor, miss?' Rose said evenly.

'Twenty to twelve,' Savage answered for her. 'I noticed because it was late for her Ladyship,' she said reprovingly. 'Her Ladyship' to Savage was always her mistress, never *that woman,* as she had been known to refer to Priscilla on occasion. Priscilla was an outcomer at Tabor Hall and always would be. 'I never got her Ladyship into bed until past one.'

'I was with Alfred in his rooms,' said Victoria brightly. She was ignoring her fiancé, Auguste noticed. 'Of course if I'd known I could be a suspect for murder by being on my own, I would never have gone to see him. I went to bed about one-thirty.'

'Why did you go to see your brother, miss?'

'I was cross with Alexander,' said Victoria disarmingly. The look she gave him suggested she still was. 'We were in the library until about twelve and then Alexander yawned and said he was going to bed. It was *our* engagement party and he didn't even want to kiss me goodnight. Can you imagine that, Inspector?'

'It certainly seems strange to me, miss. Why was that?' Rose demanded of the recalcitrant suitor.

Alexander looked hopefully at Victoria. 'It may seem strange to you, Inspector, but I can only say that my fiancée is so beautiful that it takes a great deal of strength *not* to kiss her. In short, considering the lateness of the hour, I was fearful that I might find her quite irresistible.'

'Oh!' Victoria was highly pleased. 'I forgive you then.'

'And then how did you come to be in the smokehouse with Mrs Didier three hours later?' Rose asked, uncharmed.

Auguste stiffened.

Alexander answered promptly. 'I was returning to my room when I met my cousin. We began to talk of Mother Russia in the way that Russians do and adjourned to the Blue Salon to talk further. In the course of our conversation, Tatiana expressed a great desire to have a—' he hesitated and Tatiana nodded brightly, 'smoke, and as I did too, we obediently adjourned to the smokehouse through the kitchen entrance to indulge our filthy habits. We took a lantern, opened the door of the smokehouse and found – well, you know what we found.'

Auguste glanced worriedly at Egbert whose face betrayed nothing. Did he think this explanation strange? For a newly married woman there were supposed to be attractions in going to bed that should surely supersede conversation with a cousin.

'Tiring talking into the early hours, was it?' was all Rose asked Tatiana, however, to Auguste's relief.

'No,' she replied simply.

'We Russians, even half-Russians like myself, are never tired,' Alexander amplified.

'Good,' his fiancée commented brightly. 'That bodes well for the future of the Tully-Rich line.'

A complacent cackle from the Dowager Lady Tabor. 'She takes after me, Priscilla.'

'I trust not, Mother.' Priscilla was stung into tartness.

'Her Ladyship and I retired just before twelve,' put in George Tabor quickly, anxious to intervene between his womenfolk. 'What about you, Cyril?'

'Gertie and I were in bed before twelve, weren't we, kitten?' The look he gave Gertie suggested the reason should be obvious. Kitten giggled nervously.

'Mr Carstairs? Mr Didier left you just before twelve-thirty, he tells me.'

'Correct. I would certainly have had time to jump out of a window, rush over to the smokehouse in the dark, and shoot this fellow. But so, by the same token, would Mr Didier,' Oliver pointed out cheerfully.

'In theory, that is so,' Auguste replied swiftly. 'And I could then have shot my own ear.'

No one it seemed, save Tatiana, was interested in his ear. Rose simply continued: 'Mr and Mrs Janes?'

Harold Janes' face was suddenly the colour of Camembert. 'My wife and I slept in adjoining rooms,' he said airily, 'as is usual when visiting Tabor Hall.'

Perhaps in the Janes' case, Auguste thought amusedly. Thankfully this rule, if it existed, had been waived in his case, and from the look on Gertie's face, in her case too. She was blushing, as if sharing the same bed as your husband was yet one more breach of etiquette. 'We left the dance shortly after His Majesty. I took a whisky and went to bed,' Harold announced. 'My man will vouch for that.'

Beatrice Janes rushed in to amplify his story. 'My husband has a distressing habit of snoring,' she informed the company shrilly. 'However, I decided to join my husband – how can I put it – for a goodnight kiss. I stayed some time. In fact, all night, didn't I, Puppikins?'

Puppikins, still ashen, muttered something to the effect that she did.

'Thank you, ma'am,' said Rose stolidly, wondering whether he and Edith would ever be reduced to trotting between rooms, and disinclined to believe a word Beatrice Janes said.

'Thank you, ladies and gentlemen.' Rose looked round at the relief spreading over his audience's faces. He decided to quell it. 'I'll be talking to you all individually, and we'll need your fingerprints.'

The implications did not take long to sink in. Priscilla Tabor rose majestically to her feet.

'Do I understand, Chief Inspector, that when you say someone in the Hall must know who this man is, you imply not the servants, but *ourselves*?'

'It's murder, your Ladyship.'

'But none of us could have been involved,' George spluttered indignantly.

'It's amazing at this stage of an investigation, sir, how often I find a corpse must have murdered itself.'

Was there a more calming place on earth than a walled vegetable garden? Auguste asked himself – save of course when somebody chose to shoot at you. But in general, with the rich smell of harvest in the air, and the promise of delights yet to be tasted, here indeed was the peace he needed to arrange his thoughts in more orderly fashion, like ingredients for a recipe. There were major problems that needed solving: who was the corpse; why had the murderer then shot at him; and whose body had Tatiana expected it to be? He puzzled over this, considering and rejecting the thesis that Tatiana had been worried lest it be his. He was not so old nor so fat. Moreover, he did not have a beard.

There was another problem too: why was the Tabor family so very cooperative in some ways and so obstructive in others? There could only be one answer;

they knew whose the body was, but did not wish the police to know. He turned this idea over in his mind, and found it worked. He began to think further about Uncle Oscar and Robert Mariot.

Egbert's comments about his being splendidly placed to find out the servants' point of view came back to him. So far he had only talked to the Breckles. He would pick some herbs on the pretext of explaining to the chef just how one made a *boeuf provençale* in which Breckles had expressed some mild interest. It was strange how up here in Yorkshire he did not feel the need for so many herbs in his food. Furthermore Egbert, when asked this morning by Mrs Breckles what he might like for supper this evening, had treacherously chosen Breckles' boiled beef in beer in preference to his own suggestions, not to mention claggy toffee pudding over his own delicate *îles flottantes*, to which Egbert had previously been partial. Yorkshire was indeed a strange place, where gastronomic tastes were changed so speedily.

Or was it himself? Was Breckles not an incompetent cook of London cuisine but the maître of Yorkshire? His step quickened. He now had two objectives for the rest of the morning: investigation of Yorkshire cuisine as well as picking up any items of relevant gossip from the kitchen staff.

Both quests were destined to be thwarted. Tatiana came hurrying up to him, skirts brushing aside cabbages and leeks in her impatience.

'You should not be walking here alone, *mon chéri*. You are not Mr Kipling's Just-So story cat.'

'No one would risk shooting me in broad daylight,' Auguste said uneasily, suddenly conscious of the vast empty hills behind him. 'Our murderer is a night bird.'

'You do not understand,' said Tatiana anxiously.

'You *must* take care. You would not wish to make me a widow so soon?'

He would not – on both their accounts.

'Please promise me you will not go anywhere alone again until we leave.'

His heart was touched by her concern. 'Very well.' He kissed her. 'That I promise.'

His visit to the kitchen did not begin auspiciously, however. He asked Breckles if he might participate in servants' dinner and moreover if he might observe Breckles preparing one of the local specialities he had heard about, the Yorkshire Christmas pudding.

Breckles roared with laughter. 'Daft outcomer,' he said amiably. 'Do tha know what tha's asking?'

'No,' answered Auguste humbly, perceiving he had made a mistake somehow.

'Why, it take an age. The walls be ez thick ez Jericho, and inside be a goose, partridge, pigeons, and last of all be the turkey. All boned and spiced one on top o' t'other. Tha'd have to be here day and night for a month o' Sundays.'

He watched Auguste digest this information, and then gave him a friendly dig. 'You can eat servants' dinner here and welcome, but that won't get thee what tha's seeking.'

'No food?' asked Auguste, the Frenchman in him leaping to the worst possible conclusion.

'Talk, that's what tha's after.'

'And for good reason,' Auguste explained firmly. 'They might talk to me when they might be nervous of talking to police.'

'Nothing to tell. None o' the lower servants has anything to do with the quality.'

'But just to know what their impression is of the family. I recall when I was in your position—'

105

Breckles cleared his throat. 'And that's the point. You aren't in my position now, are you?'

Auguste was taken aback. Surely he could still mingle in both worlds, at least be a permitted visitor, if not accepted resident? Reflection told him it was not possible. 'Then tell them to *think*, Mr Breckles: think of anything unusual they saw or heard,' he compromised.

'Thought here's like Christmas pudding; a long time a-coming, so 'tis better in the eating.'

And with that Auguste was forced to be content. Baulked of the honour of dinner with the servants, and unwilling to contemplate luncheon with the Tabors, he would eat with Egbert (thus avoiding the necessity of deciding whether for the purposes of the midday repast he was a gentleman who took luncheon or a servant who had dinner).

Meanwhile Chief Inspector Egbert Rose was doggedly embarking on his programme of interviewing Tabors, beginning with the less obstreperous. However, even the Honourable Laura Tabor was proving more difficult than he had anticipated.

'I believe the suggestion has been put to you, Chief Inspector, that this corpse might be that of Mr Mariot, my former friend.'

'Former?' asked Rose politely.

'It is true that we still correspond,' Laura continued steadily, not in the least thrown, 'and it is true he talked of coming to visit me. He is recently returned to Europe after assisting the archaeologist Koldeway at Nebuchadnezzar's Babylon. It is also true that, when my brother mentioned the corpse had a sunburnt appearance, I thought by some terrible chance it might be his. However, it was not.'

'You're sure of that?'

106

'As far as I can be.' She hesitated, then drew a photograph out of her bag. 'This is a photograph of him taken in Babylon eighteen months ago.' She pushed it across to him.

'Good of you to think of showing it to me, ma'am.' There was no hint of sarcasm in Rose's voice.

'Chief Inspector, it is not good of me at all, as you are well aware. I have no doubt that much better photographs are at this very moment speeding on their way to you.'

Rose grinned, then the grin faded.

'What if other friends of yours thought it was Mr Mariot, though?'

She lost colour. 'That is not possible.' she said quietly. 'What reason would these friends have for thinking that?'

'Suppose someone told them, ma'am.'

'That is nonsense,' she said violently. 'Do you wish to take my fingerprints, Chief Inspector?' she continued coldly, and was silent as she allowed her fingers to be pressed into powdered blacklead.

'Just one thing, ma'am,' Rose said as she was about to leave the room.

She hesitated and reluctantly turned.

'If it didn't occur to you that one of your friends might have murdered Mr Mariot, just why did you think it might be Mr Mariot's corpse? Did he have any reason to commit suicide?'

'No – yes. I wasn't thinking clearly,' she eventually managed to say and he did not press the point. Let her stew, he thought. If she was lying to protect herself or Carstairs, the meat might grow the tenderer for the cooking. All the same, he would put enquiries in hand as to Mariot's whereabouts.

'What on earth's got into you, Laura?' Oliver asked impatiently, as he escorted her down the stairs for luncheon. He had never known her so moody.

'I've just seen Chief Inspector Rose, Oliver,' she told him jerkily.

'And?' he asked sharply.

'He was questioning me about Robert coming back to see me. I had to tell him I thought at one point the corpse was Robert's.' She did not look at him.

He groaned. 'Now he's going to think that it was pistols at midnight for me and the corpse. Thank you, Laura.'

'I had no choice.'

'You could have told him you didn't love Mariot, and so I had no reason to kill him. That's true, isn't it?'

She stared at him and did not answer.

'Isn't it?' he demanded again.

'Is that what you'd like to think, Oliver?'

'Of course it's bally well what I'd like to think. And it's what I've always thought.' He pulled her round to face him. 'Aren't I right?'

'Whether you're right or wrong, I didn't tell the inspector anything about my feelings for Robert.'

'Why on earth not? Now he's going to think I slaughtered him in a jealous rage.'

Auguste, coming through the entrance hall on his way to see Egbert, stopped short – Laura glanced at him, but it didn't stop her crying out, 'You didn't kill him, did you, Oliver?'

'*What*?' Oliver grabbed her by the wrist to detain her, but she forced herself away. She marched towards the library, a flush on her cheeks.

'Women!' muttered Oliver, brushing past Auguste as he strode off in the opposite direction, completely unlike the serene professional bachelor he purported to be.

Four more Tabors, and two guests, succeeded Laura

in submitting to ordeal by fingerprinting. The Dowager extracted most enjoyment from the process.

'Now what, exactly, will happen to these impressions?' she enquired earnestly, eyes dancing. 'Shall they join your Black Museum, dear Chief Inspector?'

'No, ma'am, rather duller than that. They'll be disposed of once—'

'Once the mystery of this poor man is cleared up.' Her eyes were grave. 'I hope it is quickly. Tabor Hall is precious to me, as the home loved by my late husband. I cannot bear to see it stained by blood. You will find your murderer quickly, won't you?'

'I'll do my best, ma'am,' Rose replied gently. 'Whoever it is.'

Auguste, coming in to find Egbert, all but collided with the Dowager as she left. 'Ah, Mr Didier,' she cried, 'how pleased I am about your poor ear.'

'Pleased, Lady Tabor?' Auguste repeated blankly.

'But of course. Because of it, you are still alive.' She tripped off along the corridor lined with Tabor faces of the past, specially placed there by her daughter-in-law to impress His Majesty with the Tabors' pedigree.

'There's still our Priscilla to face,' Egbert told Auguste with some relish for the fray. 'Not to mention the likeable Mr Alfred.' But it was Beatrice Janes who next arrived.

'Of course I don't mind speaking in front of dearest Auguste,' she said, turning practised artless eyes on him, as Rose formally asked if she had any objections to his staying. 'He is related to His Majesty now.'

Auguste allowed himself a brief moment of pride. From apprentice cook in Cannes to Related to Monarchy was indeed an achievement. How impressed his maître Auguste Escoffier, in full reign at the Carlton Hotel in Pall Mall, had been. He had hopes that the maître might even create a dish for Tatiana, as he had for Dame Nellie Melba.

'I feel, Chief Inspector,' Beatrice said, 'that I ought to correct my earlier statement. I was not with my husband on Saturday night. Naturally I had to say I was, because I *almost* was,' she explained conspiratorially. 'Do you understand?'

Rose apparently didn't.

'I was with Another Gentleman,' she was forced to tell him crossly.

'And he would be?'

'Oh, Chief Inspector. Do I really have to spell it out? You disappoint me, you really do,' she said archly. Her fingers plucked nervously at the pale blue *bébé* ribbon adorning her blouse.

'I think Mrs Janes wishes to convey that she was with His Majesty,' intervened Auguste tactfully.

'He would confirm you were with him all night?' Rose asked, unimpressed, since Auguste had told him long since.

'Oh, but—' she hesitated.

'Don't you worry, ma'am. I've no qualms about asking him. What about your husband?'

What about him indeed? she thought quickly. If Harold had gone off in one of his jealous rages and done something foolish, she wished to be safely distanced from it. Life was too delightful with not only Bertie at her feet, or, rather, at more intimate portions of her body, but other cavaliers swearing they would follow her to the ends of the earth. Life was less delightful when she feared one of them might have interpreted the ends of the earth as Yorkshire. True, that horrid corpse hadn't looked like anyone she knew, but Harold might well have got the wrong impression.

'He doesn't mind,' she answered sweetly. That wasn't what the inspector meant, and she knew it. She

110

managed to convey that any more questions would be detrimental to her fragile composure.

Auguste watched in amusement as Rose placed the chubby rose-pink fingers firmly and squarely in blacklead. So he didn't like Mrs Janes one little bit.

Lady Tabor's bosom seemed to enter the room even further in advance of the rest of her body than usual, complemented by the large purple feather that topped her coiffure and flourished forwards like colours borne before a regiment. Only Priscilla could enter, so *completely* attired in formality, Auguste thought half admiringly, half repelled.

'Were you with your husband continuously after the house had retired, your Ladyship?' Rose enquired politely.

'Naturally I was with my husband,' replied Priscilla haughtily. 'Whom else did you expect me to be with?'

This was voiced as a rhetorical question and Rose put forward no contenders.

'Your brother Oscar, your Ladyship.' Rose pushed forward the photograph Auguste had mentioned to him.

Priscilla turned the glare on Auguste, clearly seeing a traitor. 'That is a family matter, Mr Didier.'

'No such thing in a murder enquiry,' Rose informed her.

'Indeed. Then pray explain just why poor Oscar is being connected with this so-called murder enquiry, when none of *us* recognised the corpse as being my brother.' She glanced at the photograph in front of Rose.

'When was the last time you heard from him?'

'Shortly after he left here in 1889.'

111

'How old would he be now?'

'I believe fifty-seven. He was older than me.'

'Could he have come here to ask for money?'

'Possibly, but he did not. There has been no sign of him, and you have no evidence to the contrary. That photograph is so indistinct it is no evidence at all.'

'All the same, I'll have his last known address if you please.'

'I have none. You may ask Richey for my parents' address.' She paused, then added, 'In fact, were it Oscar, which is highly unlikely, there is a far more likely explanation than that you are obviously contemplating. I trust this will go no further?' She fixed Auguste with a forbidding eye. 'When Oscar visited us in '89, there were a few unfortunate incidents. One concerned a housemaid, another a beater accidentally shot. He then borrowed money from my mother-in-law and from George – against my knowledge – and with the proceeds went to join the gold rush at Cripple Creek.'

'Successfully?'

'Highly. He is now very rich, I understand. Unfortunately he gained these riches by controversial means. Instead of digging for nuggets, he salted mines.'

'He did what?'

'I understand one buys a worthless claim, puts a few high grade lumps of gold not too far down to raise confidence, and then sells the claim to the first dunderhead who comes along. Unfortunately Oscar was never a good judge of character, and did it once too often. His victim swore revenge and Oscar disappeared. I understand, however, his pursuer is still after him. It is possible that, in lieu of Oscar himself, he might have decided to visit me to seek his lost fortune.'

112

'The corpse's shirt came from New York,' mentioned Auguste.

'Then who shot him and why?' asked Rose unemotionally.

'I have no idea,' said Lady Tabor. 'That is your job, Chief Inspector, not mine.'

'And so is this, your Ladyship, unfortunately,' as he introduced an indignant Lady Tabor to the mysteries of fingerprinting.

Her son followed her, sporting a raffish double-breasted spotted waistcoat, a hint of red braces and a gleam of vicious excitement. 'Ma says she's told you all about dear Uncle Oscar. She's still in touch with him, of course. She's canny, is Ma. Plays her cards close to her chest.'

Not that close, thought Auguste irreverently of the Valkyrie bosom.

'Personally I still think the corpse is Uncle Oscar. Catch Ma owning up, though.'

'To murder?' asked Auguste, startled.

'Good lord no,' Alfred said, shocked. 'But if it was Oscar or someone about to spill the beans on him, the murderer could be old Handsome Harold. Last thing he wants is the gold market rocked by another scandal about salted mines just now when the unions are playing up in Colorado. With South African gold still uncertain because of the war, Colorado is pretty vital. So get rid of him. Much easier. There, what do you think of that?'

'An excellently thought-out theory, Mr Alfred,' Rose said genially. 'Good to see you young folk so willing to assist the police.'

'Not at all.' Alfred took this graciously at face value. 'After all, I'd rather it was old Harold than dear old Cyril.'

Rose eyed him thoughtfully. 'Your uncle? Why should

he want to murder your Uncle Oscar?'

'He wouldn't. But he might well have had a go at old Simpson.'

'Who?'

'Colonel Simpson,' Alfred told him innocently. 'Didn't anyone mention him? As Ma always says, Unky Cyrie is a gentleman of distressingly frivolous tastes. Before Gorgeous Gertie, he took a shine to Alluring Alice, daughter of one Colonel Cuthbert Simpson of the British Army in India. Quite smitten was Cyril and so evidently was Alice, for she opened the oven door before she should have, if you take my meaning, and was cooking up a little Cyril. By that time our Cyril had met Gertie, so he turned poor old Alice away without a second thought. The gallant Colonel threatened fire and brimstone – and what was worse to the Tabors, exposure. He lives at Skipton. Fell Hall.'

'And you think your uncle murdered him?'

Alfred looked shocked. 'Good God, no. Cyril wouldn't do a thing like that, except by accident. If it's him, he might have come here looking for Cyril – but for a murderer my money's on Carstairs.'

Rose said nothing, but firmly pushed the powdered blacklead towards him.

'Everyone is very anxious to help,' he remarked as the door closed behind a newly fingerprinted Alfred. 'A case of too many cooks, you might say. Where best to hide a piece of straw, Auguste?'

'In a haystack, Egbert.'

He dined well off chicken and mutton casserole and bilberry pie, after which Egbert announced very casually his intention of having a word, not only with Cyril Tabor, but with Tatiana and Alexander during the afternoon. He wondered if Auguste would fancy

114

going to Skipton to see whether by any chance Cyril's gallant colonel were fact. Reluctantly Auguste agreed, since he could think of no valid reason for demanding to be present while Egbert interviewed Tatiana.

His plans, however, were delayed by the unmistakable sound of someone sobbing in the Blue Salon. Cautiously he opened the door, chivalry to the fore, hoping it was not Beatrice Janes. It was not. It was Gertie, who leapt up when she saw him and flung her arms round his neck, while Cyril stood embarrassedly by the window.

'He's just told me he was in love with someone else,' she sniffed. 'He went on seeing her after we were married. He was going to *marry* her.'

'But I married *you*,' Cyril shouted, pink with anger.

She raised a cautious eye, then collapsed again on Auguste. 'But he *loved* her once. She told him she was going to have a baby, Priscilla said. How could he do such a thing?'

Auguste's jacket was getting distinctly damp and he gently removed Gertie's arms.

'There wasn't a baby and I didn't love her.' The shout increased in volume and anguish.

'Then that proves you're a cad. Why get betrothed if you didn't want to marry her? And now you're probably a murderer. What happened to your first wife?'

Cyril tried to control himself. 'She died of measles, as I told you. I don't know how you can think such things, Gertie. You're not the kitten I married.' And he walked into the adjoining room, clutching in vain at the remains of his dignity.

With a howl Gertie flung herself with renewed gusto back into Auguste's arms – just as Tatiana entered, and took in the touching scene.

'Housemaids,' she said darkly and went out again.

Putting Gertie aside as soon as he decently could,

Auguste hurried after her, feeling much misunderstood. Gertrude's presence in his arms was so easy to explain. He followed Tatiana's flying figure down the front steps of Tabor Hall, still finding a childish pleasure at transgressing rules that had once, as a mere chef, applied to him. Now they were waived for ever, though only to be replaced by depressingly different and more stringent rules.

To his trepidation, he saw Tatiana jumping into Alexander's De Dion Bouton. Even more ominously, she was sitting at the wheel. 'Start it up,' she cried, as she saw him.

'But—' his protest came out as a squeak.

'Do not worry.' She raised her eyebrows. 'Alexander has shown me how to drive it. You are not scared for me, are you, oh brave protector of all lovely ladies?'

'You don't understand. Egbert wishes to speak to you.'

'*Non, mon amour*, it is you who do not understand,' she muttered darkly, handing him a piece of iron.

He stared at it blankly, till he realised it was the motor starting handle.

'Crank it,' she ordered.

'I cannot. He wishes to see you.'

'I will be back,' she shouted at him.

'Then I will come too.'

It was useless to protest that one lesson from Alexander was perhaps not quite enough for a lady to be in charge of a powerful engine of 4.5 horsepower. Unfortunately cranking was not so simple as it seemed.

'Faster,' his wife ordered, sitting imperiously above him as he toiled. 'Slower.' But still the sparks were failing to ignite – whatever that meant – save between them. A scathing look at her husband and Tatiana descended, a muttered Russian endearment to the

116

motorcar, one swift jerk and the engine immediately started. She jumped back in, and the motorcar proceeded to lurch into motion before he had climbed in. A lurch to one side threw him off the running board. He could not believe it. Regaining his balance, he ran furiously after the motorcar and managed this time to climb aboard, much to Tatiana's displeasure. Sheep scattered with unusual alacrity as Tatiana careered from one side of the road to the other. The De Dion Bouton lurched perilously near disaster, as it prepared to cross the River Aire apparently under the impression it was a ford. Only belatedly did Tatiana jerk it on to the narrow bridge.

'Why did you come?' she asked crossly.

'Because this morning you said I should not be left alone,' Auguste pointed out.

She took a deep breath. 'I do not want you with me this afternoon.'

'Why not?' He had had no intention of staying with her, but his hackles were immediately aroused. He breathed again as the motorcar left the Tabor drive and joined the Kirkby Malham road.

'You see,' she crowed, changing the subject. 'I can drive a motorcar.'

Auguste disagreed. The De Dion headed straight for a ditch after failing to take a corner sufficiently sharply enough, but a yank at the wheel which almost threw him out kept the motorcar on the road.

'I love this,' she shouted over the noise of the engine and the wind whistling past their faces. She had tied a huge white veil over a wide-brimmed purple hat which, with Alexander's goggles, made her a curious vision. She caught sight of his face. 'What's wrong?'

What was wrong was that coming towards them was a caravan of steam wagons, belching into the autumn air. The fair was leaving town. Tatiana

117

hunched over the wheel; a challenge had to be taken at full speed. Auguste covered his eyes as they rushed towards imminent impalement on a monster of an engine. He was flung violently to his right, then to his left, as the De Dion lurched on at a strange angle to the road. Above him, on the wagons, strange voices shouted encouragement to Tatiana. She needed no encouragement, he thought bitterly. It was victims like himself who most needed some hope of survival. He uncovered his eyes to find miraculously that they were back on the road.

'*Voilà*' Tatiana appeared pleased with her prowess.

When they arrived eventually in Settle, Auguste complimented her, from a full heart humbly grateful for his survival, and for the moment forgetting the rift between them. He jumped down to terra firma in the courtyard of the Golden Lion. 'You will come with me?' he enquired. He had no intention, in fact, of leaving her.

'Yes,' Tatiana declared after an unflattering pause, and picked off a few dark hairs from his ulster in wifely consideration. 'You are right, I should stay with you. You will lose no more hair, and I will drive back very carefully.'

The parlour of the Golden Lion was comfortable and inviting, a blazing log fire in the hearth. Tatiana had expressed a preference for the Public Bar and Theakston Ales on the basis that these were new experiences, but he had remained adamant. There were matters that had to be discussed privately.

'Tatiana, are you avoiding Egbert?'

'Avoiding him? Of course not. I wanted to drive the motorcar, and to buy some stockings. You would not be in the least interested.'

'I will come with you.'

'Why? Do you suspect I am meeting a lover? No, my

friend, it is you who are so good at that.'

He ignored this. 'You must tell me, *and* Egbert, what the mystery is about the smokehouse,' he said seriously.

Her eyes widened. 'You think I have a lover.' She leapt to her feet. 'Me, Tatiana Maniovskaya Romanov.'

'You are Mrs Auguste Didier.'

'*Eedee kchortoo!*'

His Russian did not extend to this, but the meaning was roughly clear as she swept furiously from the room. The door opened again, but it was only the landlord with a tray of tea, scones and jam. Never had food looked less appetising. Outside he heard the chug of a motorcar, then saw a green shape flash past the window. He rushed to look out. The De Dion Bouton was on its way without him. It was not going in the direction of Tabor Hall.

'Where have you been? The Tabors expected you at dinner.' Egbert Rose looked up from his evening meal, in none too good a mood, apparently. Nor was Auguste. He was cold, hungry and footsore.

'Pursuing your enquiries,' he answered grumpily.

Egbert regarded him more kindly. 'Tell me.'

'I took the railway train to Skipton, as you asked. It is a most attractive town. I learned much of local lore, but nothing of our corpse.' He had not expected to in fact, since Cobbold's men had scoured every hotel for miles around.

'What about the Colonel?'

'I went to Fell Hall, but the house was shut up. The Colonel left last Friday for India, so I gathered from his housekeeper who lives in the lodge.'

'And the daughter?'

'She died a year ago of what the housekeeper described as a wasting disease.'

Egbert sighed. 'I suppose we'd better set the wheels in motion.'

Auguste shuddered. He preferred not to think of wheels, after his manic ride to Settle. Coming home from Skipton there had been no cabs available, and he had therefore been obliged to take the branch line to Bell Busk, where there had been no cabs either. Two miles in the twilight, with every sheep appearing a monster, and every tree a wicked witch who placed holes in front of unwary feet, were not amusing.

'Have some of this Yorkshire pudding and beef, Auguste.' Egbert saw it was time for compassion.

'It is not precisely an exquisitely mixed *salade niçoise*,' Auguste said, unmollified.

'Tabor Hall isn't Cannes either. Horses for courses, Auguste.'

'This beef is like horse, too,' Auguste rejoined belligerently, taking some and finding he was wrong. He sent a mental apology to Breckles.

'Mrs Didier didn't come to see me this afternoon, Auguste.'

Auguste flushed.

'Tell me what's wrong.' It was an order.

Egbert was the police and he was being interviewed, no longer the trusted confidant.

'I cannot.'

'If Edith were mixed up in something I'd feel the same.'

Auguste's first reaction was relief, his second was anxiety for Tatiana. Almost as fear flashed through him, she appeared within the doorway, and he and Egbert rose to their feet.

'I believe you wished to see me?' It was Egbert she was looking at, not Auguste.

'Yes, Mrs Didier. Please do be seated.'

'Very well, Chief Inspector Rose. I hope when I have

120

explained, I may call you Egbert again.' She moved gracefully to an armchair and seated herself. 'I wanted in any case to see you.'

'To tell me you and Mr Tully-Rich moved the body?'

'More than that. To tell you why.'

Auguste felt numb; half dreading, half welcoming what was to come.

'I am Russian, Chief Inspector, and the majority of the Russian community in Paris remains far more Russian than the Russians themselves. It jealously guards the purity of its Russian blood – and its adherence to the Tsar is absolute, even though many came to Paris through incurring the displeasure of one Tsar or another.

'My father was one such strict authoritarian, and this prevented my marriage to Auguste for so long. Auguste is a commoner and I am a princess, and that meant to my father that we could not marry. I do not share these opinions on differences between people, Chief Inspector. As I am of royal blood, Mr Marx would say I am of no value to society, but I cannot quite agree with that either.

'However, when my father died, the Russian community took his role upon themselves, and one member of it in particular. The Tsar has his secret agents, the *Okhrana*, and my half-uncle is one of the leaders outside Russia. Only the fact that he was away on a mission at the German court meant that I could leave Paris and marry Auguste.

'I hoped that, once removed from Paris and under the protection of His Majesty Edward VII, we would be safe. It seems not. When we arrived here, my cousin Alexander had bad news for me. His Majesty has, as you know, just returned from a visit to Denmark – a visit extended beyond the eight days he originally intended because of the simultaneous visit of the Tsar and Tsarina. The two emperors met, and one of the subjects they discussed was my marriage. The Tsar and His Majesty are satisfied. Unfortunately my half-uncle is not. Hearing in Denmark for the first time of the marriage, and of our visit here, he decided to show his displeasure, and one obvious conclusion was that he would show it while His Majesty was present. Tabor Hall provided a superb opportunity.

'Alexander learned his plans through his mother who was in Denmark at the time, and warned the Tabors and myself. Poor Lady Tabor. I fear she was not happy. She insisted that nothing must happen under her roof, and gave her family instructions that you, Auguste, were not to be left alone. I fear this is why the Tabors might seem to have been behaving oddly. They were indeed looking out for strangers. When I met Alexander that night, it was to keep a watch on the approach to our window, as my uncle had made no move yet. Then just after half-past two we saw a light in the smokehouse. I was sure it was my half-uncle. I believed if I could talk to him, I might reason with him. Alexander insisted on coming with me. There were no lights on when we arrived, so Alexander swung the lantern, to make sure he had gone. Then we saw the body. I was *glad* that my uncle was dead. I thought he had shot himself in remorse, or by accident. Then I saw that he was of sturdy build, and unless he had changed greatly in the three years since I had seen him, it might not be my uncle. So we decided to turn the body over.'

'How could you not tell me, Tatiana, that you were in danger?' Auguste cried.

'You haven't been listening carefully enough,' she replied soberly. 'My uncle would never kill a Romanov. It is *you* Pyotr Gregorin intends to kill.'

Chapter Five

'This puts a different sauce on the goose,' Rose grunted after Tatiana had left them.

It certainly did, and it was not one Auguste found digestible. He shivered, as if a Russian assassin even now stood behind the deep rose-red velvet curtains armed with Webley and poisoned samovar. He sipped his brandy and soda gratefully, as the fire glowed comfortingly in the lamplight.

His brain was numb, pinioned on the concept that somewhere, somehow, sometime, a Russian was about to kill him. Tatiana's account had brought the reality of the attack home to him. No happy fantasy of mistaken shots at rabbits could delude him now.

'So the Tabors were protecting me, and I thought they suspected me of having designs on their teaspoons.' He spoke as lightly as he could.

'Not all diamonds and foie gras marrying royalty, then.'

'Too rich a diet for me, Egbert. Like eating Mr Breckles' toffee pudding every day.'

Egbert grinned. 'Not to be compared with your *bavarois de framboises*, but naturally, when in Yorkshire, eh?'

'You are a true friend, Egbert.'

'Policeman too.'

His meaning was lost on Auguste as his eyes gently began to close . . .

'But the Tabors must have known that body wasn't Gregorin's,' Rose muttered as much to himself as Auguste. 'Alexander would have told them when he went to rouse them.' He frowned. 'That might lead to another conclusion . . .' He glanced at Auguste, who dozed in happy ignorance of Egbert's deduction. It wasn't entirely sound but he couldn't afford to ignore the possibility, or, at least, the detective in him couldn't. The man could quite easily.

A sudden tap on his shoulder. Auguste spun round in the Tabors' morning room, his nerves still not steady. It was not Gregorin, but it was a face he knew well. Sergeant Stitch – no, Inspector, he must now remember. How strange to think that Twitch, to use Rose's not too affectionate adaptation of his name, had now attained the rank that had been Rose's when Auguste first met him ten years ago at Stockbery Towers.

'Morning, Mr Didier.' Something that was almost a grin stretched across Twitch's face. 'Didn't expect to see me, eh?' Promotion had made his heart a trifle fonder towards Auguste, hitherto regarded as an interfering Frenchie.

'No, indeed. Chief Inspector Rose told me he had sent for a sergeant. We are fortunate indeed.'

'Came myself,' Twitch said obviously. 'Can't get along without me in a major investigation of this kind. Royalty,' he summed up succinctly. He eyed Auguste as if expecting him to challenge his statement. Indeed perhaps it was true. Where routine and painstaking thoroughness were concerned, there had been few better than Sergeant Stitch. Whether he would exhibit new dramatic qualities as Inspector Stitch remained to be proved. True, there had been the affair of Charlie Harbottle and the Earl of Doncaster's Rubens, but as Twitch had in fact arrested the villain in connection with a daring raid on Perkins' Pie Shop, the Rubens could be said to be a fortunate bonus.

'I'm at the Temperance Hotel.' Twitch eyed the glories of Tabor Hall wistfully.

'I am sure there is plenty of room in the royal wing,' murmured Auguste generously on behalf of his hostess, leading the way to Rose's quarters.

Egbert Rose glanced up from his peaceful survey of the *Craven Herald* where a demure paragraph announced the discovery of the body of an unknown man in the grounds of Tabor Hall. 'Solved the crime yet, Stitch?'

'On the trail, sir,' Twitch replied woodenly.

'Fortunately Mr Didier was staying here as a guest. That's a help, isn't it?'

'Yessir,' Stitch replied without batting an eyelid. He never quite knew how to take the Chief.

'What have you got for me?'

'The Frenchie tailor can't be found, so Chesnais says.' Twitch relished the fact that he was now of equal status to Rose's friend in the Sûreté. No more 'Inspector Chesnais' for him.

'And the shirt?'

'There's a shirtmaker of that name in New York. None too grand, so they don't keep records of every batch of shirts they produce. They have a regular clients' list,' Stitch told him, carried away by his achievements, 'so if we could let them have a name . . .' His voice trailed off weakly as his chief looked at him scathingly.

Rose decided to let him off. 'Underwear?'

'The same.' Twitch began to get nervous. 'They need the name—'

Rose pulled a face. 'Why don't I ever get told, "That shirt's one of two made for the Marquis of Yorkshire Pudding." No, it's always if we send them the name of

125

the client, they'd be happy to check their pneumatic cash carriers to see if some old bills have decayed inside.' He sighed. 'Get the lists, Stitch, check 'em against the missing persons list we sent you.'

'I did, sir. And against the Yard's lists.' Pride animated his voice.

'And?'

'Nothing, sir.' It deflated again.

Rose sighed.

'I've brought details of steamship arrivals from the United States in the last few weeks,' Stitch offered hopefully.

'Better than nothing, I suppose,' Rose admitted grudgingly. 'Though the fellow can't have sailed right up and docked outside the gates. Even if he hopped over the wall, he had to have arrived at one of the local villages or towns at some point, and that's where we stick at the moment. *Somebody* must know the fellow,' he continued irritably. 'Poke round the city, Stitch. See if there's anything in these rumours about the gold market falling, and its affecting Janes. And telegraph the Colonial Office and Army HQ on Simpson. There's plenty of leads in this case, that's one thing. Like that children's game, the Labyrinth. Ever played it, Auguste? Edith's eldest sister's middle one used to be fond of it. You wind balls of string or wool in and out of trees and bushes in the garden, or if you're unlucky, all around the house. Everyone takes the end of a piece and follows it. At the end of one of them lies the buried treasure. Like detective work really.'

'And like Fair Rosamund, born to William de Clifford in Skipton Castle,' Auguste laughed, glad his time in Skipton had not been entirely wasted. 'King Henry II set his love in the midst of a labyrinthine maze so that his jealous wife could not find her. But Queen Eleanor managed to find the way in and poisoned her.'

'Did they get any evidence on this Eleanor?' Rose asked disapprovingly. 'More likely to be the King up to no good if you ask me. Ladies in bowers could be demanding. Probably blackmailing him.'

'It is but a legend, Egbert. In Skipton I learned many – like that of the green fairies haunting Ilkley bathhouse. They have not been seen for some years, though.'

'Add green fairies to the missing persons list, Stitch,' Rose grunted.

'Do you forgive me, Auguste, for not telling you? It was for your own good.' Tatiana hurried to catch up with him as he strode towards the smokehouse, and finally caught his arm impatiently. 'I did not tell you because I thought if I spoke to Gregorin I could persuade him to forgive me. Alexander and I were so sure he would come on Saturday night. On Friday we escorted you everywhere, and at night I locked our windows and doors once you were asleep. I slept with a gun beneath my pillows. I would have—'

'*Gun?*' This was getting worse.

'It was loaned to me by George. It was not the Webley, Auguste,' she added reproachfully. 'On Saturday we watched all day without success, and at night I locked you in as soon as you came back, and closed the windows again. Alexander and I searched the house, and then went back to the Chinese Blue Salon directly underneath our room. We were so sure it was Gregorin in the smokehouse.' She paused. 'I told Egbert the truth, *ma mie.*'

'Were you going to see Gregorin yesterday in Settle?' asked Auguste, enlightenment dawning.

'Yes. I believed my uncle might well be staying there.'

'Did you find him?'

127

'Yes.'

'*Yes?*' A shiver ran up his spine.

'But I fear, I very much fear, Auguste, that I talked in vain.'

Auguste swallowed. 'Do not worry,' he told her, more bravely than he felt. 'Egbert can discuss it immediately with Special Branch and Gregorin can be made to leave the country. Special Branch are most particular about other countries' secret agents working here, ever since a body turned up in Strutton Ground about fifteen years ago. That was the work of the *Okhrana* too,' he told her, trying hard to sound matter of fact.

'It is not Gregorin's style to leave bodies lying around. He usually disposes of them.'

'The sooner this gentleman leaves England, the better.'

'Then we can never go abroad again.'

Could he cut himself off from La Belle France? Auguste sighed. 'I suppose it is better to face these people.'

'He prefers it,' she informed him soberly. 'His favourite method is a stiletto in the breast.'

Auguste gulped. 'Pray tell me more about your delightful uncle.'

'I think he is now about forty-five, but always he seems the same age to me. He is slim, dark, not tall, and moves like a cat. And like a cat, he works best alone. He has no friends that I know of, merely associates. Those who use his services, the Tsar, the Kaiser and others, trust him. He has a code of honour to those for whom he works.'

Auguste tried to grapple with the notion of an assassin who pounced like a cat with a stiletto. 'Good.' He attempted nonchalance.

'I tried to convince him I am not worthy to be a

Romanov, and that I would renounce my rank and live privately, so it is just possible he might dismiss you from his list,' she said thoughtfully. 'Or else—'

'Yes?' he asked eagerly.

'He might kill us both.' She watched him, then added wryly, 'He will wish you to know who killed you, however. He will introduce himself. He is, after all, a gentleman.'

'I am glad to hear it. It makes the prospect of sudden death much more appealing.'

She ignored this. 'Russians are patient, of course. He may wait five hours, five days or five years before striking again. But I know he will return.'

His heart sank. 'Why did you not tell me before?'

'I was afraid you might not marry me if I did.'

'I would not have hesitated,' he said truthfully, taking her in his arms. The rarest truffles of Périgord were beyond price.

'Auguste,' she said, her voice muffled against his cheek, 'when we go back to London I shall stop being a princess. I have been one for thirty-three years and it is time to change. There are many more interesting things to do in the world. I do so hate At Homes. I never wish to be At Home again. Moreover, I do not think Mr Marx would approve of Nainsook knickers or bust improvers modelled on the Venus de Milo, and that is all the Mrs Janes of this world can talk of.'

'*Ma mie!*' Auguste's heart melted at her patent efforts to cheer him up. 'You can never not be a princess, any more than I can say I will not be Auguste Didier born in the fishing village of Cannes. We carry our past with us.'

'Only if we let it.'

'Society does not yet permit otherwise,' he said, despondently.

'But *we* make Society,' said Tatiana obstinately. 'It

is all brazen pretence. It accepts whom and what it chooses, regardless of its own rules; like Lady Tichborne acknowledging that fat old butcher as her son in the famous Tichborne Claimant case, even though he was nothing like the missing heir.'

'That is not Society, that is the human heart.'

'So *that*,' said Tatiana triumphantly, 'is the most important. Is it not, Auguste?'

He laughed at having been caught out, hugging her and swinging her round. 'Once I would have thought so, and between us two it is. But we live in the world, and regretfully the world is not yet at a stage when Society can be entirely disregarded.'

'But what shall I do, when we return to London? I cannot be At Home for ever. I *cannot*.'

'What would you want to do?' he asked gravely. Marriage was producing unexpected problems. Love might not necessarily solve everything. What would his wife do? Between breakfast and the marriage bed there was much time to fill. (Assuming Gregorin permitted him to fill it, he thought uneasily.) For him there was the ten-volume work on cuisine. But for her? 'What would you like to do?'

'I would like to have a profession, like you.'

'Cooking?' asked Auguste guardedly.

She laughed. 'No. I do not have the patience.'

Relief flooded over him, until an equally appalling prospect struck him. 'Not detection?'

'No, I do not have the logic.'

'What then?'

'I don't yet know. But I will soon. I am simmering the pot, Auguste.'

They had arrived at the smokehouse, and Police Constable Walters eyed them suspiciously.

'What have you come for?' Tatiana asked Auguste. She seemed unwilling to enter.

'To meet Egbert.'

'Oh. Then you will not need me.'

'On the contr—' but Tatiana was already hurrying away. Auguste watched her, in some surprise at her lack of enthusiasm for meeting Egbert again now all was well between them, and idly wondered why.

In the morning greyness, the ladies of the smokehouse seemed to have donned a veneer of respectability as though they wore their morning faces. The smell of stale smoke hung in the air, reeking from ashtrays untouched since Saturday night by police orders. His matches marking the position of the body had been replaced with a chalk outline; in any case his careful work was now irrelevant, since the body had been moved before George Tabor touched it.

'Morning, Walters.'

'Morning, Chief Inspector.' The reply came as eagerly as if Walters was envisaging a rapid removal to the very pinnacles of Scotland Yard. Egbert had arrived.

'Come alone, did you, Auguste? Brave of you.'

'No. Tatiana felt she should accompany me.'

'Ah.' Rose made no comment on her absence.

'If Gregorin is to come, then he will,' Auguste said, not knowing how to interpret this.

'Twitch is checking what Special Branch has on him. These foreign agents are lying low at the moment, now we've got the anarchists and nihilists at least temporarily under control. But you can never tell. I've heard of Gregorin.'

'What?'

'I can see why Tatiana's worried,' Rose told him soberly. 'Feel like Sherlock Holmes with a Moriarty dogging your footsteps, do you? No villain is a true Moriarty, Auguste; everyone has his weakness – if you can find it.'

'Do you know of any particular weaknesses attached

to Gregorin?' Auguste asked, trying not to sound too interested.

'No.'

'Oh.' Auguste swallowed. 'Then let us return to the dead man.' It was a brave start.

'You know, Auguste, the Yard is full of Twitches, from top to bottom. Excellent once they've a lead along a well-known path. But they don't listen to what's happening in the undergrowth to right or left.'

'The call of the cicadas?'

'Not to mention frogs. In the undergrowth nowadays are the scientists in the medical laboratories, as we were saying earlier.' He rummaged in the pocket of his overcoat and produced photographs of the smokehouse before and after the body had been removed. 'Look at this—' He pointed to a shape on one photograph, a dull grey shadow on a rug about two feet from where the corpse had lain on the carpet. 'What's that? There's nothing there now.'

Auguste dropped down on his knees to examine the rug.

'But there is,' he said excitedly. 'Egbert – see. The photograph picked up what our eyes couldn't. But if you look very closely indeed, there's the faintest of stains on it in the pile. As if it had been washed.'

'Blood?' said Rose dubiously, squatting beside him.

'It could be. Yet why should the murderer wash away one stain and leave the other?' Auguste pointed to the dull brown patch where the head had lain.

'To make it look like suicide.'

'Probably. You mean he fell here, and the murderer shifted the body to where it was found?'

'But why move the body to one side like this and try to obscure the fact?'

Auguste glanced up when Egbert said nothing more. 'Alexander denies altering the position; he merely

132

lifted it slightly and let it drop.'

'We've got a test now for the presence of blood. Some chemical turns blue. Cobbold's got a chum at a Leeds hospital who's a Home Office pathologist. I'll get him to send the rug along. If there's anything at all left, it might work.' Rose paused. 'Cobbold's been up this morning. He told me the Denver police have telegraphed about Uncle Oscar. They tracked him down to the Yukon. Running a gold assay office there under the name of Percy Smith. Last seen a week ago. If that's reliable, there goes one bright idea and Lady Tabor's whiter than white. They've confirmed the mine-salting story too, but the chief victim died two years ago. Uncle Oscar doesn't appear to be short of enemies, but they can't suggest any who'd be up to tracking him down here, New York shirt or not.'

'So Mr Janes' motive disappears too,' Auguste said glumly. 'Yet he is certainly nervous about something.'

'His wife, most like,' grunted Rose. 'You're not going to suggest a jealous Harold Janes shot the man in mistake for the King, are you? Midnight assignations in the smokehouse? About as far-fetched as vengeful fathers from the Indian Army. The Colonial Office telegraphed details of Colonel Simpson, and Mr Cyril Tabor has admitted he did know his daughter, though he fiercely denies he got her in the family way. The housekeeper fainted at the photograph of the dead man, then said she couldn't say for sure if it was the Colonel or not. Very helpful. The clothes might have been his. She couldn't say for sure, we'd have to ask his batman.'

'And what of Robert Mariot?' asked Auguste hopefully.

'The Case of the Missing Archaeologist, eh? His London housekeeper hasn't seen hide nor hair of him, and we're waiting to hear from Cairo where the Babylon expedition has a base. Anyway, Twitch brought up another photograph of Robert Mariot, which confirms what Laura Tabor said. He's not our man. Mind you, Carstairs could have *thought* he was.'

'Why should he have thought a stranger in the smokehouse was Mariot just because he knew Laura was expecting to see him sometime or other?' Auguste said.

'Another red herring most likely. We've a fine shoal of them.'

'Mine was a real herring, *mon ami.*' Auguste ruefully touched his painful ear.

'He missed, didn't he?'

Auguste stared at him unbelievingly. It wasn't like Egbert to be irritable. 'He *meant* to kill, Egbert.'

'Perhaps.'

'He must have been an excellent shot then,' Auguste replied angrily. 'Buffalo Bill perhaps.' Then he saw Rose's implication. 'You surely cannot think the Tabors murdered this man, believing it to be Gregorin, and then staged the attempt on my life to cover it up? No, no, my friend, the Tabors are not so fond of me as to murder for my sake.'

Rose said nothing.

'You think they have been producing these so-called red herrings deliberately?'

'It fits.'

'For my sake?'

'Or their own safety. Or that of one close to them. Mr Carstairs, for example.'

'But, Egbert,' Auguste exploded, 'they *cannot* be red herrings.'

'Why not?'

'Because they have told nothing but the truth. They said it was not Oscar, and it wasn't. They said it wasn't Mariot, and it looks as if they were right again.'

134

'Hell's bells,' commented Rose graphically. He thought for a moment. 'But it's all too pat. They're hiding something, I'm sure of that. Keep an eye on them, Auguste. If you can't pump the servants, start the other end. Try your charm on the Dowager. Get her to chatter about her family – away from the presence of Priscilla Tabor.'

'I'll try,' said Auguste dubiously. 'But it's hard to pin her chatter down to anything definite.'

'There's one thing definite we do know about her family. One of their prints matched that thumbprint on the Webley nicely.'

'Ah, Didier, fancy taking a gun, do you? Can't miss the first day of the pheasant season, eh?' His host pounced as Auguste was making his way stealthily to the kitchens to investigate the use to which that delightful pork he had noticed yesterday was being put. He had forgotten his route took him past the gun room. He tried to look enthusiastically regretful, but failed. Luckily his host ascribed his reluctance to another cause.

'Sorry, old chap. Tactless of me what with you having a Russian assassin after you. I don't approve of that sort of thing at Tabor Hall.'

Harold Janes frowned. He didn't approve of that sort of thing in the City either. These Russians were known to be excitable people and might well take their vengeance on the first unsuspecting back they could see. And his new scarlet flannel and chamois chest and back protectors weren't going to be much help then.

Auguste clutched metaphorically at the air for inspiration. 'I regret, sir, Chief Inspector Rose needs my assistance.'

'You're right there,' George told him. 'The fellow

asked me why my fingerprint was on the Webley. I told him it was probably because it was my gun from my gun room. He couldn't answer that,' he said triumphantly. 'Is he up to his job? Doesn't seem to be making much progress.'

'I can't live here for ever,' Harold Janes put in.

George Tabor seemed to be in full agreement with this point of view. 'Found out who he is?'

'Not yet – er, George.'

'I think you'll find he was one of the servants' relatives,' his Lordship told him confidently.

'He wore good-quality clothes.'

'Hand-me-downs,' said Lord Tabor dismissively, and strode off to more important matters. Such as the English pheasant and how many might be destroyed before dinner.

Auguste had spent a most enjoyable hour as guest at the servants' luncheon, where a compromise had been tacitly agreed. The world of the upper house was not mentioned. The mystery of the pork was solved: a wonderful casserole of vegetables, forcemeat, bacon, spice and pork, called a mitoon, was forthcoming. How he pitied the Tabors, merely eating *homard au gratin* and *blanquette de veau*. Grinning at his praise, Breckles permitted him to superintend the arrangements for dinner, including the merest hint of advice over the cooking of the fillets of partridge *à la Villeroi*, an occupation so entrancing he realised with horror that he was shortly expected by the Dowager to meet her in the entrance hall for a drive in his Lordship's Daimler.

First he must find Tatiana and explain where he was going. This did not take long. She was closeted with Beatrice Janes in the small Chinese Salon, surrounded by mandarins and willow-pattern ladies. Judging by the agonised expression on her face, Tatiana was not as fascinated as Beatrice by the conversation.

'Pray, do you recommend Madame Bellanger's Corsets Stella or Guillot, dearest Tatiana? Paris is such a long way to go when one breaks a bone but now one can get those useful Albany Corset Splints, it is not quite such a risk. Which do you favour?'

'I do not favour them at all,' declared Tatiana, at the end of her patience. 'Like calling cards, stays are a boring necessity. At present,' she added darkly. 'One day women will not be so foolish. Corsets are cages designed by men, for man's benefit, to keep us locked into the shape they wish to see, a shape that makes it totally impossible for us to enjoy the same benefits of life as they do.' She glared fiercely at Auguste, who could not remember ordering her to achieve any shape at all.

'Oh, are you an aesthetic lady?' Beatrice asked vaguely and returned to safer ground. 'Perhaps I'll go to both Bellanger and Guillot, when Uh-huh takes me to Paris next.'

'Uh-huh?' asked Tatiana blankly.

Auguste coughed. 'Doubtless Mrs Janes refers to Mr Janes.'

Beatrice giggled. 'Of course. Oh, Mr Didier, pray do not take your dear wife away from me. Does she help you in your little cases? And I understand you are a cook? How sweet.'

'A maître chef,' said Auguste through gritted teeth.

'Oh.' Beatrice looked nonplussed. 'Isn't that the same thing?'

'Not precisely.' Auguste's pleasant smile became a trifle fixed.

'Now do join us and tell us who *you* think that poor corpse is,' Beatrice continued brightly. 'I believe,' she rushed on before he had a chance to speak, 'he is some unfortunate fellow from the Tabors' past. Most unfortunate for dear Priscilla—' she said eagerly, 'to have him call after she spent all that time preparing for His Majesty. I think she wished to avoid some *scandal*.'

'You think she shot him?' asked Tatiana, interested.

Beatrice giggled. 'Oh, I wouldn't go so far as to say that.' Her hand played nervously with the buttons of her gloves.

'I would have thought,' Auguste said mildly, 'shooting him would bring upon her Ladyship the very problem she was trying to avoid.'

Beatrice could not follow this, but she was satisfied she had done her best to deflect suspicion towards where it must surely belong. After all, Harold would never . . . would he? She returned to the subject of real importance. 'And now, Tatiana, I want you to give me your opinion on which gown I should wear this evening. The flounced blue silk with the darling lace godets, or the pink glacé?'

'It is time for my walk,' said Tatiana firmly. 'Russians always take a walk after luncheon.'

'Then I will come with you. I am so fond of air. We could walk all round the outside of the house, and take Boofuls.' Boofuls, it appeared, was her dog. 'I bought him the sweetest little India-rubber Wellington boots with back lacing.'

'I am going through the woods. There may be *mud*.'

On this happy note, Tatiana gracefully excused herself to go to change, but Auguste seized the opportunity to detain Beatrice, which she unfortunately took as a tribute to her feminine charms. His Majesty's aide-de-camp had now been authorised to speak, but it was a delicate matter to pass his information on to the person it most concerned. 'Er – Mrs Janes, we have been told that in fact you did not remain throughout the night with Uh-huh, as you mistakenly thought.'

138

'Didn't I?' She looked up at him archly. 'I was bemused by love, I must have forgotten.'

'Can you remember now, Mrs Janes?' Auguste said firmly.

She reached for his hand and drew him down beside her on the sofa. 'I believe I left about two o'clock,' she said airily, leaning towards him. 'Perhaps a little earlier.'

'We were told you left at about a quarter to one.'

'Perhaps,' she snapped, sitting upright again.

'Why did you leave? Had you quarrelled?' Auguste asked as gently as possible.

'No!' Two red spots of anger flushed her cheeks.

'Then why?'

'You can't think I had anything to do with shooting that poor man—' she wailed, changing her tactics. 'Oh, Mr Didier, you are a gentleman, so I will tell you. It is not my husband who has the problem, but me.' She tried a giggle.

'You mean?' Auguste tried to fathom this little problem, 'you needed to visit a bathroom?'

'I snore,' she snapped again, angry at such obtuseness.

The Dowager Lady Tabor, as Auguste reached the entrance hall, was sitting waiting for him with Savage.

'Ah, Mr Didier, here I am. Ready to be unleashed on the outside world.'

'I hope I am not late?' he asked anxiously.

'Not in the least. I had a delightful conversation with your wife.'

Tatiana? What was she doing here? Auguste had a feeling he wasn't going to like it whatever it was. His worst fears were confirmed, as he escorted Miriam down the outside steps. His Lordship's Daimler awaited them as planned. What was not planned was the fact that Tatiana appeared to be sitting in the driving seat instead of the Tabor chauffeur.

'There now. Isn't that a delightful surprise?' Miriam beamed.

Surprise, yes. He was less sure about how delightful it was. He had planned a quiet talk with the Dowager: a sharp-eared Tatiana might not be an asset.

Hardly to his surprise he found himself gripping a starting handle, after he had helped Miriam into the back seat. A scowling Savage tried to follow her, but was thwarted. 'Mr Didier is to sit here, Savage.' Savage began ponderously to move to the front as Auguste held the door open for her, but before she could enter, Beatrice came flying down the steps in lavender silk, grey frills and white lace, dragging a reluctant black pug dog complete with Wellington boots.

'I shall come too,' she announced happily. 'Such a nice way to walk, isn't it, Tatiana?' Without a glance at Savage, she rushed past and into the front seat, handing the pug's lead to Auguste.

'No room, no room, Savage,' shouted Miriam, taking pity on Auguste and making room for Boofuls. 'Never mind, you can take me to church next Sunday, you dear thing. She so wants to drive in a motorcar,' she explained to Auguste as the Daimler lurched off. 'But George will never take me out in one. Priscilla won't let him. She *would* be cross if she knew. Some nonsense about its being dangerous. It's far more dangerous being next to her shooting pheasants. Tabor women have always handled a gun well, even Laura, but Priscilla is convinced she's Annie Oakley. Or do I mean Calamity Jane?' She laughed.

Auguste resigned himself to the prospect before him as the Daimler bounced in and out of holes and ruts, and Boofuls, not content with his own boots, took a slobbering interest in Auguste's. Why worry about

Gregorin, he wondered dolefully, considering he was doomed to death under Tatiana's patronage anyway? Why had the English abolished the rule for a man with a red flag to walk in front of these fiendish contraptions?

'Are we going to Settle?' he asked.

'No, I want to revisit the Barden Tower. I haven't been there since I came with my darling Charles in '45. He proposed to me there. Do you know Mr Wordsworth, Mr Didier?'

'The poet?'

'He was such a *dull* man,' Miriam observed. 'A worthy fellow, but, I suspect, not much fun to have to dinner. Now whom would *you* choose to entertain at dinner?'

'Brillat-Savarin,' Auguste replied promptly, glad to be on familiar ground, here at least.

'Karl Marx,' contributed Tatiana.

'Who is he?' asked Beatrice, puzzled. 'Is he in the Marlborough House set?'

'Yes, Mrs Janes,' Miriam assured her blithely. 'Just talk to His Majesty about him. Such a good chum of the King.'

The motorcar abruptly turned left, hitting a grass bank, reversing, hitting something else, and then roaring under an arch triumphantly ahead to the great alarm of a farmer peacefully ambling towards his fields in the wooded valley they were entering. Tatiana promptly yanked the wheel to swerve round him, though she did not trouble to decrease her speed.

'Oh, splendid,' carolled Miriam. 'What a good driver you are, Mrs Didier.'

Auguste momentarily toyed with the idea that the Dowager Baroness Tabor was a madwoman kept by the Tabors under restraint, since she seemed as drawn to murder as Tatiana.

'Why ever does George believe motorcars to be

dangerous? I sometimes think he is like the Shepherd Lord, of whom Mr Wordsworth wrote. Like him, he would be quite happy living out here with a few sheep and the occasional pheasant or grouse to shoot. Dear Priscilla can be just a little demanding, and just as the Shepherd Lord disliked Skipton so George dislikes the London season.'

'Who is Lord Shepherd?' Beatrice enquired, pricking up her ears at the idea of an unfamiliar member of the peerage.

'Shepherd Lord, dear Mrs Janes. Such a romantic story. His father was The Butcher, Earl Clifford The Butcher, that is.' Miriam laughed. 'After their defeat at Towton Moor, many Lancastrians forfeited both their estates and many, their heads too. Earl Clifford was dead, and his wife, fearing for her infant son's life, gave him into the care of a shepherd in Cumbria. Mr Wordsworth highly approved of the fact that when he finally claimed his inheritance, he lived in none of his splendid castles but instead restored the twelfth-century Barden Tower, buried deep in the countryside, and studied alchemy and astronomy.'

The Daimler stopped with a jerk that threw Miriam into Auguste's arms. He politely disentangled himself and disembarked, relieved to be on solid ground once more.

'This?' asked Beatrice, disappointed at the bleak towering building. 'But it's muddy. Boofuls doesn't like mud. I'll have to stay in the motorcar with him.'

Relieved, Tatiana hurried after Miriam, who was already walking spryly to the ruins.

'He was a recluse?' Tatiana asked with such interest that Auguste wondered whether she had notions of taking up alchemy.

'Fortunately for the future of the Clifford line, he seemed to have learned the secret of procreation – and also of fighting, for he left his tower to fight at Flodden nearly thirty years later. I can quite see George doing the same. Priscilla would be at his side, of course. Perhaps even in front,' she added. 'Or Laura,' Miriam added. 'I can see Laura marching into battle.'

'And why not?' Tatiana said spiritedly. 'If women so wish, they should do so.'

'I fear my Charles would have been shocked at that idea.'

Looking at her feminine figure and demeanour, Auguste could only agree with her late husband. He could see no military qualities about her at all.

'Laura was always Charles' favourite. Such a quiet little thing, but so passionate underneath. She feels things deeply. And like Charles, so devoted. I have been fortunate in my children. Of course one could not call Cyril devoted, but he is a Tabor through and through. George has his pheasants, Cyril his young ladies. Such an attractive boy, always pretending to be so much in awe of George, his elder brother, but in fact the leader. Cyril always gets what he wants, and always did. That's why Priscilla doesn't get on with him. Now aren't I a chatterbox?' She stared up at the ruin towering over them. 'Over fifty years and it hasn't changed.' There might have been a tear in her eye. 'I am glad to have seen it again,' she said quietly.

'Shall we take tea at the inn?' asked Tatiana brightly as they climbed back into the Daimler. Boofuls had been returned to the back seat, Auguste noted with some amusement, and was looking crestfallen – a state of affairs that rapidly changed when Auguste climbed in.

'An *inn*?' asked Beatrice in alarm, her eyes round. 'But I cannot enter a public house.'

'Auguste will protect you,' said Tatiana cheerfully, swerving to avoid a pheasant that had forgotten it was

1 October and was peacefully ambling across the road. 'It will be something *new*.'

'Will I like it?'

'Undoubtedly not, dear Mrs Janes,' Miriam informed her. 'Just like the Shepherd Lord. He couldn't adapt to the life of a gentleman any more than you could to the life of a scullerymaid.'

Beatrice shuddered. 'But he had all that money. Just think of the clothes he could have bought.'

There was just time to slip down to the kitchens, merely to check that all was in order. After all, his reputation was at stake, for Breckles had given permission for him to organise such meals as he wished, and whatever his own opinions as to the preferability of Yorkshire dishes in Yorkshire, a maître's first duty was to please his customers.

'I wonder if I might prepare a turtle soup?'

'Aye.'

'And the dessert. If I might—'

An almighty crash as Breckles brought down a warning fist upon the table. 'Don't you touch puddings.'

'No, no,' Auguste assured him hastily. 'Only the Nesselrode pudding. Do please try it yourself.'

Mollified, Breckles took the proffered taste. 'Mmm.'

'You like it?'

'Aye.'

'With Yorkshire chestnuts, eggs and cream it could almost be said to be Yorkshire,' Auguste pointed out craftily. 'As Yorkshire as spotted dick, anyway.' He was rewarded by another crash of the fist.

'*Spots*! Mr Alfred. I was going to tell you, then I forgot.' Breckles was crestfallen. ''Tis loudest criers in the fair have least on their stalls, and there's talk of how Mr Alfred lost a lot of money gambling, and how his creditors are getting pressing.'

'Well?'

'S'pose one of them got too pressing?' Breckles was pink in the face at this new excitement of detection.

'Mr Breckles, you are a wonder,' said Auguste admiringly. 'I always say that the art of true cuisine and the art of detection go hand in hand. Not only can you produce a Yorkshire pudding as light as a soufflé, but miracles of logical detection as well.'

Well pleased, William Breckles dried his hands on his apron and shook Auguste's hand. Then he returned to the more important matter of batter.

'Where have you been, Mother?' Priscilla asked querulously, with a none too friendly glance at Tatiana and Auguste, obviously finding them guilty of leading her mother-in-law astray, since the Dowager had appeared belatedly in the dining room.

'We went for a drive,' her mother-in-law announced airily, 'then I fell asleep. Now don't fuss me as though I were a child, Priscilla. We didn't discuss the murder, if that is what worries you.'

Priscilla stiffened, waving aside the soup. 'Since we do not know who the dead man is and the police are apparently unable to enlighten us, I cannot see there would be anything to discuss.'

'I do. I think it was all a plot to steal the naughty Sickert drawing,' suggested Alfred lightly.

'Alfred, be silent, sir,' barked his father nervously.

'And the burglar wore dress clothes in order to blend into the background if anyone came into the smokehouse whilst in the midst of his erotic deed,' said Victoria, taking up Alfred's cue.

'Then somebody shot him to prevent the awful secret,' Alexander concluded indiscreetly, 'of the presence of a Sickert nude in your smokehouse becoming known throughout Society.'

'I would have paid him to take it away,' Priscilla announced logically, without a glimmer of humour, 'not shot the man.'

'Perhaps Auguste's Russian enemy,' volunteered Gertie brightly, 'found the art thief in the smokehouse and shot him thinking it was our dear Mr Didier.'

'Rather careless of him, wasn't it, kitten?' enquired her husband. Marital relationships appeared once more to be harmonious, although there was a distinct frostiness still towards his sister-in-law.

'I think Mr Didier shot the man to provide himself with a nice piece of detective work,' announced Miriam. 'Or Mrs Janes protecting her – um – husband against a blackmailer.'

'Mother, be quiet,' thundered Priscilla, before Harold could comment on this theory.

Miriam meekly turned to wheedle Harold back into good humour.

Society dinner was a strange affair, Auguste thought, as full of wind as artichoke soup. He felt he was on a stage in an unknown play while the real work was carried out beneath their feet and in the wings. Around him the enamelled faces of the women, rouged and powdered and eye-shadowed, looked like painted masks as they talked and chattered. What were their real thoughts? He had found to his surprise that he was developing a strange admiration for Priscilla. With Laura he had struck up a friendship; he was beginning to treat Alfred, Victoria and Alexander with familiarity. It dawned upon him that he was getting used to Society, just as Tatiana increasingly resented it.

Alfred appeared, undismayed at his summons, in Rose's quarters, and interrogated him on whether everything was satisfactory, as a host to an honoured guest.

146

'I gather you've had some financial worries, sir?' Rose suggested blandly, when the inquisition was over.

Alfred twiddled his brandy glass. 'Yes,' he agreed, after some consideration and without much surprise.

'Serious?'

'Not in the least.'

'Then you won't mind showing me your accounts.'

The brandy glass was abruptly put down on the table. 'Yes, I damned well would.'

'I could ask your mother.'

Alfred considered this prospect for a moment. 'The fellows were threatening to sue,' he said sullenly. 'It was only roulette and cards, dammit. I hadn't robbed a bank.'

'Did they come here to see you?'

'*No!*'

'So what happens if they sue?' enquired Rose.

Alfred beamed at him. 'I've paid them. I had a win, as it happens, and could pay them off.'

'That's most fortunate, sir. One could say too fortunate.'

Tatiana shot in the front door at eleven-twenty-nine beaming at Priscilla who stood, key in hand, ready to execute summary justice at eleven-thirty. Auguste blushed at the odd sight it must present to Lady Tabor to see himself passing through on his way from Egbert's room to bed and his wife clearly returned from a nocturnal excursion. Had she seen Gregorin, was his immediate fear.

'Where have you been?' he hissed as soon as they were out of earshot.

'I have been to see that very nice man called Walter Tompkins,' she told him with dignity.

'*Who?*'

'The Tabors' driver. He and his wife live over the

motor stable. I drank something interesting called Stout.'

'What for?' Auguste was relieved to hear, for the sake of the last shreds of Tatiana's reputation with the Tabors, that at least Mrs Tompkins appeared to have been present.

'I wanted to know how motorcars work, of course,' explained Tatiana, surprised he should have to ask. 'Did you know, for example, that there is something called a sparking plug? Or that one may experience a backfire on the arm due to premature ignition? I shall ask Alexander if I can take the De Dion Bouton out again to give close study to the petrol-engine.'

'Why not the Daimler?' asked Auguste irritably.

'George was not very pleased that it was just a little dented where I unfortunately hit the milestone when I went backwards so expertly.' She broke off. 'Where are you going?'

'To play billiards and have a brandy,' announced her husband grimly. His arm was not going to experience any backfires. He would ensure that.

'Evening, Didier.' Oliver examined his cue carefully. 'I am not on good terms with Laura – I am also rather drunk.'

Auguste eyed him warily, and agreed that Oliver appeared to be correct in his self-diagnosis. 'The devil of it is,' Oliver laid down the cue and searched for his glass, 'I'm beginning to realise I really do want to marry her, but she won't believe me.'

'If she is in love with this archaeologist—'

'Poppycock, taradiddle and bull,' shouted Oliver. 'How could she be in love with a sack of old bones when there is me?'

'It is unlikely,' Auguste hastily conceded. 'Nevertheless I have often noticed that women have long memories, and if she is still in touch with him—'

'I don't believe it,' declared Oliver robustly, though slurring his words slightly. 'But that detective friend of yours thinks I shot that chap in the smokehouse thinking it Mariot. *Me!*'

'Did you?' Auguste asked incautiously.

'Of course not,' Oliver replied with dignified control. 'Fellow isn't a gentleman, dammit,' he pontificated in weak imitation of their host.

'What makes a gentleman?' Auguste enquired, the brandy beginning to relax him from more pressing problems of murder. (Even his own.) 'Am I one, would you say?'

Oliver thought about this. 'By whose standards? If I say it's a fellow who can hold his brandy, for instance, I'm lost, reduced to the ranks.' He took another one to test his theory. He finished it. 'As one gentleman to another, Didier, let's have another.'

What did a gentleman consist of, Auguste considered gravely, none the wiser after the passage of an hour and two more brandies, as Oliver fell asleep in an armchair. He sank into one of the leather chairs and considered the matter once more. A gentleman was more than his appearance, he told himself. He stood up and bowed deeply to his reflection in the mirror. This suit, exquisitely tailored by Redfern, proclaimed he was a gentleman. But if he transgressed the code of conduct, he would not be one, though he would still be in the suit. He bowed deeply once more in a manner befitting a gentleman. He smoothed down an errant wave of his hair, examined his shirt and black tie and waistcoat – he wasn't quite sure now for whom Tatiana said they were in mourning. The King's mother, sister? McKinley? Someone anyway. Perhaps himself.

In the old days, he told a dress-suited Auguste in the mirror, a maître chef's clothes suggested he was a cook. Doubtless a Yorkshire clogger's clothes told the

149

casual bypasser that he was a clogger. Thus by the same token must a suit by Redfern proclaim he was an English gentleman. And yet he was not. He was half-French, and only half a gentleman. He frowned. It was an extremely complicated matter. If he walked out of his suit, who was he then? If stripped like that corpse . . .

He ordered his train of thought to stop immediately. He had said something of immense significance. No, of great simplicity. If one took the dead man's clothes off, would he remain a gentleman? That was the question.

Auguste peered anxiously in the mirror. Then rising excitement drove the befuddled sensation of too much brandy from him; it was the victory of a point well argued. His detection powers were not extinct, they were at their height, he told himself immodestly. They had assumed the dead man to be a gentleman because of his clothes. Suppose he were not. Just suppose that they *were* good quality hand-me-downs?

Or even suppose they were not his at all.

Chapter Six

'Why?'

Rose regarded Auguste sourly over a plate of sautéed kidneys. He had avoided the battered anchovies in view of last night's over-indulgence in venison *à la St George*, but even the kidneys were looking triumphant at the prospect of final victory over his stomach. A wistfulness came over him for the familiar things of home: the porridge you could count on to have just a hint of burnt smokiness, the egg that mysteriously broke itself en route from kitchen to table, the tea that conquered all in its strong sweetness. That was the trouble with this job, you got the worst of being away from home but not the best. The worst, for instance, was Auguste eagerly bursting in before one's eyes were fully open, like a bouncy puppy wanting to be off and doing. Or, in this case, telling.

'Why what?' Auguste was somewhat taken aback at Egbert's chilly reception of his brilliant detective work.

'Why bother to dress up in good-quality dinner clothes if he was a tramp?' Rose continued his breakfast.

'So many reasons,' Auguste explained eagerly. 'He might have been a burglar, trying to avoid notice, as I believe was suggested. Or a prospective assassin,' he added firmly, 'as we first thought. He could come over the fells with impunity after dark.' Like Pyotr Gregorin, he was disagreeably reminded.

'No mud on his shoes. He'd have had to have carried

them, *and* the suit. And where's his overcoat?' Rose was not convinced. Far from it.

'He could have walked from Malham, or even from Kirkby Malham. Cobbold's men only made enquiries about gentlemen.' Auguste heard himself saying this with alarm. He who had always believed that gentlemen could be found in pig-sties and villains in marbled halls!

'Cobbold's men haven't found any trace of anyone missing around here that could fit our party, gent or no gent. No carriers report any passengers that evening.'

'Perhaps he has not yet been missed because there is no one to miss him,' shouted Auguste, goaded by Egbert's dismissive tone.

'A local assassin, then. Unusual for a man to decide to pop out and kill the King because he's staying next door, ain't it?'

'That is ridiculous, of course.' Auguste glared. 'But my theory opens up possibilities,' he insisted, although his certainty was rapidly fading. He strolled to the window to try to think, undisturbed by Egbert's ironic eye. There in the distance beyond formal rosebeds he could just see the walls of the vegetable garden. Somewhere among those hills was Gregorin, somewhere in a remote village or a hamlet; hidden in a deserted house, even in a cave, was the hunter, biding his time for his quarry to break cover in his direction. And there was nothing the quarry could do about it. The hunter had all the choices. And the gun. He tore his mind quickly away.

'There is a lump in this sauce that we are discussing,' he told Rose regretfully.

'It's your sauce.'

'If you don clothes as a disguise, you put on the trousers, the jacket, the waistcoat, the tie, the shirt, perhaps gloves, but not necessarily the underwear. Especially if you are an assassin. But on this corpse, *mon ami, all* the clothes were good, and hardly available to a Yorkshire shepherd.'

'Hand-me-downs.'

'Would he dress *completely* in hand-me-downs? His socks, his suspenders, his underpants?'

'Unlikely, I'll admit.'

'He had a sunburnt complexion, rough hands,' Auguste reasoned, seeing he had Egbert's attention, 'not because he had been in Babylon, or Colorado, but because he was a working man, or at least a man used to being in the open air much of the time.'

'His hair was neat.'

Auguste dismissed this. 'He might have cut it for the occasion, and put Rowland's Macassar oil on it.' A stray memory came back to him. 'Tatiana found a few dark hairs on my ulster. I thought they were mine, but just suppose—'

Rose abandoned breakfast, his attention suddenly caught, and went over to his desk. 'There were a couple on the floor of the smokehouse too,' he said, reading through the medical laboratory report.

'I must have picked up some as I lay on the floor the following day,' Auguste remembered with distaste.

Egbert roared with laughter. 'Our chap really has an evening out. Maybe he decided to use the smokehouse for a wash and brush-up, and cut his hair into the bargain. Probably trimmed his beard too.'

'Suppose, Egbert—' an idea began to blossom in Auguste's mind, 'suppose this murder is like a *soupe au pistou.*'

Rose had happy memories of *soupe au pistou* in Provence, but he could not see the precise resemblance.

'Explain,' he said resignedly. Cooking analogies tended to be more helpful to Auguste than himself.

Auguste struggled to concentrate his thought processes. 'Instead of this vegetable soup following the normal pattern, where all the ingredients cook together, suppose these dress clothes are the *pistou*, the garlic, basil and pine nut mixture, which was stirred in at the last moment.'

'I'm not sure I follow.'

'The murder took place and the clothes were changed *afterwards*.'

'Difficult for the corpse to manage, wasn't it?'

'By the murderer, Egbert,' Auguste howled.

'What about the blood?' Rose asked promptly. 'If the clothes were changed after death, what happened to the old clothes, and more importantly, how did these new clothes get covered in blood?'

'Suppose the murderer added blood?'

'Whose?'

'An animal's—' Auguste broke off. 'The missing blood from the larder.' He was right, he *must* be. 'Breckles could not find the blood for the black pudding the following day, Egbert – the mad carpenter?'

'Eh?' Rose looked startled, then caught up. 'The new test.' He thought it over. 'I'll get the shirt on its way to Cobbold's pal. Mind you, I don't know that I'm convinced. Still a few questions. Like my first one. Why?'

'To obscure his identity,' Auguste replied promptly.

Rose considered this, then shook his head. 'That doesn't add up. If he's a local man, sooner or later he'd be identified. If he wasn't, why bother to change the clothes?'

'So that the murderer had time to leave the district,' said Auguste, inspired.

'His Majesty perhaps?' enquired Rose drily.

'There were guests in the house,' Auguste replied with dignity. 'And servants.'

'With access to top-quality clothes?'

'Valets,' Auguste pressed on. 'They often inherit clothes. And there's Mr and Mrs Janes too.'

Rose shook his head, dissatisfied. 'Makes it premeditated. Call your victim to a midnight rendezvous, have a spare set of clothes handy, take all that time to change his clothes, and cut his hair, when for all you know the shot might have alerted the household. No, there must have been some strong motive for changing them. *If* they were changed,' he added cautiously.

'Sometimes the dishes that look most complicated, turn out the simplest,' observed Auguste. 'Take for instance, a *brandade de morue* or possibly a *gratin dauphinois*—'

'Not at the moment, thank you,' Rose interrupted; memories of the venison welled up all too vividly. He hesitated. While disagreeable associations were on his mind, he might as well get it over. 'Auguste, you realise that at this stage everyone's a suspect, don't you?'

'Naturally.' He was somewhat hurt. 'I had as much opportunity to kill this man as anyone. Furthermore I was alone with him for some time, able to remove any incriminating evidence—'

'I wasn't thinking of you.'

Auguste stared at him, horrified, unbelieving – then remembering all Egbert's odd silences. 'But you cannot still think Tatiana was involved, Egbert?' he asked slowly.

'I have to consider everybody.'

'But she did not recognise the corpse.' Auguste tried to keep emotion from his voice, to speak rationally. Since Tatiana's explanation, he had dismissed his own worries about her part in this death as the product of an over-active imagination working in fearful circumstances. Why had he assumed that Egbert had done the same?

'Ever occur to you the corpse might *be* Gregorin?' Rose continued simply. 'I'm only telling you because Twitch is down in London now checking with Special Branch.'

Auguste's face turned black as thunder. 'You asked him to check on *my wife?*'

'I have to.'

Auguste desperately sought to see things through Egbert's eyes. Tatiana was the only one who *knew* Gregorin. Suppose she had lied about the corpse? Egbert was right, he had to concede. And yet something inside him rebelled. Egbert should as soon suspect Queen Alexandra herself.

Reason reasserted itself. 'How,' he asked, 'could Gregorin have shot at me the following evening if he'd been murdered the night before?'

'That's simple. Young Alexander and . . .' he hesitated before Auguste's reproachful eye 'the Princess could have shot Gregorin before he could do any damage here, either to you *or* His Majesty. You never know with European politics, and Gregorin has recently been at the Kaiser's court. Suppose the King's assassination was his mission, not to kill you at all? Then the next night Alexander could have taken a pot-shot at you but deliberately missed—'

'Only just.'

'Nevertheless, missed. He's prepared an escape route up the fell, skirts round and down the slopes of Willy's Brow into the house again. He's now established Gregorin's existence. *Then* they feel free to tell us about this notorious assassin. Or, I might remind you, Gregorin himself might have shot our corpse, who might have come for some innocent purpose and got in his way.'

'Yes,' agreed Auguste eagerly.

Rose regarded him dispassionately. 'Then prove it quickly, Auguste, or I'm going to have to move if Stitch comes back with a report or photograph of Gregorin which in any way resembles our body.'

'I can begin now,' Auguste hurled at him. 'If that pathologist's report shows animal blood, then the corpse *can't* be that of Gregorin. Why should Tatiana and Alexander bother to change his clothes?'

'Good point. Gregorin might well change them though if he murdered a stranger,' Rose came back instantly. 'Twitch reported that Special Branch knows that Gregorin favours disguise. Suppose he murdered your tramp for the sake of swapping clothes?'

He wanted to agree. He wanted to agree so much. But he couldn't. 'Why go to the bother of cutting his hair?'

There was a long silence. 'Well done, Auguste,' Egbert said quietly.

A knock at the door, and Cobbold came in, escorted, in no way to his discomfiture, by an extremely tall Tabor-liveried footman. He nodded to Auguste before sitting himself carefully on the balloon-back chair opposite Rose, and announcing that every village in the dales now had a reconstructed drawing of what the corpse must have looked like pasted up in Post Office windows.

'Mr Didier here,' Rose told him, 'has a notion our fellow ain't such a gentleman as he appears. The clothes were changed after death. He reckons he might be a working man from round these parts after all. That possible?'

Cobbold considered. 'I can't rule it out. It's a time of year when men are on the move, sheep-salving, winter log cutting, re-tiling, wall repairs, peat-cutting and so on. Could be away days at a time. I'll check with the

157

cotton mill and the tannery.' A resigned look came over his face. 'So you'll be wanting a search of the land round here for the clothes?'

'Quickly. I'll have to let the guests go home after the Coroner's Enquiry,' Rose told him regretfully. 'I don't want the royal telegraph wires tapping because Mrs Janes is unavoidably detained.'

'This would naturally include myself and my wife?' Auguste said stiffly.

'Not yet, if you please.' Egbert paused. 'I need you.' That note in his voice again, Auguste noted dismally. *Not yet. Not till I'm sure your wife isn't a murderess.*

Even if he proved the clothes had been changed, the hands that changed them remained to be found, and he, Auguste, was going to have to find out whose they were. It would be a lone hunt now and lone hunts started on home ground.

'There was one of them detectives on our door all day Friday and Saturday,' Mrs Breckles supplied helpfully. 'The shirtmaker came,' she remembered. 'Mrs Waites. She were quite put out that detective thought she might have a gun in her sewing bag. Very patriotic is Mrs Waites. But no one like that.' She looked at Auguste's carefully doctored picture, with longer hair, old jacket, scruffy necktie and beard. 'Some of them—' she looked scathingly at the picture, 'call at the front entrance and Mr Richey sees them off.'

Caught in the midst of a quiet smoke, thus transgressing rules that even His Majesty had been forced to observe, Mr Richey had no option but to be gracious to Mr Didier. He gave a brief glance at the drawing.

'Trade entrance, Mr Didier.' His offhand tone implied Auguste would know that door well. Diplomacy was needed.

'My senses, Mr Richey, specialise in taste. My sense of smell is very undeveloped,' Auguste announced casually. It was not true of course – why, he could smell a sour stock at forty paces – but Mr Richey took the point that Auguste's sense of smell might easily and swiftly improve. This time he studied the drawing carefully.

'It puts me in mind of a ruffian who called here five or six weeks ago. The Chief Inspector was interested in callers during the last week, and then only in gentleman visitors. That's why I didn't think to mention it to him.'

'What did he want?' A sort of strangled gulp emerged from Auguste's throat in his excitement.

'Of course, I may be wrong. This person I refer to claimed to have business with the family; indeed, personal to her Ladyship, or if not her, his Lordship. Her Ladyship came back from her drive at that moment, and he thrust a letter into her hands. When she opened it, she said: "That'll be all, Richey," and beckoned this fellow to follow her. I did mention it to his Lordship,' he added unctuously, 'being concerned for her Ladyship's safety with such a person.'

'Naturally,' breathed Auguste fervently, a sudden convert to the merits of Mr Richey.

'Are you sure you haven't met him, Lady Tabor?' Auguste pressed on inexorably, regardless of diplomacy. 'Mr Richey was very certain you had. He called five or six weeks ago, asking to see you.'

He showed her the drawing again. Priscilla gazed at it and tapped impatiently at her rosewood writing desk. Then, as if realising that this annoyance would not disappear, she announced: 'It is possible Richey may be thinking of a terrible person who presented me with a statement of Alfred's debts.'

'But neither you nor Mr Alfred recognised the body.'
Priscilla fixed him with steady eye. 'There is a quite simple reason for that, Mr Didier. The body was not that of this man. It had shorter hair, and was of quite a different class.'

'Did your caller leave a card or address?'

'Address?' The stays creaked, the eyebrows rose. 'That sort of person has no abode, Mr Didier. He travels from shire to shire. I imagine if the police—' Did he imagine a slight emphasis on the word police? 'Wish to pursue this enquiry they might shortly find him at Newmarket. The race meeting is often a suitable venue to meet gullible young men who are foolish enough to indulge in unlicensed gambling games.'

'His name?'

'Mr Didier,' Brünnhilde rose, 'that sort of person does not have a name. He merely requires payment in Bank of England notes. My son provided it.'

'Did I?' Alfred Tabor paused momentarily in the all-absorbing task of pouring Auguste and himself a stiff whisky and soda, uncalled for on Auguste's part. 'If you say so, my dear fellow.'

'It is not I who say so, but your mother.' Auguste was irritated.

'Ah. Then I expect she's right. Yes, by Jove she is. About three weeks ago. Terrible check suit. Big boots. That the chap?' He glanced at the drawing. 'Might have been. Couldn't say. Thought of telling him to push off, but he'd only come back. Creditors do, you know.'

Auguste did.

'So the body in the smokehouse could have nothing to do with him?' Auguste enquired politely.

'Nothing at all,' Alfred told him vigorously. 'True, I was a touch worried at first that this smokehouse fellow might be something to do with the old spinning wheel. You know how it is, or perhaps you don't.' He recalled Auguste was a chef and his confidential voice adopted a somewhat more airy note. 'Black Jack, roulette, baccarat. Got a bit behind because I had to go on "tick" at one place, but then had to pay fellow two there, because news leaked I hadn't paid fellow one and that meant I hadn't the money to pay off fellow one. That must have been who old check suit was working for. Yes, by Jupiter, Ma's right. I paid the fellow off. Half expecting fellow three to turn up here, as well, but he hasn't.'

He beamed at Auguste, and confident everything was now explained, continued with a somewhat forced laugh, 'I say, you didn't really think I made an assignation in the smokehouse and crept out there and shot that chappie?'

'Not so funny for the corpse,' Auguste pointed out with some asperity.

'That inspector chum of yours isn't exactly a man of the world,' said the twenty-one-year-old of the veteran of the notorious Radcliffe Highway beat. 'So tell him from me that shooting a bailiff don't let you off the debt. Thought of that?'

Auguste hadn't.

No receipt, it transpired, was to hand, though Alfred was adamant that it had existed. Generously he offered to search for it, and with that Auguste had to be content. Reluctantly he discounted Alfred as a suspect. What possible reason could he have for dressing a bailiff up in dining clothes, thus bringing suspicion nearer to the family – and on *that* night of all nights?

His brain seemed as foggy as the mist over the fells that greeted his eyes each morning. Whereas the latter was satisfying, full of promise for the rich autumn day to come, he could not say the same of the horror that

161

he found now himself pitchforked into.

George Tabor regarded him suspiciously, as for once Auguste presented himself with Tatiana in the morning room to await luncheon. 'Your inspector chum has told us our home is to be searched. I'm not too keen on that at all. Not that we've anything to hide,' George said hastily, 'but our guests aren't taking kindly to it. Nor,' he added gloomily, 'is Priscilla.'

The door was flung open and his wife bore down on cue. 'Mr Didier, is there *nothing* you can do?'

'I regret not,' Auguste said truthfully. After all, he was on their side. His room – and Tatiana's – was also to be searched. He was painfully aware that Egbert might be avoiding him just as much as he was avoiding Egbert. 'George,' he said, grasping the nettle, 'I wonder if I might ask you more about the clothes the dead man was wearing?'

Priscilla swelled. 'We have just told the police, Mr Didier, that nothing is missing from my husband's wardrobe, if that is what you are implying. If you doubt our word, I suggest you speak to Johnson, my husband's valet. He is a Quaker.' The bell was rung vigorously.

One look at Johnson's austere face, and there was no doubting his honesty. Or his smugness. 'Nothing is missing, sir, from his Lordship's wardrobe. His suits, shirts, socks, shoes, undergarments are in perfect order.'

'The laundry?' Auguste asked hesitantly.

Johnson permitted himself a thin smile of self-satisfaction. 'Naturally, I made a point of checking it as soon as the Chief Inspector made his interest known. Nothing is missing. Moreover, all his Lordship's suits are English, sir, as are his socks, underpants, shoes, shirts and ties. His Lordship does not favour France, sir.'

George gave a deprecating cough. 'Nothing against the French, of course, Didier. But nothing to beat home cooking, eh?'

'Indeed not, George. Save in pork,' Auguste added mischievously.

'Pork?' George asked, puzzled.

'The richness and variety of pork cuts is not appreciated here. Though Mr Breckles' mutton presents—'

'And now, Mr Didier,' Priscilla intervened sweetly, 'Johnson will escort you on a tour of all the valets. *Before* luncheon. You must of course *fully* satisfy yourself. I presume we may leave your own valet to you?'

He had no valet, she *knew* he had no valet, he squirmed.

'And Miss Savage, too, I trust,' he gamely made a comeback. 'I understand the Dowager Lady Tabor retained all her husband's clothes.'

'Certainly, if you wish.' Priscilla was clearly bored by domestic talk now.

Messrs Harbottle and Watkins were a surprise. He had put down the pleasant middle-aged Harbottle as Janes' man and Watkins, an alert twenty-one-year-old with ambition, as Oliver's. It proved to be the other way around.

'My gentleman,' Harbottle informed him smugly, 'obtains his shirts and whatnots in Paris, and his suits in London. He has a very busy life,' he said with pride. 'Some folks think that it's the ladies have all the luggage for these visits, changing five times a day. I know different. My gentleman has to consider very carefully what suits to take. Is he going to be a-courting, for example? Is he going to be a-dancing with maiden ladies? Is he going to be the spot of entertainment in an old folks' household? Is he—'

'And what was this visit?' enquired Auguste, diverted,

163

thinking of his own hasty packing and sartorial shortcomings.

'This was a mourning visit, sir, with a spot of courting thrown in. Courting, sir, not murder.' Harbottle grinned. 'And nothing's missing. My gentleman still has everything he came with. How about yours, Mr Watkins?'

Watkins gave him a look of slight disapproval. 'When going anywhere where we expect to meet Royalty, we are naturally particular. My gentleman always brings ten suits. *Ten*, Mr Didier. Ten come with us, and ten are still here.'

Savage would make a good candidate for a Holloway prison wardress, thought Auguste, as he moved on to the Dowager's quarters where Savage also had her bedroom and one small sitting room to be at hand to tend her mistress. He found her carefully placing an embroidered cloth on a coffee tray, ready for her Ladyship.

'Um – is that the Tabor crest?' he asked, admiring the hand embroidery. 'Your own work?'

'Miss Laura's.' Her tone indicated that charm would make little impression on her.

Undaunted, he pressed on: 'I wonder if I might look at his late Lordship's clothes—'

'I told them perlice nothing is missing.'

'Would you be so very kind as to show me?' Auguste's voice tailed off under her indignant eye, but she obediently led the way into a dressing room adjoining the Dowager's bedroom.

'Here,' she said scornfully, flinging open a cupboard. 'His Lordship's suits. Every one of them made in Harrogate. A good Yorkshire man he was.' She turned out the breast pocket of one to flourish a label: Haycock of Harrogate. 'And his shirts was made by Mrs Pumps, the mother of her that travels round now. She were a good worker.'

'So you have been with Lady Tabor a long time?' he asked politely.

'Since she were a girl, and came as a bride to this house. A slip of a thing then, but could twist you round her little finger like she still can.' An almost human look crossed her grim countenance.

'My dear Mr Didier, how sweet of you. You're looking at Charles' clothes.' Miriam came into the small room, laughing. 'Dear Charles. It makes me feel just a little closer to him to have his belongings around me. Savage understands, don't you, Savage?'

A blush of pride came into Savage's cheeks. 'Indeed I do, milady.'

Smith, Cyril Tabor's valet, was employed in pressing Mr Cyril's dress clothes for the evening, and informed Auguste that Mr Cyril would shortly be here to change for luncheon. A matter of seconds could, however, be spared from Smith's busy agenda. 'I explained to the police,' he told Auguste tonelessly,' that Mr Cyril brought six suits with him, and three sets of dress clothes. I'll show you.'

With the world-weary attitude of one tried beyond endurance, he opened the wardrobe in the dressing room, and speedily lost his composure.

'This is strange, very strange. There does seem to be one missing.'

'You were very quiet at luncheon, Auguste,' Tatiana pointed out. 'Did you not approve of Mr Breckles' plum charlotte?'

'Perhaps I prefer his Yorkshire cuisine.' Auguste tried to give her a quick smile as if to reassure her that this was all that was amiss. It failed.

'Egbert is looking for you,' she told him casually, but watching him closely.

'I would prefer to walk with you.'

165

The early October sun was pleasant, as they walked towards the wooded valley leading up to the track from Malham to the high moors. A path led by the side of the gushing beck, which gurgled over stones and huge boulders in its haste to join its fellow becks and springs to form the River Aire. Large mossy boulders clung to steep hillsides on either side of the path. Only a few hundred yards from the house and they were in a different world. Yet it was still a world in which issues must be faced.

'Why are you avoiding Egbert?' Tatiana asked bluntly.

'Because he is working closely with Inspector Cobbold.'

'That would make no difference. It's because of me, isn't it?'

He wanted to lie but he could not.

'He is trying to do his job. It cannot be easy for him, Auguste.'

'Perhaps not.'

'Then don't hold it against him. He still thinks that corpse could be Gregorin's. While he has no other solution he *must* suspect me and Alexander.'

'That is why I am going to find the true solution quickly,' he told her firmly.

'Behind there,' Tatiana shouted against the noise, pointing to a cave behind the waterfall tumbling over an overhanging rock, 'lived Janet, so they say in the village.'

'Who is Janet?' It seemed a very wet abode for a lady.

'The Queen of the Fairies. Queen of magic spells.'

'Could she cast one to make Gregorin change his mind about me?'

'We could ask.' Tatiana turned to the waterfall. '*Pazhahlsta tsaritsa—*'

166

'She might not understand Russian.'

'Then speak in Yorkshire.'

'Hickity O, pickity O, pompolorum jig.' Auguste was suddenly lighthearted, remembering Breckles' charm. 'That's to remove the threat of evil.'

Beyond them in the hills the sun still shone, but here enclosed by huge rocks and overhanging trees it was easy indeed to believe in evil, in the Fairy Queen who lived behind the waterfall.

'It is strange to think,' Auguste said soberly, 'that if Gregorin were to appear, I should be dead, but you would be free of suspicion.'

'And if he disappears, then I am arrested but you live.'

He laughed. 'This is what they call balance in marriage?'

He looked at his wife. He saw her as she was. Not the princess in the ivory tower he had dreamed of for so many years; she was Tatiana Didier and, by all the pickled eggs in China, he loved her!

The sting of the water was on their faces as he kissed her, until she firmly pushed him away.

'*Alors*, Auguste, I am a practical woman, the ground is damp. We go back to our bedroom, *hein*? And let us hope Egbert is not searching it.'

'What *does* one wear for a Coroner?' Priscilla demanded the following day. The gathering had taken on a new intimacy through the common scourge that had fallen on them, as though this might maintain the pretence that nothing unusual was happening, despite the presence of policemen in the house.

'We don't have to wear full black again, do we?' cried Beatrice, alarmed. 'Not now His Majesty's left.'

'It *is* a death — of sorts,' Priscilla pointed out dubiously.

167

'Wear your Queen Victoria gown,' suggested Victoria. 'That black crepe one with the black lace sleeves and matching veil. They wouldn't dare arrest you then.'

'Really, Victoria,' protested her mother, but there was no heart in it.

'I think we should look our prettiest,' said Gertie simply.

'You'll melt the Coroner's heart, kitten,' said her husband lovingly.

'He can't suspect me, can he?' Gertie's large eyes looked anxious.

'No. You haven't got the brains, Gertie,' answered her nephew-in-law airily.

'That's all right then.' Gertie was relieved.

'I thought the corpse might be something to do with the stage,' said Beatrice. Every pair of Tabor eyes fixed on her indignantly. In the last resort, even Gertie was regarded as one of them. 'The police seem to think he was dressing up in someone else's clothes,' she added nervously, 'so it seems an obvious deduction.'

'Only to you, Mrs Janes,' remarked Priscilla coldly. Beatrice might be the King's favourite, but she was not hers.

'And me,' said Harold heavily, all too eager to support his wife. 'After all, we're only visitors here,' his tone implied it would be the last time, 'we would hardly come here prepared to commit a murder.' He waxed indignant. 'We are innocent bystanders. Like His Majesty himself.'

Priscilla paled at the implied threat that tales of the enforced hospitality of Tabor Hall would come to royal ears. But for once her husband rode gallantly to the rescue.

'Bertie understands. Said he'll be back for the pheasants next year.'

Beatrice and Harold exchanged glances quickly and reconsidered their position.

'He wouldn't be allowed on stage with those whiskers!' Gertie had been thinking things over.

'His Majesty never appears on stage,' said Beatrice, astounded.

Gertie looked puzzled.

'The corpse,' explained Cyril kindly.

Auguste eyed him hungrily. Cyril was the only one with a suit missing and only he knew it. It might mean nothing, he told himself in excuse, for anyone might have taken it. Of all of them, Cyril would have had least reason to change the corpse's clothes, for the suspected victim in his case was an Indian colonel who would surely be in evening dress anyway. Unless he were in uniform of course, which would be an immediate betrayal of who he was. A small voice inside him pointed out that an Indian colonel wouldn't have long hair. It was told that a few black hairs meant nothing . . .

He manufactured an opportunity to speak to Cyril that night when Cyril, braving Priscilla's eye, declared his intention of having a good smoke, now that the police had formally declared the smokehouse open again.

Surrounded by the artistic delights of the smokehouse, as creature comforts of brandy and leather armchairs reasserted their attractions, Auguste found it hard to imagine the terrible scene that had taken place here only a few days ago.

'Your valet tells me, Mr Tabor, that one of your suits has disappeared,' Auguste began, unable to think of a more subtle way to introduce the matter.

'Yes, he told me that too. Rum thing, isn't it?' said Cyril indignantly. 'I'll ask Smith to have a look at the

169

suit that poor devil was wearing, just in case he got hold of it somehow.'

Auguste blinked. Guileless or subtle? 'How could he have done?' he enquired cautiously.

Cyril shrugged. 'No idea. Priscilla doesn't encourage odd vagabonds to wander in and out of the Hall.' He yawned. 'Sorry, old chap. Must be those damned puddings Breckles suddenly seems to be serving up. Toffee puddings, spotted dicks. Can't think what's come over him.'

Auguste kept a discreet silence. Talk of puddings led him to think of Breckles' black pudding. How long would that report from Leeds take to come through?

'Chief Inspector Rose would like to see you, sir.'

Auguste paused in the midst of adjusting his tie. This time he could not ignore the summons. Besides, it might be the report.

It wasn't.

'You aren't avoiding me, are you, Auguste?' Egbert demanded. He was not at breakfast, but already at his desk, very annoyed, and with Twitch in attendance. It did not bode well.

'No,' said Auguste. 'I was involved in my duties as a guest both yesterday and today.' He had in fact spent the greater part of yesterday undergoing tuition in Yorkshire cuisine in the kitchens. He had also taken the opportunity to let the entire servants' hall hear of the discovery of the pig's blood, watching keenly for signs of guilt or over-interest. The main comments seemed to focus on how anyone could so brazenly offend Mr Breckles. The only other obvious emotion came from the pantry boy who had been wrongly accused of mislaying the pig's blood, and now saw a glimmer of hope that one day he might rise to the exalted status of third vegetable chef.

170

'If any of these duties throw up anything interesting, no doubt you'll let me know,' Egbert said ironically.

'Of course,' Auguste lied.

'Such as prising out the information from Cyril Tabor's valet that one of his suits *is* missing. And a shirt. When I was *eventually* told, I found the labels don't tie up with the suit on the corpse. Stitch here has turned in some excellent work on *that*.'

Twitch glowed.

'And, moreover, Colonel Simpson didn't arrive on board the ship for India as he should have done. He missed the boat, as you might say.'

Egbert might well be barking up the wrong tree, but Auguste was not going to encourage him to leave it. It meant Tatiana was temporarily free from suspicion.

The Coroner's Enquiry held on Friday morning in the Court House next to the police station was an exciting event in Settle. The Tabors had not appeared in the town *en masse* for centuries. The formidable Lady Tabor was usually only encountered thrusting open the doors of their houses without warning with large bowls of unwelcome succotash for the sick. Not that the sick knew what it was called, but it made them decide to get well quickly.

The visiting Skipton Coroner was well aware of the importance of an inquest on a stranger found dead at Tabor Hall when the King had been present, and an array of Tabors and outcomers as he'd never seen before. One by one these august personages announced that they had no knowledge of the gentleman whose corpse had so inconveniently turned up in their midst. They fascinated both Coroner and jury, more by their appearance than by their testimony. Skipton shops did not display Worth models, nor had the new female outline yet swept the dales by storm. Compromise had won. The Tabor party was in complimentary mourning colours.

The jury listened stolidly to information on guns, powder burns, animal blood tests, eradicating blood-stains on the carpets, and much other material painstakingly assembled by Cobbold, and duly brought in a verdict of murder by person or persons unknown.

'Hard to believe we're all free to leave the Hall, eh, Didier?' Carstairs said somewhat wistfully. There was a distinct sense of anti-climax in the Tabor party.

'Then stay on,' said Laura, overhearing. 'If,' she continued lightly, 'your engagements permit.'

'It so happens I'm free till the Duchess of Hogbury's funeral the week after next,' retorted Oliver gravely.

Laura actually laughed, the first time Auguste had seen her do so. 'Splendid. Perhaps she'll postpone it a day or two to be on the safe side.'

'I want to stay on to see what happens next,' declared Gertie with an enthusiasm apparently not shared by her husband.

'I think we ought to be getting back, kitten,' he told her quickly.

'You can't desert the family in its need, Cyril,' Miriam announced. 'Can he, Priscilla?'

'Thank you, Mother, but we are not in need, as you put it. Victoria has just become engaged to a highly suitable young man, the King greatly enjoyed his stay with us, and as soon as this wretched man's identity is cleared up, the police will be leaving us. They are merely using the Hall as an office while they make a few little enquiries in the neighbourhood. We at Tabor Hall are quite above suspicion.'

Not quite. Egbert Rose was debating if he had enough evidence yet to arrest Cyril Tabor for murder, and Stitch was congratulating himself that at last he was 'one of them' – a man with ideas. Following up the

172

French police's report that there never had been a tailor by name of Noire or Poire in Paris, he had suggested another look at the label. It had proved to be stitched in by hand over the place where an original label had once been. Why switch it, Rose had puzzled out loud. Why not merely cut out the original?

Twitch surpassed himself: 'To hide the fact something fishy was going on. By someone close at hand, who could be questioned.'

'Like Cyril Tabor,' grunted Rose.

'Auguste!' Tatiana had appeared at last. After giving evidence at the inquest, to which Auguste had listened heart in mouth, in case she might, with less than perfect English, inadvertently set up suspicion in the Coroner's mind, or, worse, increase Egbert's, she had rejoined him on the public benches only to disappear after the verdict. The Daimler, De Dion Bouton and sundry carriages set off back to Tabor Hall, leaving only the pony trap, under the watchful eye of a local urchin in pursuit of a threepenny-piece reward. Its driver had an important errand in the Lion Inn and had lost count of time.

'I met the clogger's wife in the Thistlethwaite tearoom,' Tatiana informed him, when she eventually returned. 'There is a lot of information to be gained in tearooms. As well as good gingerbread,' she added.

'Who is the clogger's wife?' he asked politely, refusing to be diverted.

'The wife of the clogger.'

'*What* is the clogger?'

'He makes clogs. With wooden soles, and Mrs Clogger says I should have some made. We can go now.'

'But we shall miss luncheon,' said her husband, alarmed at the impending catastrophe.

'He thinks he recognised your corpse.' She played her trump card.

'He did not report that to Inspector Cobbold,' Auguste said suspiciously, doubting her motive.

'Because he was too busy clogging. It's the cloggers' main season, preparing for the winter.'

Auguste accompanied her somewhat reluctantly, cheering himself with the thought that Gregorin could hardly be disguising himself as a clogger!

The clogger, Jeremiah Taylor, was on Castle Hill, next to Edmondson's the bootmaker, Tatiana informed her husband knowledgeably, known in the town as Boot and Clog Corner. He was a small man, bent over his stiddy, hammer in hand. Two walls seemed to be decorated with lumps of tree, in various stages of becoming clog soles. Clogging irons adorned another wall, and finished clogs united with their uppers awaited collection on the fourth.

'Good morning,' began Auguste companionably. 'My wife requires some clogs.'

Taylor removed some nails from his mouth. 'Aye. Her would. Coming here.' He replaced the nails.

Not a good start.

'I was talking to your wife,' Tatiana said, rushing straight in where Auguste feared to tread, 'and she said you thought you recognised the dead man in the poster outside the police station.'

'Mebbe. Brass clasps?'

'What is his name? Yes, please. And red leather uppers.'

'Don't know. Only black – or,' a moment's consideration, 'brown.'

'Who is he, then? Black, please.'

'Outcomer. Do come here once, twice a year, mebbe. Alder?'

'Where from? Yes.'

174

'Travelling man. Sit tha down.'

Tatiana extended her foot and removed her boot, while the clogger struggled over with a large piece of wood.

Luncheon and the delights of William Breckles' Yorkshire cuisine receded further. At least, Auguste thought optimistically, there was evidence now that the corpse was not that of Gregorin but of a passing stranger, a *regular* passing stranger. Why should a regular passing stranger wish to visit Tabor Hall? And why should anyone wish firstly to murder him and then to obscure his identity? Though it had only been obscured temporarily, for Auguste Didier was on the trail, luncheonless or not.

But that, perhaps, was all the murderer wished to achieve – to obscure the corpse's identity until the townsfolk would no longer expect to see him, and he would pass from their consciousness like yesterday's breakfast. But one person had remembered him – the man who had sat before him shaping a pair of clogs just as he was doing for Tatiana. To the rest of Settle and the Craven district, the dead man had merely been a face, like so many others that passed through this busy market town at this time. *At this time?* What was so special about this time? Sheep-salving time? Or, better, the shooting season? Extra beaters drawn in for the Duke of Devonshire's estates, for Ingleborough Hall, perhaps even for Tabor Hall . . .

The clogger was whistling as he worked. Slowly Auguste identified the tune as an old English folksong he'd been taught by his mother, 'Oh dear, what can the matter be?' Why did he connect that with the legend he'd been told about Henry II's mistress – no, that wasn't quite it. Excitement rose in him. He connected it with their arrival, their first sight of Settle, and with their coming into town on Monday.

175

His memory regurgitated colourful, exotic sights and sounds. Which would only come to Settle once or twice a year.

In a voice that almost squawked in anticipation, Auguste asked, 'Did he come to claim his clogs?'

The clogger shook his head. 'Can't trust no one or nowt nowadays. Expected him Monday.'

Monday, the day the fair left town.

Chapter Seven

Smuts flew into his face. Auguste was in an agony of excitement as if it were a prized turbot that he awaited rather than a steam train at Settle railway station. The smoke belching from the huge engine bearing down on him was the triumphant music of a victory possibly within his grasp. Never had luncheon seemed a less desirable meal, never had a gastronomic discussion (in this case with Tatiana on what species of *grenouille* was contained in this toad-in-the-hole) been of less interest. He had been sidetracked but for the merest few minutes to explain that toad-in-the-hole was a simple Yorkshire batter surrounding sausages, although, true, that led him to another discussion on the rival merits of the saveloys of Navarre versus the Toulouse sausage.

Time was passing, precious time. He had asked the landlord where the fair had gone, but to no avail. ''Tis busy as bees on the moor when they're here, nothing but muck when they're gone,' was all he could offer at first, but complimenting his apple pudding had elicited the suggestion that Mrs Polly at the Post Office might know.

Of course. The telephone exchange was the nerve centre for information in any town or village. Mrs Polly provided information but more anxiety. 'They was making for Skipton, but the fair was yesterday, honey.'

Yesterday! In his mind's eye Auguste had seen the cavalcade ambling down a long road forever out of his reach. He might never be able to clear Tatiana's name, was his immediate fear. He climbed aboard the train with the alacrity of Stephenson boarding his Rocket.

The train ponderously belched into movement once more, and steamed on its way to Skipton. Auguste stared out of the window, but he did not see the high fells and peaks in the distance; he counted the telegraph poles flashing by, seeming to undulate up and down to the rhythm of the train over the rails. There was no point in trying to reason out the purpose of his journey. Only his cook's nose told him this was a flavour worth pursuing. And never had a flavour been of more importance.

Skipton wore the bedraggled appearance of a kitchen where the plates of satisfied diners still awaited washing. A sense of momentous events still lingered, but events that were fading into memory. The wide High Street was cluttered in places with litter, and the smell of the cattle market, to whose coat-tails the fair clung, lingered in the air. He was too late; the fair must have gone, not long ago, but gone all the same. Frustration hit him like lukewarm soup. Suddenly at the far end of the High Street he glimpsed a traction engine, and as he rushed towards it he saw two boarded-up sideshows being loaded on the attached wagon. Hope spurred his spirits as he pounded up to the loaders.

'I need to make some urgent enquiries about someone in the fair,' he said breathlessly.

A jerk of the thumb might have meant what the swell could do with his enquiries, or it might have indicated direction. Ever inclined to trust in mankind's essential kindliness, Auguste chose to believe the latter, and was rewarded by finding what he sought in a field behind the High Street. Though the cattle fair and smaller sideshows had lined the High Street, there would have been no room there for these huge modern roundabouts and swings, brought by the age of steam.

Here too the glory was departing. Even as he arrived, a bright red canopied dragon roared towards him, belching steam, and he hastily side-stepped. Children were busily employed carrying, fetching, dismantling, as the womenfolk, in colourful check skirts, organised departure. One or two rides were still in the process of being dismantled. Where to start? Auguste plunged in, picking an elderly gentleman in moleskin trousers, check shirt and bowler hat who was contemplating the scene with the satisfaction of one whose dismantling days were over.

'I'm looking for someone in the fair,' Auguste began politely.

A hoarse chuckle. 'So's most of Yorkshire, mush. Lost your watch, eh?'

Mush was not a word Auguste knew, but he was not to be deterred. 'Do you recognise him?' He thrust his by now well-thumbed picture in front of him.

'I thinks best over a glass of ale when her's down.'

'Her?' Auguste followed the direction of his eyes. The man grinned, his meaning unmistakable . . .

The ale Auguste clutched two hours later tasted good. Anything would have tasted good after his part in the dismantling of the 'Flying Pigs'. Flying pigs were no lighter than real pigs and of far less practical value, he had thought savagely. Trotters were for *pieds de porc à la Ste Ménéhould*, not for thudding into unsuspecting backs. And that had been just the beginning. The magnificent mechanical organ had to be removed from the centre of the ride, then the roof; after that he had found himself perched perilously

179

high on a truck, helping to remove the gaudily painted running boards.

'I'll take that beer now,' his tormentor had informed him generously, as dark began to fall. All the fun of the fair was now carefully packed in wagons, like a magician's hat waiting for the next performance. Only hats were less tiring than wagonloads of heavy fairground rides, thought Auguste wearily, with scarcely the energy to lift glass to mouth. Hitherto he had disliked British ale. Now it was nectar.

'Who was you asking after?' A toothless grin from his drinking companion at the Black Horse. Auguste fished the picture from the ruins of what had been the jacket of a smart lounge suit, and showed it to him, by now convinced his quest was hopeless.

'Could be Big Fizzer. Or again it might not.'

'Is he missing?' A spark of hope managed to force its way up through exhaustion.

'Missing what?'

'From the fair.'

'He ain't at this gaff, mush.'

'So he's missing? Might he be dead?' Tiredness made subtlety beyond him.

'Dead?' The old man was astonished. 'Only saw him last week.'

'Then he *is* missing.'

The old man set his glass of ale down. 'Travellers don't keep together like them flying pigs, mush. The first ride to set up on the gaff, gets it. If there's too much stuff you goes somewhere else. Black Rufus' three-abreast got the last pitch, so I reckon Big Fizzer – he helps Blackboots on the galloper – made off somewhere else.'

'Where?' Auguste's head spun like a roundabout at full speed, but he managed to clutch at the dismal words 'somewhere else'.

'Depends. Maybe Horsham.'

'Horsham? In the South?' His spirits plummeted to the level of the ale.

'This is the back-end-run, mush. Not much doing this time of year. 'Course, there's Harrogate. *If* he was lucky.'

'When's that?'

'Tomorrow. That's if Black Rufus don't get there first.'

'Who *is* this Black Rufus?'

'He hates Blackboots. Goes back generations,' the old man said with relish. 'And that goes for Big Fizzer too. That's him now.'

The door of the pub opened with a crash. The space it left was entirely filled with the trunk clad in bright red check shirt and corduroy trousers, then the head came into view as its owner ducked to get in. All six foot four inches directed hate at Auguste: 'Who's asking for Black Rufus?'

Auguste hauled himself wearily up into the carriage that to his great relief was waiting at Bell Busk to greet him. This was no thanks to Tatiana, who had been annoyed at having to drive back to Tabor Hall and miss the novelty of a real fair. It was solely his own efforts conveyed through Mr Bell's wondrous invention that had led to the carriage being here. The coachman looked askance at Auguste who, despite his best efforts at cleaning himself up in the Black Horse, smelled of smoke, looked grimy, and whose clothes were dirty, torn, and missing one lapel. The latter was due to his encounter with Black Rufus, who had seized his jacket to emphasise a less than subtle point. He had brought his bearded black face, smelling strongly of drink, tobacco and lack of dentistry, close to Auguste's. 'No friend o' Big Fizzer gets out of

181

here alive. I hates Big Fizzer.'

'Why?' Auguste had bravely enquired. Could a midnight encounter between Big Fizzer and Black Rufus have taken place in the smokehouse?

'And Blackboots.' He spat towards the floor, but failed to miss the shoulder of Auguste's ill-used jacket. 'If you sees 'em, tell 'em Rufus will get 'em. *And* you,' letting him go. 'Nothing personal, o' course,' he added more amiably.

Perhaps Black Rufus was in league with Gregorin, Auguste thought desolately, as the train chugged its way back to Bell Busk.

A bath at Tabor Hall seemed the most urgent necessity. Once again, however, his plans were destined to be thwarted.

As he walked towards the front entrance of the Hall, he could see Richey standing at the top of the steps. Richey could smell a non-gentleman at a hundred yards, and in this case other smells were going to make his task easier.

'I'll call your valet, Mr Didier,' he said impassively.

Auguste glared. They both knew the truth. He took revenge. He deposited deerstalker and grubby gloves in Richey's care. 'I'm sure you'll do your best for them.'

Richey's reply was forestalled by a distraught Gertie. Almost knocking him off his feet, she rushed like a whirlwind through the door and flung herself into his arms. Behind her followed Tatiana, eyeing this touching scene somewhat sardonically.

'They've arrested Cyril,' Gertie howled into Auguste's shoulder (fortunately not the one Black Rufus had honoured).

'It is true, Auguste.' Tatiana firmly detached Gertie and put her arm round her, either to restrain further outpourings or in sisterly compassion.

'Why?' Auguste asked astounded, and grateful for

her intervention since the feather of Gertie's evening coiffure had been tickling his nose. He was also greatly relieved; this must surely prove that Egbert no longer suspected Tatiana.

'I don't know,' bawled Gertie. 'Priscilla thinks it's my fault.'

'How could it be, Gertrude?' asked Tatiana briskly. 'You didn't know the dead man, did you?'

'Priscilla thinks *everything* is my fault,' Gertie told her mournfully, overcome with the sorrow of life, clearly wishing she'd never left the Galaxy where her greatest problem had been which of the stage-door johnnies to choose to accompany to dinner. She buried her head in Tatiana's shoulder.

'*Calmez-vous*, Gertie,' Auguste told her, quelling an instinctive movement to put his arm compassionately round her. 'I am sure this is some mistake. *I* will find out the truth for you.'

Gertie disengaged herself from Tatiana's angora shawl, and allowed herself cautious hope. 'Oh, Auguste, you are wonderful,' she breathed. 'No wonder the girls at the Galaxy all loved you so.'

Something that might have been an unprincesslike snort escaped Tatiana. It might have been laughter or fury; Auguste did not pursue it.

The leisurely bath was reduced to three minutes, and Auguste prepared to meet the Tabors at dinner, wondering what protocol might dictate on the matter of one's host's brother having just been arrested for murder.

Tatiana enlightened the table with an account of the joys of the English sausage. Gertie sobbed quietly, disregarded by her hostess. Priscilla and George were unusually quiet with only the occasional remark on the recalcitrant pheasants, or the recent celebrations on the millenary of King Alfred at Winchester.

(Beatrice's reference to Excalibur puzzled the company, until Alfred unkindly pointed out the difference between King Alfred and King Arthur.) Victoria and Alexander were not present. Laura did not appear to be on speaking terms with Oliver and the Dowager was dining in her rooms.

What *did* etiquette demand? Should he wait, Auguste wondered, until the ladies had withdrawn? But then the gentlemen would go to the smokehouse perhaps, and he could not say what he wished. Should he speak over dessert or cheese? Finally he could wait no longer.

'I regret, George, Lady Tabor, to hear the news about Cyril.'

A huge tear plopped into Gertie's soufflé.

He had done the wrong thing. The icy calm that greeted his statement told him that.

'Thank you, Mr Didier. Did you enjoy your visit to Skipton Castle?'

Auguste blinked. Surely Priscilla could not be *so* calm, surely etiquette could not prevail *so* strongly? Apparently it did. Tatiana came to his rescue.

'But why have they arrested him?' she asked with genuine concern.

'Your friend, Mr Didier—' Priscilla's emphasis was unmistakable on the *your*, 'will not enlighten us. Cyril has been hauled away like a common criminal. At dawn a tribe of policemen are apparently coming to search the house and grounds yet again. They seem to forget we are Tabors.'

'I think it affects me most, Priscilla,' Gertie said bravely.

Priscilla looked faintly surprised, as if she had forgotten her presence. 'This unfortunate occurrence took place here. How could Cyril have been so careless?'

'But he didn't do it,' Gertie wailed.

'If he was with you all night, Gertrude,' Tatiana

184

pointed out, concerned, 'then of course he couldn't have done it. Was he?' she asked, perhaps untactfully, but to Auguste's gratitude.

Gertie's face grew pink and she appeared uncommonly interested in the Wensleydale cheese.

'I expect he'll be released,' Alfred announced cheerfully. 'Cyril hasn't the spunk for murder.'

'Oh!' This seemed to cheer Gertie up.

'Mr Didier,' Priscilla was not amused by this argument and fixed Auguste with the power of her personality, 'kindly use your influence to get him released.'

Appalled, Auguste bowed slightly. From his hostess's approving smile, it seemed he had at last met her standards of etiquette.

The smokehouse was a sombre place, despite the best efforts of the cavorting ladies. It was all too easy to remember that sprawled figure on the floor now that there was a gap in their own ranks.

'Priscilla's worried, you know,' her husband informed Auguste.

Was there a note of reproach in George's voice? Auguste ignored it if so. 'Naturally.'

'The Tabors have been here hundreds of years,' George pointed out. 'We're part of the fabric of the Craven area. We have to set an example. Murder doesn't look good, you know.'

Auguste did know. 'Cyril will be released, once the police have found out the truth.' He tried to sound confident.

George gave him a sideways look. 'It was suicide, of course,' he said loudly. Even he could see this didn't go down very convincingly. 'Murder by one of the servants,' he continued. 'Tripped over the gun. Who was the fellow, anyway?' he added, aggrieved.

'The police will discover soon.' It was a placebo and even George recognised it.

'The family will stick by old Cyril, of course. Priscilla's very hot on family loyalty. That's the Tabor motto: Loyalty to the End. Seen this one, have you?' Obviously hoping to lighten the atmosphere, he swung back a panel to reveal a lady standing in her bath indulging in contortions highly unlikely to have been called for in the pursuit of daily hygiene.

'I still think the fellow was Mariot.' Harold's voice fell into the silence while this study was being appreciated.

'Aunt Laura told me she's just had a telegraphic message from him,' announced Alfred with relish. 'So it can't be.'

'Impostor.' Harold was adamant.

'No,' said Oliver quickly. 'The police told me they'd had confirmation from Cairo that he set off for England weeks ago. He must be here by now. Somewhere.' He seemed rather gloomy at the prospect.

'Laura wouldn't marry a chap who wasn't a gentleman,' George assured him. 'It would upset Priscilla.'

Oliver began to laugh hysterically. 'A famous archaeologist and Laura can't marry him because he isn't in Burke's Peerage. Can you believe it, Didier?'

'Yes.' Auguste could. He, Auguste Didier, maître chef, would never be a gentleman by Tabor standards. Fortunately, from what he had seen so far he had little desire to be one.

'This is a salted herring in a *salade de fruits de mer*,' he told himself later, after he had been released from ordeal by smokehouse. Was it not bizarre that nobody seemed unduly concerned about Cyril – almost as if by consensus? Was this Society's way of coping with disaster, or was it something more sinister?

186

* * *

Rose returned by the police carriage late that night, and Auguste roused himself from the settle in the entrance hall.

'Had a good day, Auguste?' Rose asked grimly. 'Pheasant shooting, visiting local beauty spots, eh?' He stalked upstairs towards his quarters.

'No,' cried Auguste truthfully, following in his wake. He had no intention of telling Egbert about Big Fizzer yet, but he was convinced his theory added up. The corpse's clothes had been changed not to delay identification indefinitely, but to the point when no one would miss him, and that would be when the fairground workers would be supposed to have passed out of sight and out of mind. But theory was theory, and this one would not, he knew, impress Egbert without further information.

'Why have you arrested Cyril Tabor?' Auguste asked Egbert's unresponsive back.

Egbert marched on, and then stopped so suddenly that Auguste cannoned into him.

'He's not arrested, only being questioned.' He paused. 'The gallant colonel's still missing, and now your Cyril's admitted he and his wife had a tiff that night – over you as it happens – and he slept in the dressing room, so she can't vouch for him. Satisfied?'

'You're hoping to find the colonel's uniform buried in the grounds?' (Over *him*?) Suppose after all Egbert was right about Cyril. It was as likely as his own wild theory.

'You got anything better to offer?'

Auguste did not reply.

'Where have you been, Auguste?' Egbert shot at him.

'In Skipton.'

Egbert Rose was exasperated and showed it. 'Look

here, Auguste, I don't think Tatiana's guilty, but until we know whose that body is, I have to bear the possibility in mind. I'm a policeman.'

Motorcars had their uses. Auguste yanked the starting handle round almost with pleasure. There was no doubt that to travel along the Harrogate Road was a great deal pleasanter than the roundabout route of the railway train. Even adhering to the maximum permitted speed of 12 mph, three hours would see them safely there. The day was fine, and both he and Tatiana were warmly equipped with fur rugs. And to add to his optimism, Walter Tompkins, at his Lordship's insistence, sat behind the driving wheel.

Tatiana's small blue glengarry cap was covered by a gauze veil, not only over her ears but at Beatrice's insistence over the whole of her face and goggles as well. Her complexion would otherwise apparently be ruined for ever.

'I look like a toad-in-the-hole,' Tatiana announced crossly to Auguste, ripping off the veil, 'and you look like a rather bad burglar.'

The sleeves of his tweed jacket were secured, on George's advice, to prevent the wind whistling up them, and his felt hat was pulled firmly over his ears inside the collar. He had always understood that a wife's duty was to admire her husband at all times and in all situations. Apparently he had been misinformed, as in so many ways in this mysterious new world of marriage.

As the Daimler moved on to the Harrogate Road he relaxed. Behind them lay Tabor Hall and the shadow of murder; before them lay the excitement of the hunt. The hunt that might prove Cyril innocent. Not to mention Tatiana herself.

'Cyril always gets what he wants.' That's what

Miriam had said. Yet in this case he had already *got* Gertie. Nothing could change that. What else might make Cyril turn to murder? Nothing that would involve British Army colonels in India, of that he was sure.

The Daimler almost purred under Tompkins' steady hands. Tatiana had abandoned Auguste in order to sit by Tompkins and discuss motorcars, and was listening to an incomprehensible (to Auguste) account of combustion chambers, pistons and side-slipping.

Left to himself, he pondered the beauty of bracken-covered hillsides, topped with outcrops of limestone crags, under the blue autumn sky. To his right lay valleys of green fields like a *salade de mesclun* – until this peaceful scene was shattered by a sharp explosion.

'Gregorin!' It was Tatiana that cried out his fear.

Then his jumping heart subsided, as he saw Tompkins getting calmly down from the Daimler with the air of one to whom this was not an unusual occurrence.

Having satisfied herself of Auguste's survival, with a quick kiss, Tatiana followed suit.

Auguste leapt out after them, but there was now little to be seen of wife or driver save their lower halves.

'You don't die from exhaust stems snapping, Mr Didier,' Tompkins called out a moment later.

'It fell into the compression chamber and shattered a piston,' Tatiana's voice informed him knowledgeably.

'Is it serious?' Auguste asked with foreboding, seeing the Harrogate fair receding yet further. The good thing about railway trains was that by and large they went, he thought savagely. Motorcars did not. Like wives, they only went if they wanted to.

'It won't be, if I've another one.' Tompkins was covering the Harrogate Road with the mysterious contents of his tool case.

'Have you?'

'Nay.'

It was not the way Auguste would have chosen to arrive in Harrogate. True, they were there, a mere nine hours later, but to the great delight of a cheering populace the Daimler was being towed by a carthorse. Tempers were frayed, particularly that of the horse. Replacement valves being unobtainable in the time, a farmer had been persuaded to lend his horse, who had obligingly begun his task in good spirits. Unfortunately he was a village horse and was used to nothing more alarming than one of his own kind approaching him. When a motorcar roared towards him at 10 mph, he had taken great exception and stopped in his tracks. The Daimler had run into his rear quarters, which caused him even greater surprise, so that he sat on the bonnet in disgust. The Daimler had come off worst, and once in Harrogate Tompkins declared his intention of not being parted from it till it was restored to its pre-horse condition by a reliable engineer.

Tatiana, torn between the rival attractions of motorcars and fairs, somewhat reluctantly accompanied Auguste to the Majestic Hotel, since an overnight stop was now inevitable. An hour later they were hurrying towards the sound of 'Two Lovely Black Eyes' roaring out from a fairground organ.

'I would like to see a flea circus,' Tatiana said hopefully.

'Later.' The middle of the Saturday evening festivities might not be an ideal time to see Blackboots, but he must speak to him as soon as possible, fleas or no fleas.

190

The difference between a fair being dismantled and one in full swing was as a chicken bone to a *poulet à la Dauphine*. This fair was on the outskirts of the town in order that elegant, fashionable Harrogate might blinker its eyes to the excrescence it had temporarily grown. Its lower orders might creep out to enjoy the fun, but their betters could ignore it. Fortunately there were many lower orders in this affluent town.

On the far side of the road Auguste paused, taken aback by the dark noisy hubbub in front, pierced by bright lights, the air full of laughter, screams, and the noise of songs from conflicting organs.

'Hold on to my arm, *ma mie*,' Auguste yelled. 'Let us advance.'

'*Impossible*,' she shouted back. 'I'll hold your coat.'

She was right. There was no room to force a way side by side in the hustling crowds. They had to push one behind the other, and every so often he felt himself yanked to the right or left, as Tatiana saw something that caught her eye, and then recollected duty.

Eventually, on the far side of the ground, they found a Savage three-abreast galloper with prancing horses. The magnificent steam organ struck up: 'Ta ra ra boom de ay', and riders were lifted high above the everyday world in their painted heaven. And there in the middle was the owner, dexterously swinging out to collect fares as the platform rotated. He hardly allowed time for eager riders to mount before he was off again.

'We'll have to take a ride.' Tatiana eagerly led the way, climbing up to ride side saddle on a huge white horse with scarlet trappings and a lascivious leer in its eye for the dainty yellow mare in the inside stream.

Resigning himself, Auguste chose the mare in order to be nearest his prey. Up and down, up and down, music blaring out, excitement gripped him as the music grew louder, swamping him in the febrile atmosphere

191

it created. The owner swung round, and Auguste reached down to pay him their sixpence, trying to quash a distinct feeling of queasiness from the motion.

'Are you Blackboots?'

'Aye.'

He was a big man, elderly but moving with agility. He was gone again, swinging off one horse after another to take in more threepenny pieces. There was nothing for it but another ride.

'Does Big Fizzer work for you?'

'Did!' A suspicious look now.

'Is he missing by any chance?' Auguste in his excitement let go of his pole and nearly slipped from the horse.

'Might be.'

'I need to talk to you.'

Blackboots was gone again, the roundabout slowing down. His stomach, empty or not, would not take another ride. Blackboots pushed his way towards him. 'Come round to the living wagon tomorrow. Early, mind.'

'What's Big Fizzer's real name?' Auguste yelled, hardly expecting a reply as Blackboots restarted the organ.

'Tom Griffin. Poor old Tom Griffin,' came the answer, barely audible over 'You Are My Honeysuckle'.

'Poor old Tom Griffin,' repeated Auguste contentedly. At last the corpse might have a name. It might not be the right name, but it was still a possibility. And tomorrow he would know. Still staggering from the motion of the roundabout, he whirled Tatiana around. 'Tonight, my love, we share a goosefeather bed,' he crowed in triumph. He kissed her in the shadows of the Haunted House.

'After we have been to the flea circus,' she murmured lovingly in his ear.

'Very soon after,' he compromised, happy in the knowledge that sex had been the first – and he trusted the longest-lasting – of Tatiana's new passions.

Chapter Eight

Early for the travelling showmen would mean just that, Auguste decided, with some relief. For much of the night he had tossed about in bed restlessly, his mind turning like beef on a spit between the beckoning will o' the wisp of Tom Griffin and wondering whether it was not his fear for Tatiana that sent him rushing irrationally in pursuit. As he walked under a gradually lightening sky in the mists of a Yorkshire October morning, the air damp in his nostrils, he could see ahead dim shapes of loaded wagons and human activity. They must have been working all through the night from the time that the fair had closed at midnight, for few towns tolerated the defilement of their territory on a Sunday morning. God-fearing folk were then bound for Church, no matter if those same folk had been throwing balls at coconuts with gusto the evening before. Either it must remain silent and unprofitable until Monday, or like Mr Carroll's Snark, the fair must softly and silently vanish away.

Auguste had invaded the hotel kitchens in search of life-restoring coffee before leaving, trusting that the kitchen staff would put down any disarrangement to laxity of preparation the evening before. He had been strongly tempted to linger, for the sights that greeted his eye in the larders looked most interesting. What, for instance, had been the basis of that sauce? From the colour, soya was widely employed.

Auguste firmly directed his mind back to the matter-in-hand. Where the Golden Galloper had proudly stood only a matter of hours before, ablaze with lights, only a muddied grass ring was to be seen. That and a trail of discarded fish papers and lollipop sticks were the only signs of last night's magnificence. He made his way towards the living wagons, attracted by the smell of frying bacon.

As he drew near, he could see a woman cooking on a small stove, set on a trivet on the ground. Travellers setting off into the gloom of the winter break did not do so on an empty stomach. Trying not to stare too enthusiastically at her frying pan, he asked the woman for directions to Blackboots' caravan.

Blackboots too was at the business of breakfast, sharing a stove with his neighbour. He interpreted Auguste's wistful look correctly, as he hovered on the damp grass. 'Plenty here. Help yourself.'

Never had breakfast tasted better. Auguste's feet were wet, his perch on the wooden steps leading up to the living wagon was uncomfortable, but the greasy bacon and the fried potatoes were ambrosia, washed down by a mugful of nectar in the form of hot, sweet, strong tea. Hitherto tea had not been a favourite drink of Auguste's. Now he began to appreciate its pleasures, not as an afternoon drink to break the monotony of the hours between two and eight, but as a restorative in its own right.

He wondered briefly what Brillat-Savarin might have thought of this none-too-clean mug of delight, and decided that he might approve of the principle while disliking its execution. Soyer, he ruminated, his body glowing with renewed warmth and love of mankind, with his grasp of what might comfort the stomachs of the majority of his fellow-men, would certainly savour this delightful drink. For the first time, Auguste felt that Soyer and himself, were they to meet in some future heavenly kitchen, might have subjects in common to discuss.

'Nah,' Blackboots drained the dregs of his mug with audible gusto. 'I got half-an-hour, then I got to clean my tubes.'

Auguste eyed him doubtfully. His unspoken question was answered when Blackboots continued, 'You can give me a hand loading up.' He pointed to a load of coal at the side of the field.

Auguste's heart sank, as he tried to convince himself that the total destruction of another suit would be worth it if this companionable activity led to the identity of the body in the smokehouse.

Blackboots knocked out his pipe on the side of the step where Auguste was perched. 'What's all this about Big Fizzer?'

'Who is he?' Auguste asked eagerly. 'Was he at Settle with you? Did he leave with you?'

Blackboots carefully cleaned his pipe with the stick he'd stirred his tea with. 'What's it to do with you?'

'Mr Blackboots, I am a guest at Tabor Hall near Malham, not far from Settle, and on Sunday morning an unknown man was found dead in the grounds – murdered, so the enquiry has decided.' He took the now dog-eared picture from his pocket, almost daring to hope that this time, he might be rewarded.

Blackboots studied it, his fingers packing tobacco into the foul-smelling pipe. 'Could be Tom,' he said at last. 'But he didn't have hair hanging down like that. Not Tom.'

'When he was found, the corpse's hair was short, and he was in evening dress, his beard trimmed, his hands were—' Auguste sought for a tactful word, '—manicured. In short, this man did not look like a traveller of the world.'

'What's it to do with Big Fizzer then?' Blackboots asked reasonably.

'I believe his clothes were changed after he was dead, his hair cut and his hands attended to, in order to disguise his identity.'

He glanced at Blackboots, aware of how fantastical this theory sounded, out here in the cool morning surrounded by evidence of the hard life of the travelling showmen and their families. Blackboots stuck his pipe in his mouth and took the doctored picture again from Auguste. With only a side view, and Auguste's artistic embellishments added, it was not much to go on.

'Could be. Daft old bugger.' Blackboots' eyes were moist.

'Is it like Big Fizzer to go off on his own?'

'No, it ain't. I were expecting him 'ere Thursday or Friday. "I'll be with you for the build-up," he says. "I've somewhere to go when we close on Saturday," he says. "I'll catch you on the road if I'm not back before." Full of importance, silly old fool,' Blackboots added affectionately. '"What you going to do – tow your wagon yerself?" I asks. He ain't got no horse, see, but hitches his living wagon to the back of Black Beauty.'

Auguste looked bewildered.

'That's my steamer, there. It tows the galloper and three or four living wagons. Fine old lass is Black Beauty. "The travelling gingerbread man's taking me tonight," he says, "and I'll be coming back by carriage. You take the wagon, and if I don't catch you, I'll take a train," he says. That's what money does for you. Never been right since the Leather and Nails, he hasn't.'

'Leather and Nails?' Auguste asked blankly, struggling to cope with accent and jargon simultaneously.

'Big fair at Settle at Lammas, 19 August. Cobblers and suchlike come from all around. We were lucky.

198

Got the gaff before Joe Peg-Leg could get his thieving peacocks in.'

'What happened to Big Fizzer?'

'We gets to the gaff day before and off he goes. Something to do, he says, mysterious-like. He were back to put up the galloper, but his mind weren't on the job.'

Blackboots heaved himself out of his chair, and clambered past Auguste into the living wagon, returning with a photograph in a cheap frame.

'That's him.' Blackboots was posed on the platform of the galloper, with his arm round the neck of a bowler-hatted black-bearded Big Fizzer.

Was this the corpse? It could be. The size and build were right. 'Was – is – he married?' Auguste asked, trying to subdue excitement.

'No. Tom's *dinilow* – a little simple-like. Nothing wrong with him, but he hasn't much beef in him for all his size. The ladies round here—' he paused as a crash and shrieks came from a nearby wagon '—like spice. He might be called Fizzer but he looked like he were going nowhere, poor chap. He got his name because he started out with a Big Fizzer sherbert stall. I remember him at Windsor Fair as a nipper. Always hoping Her Majesty would drop in. Day she did, he were down with the fever. That'd be like Tom. Unlucky.

'He stuck with the sherbert twenty year or more. Then I goes to the Nottingham Goose Fair, and there was old Fizzer, helping with a knock 'em down. Coconuts. He did well at that, had his own game, then he fell ill, went into the workhouse. Next thing I heard he were out again, turning his hand to anything he could. He had showing in his blood. Told me his ma died when he was a small nipper Clapham way. She'd been in Wombwell's Travelling Menagerie, leading the elephants round to the music. That would be back in the thirties, long time ago now.' Blackboots mused briefly on the transitoriness of life.

'Anyway, then poor old Tom runs into Black Rufus, and next thing I hear is that Tom's looking after his midgets for 'im while Black Rufus gets on with the real work, the roulette in the tent behind for the quality. Tom allus liked children, and them midgets were just like kids. He looked after 'em like a pappy. Black Rufus used to send 'im out to do his dirty work, collecting debts, because old Tom looked fearsome, so they weren't to know he was no prizefighter. Black Rufus took advantage of old Tom, and he got tired of working for him, so he asked if he could come and help on the galloper, me getting older. If he had one ambition in life it was to have a galloper. He's like a big kid himself: "I'll test them swings, I'll fly those pigs, I'll try that bicycle ride." Tom will always oblige. But it was the gallopers are his real love. Just a three-abreast up and down like mine. 'Course, it looked like he'd never be able to afford one and no bank was going to lend old Tom any money. So he did the next best thing and come and help me. I suppose it were because he never had much of a childhood himself. He could never get any of the girls to marry him. They could see they would end up with a dozen kids and no security. My missus died ten year ago, and Tom and I get on all right together.

'In the winter he gets a pedlar's licence, same as me, and we work together. He does pens and stationery, he's good at that, and I do ribbons and the like. I got more of a way with the young ladies than he has. Or had, maybe.' He sighed.

'Perhaps, *mon ami*,' Auguste said compassionately. 'Black Rufus was at Settle Fair last week, was he not? How did Tom get along with him?'

'There ain't no love lost between them, that's for

sure, but Rufus didn't usually go too far. Tom's good at getting money out of folk, so sometimes he'd hire him just for that. Tom doesn't like it, but it's money. Black Rufus pays him well.'

'And do you think that's where he might have been going after the Leather and Nails Fair, and last Saturday – to chase up debts?'

'Tom can be a dark horse. I weren't too pleased about it. "What am I going to do," I says, "if you go off jaunting?" "I owns the galloper now," he says. "True enough," I says, "but that don't make it right." Mind you, at the Leather and Nails, there was a right to-do with Black Rufus. "I don't like roulette and I don't like you," Tom says. Not like Tom to be that outspoken. Black Rufus weren't too pleased, so he clocks Tom one. Tom's no fighter, but he don't like being hit, so he floored Black Rufus right in front of his missus. "I'll get you," he said, and he were still muttering about it last Saturday when we gets back to Settle again.'

Auguste interrupted the flow to fasten on the salient point. 'Tom *bought* the galloper?'

'I thought he was joking, but he flashed all this dosh. I thought perhaps it might be Black Rufus', but then, that was Tom's business. Yus, I can see him now, eyes shining, beaming all over his face. "I'm going to buy her, Blackboots," he says, stroking one of the horses. He looked as if the sky were raining lollipops. I'm getting old, see,' Blackboots explained apologetically, as though only such a reason could explain his fickleness to Black Beauty and the galloper. '"Here's some of it," Tom says. "I'll have the rest of the dosh for you next week." Sure enough he did.'

'When?' Auguste asked, muddled. Blackboots' grasp of chronology needed improvement.

'August, beginning of September, thereabouts.'

'So what will happen to it now?'

Blackboots shrugged. 'I'll wait till Tom gets back.'

'And if he is dead?'

Blackboots thought this through. 'You come and tell me when you know he is.' Auguste could not budge him. Tom might or might not be dead, and Blackboots was going to wait for him. That meant not letting flatties into Tom's living wagon, forestalling Auguste's next question.

'But where will I find you?' Auguste asked, defeated.

Blackboots lumbered towards Black Beauty. 'I'll get the damper out of the chimney, while you be coaling up.' He picked up the shovel and presented it grandly to Auguste. 'Maybe I'll be heading for the Smoke, maybe Scotland. Who can tell? By the time Black Beauty's ready to belch, perhaps I might be able to recall where I was a-going – that's if you loaded enough of that there coal.'

Auguste sneaked up to his hotel room, eyed with great suspicion by a chambermaid, and prepared to face Tatiana's mirth. She was not there, but he had only got so far in his obligatory toilet as to gingerly remove his jacket when she came in, extolling the virtues of breakfast as provided by a Mrs Snipes. Mrs Snipes, it transpired, was wife to Herbert Snipes, motorcar engineer. *Then* came the laughter, as she took in her spouse's blackened appearance. 'Voilà, chéri, I know just the place for you. The Royal Baths. Did you know there are seventeen bogsprings in Harrogate?'

Auguste had no interest in bogsprings or Harrogate. He merely wanted a bath (and the Majestic's would serve admirably), a speedy snack and to be removed to Tabor Hall as quickly as possible.

Tatiana, in the front seat of a now restored Daimler with Tompkins, busily discussed the merits of the Daimler compared with the De Dion, plug by plug, and in splendid isolation at the back, Auguste digested what he had learned. Blackboots had last been seen on the Black Beauty as the cavalcade slowly made its way into the misty but infinite possibilities of the open road. He had only partly kept his promise of declaring his route: it might be Selby; it might be Whitby; or it might be the Great North Road. He'd find him all right, if he needed to, seemed to be Blackboots' attitude.

Had the odds shortened on the corpse being that of Tom Griffin? Some part of him didn't want it to be so. Blackboots had brought him to life. A nameless corpse now assumed a reality of wasted hopes and dreams. Another part of Auguste's brain was quickly working out what might have happened. From 'what' he might then reach 'why'. Tom's clothes would have to have been hidden somewhere, probably in the grounds of the Hall, given the time available. Unless of course Gregorin were the murderer. Tom had thought he might be gone a while – where then was his overnight bag? How would he get back to Settle? Walk? Possible by daylight, but not at night.

Reluctantly he dismissed Black Rufus from his mind. However much he disliked Tom, he would hardly follow his prey into private grounds or bother to change his clothes. Unless . . . Unless they *both* came on the same mission. And that mission could therefore only concern one person: Alfred. He and Egbert had assumed Alfred's debts were from games in the houses of friends or London clubs. Suppose they were incurred in a hidden roulette tent at a fair? Alfred admitted he gave the man who called money; Tom Griffin had had a sudden influx of money sufficient to achieve his lifetime dream of buying his own galloper. Had he 'forgotten' the money belonged to Black Rufus? Had Black Rufus himself stormed up to Tabor Hall that night to demand the money from Alfred and had Tom set off to stop him? Had there been a quarrel, an accidental shooting and a desperate attempt to disguise what had happened? Auguste turned the theory round, upside down and shook it like a jelly from its mould. It did not quite come out cleanly, but it was edible nevertheless.

As the Daimler turned into the lane leading to Airton and Kirkby Malham, Auguste became aware that he was not looking forward to entering Tabor Hall again. What was he to say to Egbert? Should he tell him about Tom Griffin or not? If not, he breached their private rules on how their professional relationship was conducted. He was not supposed to keep things to himself, in view of the privileges granted him. Yet Egbert was surely tackling this case the wrong way round, concentrating on possible murderers and not on who the victim was. And one of those possible murderers might still, in Egbert's mind, be Tatiana.

His dilemma was solved for him, for Chief Inspector Rose had left Tabor Hall, he was informed. There were still ample signs of His Majesty's police forces, however, digging tenaciously on the moor and hillsides, and in the formal garden flowerbeds. The Daimler had accomplished the journey in under three hours, a fact that endeared motoring to Auguste, since there was still a chance that luncheon might be available. His pleasure was diminished by the wall of disapproval that met him.

'Ah,' George announced with forced heartiness. 'Just in time for the cheese.'

'Nonsense.' Priscilla coolly rang the bell. 'I am quite certain Breckles can find some cold pie for Mr and Mrs Didier before they depart.'

'Depart?' echoed Auguste.

'My sister-in-law assumes you will want to return to London as soon as possible after your enforced stay,' Laura explained tactfully.

Priscilla Tabor saw little need for tact. 'Since your friend has seen fit to arrest Cyril, I see no reason that I should continue to provide an enquiry room at Tabor Hall. Presumably the matter is concluded so far as he is concerned, and I assume you wish to remain at his side. The princess is naturally welcome to remain here.' Welcome wasn't quite the feeling her tone of voice suggested. Tolerated, perhaps. Auguste seethed in fury, but Tatiana's social smile did not waver.

'How thoughtful. However, since my husband is engaged on finding the true murderer, I feel I should be at his side.'

'True murderer?' cried Gertie hopefully.

'I hope so.' There was nothing else Auguste could say.

'You mean you believe Cyril innocent?' asked Oliver, delighted.

'I'm sure we all do,' Auguste stalled valiantly. Looking round the table, he was dismayed to find, however, that on most faces there was no expression of relief at this prospect at all.

'In that event,' Priscilla said after a pause, 'I realise that you might wish to remain here.'

'Auguste,' Tatiana addressed him sweetly, 'I could be quite happy at the Lion.'

His heart rose and then sank, as the delights of the coaching inn faded before him. Tabor Hall was the heart of this mystery and here he should remain – even if one of the hands that fed him was that of a murderer. 'Your thoughtfulness is much appreciated, Lady Tabor.'

Oddly, Priscilla Tabor did not seem overjoyed that he had acquiesced.

'*Walk?*' Auguste enquired suspiciously, as Tatiana

announced her intention of joining a party on an excursion to view some waterfalls. He had long wondered at the passion of the English for striding across the countryside, when they could be admiring its beauties from a *petit restaurant* or bar.

'You are safer with the Tabors than here alone, *ma mie,*' she told him.

This aspect had not occurred to him, and the merits of muddy walks by waterfalls suddenly grew.

The journey necessitated taking one Midland railway train and then changing to another, but he noticed little of it. He was in the world of the fairground, trying to imagine the life of Tom Griffin. Only when he began to walk along woodland paths, and by rushing streams and tumbling waterfalls did he begin to take note of his surroundings. This was a different Yorkshire to that of the bleak high fells. Moreover, some kind providence or private patronage had laid out paths and bridges so that the spectacular falls could be enjoyed at their best.

'Now,' said Tatiana, as they lingered on one of the bridges, 'at last you can tell me. Can you prove Cyril is not a murderer and make your lovely Gertie happy?'

'Not yet.'

Normally he would discuss a case with Egbert. Perhaps it might help to tell Tatiana. As he did so, his sense of understanding Tom Griffin's life and what meant most to him grew stronger.

'If Tom came to Tabor Hall,' he concluded, 'we can forget Colonel Simpson. It is not a "gentleman", but poor Tom who lies dead. And only one person could have reason to kill him that I can see. Just possibly two.'

'Who?'

'Gregorin, whom we provisionally ruled out on the

grounds that he would not have cut his hair, and *him.*'
He glanced up.

Alfred was calling to them from the rocky path above them. 'I say, you fellows, hurry up!'

'He is only a boy,' said Tatiana, astounded. 'Not a very nice one, but still a boy.'

'He is twenty-one, no boy. It could explain why the Tabors were apparently so cooperative, but in fact all their suggestions led to dead ends.'

'Except the Colonel.'

'And that will too, I'm sure.'

Tatiana laughed. 'Oh Auguste, what a wonderful imagination you have. The Tabors have a great sense of family loyalty, but do you think Cyril would get himself arrested just to save Alfred?'

Put that way, Auguste was forced to admit it seemed unlikely.

'Too steep for you, Aged Cousin?' Alexander came galloping down the path towards them, Victoria close behind.

Tatiana promptly chased him up the steep steps again as Victoria called to Auguste: 'You're dreaming up murder mysteries, aren't you? Suppose Gertie rushed out and shot the poor man to stop him blackmailing her darling Cyril?'

'That had not yet occurred to me.'

'There you are, you see. I should make a wonderful detective. And an even better criminal,' Victoria added.

Auguste glanced up. Was it his imagination or was there a very strange look on Alexander's face as he heard her? It must have been, for he turned quickly with a joke to Tatiana again.

'Do you believe Cyril is guilty, Laura? You all seemed rather uninterested at the prospect of his innocence.'

She whirled on Oliver indignantly. 'How can you

say that? He's my brother. Of course I want him released. But the Colonel is missing. It's an unfortunate coincidence.'

'What do you mean by coincidence?' he asked sharply.

'Nothing.'

'Laura, I *know* something is wrong.'

'That should be of no concern to you, Oliver. You have no commitment to me, none at all. Is that clear?'

'Yes,' he answered slowly. 'Very clear. Do I take it you do not wish any commitment?'

'I am afraid, Oliver, that's precisely what I mean. I am sorry if you formed any other impression.'

'Pussikins.' Harold Janes did not like walks, even those laid out with every assistance to victims of over-indulgence in claggy toffee pudding. 'Let's leave tomorrow, shall we?'

'Oh, Puppikins.' Beatrice was heartbroken. 'But it's all becoming so exciting.' Now that there was no risk to Harold, she was enthusiastic about finding out which of the Tabors knew more than they were telling about the murder. If her stock should fall at Court (and there were just a few small signs that it might) she needed to increase her value to Society. 'Pussikins wants to stay.'

'We're going,' he replied curtly.

The water tumbled and splashed by his side, but Auguste was now oblivious to the glories of nature, absorbed in the results of his thinking. Tabor family loyalty and Tom Griffin. He must see Egbert immediately. Perhaps Alfred was not the only candidate among the Tabors after all.

Immediately took a little longer than he had hoped. Halfway round a circular walk in the wilds of Yorkshire was no place from which to get anywhere immediately. Auguste was forced to curb his impatience while the wonders of Thornton Falls, then the moorland, then Beazley Falls, the Snow Falls and finally the glories of Ingleton village and its obliging teashops were enjoyed.

Reaching Settle station at last, he leapt eagerly from the train. Tatiana had accepted his abandoning her suspiciously easily and it was only belatedly that it occurred to him how deep she had been in a discussion with Alexander in which the price of De Dion Boutons seemed to be under review. He quickly forgot it again.

Once at the Golden Lion, he was forced to curb his impatience even longer. Chief Inspector Rose, he was told, was out.

Tired of waiting for results from the digging, Rose too was sightseeing. He was on the other side of the Ingleborough Hill from the Tabor Hall party, taking a trip round Ingleborough Cave. He too needed to think. He wasn't happy with the present situation: not with Cyril Tabor as murderer – or with the first cave they entered. Perhaps he'd seen too much of the London underground railway system to be impressed by brown-coloured stone and dim light. He thought wistfully that Edith might have liked it, though she'd have to take care of her Sunday best, and wouldn't have taken to all these puddles. The next cave and those after that did impress him, for there was nothing like this on the Central Line. Stalactites, stalagmites, lakes of water. Very pretty.

By the time he emerged, after seeing cavern after cavern, he was highly satisfied with his afternoon, and even disposed to admire the scenery on the walk back to the village. He had come to a conclusion and not about Ingleborough Cave. He was not pleased to find

Auguste waiting for him in the Golden Lion. He wasn't
quite ready yet.

'I have something to tell you, Egbert.'

'Good of you.'

'May I buy you a drink?'

Egbert relented. 'Yes. *And* supper. You've been
holding out on me, haven't you?'

'No. Yes.'

'You can tell me *why* I've got the wrong man. *Before*
we have supper.'

Auguste looked at him soberly. 'You agree Cyril is
innocent?'

'I don't know what I think until those blasted clothes
turn up. I'll have to charge him or release him,' Egbert
told him irritably.

Seated in the snug with ale in front of them, Auguste
related the story of Tom Griffin.

'And you didn't think to mention this to me earlier?'

'How could I, Egbert?' Auguste ignored a pang of
conscience. 'There was no proof. There is still none. It
is but a wild theory. You would have told me as usual
that I was putting two and two together and making
forty.'

'Maybe, and maybe not,' Egbert said shortly. 'What
concerns me is that this case is the wrong way up.
Normally you can't be certain who the murderer is
until you're sure who the corpse is. Your theory tells
us that. Mine doesn't. The funeral took place after the
inquest so all I've got now are photographs. Colonel
Simpson's housekeeper can't identify them one way or
the other, as you know, so I haven't a hope of getting
the case on Cyril Tabor tied up unless those blasted
regimentals turn up.'

'Or the Colonel.'

Egbert shot a look at him. 'Get that beef and
Yorkshire pud ordered, Auguste, and be quick about

it. *And* an apple pie, as you're paying.'

'You will be as plump as a dumpling when you return to Edith,' Auguste laughed.

'You're putting on weight too. Marriage, is it?'

'I am not *enceinte, mon ami.*' Auguste was unreasonably cross at this aspersion against his figure. 'This healthy Yorkshire air overfeeds your imagination.'

Sustenance was speedily followed by Cobbold, accompanied by Constable Wright glowing with pride, and carrying a bag. Auguste thought he discerned a slight interrogative lift of Cobbold's eyebrows followed by a nod from Egbert. It had been a long day, and it depressed him.

'Got something for you,' Cobbold announced.

'Regimentals?'

For answer Cobbold tipped out the bag. To Auguste and Rose the contents shouted out: moleskin trousers, check shirt, scarf, old jacket, bowler hat, and old shoes.

Auguste could not resist it. 'They do not look like regimentals, Chief Inspector.' He managed to sound disappointed.

Egbert cast him a scathing look. 'Sit down,' he invited Cobbold, dismissing Wright. Rose pushed Auguste's apple pie across to Cobbold. 'Fancy some pie? Mr Didier is leaving to return to the Hall.'

'I thought I might stay—' Auguste began.

'The Hall,' interrupted Rose dismissively.

Smarting, Auguste retreated. He reached the front entrance and reconsidered. Tom Griffin was *his*. He marched back. He sat down again and Egbert did not comment. They were indeed talking about Tom Griffin.

'His Nibs up at Balmoral will be relieved that it's not going to be a major scandal,' Egbert was saying, 'but if I know him he'll still want to know who did it, travelling man or not. And quickly.'

'I don't know what constitutes a major scandal in

London, but round here it's anything implicating the Tabors.'

Egbert Rose stared at him. 'You're right, Cobbold. We're not out of the wood. We can release Cyril, and the clothes prove it can't be Mariot, which clears Miss Laura and I suppose Carstairs. There are still other Tabors.'

'Why should they want to kill a travelling man?' Cobbold demanded.

'Auguste here reckons it's to do with young Alfred and his gambling debts.'

'But he is not the only possibility,' Auguste put in quickly. Thank goodness now there was no mention of Tatiana. Or was that merely because of his presence?

'We ain't ballet dancers, Auguste,' Egbert told him irritably. 'We go through the facts one by one. We don't leap six foot up and twirl around in the air like something out of *Swan Lake*.'

'But you must consider other possibilities,' Auguste pleaded. 'We must find out more about Tom Griffin. Suppose he was an illegitimate brother?'

Egbert laughed. 'I'd like to see Priscilla's face.'

'He is about the right age,' Auguste continued doggedly. 'Should we not ask the good Inspector Stitch to make investigations in Somerset House now he has returned to London? Tom Griffin is or was about sixty, perhaps a year or so younger: his birth should have been registered. Also Stitch could make enquiries among the workhouses and orphanages in South London where he was born. If Tom's mother died when he was young he might have been taken into one.'

Rose hesitated, but was suddenly diverted by the idea of interrupting Twitch's Sunday evening, with details of a nice job for the morrow. 'Got a telephone here?' he enquired of the Lion's landlord.

212

It was nearly nine by the time Rose and Auguste arrived back at Tabor Hall, accompanied by Cyril Tabor.

Gertie's sad face brightened; she was no longer alone in the Tabor lions' den. 'Cyril,' she shrieked, hurling herself into his arms with an enthusiasm that strained her narrow jet shoulder-straps to danger point.

'Steady, kitten. I wasn't snatched away from the gallows.'

Priscilla rose to her feet, in righteous indignation. 'I am glad that you have come to your senses, Chief Inspector. Cyril, you will need a brandy.'

'I need three,' he corrected.

'I'd be glad if you wouldn't leave the Hall yet, Mr Tabor,' Egbert Rose said stolidly, 'pending further enquiries. I'd like to have a word with you tomorrow morning in my rooms here.' He stared blandly at Lady Tabor.

'I thought you understood our rooms could no longer be at your disposal, Chief Inspector, after this unfortunate case of wrongful arrest,' Priscilla countered.

'I'm quite willing to stay on at the Golden Lion, Lady Tabor. It's a nice little place; I've taken quite a fancy to it. Warm and cosy. Especially when you're seated round the log fire with interesting folks, like the editor of the *Craven Herald,* and I believe gentlemen from the *Morning Telegraph* and *The Times* are still in residence.'

There was a pause, as Priscilla reconsidered her position.

Miriam spoke for her. 'Much more convenient for you to be here on the spot when you have to arrest another member of our family, Chief Inspector. Do keep us informed on whom it is likely to be.'

On Monday morning it rained. Grey skies hung low
over the moors, as Cobbold's men continued their search
for missing regimental uniforms, squelching through
mud on the flat land, tramping in mud-clogged boots
on the high. Nothing was found. Egbert Rose achieved
much the same result with Alfred, who clung to his
story that the debt-collector who had called had been
completely paid off, and that was the end of the matter.
It was not, but for the moment Rose let him go.
Interviews with everyone else from the Dowager Lady
Tabor down to Betty Tubbs the scullerymaid failed to
reveal anything more.

By the evening someone else had a grievance:
Inspector Twitch.

'Him and his daft ideas,' he squealed with indignation
over the telephone line, while Rose listened without
compassion. 'Do you know how many Tom Griffins
were born in South London in the early 1840s? Dozens
of the little nippers. And I had to look every one of
them up and not a blasted clue as to which one is *your*
fellow. And I bin to every workhouse, every orphanage,
but not one of them had records of a Tom Griffin. *And*
I've bin to every board school, every national school,
every old dame school, *everywhere*. I've got a list as
long as the Commissioner's face to follow up!'

'You're doing a grand job,' Rose told him cordially.
'Keep up the good work,' and went back to his supper.

Auguste mentally danced up and down in impatience.
Waiting, always waiting. In cooking there were at
least tantalising smells and tastings, to lure one along;
in detective work there was frequently nothing. Surely
Egbert could not still think Cyril guilty – yet he was
still hunting for regimentals. To whom could those
ragged garments have belonged other than Tom

Griffin? The corpse was Tom Griffin's. Surely Egbert must realise that?

At dinner he felt distinctly unwelcome at the Tabor table, which he forced himself to attend. Tatiana had vanished on an unexplained mission of her own. Something to do with motorcars, he supposed vaguely.

He also noticed the Janes' absence, and boldly asked his hostess the reason.

'Harold had a sudden call to London.' Priscilla's smile was wintry.

'He couldn't wait to get away, if you ask me,' Alfred said judiciously. 'Now Cyril's free, he was afraid the arm of the law might fall on him.'

'Why?' Auguste asked, pinning him down.

Alfred was nothing loth. 'The yellow god, jealousy, old chap. The King's one thing; but I heard a whisper at Doncaster that our buxom Beatrice had been spreading her bosom rather further.'

Auguste felt the likelihood of its spreading to Tom Griffin was unlikely, but could not say so. Not yet.

'I think *we* should leave now it's all over,' Gertie announced bravely.

'It's not all over, kitten,' Cyril told her.

'What?' She stared at him, her lip trembling at salvation so unkindly removed.

'They still think I did it. Or one of us.' Cyril stared querulously round the table. Was there some kind of warning in his words, Auguste wondered.

'They're busy digging up the grounds,' George said gloomily. 'I'll ask them to put the manure down for the winter while they're about it.'

No one laughed. Not even Victoria.

'What do you mean, still under suspicion, Cyril?' Priscilla demanded crisply.

'Stands to reason. Whoever he is, the chap died here. One of my suits is missing. They still think I did

215

it, changed his clothes, and buried his own. They just can't prove it.'

Auguste held his breath. Something hovered here, he was sure. Something that could not be spoken because of his presence, perhaps.

'Do they still think it's Colonel Simpson?' asked Priscilla at last.

'Either that or the debt collector who called here for Alfred a few weeks back.'

'I thought we had disposed of that notion,' Laura said resignedly.

'I suppose you didn't kill him, did you, Alfred?' enquired Miriam.

'Mother,' barked Priscilla immediately. 'There are those present who might take you seriously.'

'We've only Alfred's word for it that he paid the man off,' Miriam pointed out meekly.

'If I did shoot him, you'd be the first to know,' her grandson tried to joke, but his hand was unsteady on the glass.

It was hard to believe in Alfred's guilt – Auguste studied the spotty young face – but then did murderers have to be middle-aged and shifty-faced?

'I don't think Alfred's got enough blood in his veins for murder, do you, Mr Didier?' Miriam brightly made amends.

Auguste politely pretended that the dessert basket was his only interest.

'I think you'll find, Mr Didier,' Priscilla boomed decisively, 'that the poor man had some kind of delusion about the King. No doubt he followed him about all over the country.' A pause. 'Shall you be at Newmarket, Mr Carstairs?' Normal life was being resumed.

'No. I thought I'd stay on a little, if I may. I might be of help.'

'I do not require help,' Laura informed him stiffly.

216

'I meant the family.'

'The Tabors have much experience of being under fire,' Priscilla replied tartly.

'Perhaps murder has never touched you so closely before.'

'An unknown dead man does not touch our family honour, Mr Carstairs.'

'Unless it's "honour rooted in dishonour". . .'

'I *beg* your pardon!'

'Forgive me, Lady Tabor. I'll leave your house, of course.'

'You'll do no such thing.' George went pink at such robust exertion of his will.

Oliver looked at him. 'You're right. I'll stay.'

'What if Twitch fails to turn up anything, Auguste?' Egbert asked him, as he went to bid him goodnight, and report on the evening's conversation.

'But he must find something. Blackboots told me Tom was an orphan from Clapham, and his mother—' He broke off for Egbert was roaring with laughter.

'*Clapham*,' he repeated, shaking.

'What is the matter?'

'It's Twitch,' said Rose between guffaws. 'He's still searching high and low throughout South London.'

'What is wrong with that?'

'I'll tell you. And if I'm right, Twitch will have your guts for garters. You said South London. Was that Blackboots' definition or yours?'

'Clapham *is* in South London.'

'It never occurred to you there might be more than one Clapham?'

A terrible feeling came over Auguste that he was not going to like this.

'You'd better get hold of some of that Koko-for-the-hair stimulating-for-the-brain stuff,' Egbert told him

217

rudely. 'Clapham is a small village a few miles from here. You changed trains there yesterday. Clapham Junction, it's called.'

Chapter Nine

'There's such a thing as wasting police time,' Twitch screeched malevolently over the telephone, secure in the knowledge that only Auguste and not the Chief could hear him. Auguste smarted from injustice. Anyone could have made such a mistake. Yet he knew that in Stitch's strictly kept mental accounting book, this was a major entry on the debit side and would not lightly be forgotten.

On this bright October morning, Twitch sank from his mind as hopes rose. Clapham village lay a mere mile and a half away from the Midland railway line in the valley, and Auguste strode purposefully forward. A poster at the station had informed tourists that they might hire ponies for the purpose of visiting Clapham, but arrival by pony appealed to him even less than the offered Daimler.

What was the etiquette of using one's host's carriage when bound upon a task that might bring murder uncomfortably close to his family? It was hard enough living under their roof. By now the Tabors seemed less like the arrogant *aristos* from his childhood history books of the Revolution and more like a family with normal foibles. Were there no youths of twenty-one in Bethnal Green convinced they knew everything there was to know about life; no mothers as fiercely possessive as Priscilla in the back streets of Paris; no country farmers as stolid and unimaginative as George?

219

Clapham was a pretty grey-stone village, divided by a sparkling beck. Children played hopscotch in the streets and on his right was the most welcoming New Inn, but he decided to postpone this reward until further forward in his quest. Clapham's annual sheep fair had just taken place, but apart from a middle-aged man of Mediterranean extraction leading an equally middle-aged dancing bear, there were few signs of it now. He decided to go directly to the church at the far end of the village street. Inside he hesitated in the semi-gloom, looking hopefully for a verger. Suddenly the church was flooded by the harsh glare of what could only be electric light.

'Surprised, eh?' The vicar materialised at his side. 'We're the first village in England to have electric light in the streets. It's as good as an extra policeman.'

Auguste was doubtful whether it was such a dramatic improvement so far as the church was concerned. He missed the sense of ageless communion that the warmth of gas or oil bestowed. But at least the registers would be easier to read.

'Clapham is fortunate to have your farsightedness, *mon père*,' he said politely.

'Not mine. The owner of Ingleborough Hall. You'll be wanting to see the registers, I expect.'

'Do you know the name of Tom Griffin?' Auguste asked hopefully, following him to the vestry.

'No. I've only been here six years though. Lamb.'

Was this an invitation to luncheon? Auguste hesitated – fortunately.

'Canon Lamb,' his guide amplified.

Left alone with the registers, Auguste began his task with enthusiasm, convinced that the basis of the mystery lay within these volumes. If Tom Griffin were about sixty he must have been born in the early 1840s and his mother probably between sixteen and thirty years before that. He pored over handwritings from spidery to copperplate, but could find no record of the baptism of a Tom Griffin, nor indeed of any Griffin at all, father, mother or son. For thoroughness, he checked the marriage registers. No Griffin had married in the relevant period, and being illegitimate, Tom might not have been baptised of course. Or what was far more likely, he realised despondently, was that the Griffins had simply moved here when Tom was small. And if they were travelling folk, it could have been from anywhere.

Was it worth making further enquiries? Yes, he decided. There was no sign of the vicar, so he made his way to the Post Office, waiting patiently in line while small children were served with sherbert and bull's-eyes, sundry villagers with halfpenny stamps, and bookings made for telephone calls. Tactfully purchasing a dozen postcards of the glories of Ingleborough, he brought up the name of Tom Griffin, and was rewarded with the information that Old Nell might know. He tracked down his quarry to an old cottage on the other side of the beck, where Old Nell, in black skirt and shawl, was busy pouring batter on to her iron bakestone.

'That looks most interesting,' said Auguste sincerely. From Breckles' explanation of the wonders of Yorkshire baking, he deduced this must be riddlebread. Above him, the pale-brown results of previous bakings were drying over strings between wooden supports, like a clothes line, and the smell in the small kitchen area suggested it would be good.

Baking day was not conducive to idle chatter, and the name Tom Griffin brought no reaction. His last slim chance had evaporated.

'You are sure? Perhaps his mother died here, for he was orphaned while he was still a small child.'

221

'Ay knows nowt about a Tom Griffin. And my memory's as good as t'day tha taught me two and two meks four,' Nell grunted in a thick Yorkshire accent, mixing buttermilk into the batter for a new batch of dough. Auguste ignored the delicious warm smell bent on seducing him from his purpose.

'His mother had travelled with Wombwell's Menagerie—'

Old Nell stood suddenly still, the dough in her hands. She stared not at Auguste but back into the past.

'Rose!' she whispered. 'Little Rosie Moffat.'

Auguste sat back in the rocking chair, fully satisfied. Fresh riddlebread and some even more delightful haverbread, blue-milk cheese and rough ale surely constituted a feast to be rivalled by none, not by the ortolans of the Pyrénees or by the foie gras of Périgord.

Nell nodded, taking praise as her due. 'Folks are forgetting how. There's nowt like the old ways. My mother were an outcomer. A knitter of Dent, she were.'

He had heard of Dent. It must be all of twenty miles away to the north, which certainly made her an 'outcomer', he thought with amusement, until he recalled the Cannois speaking of the Niçois as though they were barbarians.

'She did teach me haverbread. Tha don't know nowt about mekking her round here. 'Tis all throwing round here. Haverbread needs rolling.' A certain complacence was in her voice. What must it have been like for Nell's mother to leave the sheltered Dent valley to cross the inhospitable moors on what was no doubt only a rough drovers' track to come to a village where people, accent, even cooking were foreign to her? It was as much an upheaval as for any Army colonel's wife facing the unknown rigours of India. This reminded Auguste of the still missing Colonel Simpson. Suppose this slender

222

thread now dangling in front of him were yet another false end?

He firmly put this from his mind. 'Tell me about Rose Moffat,' he asked Nell, as at last she stopped painfully attending to her baking.

'She sat next to me at Dame School, she did. Kitty Blake were next to her, and Billy King – he died of the fever – and Charlie Watts. He came to no good. And . . .' Auguste let her ramble on as the old days sprang to mind with a clarity the present lacked.

'Rose,' he reminded her gently.

'Aye. Poor soul, she were pretty as a picture, but strict! One of them chapel families, sheep farmers.'

Of course, Auguste realised, that might be why there was no trace of Tom in the baptismal register.

'Thoo should a' seen them Sundays. Dressed up like for a funeral, all a-setting off to service. They were that strict, she never were allowed pretty ribbons, nor to play with the rest of us. Kept themselves to themselves did the Moffats. 'Tis no wonder she did run away. "Nell," she'd say to me, "when I grow up I'm not a-going to stay." Well, we all knew what happened to girls who ran away to the big town. "Thoo wouldn't, Rose," I said. "I would," she says. "Just as soon as I can."'

'She was a lively girl, then. The village boys admired her?' asked Auguste tactfully, impatient to find the link – if any – with Tom Griffin.

Nell took his meaning. 'The lads never tried anything on with Rose, for all 'er looks.'

'Because of her family?'

'Aye. And because she were good and gentle.'

'Why did she want to leave?'

'To get away from *them*,' she said soberly. 'She loved animals, and she loved children, and she weren't going to get nowt but sheep in Clapham, her family being as

223

they were. She were going to wed for love and t'only person they had in mind for her to wed were someone like them. I never did think she'd go. And perhaps neither did she. But one day Wombwell's Menagerie came through t'village its on way to Settle. And that did it. She saw this baby monkey and an elephant, and couldn't get them out of her mind. The wonders of the world, she said. She joined me on a cart, and we rode to Settle to see t'show. Her folks didn't know, o' course. Even I didn't know Rose wasn't planning to come back. Queen Victoria herself did like Wombwell's,' she added. 'I remember it yet. Yon things with horns.'

'Goats.'

'Nay. Rhinoceros, that's she. Marvellous. Alive, too. Anyway, Rose came running up to me "I'm staying," she said. "They're giving me a job helping walk the elephants." And that were that. I pretended I didn't know what had happened to her, not till Wombwell's moved right away. Then I told her folks. Such a to-do. You'd think she'd made a pact with the devil.'

'Did they try to bring her back?'

'Not them. She were sixteen, maybe seventeen, and to her folks that meant she were already ruined by then.'

'And was she?' Interest was outstripping tact.

Nell shrugged. 'Never saw her again, not till she came back with t'babby, five, mebbe six years later. A boy it were. About two then, I reckon. What did you say your man's name was?'

'Tom Griffin.'

'Tommy,' she repeated the name, searched back in her memory. 'Aye. Perhaps it were Tommy.'

'And her parents took her back?'

'Nivver spoke to her again. Nor her brothers nor sisters. She took a cottage up in the woods. Shame it was. You could see 'em pass in the street, her hesitate, try to smile – but no, straight on by. That's the Moffats for you.'

'Because the baby was illegitimate?'

'Lord luv you, no. She were wed, she said, and now I recall she didn't call herself Moffat no longer. Could have been Griffin. No, she'd gone with the showfolk and that was enough for the family. She'd sinned. You'd think tha'd want to see their own grandchild, wouldn't you? No. Not him, nor her, nor the brothers and sisters.'

Married. Rose Moffat might have been lying, of course, but if not that was the end of the tempting theory that Tom was the illegitimate son of one of the Tabors – unless of course Rose had married after she bore Tom, or because she was about to bear him.

'What happened to the father?' he asked.

'She nivver said. She didn't talk more than she had to. Nivver a word about where she'd been.'

'Did she say why she didn't stay on at Wombwell's?'

She cackled. 'Lord luv you, it's more than fifty years ago.'

Fifty years or not, Auguste was beginning to feel as if Rose Moffat had passed through Clapham only shortly ahead of him. 'How did she manage to live?'

'She did knitting. And she helped old Ned with his longcase clocks. Nimble fingers had Rose. I can see her now tripping down the street, with that bairn. Pretty as a picture.'

'And what happened to her?'

'She died there, did poor Rose, up in her cottage in the woods. It were only a few years before she was took. Buried here she was. You'll find her in the graveyard, poor Rose.'

'And old Ned?'

'Dead these forty years,' Nell announced with the relish of one who had survived.

'All her family too?'

She snorted. 'One brother's still here, the stiff-necked bugger.'

A brother still alive? True, he did not sound entirely *sympathique* but age can mellow the harshest of souls. As Auguste took his leave, Nell called out after him:

'I do remember old Ned telling me that the night she died, the clock she'd been working on stopped. When she nivver came to the workshop, he went up to see if she were ill. Found her lying there dead. He nivver did get that clock to go. Poor Rose. Such a pretty lass.'

'And the clock stopped, Never to go again . . .' The popular song running endlessly through his mind, Auguste made his way to the Moffat family house, a huge forbidding grey building on the outskirts of the village, as outwardly dour as the woman who came to the door. A wife? Housekeeper? The house struck cold even on a comparatively warm autumn day. Or was it the atmosphere emanating from those that dwelt within? He was led down the flag-stoned passageway into an equally forbidding living room.

'Mr Moffat?'

The gaunt old man did not answer, but pointed to a chair. His own armchair was the most uncomfortable Auguste had ever seen. Like its owner, it bore a look of conscious rectitude in its upright approach to life. Moffat looked suspiciously at him as though a visitor from the outside world might threaten his fortified castle of a mind.

'I've no wish to intrude on your family's past, Mr Moffat,' Auguste began firmly, 'but I am connected with the police investigation into a murder. It is just possible the victim may be the son of your late sister, Rose Moffat.' He was painfully aware how thin the possibility was. Nothing but a Christian name to link

Tom to any connection with this dour household.

The old man said nothing.

Thinking he had not heard, Auguste repeated more loudly, 'Your sister Rose.'

'I had no sister Rose.' The voice was flat, unemotional.

'I'm sorry. I was told you had.' Auguste forced himself to be firm in the face of obduracy. 'She left home when she was about sixteen, married and returned with a child a few years later. A boy called Thomas, recently known as Griffin.'

'She was put asunder.'

'I beg your pardon?'

Moffat rose painfully from his chair, beckoning to Auguste with a thin gnarled hand. He followed him into a darkened parlour which smelled musty and unused. A sand picture of Carisbrooke Castle was the only sign of individuality, and even that seemed grey with age. On a small occasional table lay a huge family Bible. Moffat opened it on to the flyleaf and pointed to a thick line obliterating a name.

'I had no sister called Rose,' he repeated.

The smugness in his voice infuriated Auguste. 'The man who died may be your nephew,' he said sharply.

'I had no nephew.'

Auguste snatched his hat with hands trembling at the pig-headedness of the human race. Poor Rose, poor Tom.

Rose Moffat. There would be no marriage entry here, nor baptism for Tom. Then a thought struck him – her grave might reveal more information. He walked into the churchyard, and eventually found what he sought. The stone was moss-covered, and the lettering faded, but he could still read what few words there were.

'Rose Griffin, born March 1821, died August 1847. *Hic jacet rosa mundi.*'

So someone cared enough to provide a loving epitaph. Who? he wondered. There was no mention of parents, or husband, or child. Nor, with its Latin inscription, was it the usual village headstone. *Here lies the rose of the world.* The beautiful Rose Moffat, whose life had ended too soon. Was there ever a husband, or had she simply changed her name to avoid the disgrace of an illegitimate baby? If she left home when she was eighteen or nearly eighteen, any marriage would have been after the 1837 act of compulsory registration came into effect and should have been registered. Perhaps Twitch should check all marriages entered into by Rose Moffats between the years 1839 to 1844, and continue searching for Tom's birth certificate to see if a connection could be established between Rose Moffat and Tom. Perhaps, however, Egbert had better put the request to him . . .

Meanwhile other Clapham folk must surely have known her, apart from old Ned the clockmaker, long since passed to a world without time. There couldn't be many still alive, he supposed. He decided a glass of no doubt excellent ale would assist the search wonderfully.

The moment he stepped into the New Inn it was obvious that news of his mission had shot round Clapham quicker than a mayonnaise could curdle. The landlord leant confidentially on the bar towards him.

'Tha want to buy old Amos a drink.'

Did he? Auguste dutifully purchased a pint of mild and bitter and bore it to its destination. Old Amos had the shrivelled look of one who was shrinking gradually into his own roots and, in his own time, proposing to die in them. For such people, irrespective of nationality,

228

Auguste had great respect. Old Amos might not display the wisdom of ages, but he proved to have a remarkable desire to talk of Rosie Moffat.

'She were never the same after she went to Wombwell's.'

'After she returned to Clapham, do you mean?'

Amos looked at him. 'I know what I means, young man. I says after she left here for Wombwell's. Old Nell say she didn't come back until she were wed, eh?'

'Yes.'

'True enough. I had sheep at Settle market, and I saw her once. "Hullo, Amos," says Rosie. "Remember me?" Remember her, I hadn't had a day when I never thought about her. 'Course, I'd never thought them Moffats would let the likes of a shepherd near Rosie, but she knew how I felt. "I'm going to leave the Menagerie and go into service," Amos, she said. By gum, I didn't like the sound of that, not for my Rosie, but she weren't one for listening, my lovely lass.'

'Where was she going?' Auguste could hardly frame the words in his excitement.

'Tabor Hall, over Malham way.'

At last the connection! The sun shone brighter and the ale tasted even better. The ecstasy of that exquisite moment when the *brandade* is complete or when the *soufflé* rises to honey-brown could only be matched in detection at the point when logic and guesswork combine in a mixture as divinely inspired as a hollandaise sauce.

'When she returned to Clapham, she had a baby and her name was Griffin. Do you think she met this Griffin at Tabor Hall?' Surely there could only be one answer to this, the most vital of questions? And it came.

'Griffin? Nay. I reckon it were Tabor were the bebby's father. Thomas Charles Tabor,' Amos pronounced in

229

disgust. 'Him that became 13th Lord Tabor; not his present Lordship, but his father. He's long dead, but he was only a boy then. I met him once and I could've killed him. You see things different when you're twenty. Now I'm eighty-odd, I suppose he weren't so bad. He went in mortal fear of his father, who were a real terror. He turned Rosie's head, though. She left the Menagerie and off she goes to work at Tabor Hall, and I heard no more till she tells me she's Mrs Griffin, her husband's dead, and Tom's his kid. 'Course, I didn't believe her, but she were a lovely lass. She threw a haverbread as good as Nell's, she did. A good lass.' Fifty-odd years whistled down the wind. 'I thought her being back in Clapham and a widow or not, as the case may be, she might look at me, her needing a man. But all she'd say was, "I'm a married woman, Amos."'

'Yet her husband never came to see her?' Auguste tried to control his excitement.

'Nay. A chap did come once in a pony and trap just afore she died, asking after her in the village.'

'Not Charles Tabor?'

Amos could hardly conceal his scorn. 'This chap weren't quality. It were a working man. An outcomer.'

'And then she died?'

'Aye. Poor soul, she weren't happy. Her family ignoring her, and a young 'un to rear. She loved her clocks, she did. But it weren't enough and her died. It fair broke my heart.'

The weekly market had come to Settle in Auguste's absence, and the bustle and noise were overwhelming after the quiet of Clapham. He had arranged to meet Egbert to tell him his transport back to Tabor Hall; and eager to share his news he jubilantly hurried into the Golden Lion, which like every other hostelry, was crowded out. Auguste finally ran Egbert to earth, huddled in a window seat, surrounded by three broad Yorkshiremen beside whom Rose looked lean indeed. Lean, but not hungry. He looked well satisfied, and seeing the brisk business in Yorkshire puddings and pies, Auguste had no difficulty in detecting that Egbert had already partaken of them.

Auguste glanced at the Yorkshiremen but they were more intent on discussing the rival merits of sheep salving or the new-fangled dipping than in listening to the daft conversation of outcomers, so he plunged excitedly into his story.

'The illegitimate son of the late Lord Tabor, eh?' Rose said when he finished. 'It's logical, I grant you.'

'*Thomas* Charles Tabor,' Auguste said. 'The Dowager Lady Tabor calls him Charles, but if Amos is right, and it's easy to check, then Thomas was his first name and Rose named her baby for the father.'

Egbert considered. 'It's slender, Auguste. What have you got after all? On the one hand a missing traveller called Tom Griffin, whose mother probably worked at Tabor Hall sixty years ago, and on the other, an unidentified corpse in dress clothes and a pile of old clothes thrown in a bush in the grounds. Coincidence.'

'And what have *you* got, *mon ami*? Have you got Colonel Simpson's clothes?'

'No,' said Egbert sourly. 'But I *have* got the Colonel.'

'He's alive?'

'Went down with measles while staying with his sister.'

'Then surely this body *must* be that of poor Tom Griffin?'

'*But*,' Egbert disregarded this, 'we've found Cyril Tabor's missing suit. It was way out of Settle by the side of a viaduct.'

'That doesn't make sense.' Auguste frowned.

'Tell me what does round here.'

'Tom Griffin.'

'There are more loose ends to that theory than in Edith's cushion covers. If the late Lord Tabor were the father of Rose's illegitimate child, it's all very neat, but it doesn't explain why Tom was murdered in this day and age. You don't get murdered for being born out of wedlock sixty years earlier.'

'Blackmail?'

'Hardly. The gentry was more or less expected to have a few on the side in those days.' Rose paused. 'And why can't Twitch find a birth certificate that looks like our man?'

'Why not ask him to look under Moffat?' Auguste asked simply.

'He *will* be pleased.'

'And,' said Auguste, struck by inspiration, 'just in case, look for a marriage certificate for Moffat. Suppose Tabor married her? Rose told Amos she was married. Suppose she wasn't lying, and suppose it wasn't a man called Griffin.'

'Why not?' Egbert agreed evilly. 'I'll tell Twitch you asked.'

'Perhaps that would not ensure the best results.'

'In that case, I'll have another pint.'

Auguste fought his way to the bar, past one burly figure after another, his mind racing furiously. Surely now the police would order a search of Griffin's wagon? And perhaps Wombwell's would have records of former staff. Perhaps there might even prove to be a Griffin amongst them, someone Rose met and married after Tabor had made her pregnant. He acquired the beer and turned to plunge into battle for the return journey.

'A thousand pardons.' Someone cannoned into him, slopping the beer over Auguste's Norfolk jacket.

'*De rien, monsieur,*' he replied automatically, then realised in surprise that he had unconsciously picked up a French accent. *'Vous êtes français?'* he asked, delighted. The cap, unshaven face, old jacket and waistcoat looked like the dress of a market worker, hardly that of a touring Frenchman in the wilds of Yorkshire.

'Oui, monsieur. My wife is from Yorkshire and we have a stand in the market. We make pies and cheese, the best in Ribblesdale. Perhaps you have tried them?'

'Not yet. But I shall.' Cheese stalls always interested him. 'What are your specialities?'

'Blue cheese, *chèvre* and ewe's cheese. And of the pies, *lapin*—'

'I shall most certainly come.'

'Enchanté, monsieur.'

'Where have you been?' asked Egbert when Auguste returned. 'A man could die of thirst waiting for you in a pub.'

'I was detained on a professional matter with a Frenchman. *My* profession.'

'More important than solving the murder?'

'Non,' conceded Auguste, 'but important, nevertheless. After all, we are in the home of good cheese, and he produces it. And pies.'

'French?'

'Married to a Yorkshirewoman.'

'Where is he?' Egbert Rose craned his neck round.

Auguste turned, but the man had vanished. 'He must have left,' he said, wondering why he felt a chill of unease.

'Probably has,' retorted Rose. 'What did he look like?'

'He wore a cap, a jacket, a waistcoat, a scarf, he was swarthy, your build, somewhat younger than you—' Auguste broke off, seeing Egbert's face.

'That was no pie-maker,' Rose said grimly. 'I lay you a monkey that was Pyotr Gregorin.'

*He will wish you to know who killed you . . . He will
introduce himself . . .*

Dazed with belated shock, Auguste listened to Egbert
talking on the police station telephone to a highly
annoyed Inspector Stitch, judging by the squawks
that reached him every time Egbert stopped talking –
or rather shouting. Egbert was never convinced that
people could hear as well at long distances as short.
  'Moffat. *Moffat*, Thomas. Got that, Stitch? And you
might as well check Moffat, Rose, for marriage
certificates in the late thirties and early forties. Got
that? And you might take a look at Thomas Charles
Tabor's will.'
  A squeak from Stitch.
  'Moffat's her maiden name. Griffin is the name she
went under when she reappeared,' Rose continued.
'That simple enough for you? And you ain't forgotten
that list of all Tom Griffins born in the early forties,
anywhere in England, have you?' A pause. 'I thought
you'd have it in hand. Good man, Stitch.' Rose hung up
and returned to Auguste. 'That should keep him happy,'
he announced with satisfaction.
  'Busy, certainly.'
  'Same thing with Twitch.'
  'And Wombwell's? And Blackboots?'
  'Cobbold's already tracking them down.' Egbert Rose
thought longingly of the Highbury fireside, his slippers,
and Mr Pinpole's pork. He was beginning to feel he
might never see Edith again.

Each kitchen had its own evocative smell. The one
Auguste had come to associate with Tabor Hall was a
persistent smell of baking, combined with roast beef,
which seemed to give the kitchen a warmth and comfort
singularly lacking from the rest of the house.

234

Breckles shouted cheerily as Auguste entered, 'Tha looks canty.' Correctly guessing this to mean that he appeared in good spirits, Auguste beamed and duly admired the raised pie's coffin which Breckles was artistically finishing, before putting the question he had come to ask.

Breckles considered. 'Miss Savage, she's been here longest. Come with old Lady Tabor when she was wed to the old lord.'

'No one before that?'

Breckles grinned. 'Reckon they'd be in t'ground now, man. There be Tompkins' father, o' course. He do go back a long way, he and his father before him. Served the family for generations. Lives in Malham, he do. Mind you, 'e be a bit daffly daffled these days.'

Pumping Breckles' hand as vigorously as if it had been dough, Auguste hurried to the motor stable – where he found not only Tompkins but Tatiana, who greeted him with a cry of delight when she emerged flushed from investigating the Daimler's intestines.

'Have you come to take a drive?' She moved eagerly towards the driving seat.

'No,' Auguste replied hastily.

'Father?' Tompkins repeated doubtfully when Auguste had explained.

'Oh, Mr Tompkins, do let's. We could all go in the motorcar,' Tatiana interceded.

Walter Tompkins could deny Tatiana nothing, and once again Auguste found himself seated in the rear of the Daimler. It was a remarkably long way round to Malham, he thought impatiently: on foot he could have made the journey in fifteen minutes.

Mr Tompkins senior was engaged in the serious business of slaking his thirst at the Buck Inn, which, Tompkins explained, it was essential for him to attend daily otherwise he might lose his regular place by the bar. Woe betide any outcomer who might inadvertently sit there. If indeed Tompkins senior were 'daffly daffled', it did not affect his memory for the past, nor for grievances long held. He took some coaxing, however, to share his memories, seeing no need to waste his pearls on daft Frenchmen.

'He's like the police, Father.'

This was no recommendation to Mr Tompkins senior, Auguste noticed, deciding to try charm. 'I am sure you would wish to help solve a mystery, Mr Tompkins.'

Tompkins senior disagreed. ''Tis sixty year or more ago. Anyways I was only an outdoor fellow.'

Much of this was unintelligible, and needed his son as interpreter.

'But your job is so important, Mr Tompkins.' Tatiana had a better grasp of charm where elderly gentlemen were concerned. 'The driver hears all, sees much, and speaks little, but he is in control of his passengers' lives.'

Mr Tompkins beamed and, thanking the heavens for providing him with a wife, Auguste continued: 'Were you at the Hall before the Dowager Lady Tabor came?'

'Aye. Only a lad then, o' course.'

'Do you remember a housemaid called Rose Moffat?'

'There was a lot of them. Don't recall one from the other.'

'Would an ounce of baccy help your memory, Father?' Walter asked helpfully.

'It might.'

Auguste rushed to oblige. 'Did young Mr Tabor, the present lord's father, have a bad reputation with the female staff?'

'Nay. 'Twould be more than his life was worth,' declared Tompkins in scorn. 'Terrified of his father, he was. This Rose Moffat. I do recall a Rose. All the junior housemaids went by their Christian names. Never knew their surnames, half the time. Pretty she was. I were seventeen and noticing these things.' He gave a toothless grin. 'And if there's any *more* of that baccy I'll be having it, thank 'ee. Not that she'd look at me. Then she left all in a 'urry. Dismissed, so the story went, but one of the girls told me different. She was to have a baby and the story was it was the young master's. He loved her. She were a pretty young thing, as I said, and kind with it. Reminds me of her Ladyship, the present Dowager, looking back. Different class, o' course, but same pretty ways and graceful-like as she moves. Story went he wanted to wed her, but o' course his Lordship wouldn't hear of it and Rose had to leave the house that day. The whole roof nearly came off with all their shouting, so I heard. But it weren't no good. Rose went. I allus did wonder about Rose, and what happened to her. Ah well, 'tis a long time ago.'

'Possibly she did marry, but she died a few years later. She had a son called Tom.'

He paused, hoping this might spark off another recollection.

'Things weren't the same between his Lordship and young Master Charlie, as we called him, after that. He spent a lot of time away for a year or two, and whenever he was home there was quarrelling. The more he came to stay the worse it got. Terrible it was. You're right, missus. When you're driving it's amazing what folks'll say. They reckon your ears don't work. I'm the only one left of them old days. Lot of the servants left or changed when the old lord died. New ways, yer see. New mistress. But they didn't change Tompkins. Oh no. His new Lordship wouldn't have that.'

'Were the quarrels still about Rose?' Auguste asked excitedly.

'No. They was about young Mr Charles having to

wed to produce an heir. Every time he was home, he were on about it, was his Lordship. Then he met her Ladyship and wed her in '46. Lovely wedding t'was. She was so lovely, and so much in love. It was a pleasure to see 'em. His old Lordship dies in 1850 and that put an end to the bad blood.'

No sign of his being daffly daffled, thought Auguste gratefully.

The old man looked at his empty glass, and pushed it towards Auguste. 'I'll take another pint o' this cowslip wine, Ebenezer, thank 'ee.'

'There are as many possibilities as currants in a *clafouti*,' Auguste commented triumphantly, back in Egbert's rooms. 'Surely you can't doubt now that the corpse is that of Tom Griffin?'

'Probably,' Egbert grunted. 'So I take it you believe his ancestry is the key and young Alfred, Black Rufus, roulette and gents in loud check suits dunning for payment can join our distinguished company of false scents.'

'Yes.' Auguste was almost reluctant to let the unlikable Alfred go as a suspect. That meant one of the other Tabors must be guilty.

'So an illegitimate brother turns up at midnight on the very day the King was staying to threaten George Tabor with a scandal sixty years old. Why? His Majesty ain't exactly a paragon of domestic virtue, he wasn't going to be shocked out of his Balmoral socks. And why kill him and land themselves with a corpse? Why not just pay him off?'

'But just suppose Rose *did* marry Charles Tabor, Egbert,' Auguste said desperately, seeing his theories melting away. 'Just think, Tom would be the oldest son, and he, not George Tabor, should have inherited the title and the estate.'

238

Egbert thought lovingly of this horror descending on Priscilla, but shook his head. 'You forget. You say Rose Moffat died in 1847, but Charles Tabor married Miriam in '46.'

'Bigamy!' breathed Auguste, his eyes gleaming with excitement. 'George would be illegitimate. One mention by Tom Griffin of an earlier marriage, and scandal would sweep down like castor oil.'

'How about some evidence, Auguste? All those fairy stories have gone to your head. If Rose Moffat married Tabor, Twitch will dig it out.'

Feverishly, Auguste played with the idea that Twitch might deliberately be holding back to spite him.

'I grant you the corpse is most likely Griffin,' Rose said reassuringly, seeing Auguste's crestfallen face, 'and that seems to imply that one of the Tabors must be the murderer.'

Seems to imply? The qualification did not escape Auguste, but he managed to bite back his anger, saying instead, 'And Gregorin seems to have his own supply of old clothes, without murdering stray working men for the privilege.'

'Perhaps,' Egbert threw in idly, 'old Tompkins was a jealous lover, and popped down here to shoot the product of his sweetheart's love for another. Seventeen-year-old boys have violent passions.'

'Mr Tompkins is no longer a seventeen-year-old and his passion has now been transferred to the Buck Inn, its cowslip wine and tobacco,' Auguste tried to jest.

'If you're right, and that body is Griffin,' Egbert said after a pause, 'I reckon all the Tabors are in it together.'

'They *all* shot him?'

'Accessories after the fact, at least. They'd gamble I'd never arrest the whole family – much as I'd like to. That wash and brush-up in the smokehouse took time – *and* organisation, especially if it were done on the

239

spur of the moment.' Another pause. 'Cobbold's heard from his pathologist chum. You were right – it is pig's blood on the clothes. We've got proof of that at least.'

Auguste glowed with pride. 'And the carpet?'

'Human blood where someone tried to wash it out. The pathologist had a hard job with that one, but managed it in the end. Thanks to you, we can prove murder *and* that the clothes were changed.'

'You know it is not thanks I want.'

Rose looked at him. 'Tatiana's clear.'

'Thank you, Egbert.' All was well. Relief flowed through him. Now at last his brain could work unfettered.

'You believe the Tabors did not expect Tom's visit?'

'It's a strange time for a chap to choose for a casual call.'

'Perhaps *one* of them knew.'

'Which?'

'Not Oliver Carstairs.' Auguste was clean on that. 'Even if Oliver believed the man was Mariot, and that is surely unlikely, given the clothes, the Tabors would not put themselves to so much trouble on his account.'

'They would if they had been expecting Tom Griffin, and discovered him dead. They'd be only too anxious to conceal his identity.'

'Why not bury the body?'

Rose crashed his fist on the table. 'I don't *know*. There's a cunning mind behind this, Auguste. A Tabor mind, I'll wager.'

'But not Alfred's.'

'If the whole bally family decided to get rid of Tom Griffin, Alfred's not an obvious choice for the deed. Son and heirs have to be protected.'

'And the Dowager.'

'Right. Would you choose an elderly lady of seventy-nine to pull the trigger? Besides, Laura and Savage

240

were with her. My guess is she was left well out of it.'

'So Laura can be omitted too if she was with her mother.'

'But the Dowager said at first she didn't remember that,' Egbert recalled thoughtfully. 'It was Miss Savage confirmed her story.'

'If they acted on a family plan, surely the task of shooting Tom Griffin would be allotted to a man. Cyril or—'

'Not him again. I can't take any more of his blasted stories about the Galaxy Girls. As bad as you.'

Auguste ignored this. 'Then we are left with the obvious: George, whose thumbprint was on the gun.'

'All the Tabors would have been wearing gloves. Can't pin much on that.'

'But, as head of the family, George is the obvious suspect.'

'Is he?' Egbert grunted. 'What about Priscilla?'

'Ah, Chief Inspector Rose and Mr Didier. It is not often nowadays I have the pleasure of a visit from two gentlemen. In former times it was far from unusual, though this may now be hard to believe.' The Dowager Baroness Tabor sat in her upright armchair, a delicate hand resting on the arm, as the other gestured to them to be seated.

'*Madame*, you are beautiful still.'

'Beauty fades, Mr Didier, for all your kind words. Fortunately I still have my brains, don't I, Savage?' She turned mischievously to the woman at her side.

'Indeed you do, my lady,' Savage replied, her hands resting primly in her lap.

Rose cleared his throat. He could leave the pleasantries to Auguste. 'We believe we've identified the dead body in the smokehouse, ma'am. It seems possible it was the body of a man called Tom Griffin.'

241

Miriam looked concerned. 'I don't think we know anyone of that name, do we, Savage? Was he a friend of His Majesty's?'

'He's not what you'd call gentry, Lady Tabor. He was a travelling showman at a fair.'

'Oh, what fun, I love fairs. But such a shame.' Her face puckered in concern. 'That poor man. What did he kill himself for? No – it was murder, wasn't it? Why? Was he a thief after something here at Tabor Hall?'

'That we don't know yet, Lady Tabor,' Egbert told her noncommittally. 'But I have to ask you some questions, which may seem odd or even hurtful. How old was your husband when you married him?'

She looked startled. 'That is indeed an odd question, Chief Inspector,' she replied after a moment. 'Darling Charlie. He was a year older than me, so he would have been twenty-five.'

'Did he tell you anything of his past life, ma'am? Any wild oats, shall we say?' Rose asked delicately.

'You mean mistresses? I should think it quite likely, Chief Inspector,' Miriam replied frankly. 'Gentlemen do, you know. It is no part of a lady's task to resent what her husband has sown in his past, merely to prevent his sowing any more.'

Auguste's approval of this intelligent attitude was instant.

'He never mentioned having had any children?'

The atmosphere grew a little less warm.

'He did not.'

'I don't want to shock you, Lady Tabor, but it's possible Tom Griffin was the illegitimate son of your late husband by a girl called Rose Griffin or Rose Moffat who used to work at this house.'

'When?' The word shot out.

'The late 1830s or early 1840s.'

'I did not marry Charles until 1846, Chief Inspector, and this would have happened well before I came to Tabor Hall – with dear Savage.' She patted the maid's hand affectionately. 'Whatever happened earlier is not my concern. I did not meet Charlie until 1844. If there had been such an unfortunate business, he would not have bothered me with it, for he dealt with all business matters himself. As for being shocked—' she smiled, suddenly looking fragile, 'I am not, for I know he loved *me*. Nevertheless, I am not young, and tire easily.' She held out her hand.

Auguste kissed it. 'Forgive us, Lady Tabor.'

'You must do what you must, Mr Didier.' Her face crumpled and she looked her full age before she recovered. 'I expect you will find that Priscilla knows all about it. She usually does.'

Egbert looked very solitary surrounded by Tabors, like raw meat encircled by Wombwell's Menagerie, thought Auguste, protectively at his side. But he was armed now. Cobbold's men had tracked down the travelling gingerbread man who had given Tom Griffin a lift to Tabor Hall that night. It was all the evidence Rose needed for the moment. Auguste felt no struggle of loyalty now. One of those in this room had murdered Tom Griffin. Egbert would not have called them all together unless he was sure they were on the right track. And plumb in the middle of that track was Priscilla Tabor, whom Egbert was preparing to meet head-on. If Alfred were to be discounted, then for Auguste's money – and it seemed Egbert's too – Priscilla was the only Tabor capable of ruthlessly removing anything that stood in the way of the Tabors' security. The Dowager's voice rang in his ears: 'Annie Oakley – or do I mean Calamity Jane?'

The well-bred Tabor faces around them betrayed

nothing but polite interest. Except, that is, for Priscilla's; a Vesuvius gathering up steam to explode. Even Miriam, whom Rose had excused from attending, wore her charm like a mask. Auguste glanced at the family portraits around the room. Gainsborough, Lely, van Dyck. The Tabors might have lived discreetly over the centuries, but they had not stinted themselves. It was a point worth remembering. He was glad he had persuaded Tatiana not to come. Survival was what mattered to families such as the Tabors, and the ruthlessness it necessitated might shortly be shown in all its stark ugliness.

'It's probable the corpse was a man called Tom Griffin,' Rose told them bluntly.

There was no reaction.

'And who is or was he?' enquired Victoria.

'The son of Rose Moffat of Clapham.'

'And Mr Griffin presumably,' added Alexander irrepressibly, but was quelled by a warning frown from Victoria. Rose's face did not suggest it was a time for badinage.

'It's also possible,' Rose continued evenly, 'that he was an illegitimate son of the 13th Lord Tabor, conceived before his marriage.'

'Illegitimate?' retorted Priscilla robustly. 'What of it?'

'It's immaterial, of course,' Rose came back immediately, 'unless he came to blackmail you. It seems likely that the visitor you said was a creditor of Mr Alfred's was actually Tom Griffin, and that he came here on 18 August.'

Priscilla eyed him with scorn. 'I really cannot say. Two such persons might have called; I do not keep a record of all unwelcome callers. My impression is that the visit was later than 18 August. You may ask Richey.'

'Thank you, ma'am. I'll do that. Send for him, would you?'

Richey averted his eyes from the terrible sight of a policeman sitting in the Tabor drawing room. 'Richey, were there one or two objectionable callers who insisted so rudely on intruding into the Hall in August?' Priscilla asked him.

Richey hesitated and Egbert Rose thrust the picture, now doctored somewhat more professionally than Auguste's efforts had achieved, towards him.

'That's the man that came,' Richey said, baulked of any guidance as to how her Ladyship would wish him to reply. 'I don't recall another.'

'Thank you, Richey, that is all.'

'I don't recall saying I'd finished talking to him, ma'am,' Rose said pointedly.

'There is no need to detain Richey now I have seen that picture,' Priscilla told him coldly. 'It strikes a chord more vividly than the first picture you showed to me. It is immaterial whether there were one or two callers. I realise I did see this man several weeks ago. It is true that impertinently he came to this house to collect a debt from my son, but he was also eager to impart his fantasy that he was also the son of my late father-in-law. One meets such people.'

'You lied to us then?'

'Lied, Chief Inspector? I did no such thing. Since the man achieved his purpose in August, he had no reason to come again last week. I could hardly be expected to appreciate that the body of a well-barbered gentleman found in our smokehouse was the same scruffy individual who had left here well satisfied many weeks before.'

Egbert Rose looked up from his file. 'Richey stated he didn't recall escorting that caller out of the house again.'

'Possibly not, Chief Inspector. The man was so well satisfied, he produced,' she shuddered, 'a most obnoxious pipe and as it was raining I showed him out *myself* through the garden door, pointing the way to the place where he might indulge his filthy habit. I could not be expected to presume he would remain there for four or five weeks.'

Auguste watched as Egbert was dealt this blow, of which Jem Mace himself would have been proud. But he showed no signs of retiring to his corner yet. 'Glad it all came back to you, ma'am. Now,' turning to the rest of the family, 'you were all very helpful with your various suggestions as to who the corpse might be. The police were much obliged to you. Of course, if I were an imaginative sort of chap, I might think you were trying to pervert the course of justice by sending us off on enough wild goose chases to stock my larder for six months.'

'Why would we do such a thing when we didn't know who the man was?' Laura asked, unruffled. 'Not even Priscilla recognised him, and she tells us she had in fact met him once.'

'Maybe because you're Tabors,' Rose replied. '*Loyalty to the End* is your motto, I gather. Between you, you've misled the police and buried the truth deeper than someone did Tom Griffin's clothes.'

There was a reaction at last. But from whom? Auguste could not be sure.

'Why should we?' Cyril asked plaintively.

'At the least, to avoid scandal. And perhaps more.'

'Now it is you wasting time, Chief Inspector,' Priscilla replied crisply. 'Kindly tell us just what you imagine we have done. I am not acquainted with the higher echelons of Scotland Yard if that is what concerns you. Nor have I any intention of appealing to His Majesty. I merely wish to remove the police presence from Tabor

Hall as soon as I can—' her eye fell deliberately on Auguste, in case he might be in doubt as to whether or not he was counted with the forces of the law.

'What I *believe*, ma'am, is that Tom Griffin visited you one afternoon in August and went home with the promise of enough money to fulfil all his dreams: a part payment on a roundabout and promise of more to come to pay the rest. A very successful afternoon's work, you might say.'

'Yes. Highly successful,' agreed Priscilla.

A strangled gulp from her husband.

'Don't make foolish noises, George,' his wife continued unperturbed. 'I see we must take Chief Inspector Rose into our confidence.

'Priscilla!' said Laura sharply.

Her sister-in-law glanced at her. 'You are English, Laura. I am American. I have no natural propensity towards unnecessary concealment of unpalatable facts. Chief Inspector, that fellow did indeed come here to blackmail us with the fantasy that he might be my husband's illegitimate brother. Fact or fiction, either would be annoying in the extreme. We were forced to cede to his demands, which fortunately by Tabor standards were insignificant.'

'Why forced?' asked Oliver slowly.

'To have a travelling showman claiming, rightly or wrongly, to be half-brother to Lord Tabor would do little to enhance our reputation at Court.'

'Suppose he decided to live in easy street for the rest of his life on you?' enquired Rose.

'I wish he had, Chief Inspector,' Priscilla pounced. 'He might have had a house on the estate for his old age, and a job, if he required it. But no. He was abusive and stubborn. It appeared he did not wish to give up his way of life. His great ambition,' she said scornfully, 'was to own a roundabout, and he only

247

wanted enough money for that. Apparently,' she added.

'You mean you realised blackmail doesn't stop after the first time.'

'I did indeed realise it,' Priscilla replied coldly. 'He was an unpleasant sort of person, but with no idea of the way of the world. A few threats of legal action of my own, and he decided to take some money away with him, and the rest later. We made an arrangement through our bank for him to collect the balance at Kendal where he shortly expected to be. Our bank manager will confirm this.'

'Nevertheless the risk remained,' observed Rose.

'I took precautions, Chief Inspector, and you shall see just why I was confident he would not return.' She rang the bell and Richey once more slid deferentially to her side.

'I would be grateful if you would avoid troubling my mother-in-law about this man's delusion,' Priscilla said, as Richey vanished again.

'I have already spoken with her about it,' Rose said promptly.

Priscilla struggled for control. 'Have you no sensitivity, Chief Inspector?'

'You'll find she took it very well,' Rose rejoined. 'She comes of a generation when ladies were not brought up to be so fragile as your sensitive generation, Lady Tabor.'

Richey reappeared with a small *escritoire* which Priscilla unlocked; she removed a document which she handed to Egbert Rose. 'There, Chief Inspector. A handwritten but legally signed and witnessed statement that Tom Griffin has no further claim on the Tabor estate or assets in any way, once he has received the balance of the money agreed to.'

'That wouldn't stop him coming back and threatening

248

you again,' Auguste pointed out as Egbert read it through.

'I am quite aware of that, Mr Didier.' Ice dripped from her voice. 'Chief Inspector Rose may now have reached the proviso in the document that the money that the fellow was given through the bank was only a loan, permanent except that it would be redeemable if he ever bothered the Tabors again. He would have lost his roundabout if he had dared to threaten us again.'

'So he had no reason to return here?' Auguste asked.

'On the contrary. Had he done so, we would have immediately started proceedings to reclaim the money.' Priscilla looked coldly round. 'The Tabors endeavour to avoid the public eye, Chief Inspector. We are hardly likely to have attracted it by murdering the fellow under His Majesty's very nose. Are we?'

As Egbert Rose and Auguste left, it was Rose who spoke first.

'I never thought I'd admit this, Auguste, but Priscilla Tabor's right.'

Chapter Ten

Refreshed by a light breakfast of kidneys, muffins and oatcake, Auguste strolled out into the yard of the Golden Lion. He was accompanied on this early visit to Settle by Tatiana – rather to his surprise until he realised her stride was increasing as they approached the groups of millgirls hurrying across the Settle market square, past the arched colonnade of The Shambles. Did Mr Marx have anything specific to say about millgirls?

Auguste was beginning to feel a fondness for this small town, snug in the protective shadow of the high Castleberg cliff. A town where over sixty years ago Rose Moffat had fallen in love with Wombwell's Travelling Menagerie and freedom, and subsequently the Honourable Thomas Charles Tabor. Just one girl of the thousands who had passed through the town since, each with her own individual story of love, tragedy, happiness, sorrow. One just like the millgirls flocking towards the river bank, in shawls and clogs.

'Are you near to making an arrest, Auguste?' Tatiana asked quietly – and then he understood the main reason for her coming.

'*Mon amour*, the *bavarois* is almost set,' he told her gently.

'And will it set in Tabor Hall?'

'It is probable.'

A silence.

'Not Alexander?'

'No,' he assured her.

'Or—'

'I cannot tell you, *chérie*.'

'I *like* them, Auguste,' she cried after a moment. 'I even like—'

'Priscilla?' finished Auguste for her.

'Yes. When she is not playing the *grande dame* of Tabor Hall, she talks about her childhood in Kansas on a cattle ranch. She is so straightforward when she forgets she is trying to be English, and remembers she is American.'

A millgirl ran past them to join her comrades; a carpenter hurried down from the small cottages built over the shops and colonnade of The Shambles; a butcher's boy bicycled past whistling.

'You see that hoop?' Auguste asked gravely, as one spun by them out of control, chased by its young owner. 'That is what this case has become.'

The hoop clattered to the ground at the end of its run before its owner could grasp hold of it, and Tatiana sighed. 'Egbert must continue,' she said at last, 'because he must follow the path of law. But you, surely you have a choice?'

'No, *ma mie*, I cannot stop, any more than I could take a half-cooked soufflé from the oven. Do you mind very much?'

Tatiana leaned over the bridge and looked at the river racing beneath. 'Once in Cannes long ago, when I was eighteen and you were our chef, you told me we would always be divided by a door, a door so strong that we could never break it down. But we *have* broken it down, and we must never build another. Only,' she added, 'when it is about to happen, please tell me.'

'Cobbold's just telephoned.' Egbert looked up as

Auguste came into the police station. He had left Tatiana disappearing in the wake of the last of the millgirls. 'Twitch has sent up a list of all Tom Griffins *and* Moffats in England born between 1838 and 1844.'

'That is excellent.'

'Glad you think so.'

Auguste's face fell. 'Ah, but if there is need to send a list, that means—'

'Thought you'd get there eventually,' said Rose sourly. 'You must have had breakfast too early. It means there is no one on the list with the father specifically named as Tabor. He's probably going to be one of those "unknown fathers". Twitch was told at that time the certificates for illegitimate nippers left a blank under the father's name unless he actually turned up in person at the registration. Very helpful.'

'Perhaps Rose Moffat and Tabor did marry,' Auguste said wistfully.

'If they were married, the chap wouldn't be registered under Tom Griffin, would he? And before you go sending Twitch off to check all the Thomas Tabors in the world, let me tell you there's no marriage certificate for Moffat and Tabor in that period, *or* Moffat and Griffin. So that's that. Tom Griffin was a bastard, father unknown. And we're not much further forward on his killer.'

'Surely the crime *must* be connected with Griffin's parentage? It's too big a coincidence for there to be another reason for killing him.'

Rose glared at him. 'We'll have one more shot, and get a permit to search old Tom's caravan. Though I don't see what it could tell us, since Queen Priscilla is prepared to admit he might be George's illegitimate brother.'

'The more we know about Tom Griffin, the better we understand the ingredients of this dish before us.'

And the less, Auguste suspected, he was going to like it.

Having established themselves in the comfort of the Londesborough Arms at Selby, where Cobbold had run Blackboots to earth, Auguste and Egbert Rose set out to find their quarry. They found the wagons parked in a field on the edge of the flat plain round the town, and Blackboots himself in the nearest pub to them.

He was ostentatiously contemplating an empty jug. Auguste, now practised in such arts, promptly removed the jug for refilling.

'Well, then?' Blackboots grunted.

Egbert eased himself on to the hard oak settle. 'I'm satisfied the body's his.'

Blackboots was silent a moment; then, picking up the now brimming jug, he held it aloft. 'Here's to old Tom,' he said gruffly.

'Mr Blackboots, did Tom talk to you about his childhood?' Auguste began, when he judged the beer level sufficiently sunken to justify interruption.

'I told yer, Clapham.'

He and Rose had combed Twitch's list of births in conjunction with Ordnance Survey maps of Yorkshire and its surrounding counties. There remained a shortlist of three possibilities: one born to a Rose Perkins, father Joseph Griffin; one born to Mary Griffin, wife of Thomas Griffin; and the third to Rose Griffin, unnamed father; the locations being respectively Ripon, Doncaster and Bolton.

'He moved to Clapham when he was very young. Did he ever suggest to you that he might be the bastard son of one of the Tabor family?'

'No.' Blackboots wiped his mouth deliberately on the back of his sleeve, having drained the last drop of beer. He delicately slid the jug forward.

254

'Old Tom, there was nothing more he wanted than a family – and a galloper. If 'e thought 'e were the son of one of those Tabors, even a bastard, he'd have told me. I was his only real pal. Nah.' Blackboots began the next pint without even glancing at its bearer. 'Old Nayler were the only father Tom ever knew and he weren't much of one.'

'Scarface Nayler?' asked Rose in sudden interest.

'Yus. In between stir, he 'ad a flea circus and a coupla' performing dogs he showed. When Tom were with 'im, so Tom did tell me, he looked after the dogs while Scarface were inside.'

'Just like Scarface,' said Rose with relish, remembering his own encounter with him. 'He'd put his own hundred-year-old granny on the hoop-la.'

"E weren't all bad,' Blackboots observed. "E took Tom on as a nipper because he knew his ma at Wombwell's. Sweet on 'er, I reckon.' Scorn for all such irrelevant fancies filled his voice. 'That's what he told Tom afore 'e died. Sent for 'im special, 'e did.'

'When was this?' Rose asked sharply.

'Matter of four months ago mebbe. Tom were a bit preoccupied-like after he came back. I even thought perhaps 'e was getting tired of the old galloper because 'e said 'e wanted to do the Leather and Nails gaff at Settle. I wasn't keen. They're too busy talking about boots to want to ride a galloper there. And there's a lot of competition. If you don't get a pitch, there's not much else around Settle then and that's August gone. "If you don't, Blackboots, I'll up and leave you," Tom said. 'Course, I roared with laughter. Reckoned Tom would never do that. Still, we went – and look what's 'appened.'

'Hadn't Scarface kept in touch with him over the years?'

'Not 'im. 'E was a mean old cuss, begging pardon of

255

the dead. Minute Tom was twelve – "you're on your own now," 'e says. 'E could see Tom were never going to do much, so he pushed 'im out, 'cos otherwise 'e'd have to start paying 'im. 'E'd bump into 'im from time to time, but 'e never sent for 'im afore; and that's only 'cos he knew he were done for. Died in August, so I 'eard.'

'He didn't tell Tom who his father was?'

'Nah. I told you.' Exasperation came into Blackboots' voice. 'Tom couldn't keep a thing like that quiet. I doubt if Scarface knew.'

'Perhaps it was him,' said Auguste.

'Nah.' Blackboots shook his head, after considering this. 'If 'e were, 'e wouldn't push Tom out. Not because of 'is loving 'eart – doubt if Scarface knew 'e 'ad one – but because 'e could have got Tom to go on working for 'im free by pulling the poor old father line.' He paused hopefully, edging the jug forward again. It was ignored.

'Ah well, gentlemen, I can see there's no more beer a-flowing.' Blackboots heaved himself from his seat with the air of one to whom great wrong has been done.

It was a strange feeling to walk into the dead man's van, which smelt musty from disuse. It was smaller and shabbier than Blackboots' own, and apart from the essential items of furniture, there were few personal effects. An aspidistra was dying from lack of water, a few dead Michaelmas daises adorned a Golden Jubilee mug, six toy soldiers battered from overuse stood on a shelf by the stove. There were only two photographs, one a studio picture of what must surely be Tom himself aged about forty; the other a duplicate of the photograph Auguste had already seen.

'Could Tom read and write?' Rose asked idly, busy

looking through a pile of papers bundled up in a rough wooden box.

'After a fashion. The fairground folk taught 'im. Not much of a writer, though. His name. Not much more. He could read a bit.'

'Yet he sold pens, ink and paper during the winter, you said. Here's his pedlar's licence.'

'Ah well, 'e 'ad a way with 'im when it come to pens and paper, did Tom. "Don't be like me, better yourself," 'e'd say to 'is customers. "Learn to write and read like I never 'ad the chance to." They fell for it every time. I tell you, Tom did better at it than many a folk who could read the whole of the Bible cover to cover.'

'He could read enough to understand this though, or did you read it to him?' Rose held out a letter written on thick yellowing paper.

Blackboots peered at it curiously. ''E never showed that to me.'

'It's written in copperplate handwriting, carefully too, though it's badly spelled. Here, read it out, Auguste.'

'"My dear son,"' Auguste began. '"Yea though I walk through the valley of the shadow of death I will fear no evil. My God is with me. He knows I have done you no wrong, and He will protect you as He will shelter me. Your father is a good and loving man and loves you too my dear son. No wrong was done to me by him though they can call you bastard. You are named for him my dear son Thomas."'

''E never showed me this,' interrupted Blackboots indignantly.

'Go on, Auguste,' Rose said quietly.

'"Thomas Charles Tabor is his name. He is a good man. Your loving mother, Rose Griffin, written this day 18th June 1847."' Auguste finished, torn between satisfaction and disappointment that his prized theory of a marriage between Rose Moffat and Tabor had been exploded.

Egbert had no such mixed feelings. 'So there you are – Tabor. Do you think Scarface gave him this, Blackboots?'

'Tom couldn't keep a secret like that to save his life,' Blackboots snorted. Then he realised what he'd said. 'If I find 'im,' he went on violently, 'the bloke what done this, I'll cut the bugger's throat from ear to ear.' A pause. 'What's going to 'appen to the galloper, eh?' No one answered.

'If that old villain is right,' Egbert reasoned, as they walked back to the Londesborough Arms, 'then Tom only recently came by that letter.'

'In that case, Egbert, there's probably only one place he could have obtained it.'

Clapham was grey in the drizzle and even the beck failed to look lively this morning. The horse's hooves pulling their trap was the only sound in the quiet village, as they went straight to the old farmhouse. Geese as unwelcoming as their master honked at their arrival.

'Master's na home.'

'Yes, he is, ma'am,' said Rose firmly to the daunting Cerberus. 'I saw him.'

There had indeed been a pale face at the window. As the trap clattered to a halt, it had immediately withdrawn behind the sheltering curtain.

Sullenly Cerberus flopped her way to the living room, where Herbert Moffat sat in his armchair. He did not turn his head as they entered.

'Why did you not tell me that Tom Griffin had paid you a visit?' Auguste began without preliminaries.

'You asked if I had a nephew called Tom Griffin,' the cold voice replied. 'I told you I had not. I do not recall your asking if this man had come here.'

'He's your nephew by your sister Rose and the last Lord Tabor was his father, wasn't he?'

'I had no sister Rose. The female person to whom you refer was cast out by the Lord. He giveth and He taketh away. In due time the female produced a bastard child, and suffered the just reward for her sin. Death.' He raised his head and stared at them.

'It's not God you're dealing with,' Rose informed him sternly. 'It's Scotland Yard, and the crime's murder. Are you going to speak to us here, or come in handcuffs to the police station?'

'Thou preparest a table before me in the presence of mine enemies,' Moffat muttered. His unblinking stare was unnerving, and Auguste shivered.

Rose was never unnerved: 'Did Tom Griffin come to see you in August?'

'A person calling himself Thomas Griffin called here, claiming to be the son of a person born Rose Moffat.' Moffat had obviously chosen his version of cooperation.

'Did you meet her husband?'

'I had no contact with that person. I speak only of what I am told took place. The person returned to this village calling herself Rose Griffin. Rose Moffat was dead.'

'*Dead?*' repeated Rose, startled.

'She died the day she left this, my father's house.'

Rose sighed. 'What did Tom Griffin want?'

'He claimed to be Rose Griffin's child, and wished information about his youth. I could give him none. He was persistent. I told him Rose Moffat was not a member of my family. He grew abusive. I asked him to leave.'

'And that's all you can tell us?'

'Aye.'

'What about the letter you gave him?'

259

For the first time Moffat showed some sign of a human reaction.

'It was found amongst his effects,' Rose continued. 'A letter from Rose Moffat. Left with you, wasn't it?'

'No.'

'Your God approve of lying, does He?'

'You mistake me, Chief Inspector,' Moffat was flustered. 'I speak the truth when I say it was not left with me. I had no contact with that woman. She left a letter with the clockmaker. When he died, the letter was passed to me in the mistaken belief I was her relative. A solicitor insisted I should have it, and that it was my duty to pass it on to this Thomas Griffin should he call here.'

'And that's all?'

'It is.'

'No,' said Auguste, infuriated by Moffat's clipped punctiliousness. 'It is *not* all. What happened when Rose Griffin died? What happened to the cottage and her personal possessions? Your family must have dealt with them, if she had no traceable husband.'

'The cottage did not belong to her.'

'Then to whom did it belong?'

'I do not know. The woman was nothing to me.'

'The boy was. He'd done nothing wrong. Didn't you think you should look after him?'

'He had gone. Run away.'

'On his *own*?'

'I have no knowledge of that.'

'Did you search for him?'

'He was no relative of mine.'

'Her effects, then,' Rose almost spat out.

'There were none.'

'Must have been.'

'It was a long time ago.' Moffat was weakening, Auguste realised with relief. 'A parcel was brought here by the curate of the parish church. I examined it, in case there were matters to do with the Moffat family. There were not. The woman acknowledged her sin and had kept nothing.'

'What happened to these effects?'

'I refused to keep them. I understand the parish church distributed anything that might be useful to the villagers, and destroyed the rest.'

A silence. Rose's face betrayed nothing, but Auguste knew him well enough to see that Egbert was as frustrated and maddened as he. There *must* be something else, some other way of reaching the heart of this mystery. And then he realised there was.

'Who erected the gravestone in the churchyard?' he asked. Surely it must have been Tabor – who else?

'I have no idea.'

'You did not pay for it?'

'I did not. I presume the parish did.'

A small country church was hardly likely to have chosen to put *Here lies the rose of the world* as epitaph, Auguste reflected. No, here at last was the link – and a link he was going to think about.

'The kind of chap who could turn you into a hedonist overnight,' Rose remarked as they left. 'Eat, drink and be merry, eh?'

'Talking of drink . . .' Auguste reined in the horse outside the New Inn.

By the time they returned to Settle, another glass of ale seemed an excellent idea, especially if accompanied by the Golden Lion's boiled beef in beer. To find Tatiana already ensconced in a private room completed Auguste's satisfaction.

'The Panhard, Auguste,' his wife informed him excitedly, 'is a wonderful motorcar. It drives at *thirty* miles an hour! Mr Williams, the owner, whom I met at the Ashfield Hotel, says it is a cheerful motorcar, because it sings "tum-tum-tum" as it drives. That's because of the double-cylindered motor. Mr Williams would take us for a drive in it,' she finished innocently.

'Very good of you, Tatiana,' Egbert replied, seeing Auguste's look of mute appeal. 'But we've a few enquiries to make, and I need Auguste's help.'

'Oh.'

Auguste was smitten with guilt at her obvious disappointment. 'Perhaps another time.'

'You would not enjoy it as much as when I drive. But if I go alone with Mr Williams, Mrs Williams insists on coming as chaperone again,' Tatiana explained with some surprise. 'The sound of her knitting needles means I can't listen to the engine properly. Apparently she finds knitting has a calming effect on her nerves in the motorcar. But she is a *terrible* knitter. Mr Williams wears a most strangely shaped waistcoat. Perhaps we should buy a motorcar of our own,' she finished offhandedly.

'*What* was that you said, *mon amour?*' Auguste asked slowly.

'Listen to the engine,' Tatiana repeated. 'The double-cylinder means it has two impulses for every two revolutions of the flywheel instead of only one.'

'No, no,' Auguste broke in. 'Something else.'

'Mrs Williams and her terrible knitting?'

'That was it!' Auguste cried triumphantly.

'Edith's knitting is terrible too, but what is that to do with anything?' Egbert asked.

'When I was with old Nell in Clapham, she told me Rose was a knitter, as she was herself. Old Nell's mother came from Dent. There is a story my mother used to read to me, "The Terrible Knitters of Dent". It is by Southey, I believe. And Egbert,' Auguste's voice rose, 'Amos told me Rose threw haverbread *as good as Nell's*. But I am told haverbread is a speciality of the

Dent area, not of Clapham. Suppose during those missing years Rose Griffin was at Dent? Suppose that's where she had Tom?'

'A lot of supposes.'

'Where did she go after she left Tabor Hall? Back to Wombwell's? Not all the time, because she bore Tom about 1842. She had to be living *somewhere* before she turned up in Clapham.'

'Maybe,' Egbert said dubiously. 'But if the Super hears I've spent time tracking down knitters, he'll have me off the case. Why not follow up the Tom Griffin registrations first?'

'Yorkshire is a long way from your Super, *mon ami*, and Dent is very close to Settle by railway train. And it is *much* closer than Bolton, Ripon or Doncaster.'

Dent railway station might indeed be close to Settle. Dent village is not, as they discovered the following morning. Auguste arranged to hire a cart to drive to the village which was several long, slow, winding miles away. Tatiana had pleaded to come with them, in order to gain further experience of how workers lived. Auguste privately doubted how the workers of Dent would receive this Marxist Mayhew in their midst, and then decided Tatiana's charm would be equal to it.

Dentdale bore little resemblance to the Settle and Malham landscape. The valley was wooded, with cottages that spoke of the softness of the West Country in comparison with their grim sisters on the other side of the moors. The village, when they eventually reached it, was a warren of small cottages, many with women sitting in their doorways knitting. The village had evidently lost none of its skills since Southey's time.

The enticing prospect of registers danced through

Auguste's brain, as they found the church by a small green. In fact, he had almost lost sight of what they hoped to find. Just something, *somewhere*, that might further illumine the lives of Rose Griffin and her son.

The verger was young and enthusiastic. The name Griffin sparked an immediate reaction. Since he himself could only be a product of the late '70s, it must be because he prided himself on his excellent custodianship of his beloved charges, the registers. Auguste's hopes rose. Much was his disappointment therefore when the register the verger produced was the marriage volume. Whatever Griffins' happy nuptials were duly recorded in it, it could not be their Griffin. True, in those early days of registration, churches were often lax about their returns, but since Rose Griffin didn't consider herself married—

'There!'

A triumphant verger's finger pointed amazingly quickly at an entry.

'Eighteen July 1841. Rose Griffin to—' Egbert Rose broke off in startled silence. Auguste craned eagerly over his shoulder.

'Who?' he cried.

'It's the permutation we didn't check. It's not a case of Rose Moffat marrying anyone, it's—'

'Rose Griffin to Thomas Charles Tabor,' Auguste read out triumphantly. 'So they *were* married. Did I not say so?' he crowed.

'Twitch checked Moffats marrying Tabors – but she married under the name of *Griffin*. So either she was married twice, or she adopted that name when she joined Wombwell's – perhaps in case her family came after her. Odd that it was she who gave the false name, while Tabor risked giving his own. He must have told his family about her.'

'Not necessarily, *mon ami*. In those days a village as far from Malham as Dent must have been a different world. Charles Tabor and Rose Griffin's secret would be safe here.'

'Popular this young lady, whoever she was,' the verger remarked chattily, pleased he'd been of help. 'It's the second time in two days someone's been looking for her.'

'Who else was looking for her?' asked Egbert sharply.

'Quality,' was the somewhat smug reply. 'Old lady, she was, for all she came in Higgins' trap.'

'The Dowager?' said Auguste to Egbert.

'Yes. I wouldn't mind betting it was our visit to her that put it in her mind.'

Tatiana was waiting for them outside the church. She had not wasted her time, though Mr Marx might not have approved. Over one arm was, so far as Auguste could judge, her endorsement of capitalist enterprise: a new white shawl, a bright red knitted dress, several tea-cosies with matching egg cosies, and an object which looked suspiciously like a knitted tie for him. She made up for this with her very first remark. 'Granny Higgins is still alive. The trap-driver's mother.'

'I'm glad for him,' said Auguste, unable to see any immediate relevance to their mission.

'She lived next door to Rose,' Tatiana told him reproachfully.

''Course I remember her.' Granny Higgins delved into her youth, as eagerly as a child into a bull's-eye jar. Her cottage was on the outskirts of the village. Beside it was another, in ruins, showing signs of occupation by only the odd tramp. It was derelict and as devoid of atmosphere as a disused barn. If there was information to gather on Rose Griffin, it would be from Granny

Higgins, not the home Rose had once made for her family.

'Rose's husband was one of the quality, wasn't he?' Auguste asked her.

She frowned. 'I don't recall that. 'E spoke different, but he were a sheep salver and clipper and that. Travelled around, 'e did. Away more than 'e were here. But talk about love. And yon babby. Fair doted on him. Often wondered what became of young Tommy.'

They did not enlighten her.

'How long did they live here?'

'Matter of three years, maybe. Yes, it were just before my Harry were born, 1844. "We're going away," says Rose. So sad she looked. "Where be tha going?" I asked, but she wouldn't tell me. "A long way," she said. Very sudden it was. Couldn't afford the rent, most like. Never heard from her again, but I'd not forget her. Not Rose.'

'She must have had other friends in Dent. Would anyone else still know of her?'

'Nay,' Granny Higgins told them complacently. 'Weren't one for mixing, were Rose. Anyway, no one would want to know her, would they?'

'Why not?'

'She were an outcomer, that's why.'

'An outcomer from all of ten miles away,' commented Egbert disgustedly, as they climbed into the trap to drive back to the Ribblesdale valley railway line. 'Makes Highbury look like the family parlour.'

'She had her husband and her baby,' Auguste pointed out. 'Perhaps she was happy. I hope so.'

'The shepherd and his true love in their country cottage,' Egbert said. 'Charles Tabor playing at Arcadia, but sometimes having to go back home to the real world. Question is: which did he like being in best?'

'A Tabor would not stay with a girl from Wombwell's if he did not wish to.'

'Three years seems to have been enough.'

'He tired of her?'

'Or of the country life,' Egbert said sourly, holding his nose as they passed a well-manured field.

'But he was *married* to her,' Auguste puzzled. 'He can't just have left her with the baby. He was his *heir*, after all. What about the estates, the title?'

'*She* doesn't seem to think she was married, not according to the letter she left for young Tom.'

'She knew he had married again. She loved him, my friend.'

'Hm.' Egbert looked dubious. 'Whatever happened,' he pronounced finally, 'it doesn't bode well for the Tabors. And especially one of them.'

In the Lion, Inspector Stitch was waiting for them, aglow with happiness.

'Unexpected pleasure, Stitch,' Rose said suspiciously.

'I thought I'd come myself, sir.' Confidence exuded from every perspiring pore on his face. 'I've had a look at the will, sir. Nothing about Tom Griffins or by-blow sons. *But*,' he flourished a certificate like a rabbit from a magician's hat, 'I found this, sir.'

His superior glanced at it.

'It was my own idea, sir,' Twitch informed him eagerly. 'You asked me to check the marriage certificates for Moffat, so I thought I might as well give Griffin a go too. Just a hunch, sir,' he added modestly.

Rose handed it to Auguste, who looked at it, and tried to keep a straight face: Rose Griffin to Thomas Charles Tabor in July 1841 in Dent Church.

'That's why,' Stitch pontificated, 'we had trouble over Tom Griffin's birth certificate. He wasn't registered as Thomas Griffin but as Thomas Tabor. Born 1842.'

Auguste held his breath as Egbert deliberated on Twitch's fate. It came at last.

'If I still had my hat on, Stitch, I'd eat it.'

'Thank you, sir,' said Twitch modestly.

As the carriage trundled over the rough path towards the grey stone of Tabor Hall, flanked by its protective fells, Auguste tried to rid himself of the feeling that he was a Judas on his way to bring doom to the house under whose roof he had slept. For there seemed no doubt that one of the people with whom he had broken bread (and many of Breckles' delightful recipes) was a murderer. Soon it would be necessary to keep his promise to Tatiana to warn her that an arrest was imminent. She had returned here earlier straight from Dent, pleading a weariness he knew she did not feel.

'The Dowager Lady Tabor, if you please,' Rose instructed Richey.

Richey glanced questioningly at Priscilla, who was bearing down upon him in a bright blue teagown. So must Tom Griffin have seen her, Auguste reflected: formidable, large, and overwhelming.

'It will not be necessary for you to disturb my mother-in-law, Chief Inspector. I will ask Savage to request her to join us later. You may put your questions then.'

'I'd like to see Lady Tabor now.'

'She is—'

'Now,' Rose repeated politely.

'Show the Chief Inspector to my mother's apartments, Richey,' Priscilla yielded.

As usual, however, Miriam was in no need of protection.

'Lady Tabor, how long have you known that your

late husband was already married when you married him?' Rose asked her quietly.

'Since your visit a few days ago, Chief Inspector,' she answered him readily. 'Something you said suggested I should check. Dear Charlie always took the line of least resistance – so like him to gloss over unpleasant facts. Whereas I—' She did not finish the thought, instead saying: 'I had no idea he had had a child, legitimate or otherwise, though I did suspect there had been other women in the past before he met me. Does George know?'

'He knows he might have had an illegitimate brother,' Rose said cautiously. 'How did you get to Dent, ma'am?'

'Savage went with me. It was not an easy journey.' She smiled. 'Nevertheless I am not an invalid, and I was determined to see for myself. I did not wish to discuss the matter with my family, nor have I done.'

'How did you know where to go?' Rose asked mildly. 'I didn't mention Dent.'

'I found out from old Tompkins. Savage brought him to the Hall for me when Walter was out. Wasn't that clever? Perhaps I should have followed your profession, Chief Inspector.'

'I am sorry to be the means of upsetting you, ma'am.'

'It was a long time ago, Chief Inspector. It was indeed a shock,' she admitted, 'but I am recovered now, thank you. You see, I know Charlie loved me and that is all I care about. He was a weak man in some ways, good and kind but easily led. I've no doubt he thought he loved the woman, but in 1844 he met me.' She smiled. 'It was love at first sight, as they say, Chief Inspector. Whatever he felt for that girl must have died from that moment, though I am sure, being Charlie, he would see that the girl and her child did not starve.'

'But she was his *wife*,' Auguste wanted to shout,

'just as you were later.' But how could he point out the appalling truth that Miriam had never been his wife, because Rose did not die until a year after their marriage?

'Now that that poor man's dead, what difference can it make to anyone?' Miriam said, as if reading his thoughts. 'Are you going to have to arrest someone, Chief Inspector?'

'Very soon, ma'am. Will you be strong enough?'

'Very little has upset me for a long time now. Charlie is no longer with me, and beside that, most other things seem rather unimportant.'

There was some delay in gathering the family together in the drawing room. Only Miriam was excused from attending this salmagundy, this dish for which Egbert would assemble his ingredients, and proceed to chop them finely. Firstly it appeared Victoria could not be found. Eventually she was discovered with Mrs Breckles, having a cut finger tended. George was changing for dinner and apparently could not be hurried. A second more peremptory summons had to be sent.

Auguste fidgeted, on tenterhooks now. He and Egbert exchanged few words now that the trail appeared so clear-cut, so obviously pointing to one conclusion.

Gertrude and Cyril were first to appear, closely followed by Laura.

'Mr Carstairs, ma'am,' a parlourmaid announced to her a moment later.

'I trust you do not object to his presence, Chief Inspector,' Laura said drily. 'Although this is going to be a matter for the family, Mr Carstairs still claims he wishes to be part of it, but I fear he will shortly change his mind.'

'I'd like you here, sir.' Rose nodded at him.

Gradually the family including Alexander assembled, Priscilla and George entering last, as if to present a united front. And that, Auguste thought soberly, they were going to need.

'In the early morning of Sunday 29 September, the body of a man was found in the smokehouse here at Tabor Hall,' Rose began, his formality causing Oliver to glance at Auguste uneasily. 'The body was that of Tom Griffin, a travelling showman, whose clothes were later found hidden in the grounds. They had been exchanged for evening clothes, not his own, and his dead body had been manicured, in an attempt to obscure his identity long enough so that those who might most easily identify him would have left the area.'

Auguste looked round as Egbert's even voice continued. Victoria appeared on the verge of tears as though a game had suddenly ceased to be one; her hand was clasped in Alexander's. Gertrude looked brightly interested but Cyril distinctly nervous. That was odd, wasn't it?

'We'll leave the matter of just how and at whose hands he met his death for a moment. Suffice to say that you, the Tabor family, found itself left with a body on its hands at approximately twelve-thirty. The murder probably took place at the time that the noise of the report would be best smothered by the stable clock chiming midnight. The family had to think quickly, and came up with the solution of changing the victim's clothes and sprucing him up; probably it was meant only as a temporary measure until the body could be otherwise disposed of. It would hardly have been safe to attempt to bury the body in the grounds that night, or to smuggle it out, with extra police and guards on watch due to the King's presence. For the same reason I don't believe it was a premeditated crime. The suit presented a problem, since one belonging to a member of the family or a guest would instantly be missed by the valet responsible.'

'It wasn't mine,' cried Cyril defensively.

'No,' Rose agreed. 'We think it was one that had belonged to the late Lord Charles Tabor.'

'None of those was missing,' said Laura quickly. 'Savage told me.'

'So she might have, Miss Laura. But Miss Savage is devoted to her mistress and the Tabor family.'

'Are you suggesting my mother-in-law sneaked down in the middle of the night and murdered this man?' Priscilla asked icily.

'I'm telling you I believe one of your father-in-law's suits disappeared. You, the Tabor family, realised you could not leave labels inside which would easily be traced to the late Lord Tabor. Nor could they simply be ripped out, thus betraying something was out of the ordinary. It was important that every detail should look as correct as possible to mislead us on the dead man's background. False labels therefore had to be stitched quickly into the pockets of the jacket and waistcoat, on the shirt, etc. That task was, I fancy, given to Miss Laura and Miss Victoria.'

Laura's face betrayed nothing save mild interest. Victoria's flushed bright red.

'The hair and beard had to be trimmed, the fingernails and hands manicured,' Rose continued. 'All at high speed in case lights in the smokehouse, however dim, or lanterns moving on the path should be noticed. It was just over two hours later that Mr Alexander and Mrs Didier came across the body by chance, thinking it was someone who was after the blood of Mr Didier.'

Auguste's stomach took an unpleasant lurch. Gregorin leapt agilely from the back to the forefront of his mind and was firmly sent back again.

'It was a remarkable achievement looked at dispassionately,' Rose finished. 'Great organisation and clear thinking were needed. Bloodstains, for example, had to appear on the suit, for which purpose, if I'm right, pig's blood was taken from the kitchens. Some of the original blood had to be removed from the carpet, in order that a fiction of suicide might be maintained.'

There was dead silence as seven mask-like Tabor faces stared politely at Chief Inspector Rose. They might have been listening to a travelling entertainer, not to a Scotland Yard detective all but accusing them of being at the very least accessories to murder, a crime which could carry a penalty of ten years' penal servitude.

'You have a fanciful imagination, Chief Inspector.' Priscilla took up her usual role of spokeswoman. 'It is a *tour de force* to recreate so vividly two such busy hours in the life of – I think you intimated – my sister-in-law Laura.'

'Oh, it wasn't one person,' Rose rejoined. 'That wouldn't have been possible. I believe you were all working together.'

A cry from Gertie. 'It wasn't me!'

'Except Mrs Gertrude Tabor, I should have said,' Rose continued unruffled. 'I don't think she was involved with this business at all. The rest of you were all very helpful in providing us with red herrings, just serious enough to deflect our attention from the truth. Mr Cyril Tabor's suit was the last of these – a risk on your part since it pointed, falsely, to one particular member of the family.'

'Might I ask,' Priscilla came in heavily, '*why* we were all going to such lengths to disguise the identity of this man, or are you accusing us of murdering him as well?'

273

'I'm coming to that,' said Rose. 'Unless you feel inclined to take over, Lady Tabor?'

Priscilla apparently didn't.

'Whatever document you may have made Tom Griffin sign, and even if he *believed* himself to be illegitimate, you knew different, didn't you? You knew that the late Lord Tabor's marriage to the present Dowager was invalid because he was already married to Rose Griffin, who did not die until 1847. Therefore you, Lord Tabor, Mr Tabor and Miss Tabor, were illegitimate. The title and estates belonged to Tom Griffin, whether he knew that when he called here or not. Nothing could preserve you from ruin if he ever found out he was legitimate. Did your father tell you about the marriage, Lord Tabor, or did you only find out after Tom Griffin called here in August, and you did a little bit of investigation? For some reason Rose Griffin thought her marriage not valid, and therefore that Tom was illegitimate, but there's no doubt it was. You had reason for murder all right. To do you justice, you might even have wanted Tom Griffin out of the way to spare the Dowager the shock of learning of her husband's misdeeds at her time of life.'

Auguste noticed a swift look between George and Priscilla. So Egbert was near the truth. Nothing convinced him of it so much, however, as the utter silence of the Tabors. Only Oliver showed emotion, but what emotion it was, Auguste could not be sure.

'So where have we got to?' Rose continued. 'The marriage of Thomas Charles Tabor to Rose Griffin in 1841 meant that the Tabor estates rightfully belonged to Tom Tabor, or Griffin as he called himself, since he was born legally in 1842, as we now know. With Tom's death the estates pass, I believe, *not* to you, Lord Tabor, since you are illegitimate, but to Tom's line. He had no direct heirs, so it reverts to the line of Charles

Tabor's brothers, and failing that, to the line of *his* father's brothers. Very remote. And no one would ever find out if Griffin were dead, would they? There was a reasonable chance he would never be missed, certainly that he could never be linked to you. Of course, by that time he had bought a thumping great roundabout which, for all you know, might have been left sitting there in the middle of Settle. But luck was with you. And against Tom Griffin.'

'Let me be clear of your meaning, Chief Inspector,' Priscilla said steadily. 'You seem to be accusing our family of murder now. Why? You have invented a wonderful story. Do you have proof that one of us committed murder? Or are we merely discussing possibilities?'

'You'll know the answer when we make an arrest,' Rose told her shortly.

Priscilla smiled. It was a challenge to battle, thought Auguste, both fascinated and repelled; the smile of one who understood her opponent and was confident of victory. 'So you have no proof,' she said. 'Suppose, for the sake of argument, this strange story about our conspiracy in the middle of the night were true? What would you propose to do? Arrest the whole family?'

Checkmate, Auguste thought to himself. The jelly that refused to jell. There was no way Egbert could arrest the whole family. He needed to single out one from the others, and he could not yet do so. He had obviously been hoping for the united front to crack, but it had not done so.

'I thought not. Even had we such a strong motive as you outline, Chief Inspector, your case is laughable without proof. Now I regret I have to disappoint you: there *is* no such motive.'

'And how's that, Lady Tabor?' Rose asked.

'We have no such motive.'

275

'What my wife is trying to tell you, Chief Inspector,' George took up the colours, 'is that my father was *not* married to this Rose girl. The marriage was invalid. This Tom Griffin came here in August believing he was illegitimate and he was. This marriage is a red herring of your own, Chief Inspector. It is true my father went through a form of marriage with the girl, and possibly believed it valid at the time, but it was not. The marriage was not known to his parents and when my grandfather discovered it two years later, he disabused my father of any notion that it was valid. When my father later married my mother, he therefore never burdened her with the pain of telling her about this boyish foolishness.

'You will have noticed my late arrival at this meeting,' he continued gruffly. 'The reason is that, thanks to you, I had to explain all this unfortunate business to my mother, who was badgering me to know all the details. I gather she discovered about Rose Griffin through you, Chief Inspector, and I was able to relieve her mind greatly as to the validity of her marriage. It had been an enormous shock to her, though she might not have let you see that. She is a lady of the old school.'

'I trust you are satisfied with the result of your meddling, Chief Inspector?' Priscilla used her most glacial voice.

'When did you first hear about Rose Griffin, sir?' Rose was impervious to ice and fire.

'My father told me about the entanglement when he was getting on in years, merely because there had been a son, and he feared there might be trouble if he ever approached the family. As indeed there has been,' George added crossly.

'Why did your father believe the marriage invalid?'

'For two reasons. Both my father and the girl were

minors, and swore falsely that they had obtained the consent of their parents. They had not. The marriage was thus invalid, not only on that score, but also because the girl had given a false name. She was married under the name of Griffin, whereas her real name was Moffat. My grandfather had naturally investigated the matter thoroughly. The girl was provided with a home and a certain amount of money to live on.'

'I trust you now see, Chief Inspector,' said Priscilla simply, 'that your work has brought you full circle. As none of us had any motive to murder the man, it is obvious he met his death, not by murder, but by suicide.'

Chapter Eleven

'It adds up.' Rose poured himself some more coffee.

'Like a butler's accounts,' protested Auguste crossly. 'It is *too* accurate.'

'Be blowed to that. Tabor marries the girl and plays at part-time shepherds and shepherdesses in Dent, but, in 1844, the family finds out and there's all hell to pay. They convince him the marriage is invalid. By that time he's met Miriam, and is only too eager to see the folly of his youthful ways. So he or the father sets the girl up in a cottage in Clapham, and breathes a deep sigh of relief.' Egbert contemplated the coffee, provided by the hospitality of the Tabors. It moved him not at all. 'One of them did it, of course, but which of them? Or are you backing Priscilla's suicide theory?'

'How could it be suicide in view of the post mortem report?' A procession of Tabors marched before Auguste's eyes, headed by Miriam, with Priscilla, George, Victoria, Alfred, Cyril and Laura solidly behind her. Somewhere at the end of the line a breathless Gertie struggled to keep up, but he quickly dismissed her. It couldn't have been Gertie. On the other hand, it couldn't have been any of the others either. Not people he *knew* and, he realised with a sinking heart, *liked*. Detection was easier from behind the green baize door.

'Fancy a visit to see the registrar?'

'We are to be married, Egbert?' Auguste tried hard.

'Very funny. Breakfast ain't a time for jokes.'

'Yes, I will come.' Tatiana had an appointment with a petrol engine, and the prospect of a day on tenterhooks did not appeal.

What they learned from the Settle sub-district registrar, however, depressed him further. The gas had now been turned so high that the *pot-au-feu* must surely boil over. He, a mere *sous-chef* in this, could do nothing to prevent what must now happen.

'Do you forgive me, darling?' Victoria looked scared.

A pause. 'No. Not when there's murder involved.'

'But it was suicide,' she wailed. 'Mother is right and the police are wrong. That horrible man came back that night claiming he was the legal heir, that he'd been misled. Father told him he wasn't and proved it, so he shot himself. What other explanation could there be?'

Victoria looked defenceless and beautiful, but Alexander still remained unable to leap the gulf. 'Perhaps,' he said noncommittally.

'You still want to marry me, don't you?'

Thus forced, Alexander ran through the scenario that might lie ahead: an alliance with a family more likely than not to harbour a murderer. But did he believe *Victoria* guilty of murder? The idea was ludicrous, of course. Wasn't it?

'Yes, I do.'

'Laura.' Oliver appeared unexpectedly from the library, catching her arm as she returned from breakfasting. 'I need to talk to you.'

With obvious reluctance, she allowed herself to be shepherded into the library and the door to be firmly closed behind them. 'What is it?' There was a note of defiance in her voice.

'I would like you to marry me.'

She opened her mouth to speak, but he forestalled her. 'I don't know what's happening here, and I know you can't tell me. What is obvious is that it isn't over yet, but that it's coming to a head.'

Laura flinched, but her voice was steady enough. 'What has that to do with you and me, Oliver?'

'Old-fashioned though it may sound, you will need my protection in what is to come. I want to be able to give it to the best of my ability.'

'Protection?' she echoed lightly. 'What an odd word.'

'You know well why I use it.'

She steadied herself. 'Oliver, I am grateful to you for your concern, but I cannot marry you, or even be affianced to you. Not now.'

At last Egbert re-emerged from the room in which he had been closeted with Cobbold. 'Fancy a pint, Auguste?'

There was nothing Auguste fancied less, but obviously Egbert had more in mind than refreshment. The *sous-chef* was rising in status.

The Golden Lion's private room was warm and welcoming after the police station, and the hot punch Auguste had chosen in preference to ale even more so.

'It all points one way, Auguste. You know that.'

'But the evidence . . .'

'The motive, Auguste. That marriage was as valid as yours and Tatiana's. The tale they spun us about the false names was true enough, but the marriage would only be invalid if both parties knew that a false name was being used. Charles Tabor did not: he thought Griffin was Rose's real name, not knowing that she assumed it when she left home to join Wombwell's Menagerie. We can prove that now from Wombwell's books, which show that a Rose Griffin worked there from June '37 to September '39. Rose Moffat ceased to be from the moment she saw those animals. And the change of law in 1822 meant that though Rose and Charles were minors, they could only be fined for having falsely declared that their parents' consent had been given. No, the Dowager's marriage was bigamous all right. Hard for her, discovering it after all this time, poor lady. But not,' he added, draining the glass, 'for our villains. They knew all the time.'

'But one thumbprint, Egbert?'

'Or a wife with gloves.'

'Which?'

'We'll soon know.'

'He is of the old school, Egbert. He would not allow his wife to take the risk of murder.'

'Our Priscilla not only plans, she acts. She's the Lady Macbeth of Yorkshire, Auguste. She'd decided the honour of the Tabors rested with her to defend.'

Don't underestimate George, Auguste heard the Dowager say again. But wasn't that just what they were doing?

'The landlord told me you were here.' Tatiana swept in, flushed and pink from the fresh air. 'I've just had an oatcake in the Thistlethwaite tearoom, but I seem to be hungry—' She broke off, seeing their glum faces. 'What is the matter?' she asked sharply.

'It is near, Tatiana,' Auguste told her.

'Ah. Can you—?'

'No,' he answered wretchedly.

'When?'

'Late this afternoon,' Egbert said gruffly. 'When I've spoken to the Chief Constable.'

'I should like,' Tatiana said to Auguste, after Egbert had left, 'to know more about Rose and Tom. I think it would help . . . when it happens. Would you come with me to Clapham? I could drive you, *ma mie*,' she added hopefully. 'Mr Williams has loaned me the Panhard.'

It was only as Auguste climbed into the Panhard that he realised to his amazement that he had not even demurred at the prospect.

The motorcar was left in the appreciative care of the landlord of the Clapham New Inn, and they followed Amos' directions. Where else to feel close to Rose Griffin than in her cottage? It was not easy to find. They walked through the village and towards the Ingleborough Cave. The pathway leading to the cottage, off the main track, was overgrown through disuse, as Amos had warned them, but a large stick and determination finally succeeded, after several twists and turns and one or two blind alleys, in bringing them to a ruined stone cottage of fair size.

They stared at it in some disappointment. What had he expected? Auguste wondered. A home, hidden from decay for nearly sixty years?

Tatiana pushed through the half-rotten wooden door. 'If the cottage belonged to the Tabors, perhaps they wished simply to forget about it, as they did Rose.'

A bird, alarmed, flew squawking out of a large hole in the roof. Inside was only damp, decay and a few pieces of broken furniture. Leaves had rotted in piles in the corners, woodland animal life had claimed the cottage for its own. Half-burnt, fungus-covered logs still lay on the hearth, a copper dolly-mop lay tarnished and cobwebbed in what passed for a kitchen.

This was the home where a girl had faced the ruins of her life, deserted by the man she had married for love, Auguste thought sadly. Or had she been so deserted? Did Charles visit her here? Charles had told her their marriage was invalid, but did she refuse to see him again? Or demand to regularise their marriage? No, not Rose. In any case, by that time Charles had met Miriam. Rose lived on in a humble cottage, not even her own; all she could boast for herself and her legally born son. She had been deprived even of the knowledge that he *was* legally born. Forced to knit and work on clocks for a livelihood to support herself and her son. The son who had turned out to be an aggressive blackmailer.

'She's not here, is she?' Tatiana said quietly.

'No.' He walked outside and breathed the fresh cool air with relief. The track wound on past the cottage even further into the wood, already covered with early falling leaves. Not quite knowing why, he turned that way, with Tatiana following, as he pushed aside branches and bracken. Several times there were cross paths, causing him to stop to consider which way to go.

'Why are we coming along here?' Tatiana asked curiously but uncomplainingly, as brambles caught at her skirts.

'I wanted to see where it goes.'

'Might Rose be at the end?'

'Only her cow. It's just a footpath to the pasture.' Auguste felt cheated, as the path emerged on to the open fell. Then at the bottom he saw a track, suitable for horse traffic if not for Panhards. 'If we turn left it should bring us to the village,' Auguste declared, with the lofty relief of one who had known his way all along. The track in fact led on to the main Settle to Ingleton road, but a branch line brought them back to the head of the village and the church.

'Come and look at Rose Griffin's grave.' He took Tatiana by the hand.

'Poor Rose,' said Auguste at last, as they stood before it. 'No "beloved wife of", no "dearly beloved mother of". And she must have had such dreams when she married Charles Tabor in Dent Church.'

'"Here lies the rose of the world"' Tatiana translated

softly. 'That does not seem to me the epitaph given by a man who did not love his true wife.'

'A man driven by guilt.'

'Perhaps. Yet I think, Auguste, that Rose is here, nevertheless.'

'This is intolerable.' There was no heart in Priscilla's protest as she tried vainly to protect her Valhalla against Scotland Yard, the Yorkshire Constabulary and Auguste Didier. Awaiting them in the formal drawing room was the whole Tabor family.

'I said just you and his Lordship, ma'am, when I telephoned,' Egbert pointed out.

'We are a family. All its members and those to be part of it must be present,' she replied.

'Very well, ma'am. If that's how you wish it.'

The Dowager was present, Savage of course by her side, and even Gertie apparently counted as a member of the family today. She winked when she saw Auguste, then subsided as Priscilla's eye fell on her.

The Last Stand of the Tabors, Auguste thought, looking at the set faces: Victoria and Alexander, Oliver and Laura – not sitting together, he noticed – Cyril and Gertie, Alfred (subdued to the point of conventionality), George and Priscilla.

They listened in silence as Egbert demolished the theory of the invalid marriage. Only Oliver showed any surprise, glancing worriedly at Laura. The Dowager sat, hands folded neatly in her lap, inured to shock.

'The marriage between Rose Griffin and Charles Tabor *was* valid,' he finished, addressing the family as a whole, 'and I'm sure you all knew it to be so. You wouldn't have let a matter like that go unchecked. You invited Tom Griffin to return that night – it had to be then for he probably told you it was the *only* night he'd

285

be in Settle – in order to get rid of him for good. We can prove the clothes were changed by you. For what other reason than that one or more of you had committed the murder?'

The 14th Baron Tabor rose to his feet. 'Touché, Chief Inspector.'

'No, George.' Priscilla's cry was heartrending and terrible.

'My dear, I have no choice.' George turned to her gently, taking her hands and holding them to him. It was the first sign of warmth that Auguste had seen between them.

'No. I will not let you.' Each word seemed pumped out.

'You *will*.'

Everyone seemed to be shouting at once. Laura's voice was the strongest: 'No, George!' Alfred was sobbing, youthful arrogance gone. Cyril, bleating, 'I say . . .' Gertie inexplicably crying, 'No.' In the end Priscilla's deep voice prevailed.

'There is one aspect you have not considered, Chief Inspector.' She sounded the calmest of them all. Yet the tiger was at bay.

'That is, ma'am?'

'We *believed* the marriage to be invalid, whether it was or not.'

'You were worried enough to tell Griffin to come back, fearing you hadn't got rid of_him for good in August. Or did he come back of his own accord, having heard the King was here, in the hope of blackmailing you further? At any rate, you were frightened enough to kill him.'

She did not give an inch. 'You have no evidence that we knew the marriage to be valid. On the contrary, I can offer strong proof that the family firmly believed it invalid both at the time and since.'

'And what proof might that be?'

'This Rose Griffin died in 1847.'

'Priscilla!' There was a warning note in George's voice.

She ignored it. 'My late father-in-law—' she began.

'One moment, Priscilla.' The Dowager tried to interrupt, but Priscilla overrode her.

'George told me my father-in-law paid for the woman's funeral and tombstone. Do you think if he had known then that his earlier marriage was valid he would not have taken steps to rectify the situation by legitimising his marriage to my mother-in-law? Would it not have been somewhat *careless* of him to overlook that detail?'

If Rose was thrown he showed no sign of it. 'He might not have realised it was necessary, or might not have wanted to cause you pain, ma'am.' A compassionate look at the Dowager, acknowledged by a slight incline of her head.

'Both highly unlikely, Chief Inspector. To me it is obvious that he regarded the marriage as invalid. That was what he later told you, was it not, George?'

'Yes,' George said unemotionally. 'He had had the devil of a row with his father, of course.'

'Charles Tabor just accepted that his marriage was invalid without checking?' said Rose incredulously.

'It may seem strange to you, Chief Inspector, in this modern age. My grandfather, however, was a hot-tempered man. It was hard to contradict him. You have to remember this was a small country district. People weren't as aware then of the minutiae of the legal system as they are today.'

'I do find it hard to believe that the heir to the Tabor estates was quite such a simpleton, Lord Tabor. Moreover, even if you are correct, there was plenty of time for *you* to check into the legalities after Griffin's first visit to you, or indeed at any time since you were told the story.'

George looked steadily at him. 'I had no reason to check my father's story. Why should I? It was all over long ago. And as for checking Griffin's story when he came to us, again why should I? He made no claim to legitimacy. We paid him off, and had no reason to summon him here again.'

'Are you now convinced you have no proof against my husband, Chief Inspector?' There was triumph in Priscilla's voice.

'Far from it, Lady Tabor. I have proof against all of you and, if it comes to it, I'll arrest you all on the charge of being accessories to murder. *Now*, Lord Tabor, will you speak?'

George rose to his feet again. He did not look at Priscilla or the rest of his family. 'Very well, Chief Inspector, I am ready to come with you.'

'No, Lord Tabor. You know that's not what I want.'

'But—' His appalled look slid to Priscilla, who sat stiffly, her face betraying nothing save exhaustion.

'I think it is I you wish to question, is it not, Inspector? George is very good in coming forward to protect me, but I cannot of course permit him to do so.' His sister stood up, her face made even paler by the dull grey dress she wore.

'Laura!' Oliver cried in anguish. 'What are you saying?'

A slight smile. 'You see how right I was to insist you would wish to have nothing to do with me, Oliver. You would not have liked to have been married to a murderess, would you?'

As Egbert Rose got to his feet, Priscilla's guard slipped. Her face crumpled and for a moment Auguste saw the woman Tatiana had told him existed beneath the mask. A woman in despair.

288

Laura turned to Oliver as Rose led her from the room. 'It was Robert,' she told him calmly. 'It always was.'

'You may think of me as a passionless woman, Chief Inspector,' Laura Tabor said, in the small airless room at the police station. 'I assure you I am not. Or, rather, I am, save in one respect – and that was, and is, Robert Mariot. I was no mere girl when we parted; I was mature, the pain was the greater. We parted through his wish, not through mine. I did not care about my social position, but unfortunately he cared about it on my behalf. His pride was offended by my late father's rebuff – ironic, is it not, in view of his own involvement with a village girl? Robert was too proud to ask my own views. He left and naturally I believed that he did not love me.

'A year or two ago I discovered the truth, and that, wonderfully, he still cared for me and was unmarried. Yet *still* his stubborn pride kept us apart. He told me he would come to me when the current expedition was over. By then, he judged – how foolish men are – that he would have made a sufficient name for himself to appease my family. He meant it, and I was overjoyed.'

'Are you telling me, miss, that you thought the man in the smokehouse was Robert Mariot?' Rose demanded. Surely they couldn't be back at the beginning again, after all this?

'Not when I *saw* him,' Laura said impatiently. 'But Robert was an impetuous romantic – and twenty years ago we used to meet at midnight in the smokehouse, Chief Inspector,' she told him, a faint flush animating her usually pale cheeks.

'I understand.'

'I heard from Robert on the Friday that the King was due to arrive. He told me he was in England and I could expect to see him very soon. I was so excited, and when I saw the light in the smokehouse at the hour at which we used to meet I thought . . . I hoped . . .' Her voice faltered. 'But it wasn't him. I had no idea who it was. He lunged at me, when I told him my name, and put his arms round me. I was his sister, he shouted, his odious breath on me. He'd found out he was legitimate, and had come back to claim his inheritance, or he would shout the truth out under the King's window. I thought he was a madman, a lunatic – Priscilla and George had not told me of his earlier visit. He was repellent, not just because he was dirty, but because he was aggressive, sly, violent. I told him he was no brother of mine, nor ever would be. He took it badly.'

'So you killed him?'

'No.' Laura was shocked. 'Not for that, Chief Inspector. He attacked me.' Her voice dropped. 'He said if I wasn't his sister, he'd have me in another way.'

Auguste, listening quickly in the corner with Cobbold, shivered. The truth at last, and how different to everything he had imagined.

'He lunged at me, tore my dress . . . I broke away . . . He came after me, pulling at my skirts – it was shaming, terrifying. He tried to push me on to the floor, but I caught a chair and wriggled free and—'

'And then?'

'I saw the gun lying on the mantelpiece.'

'Ah.'

'George had left it there by mistake earlier that day after finishing off an animal in distress. I seized it, and the man came at me again to take it from me. We struggled, then suddenly he pushed me away to take me by surprise and make me trip. I did, but as I staggered backwards and fell, the gun went off. I didn't mean to kill him . . .' She covered her face. 'It was terrible.'

'Did you get blood on your clothes?'

'One or two splashes, but most missed me as I fell. I got to my feet, and saw he was quite dead. It was an accident,' she pleaded, 'so I went back to the house to tell George to call the police. But then he and Priscilla told me who the man was . . . It was a terrible shock. They took charge – with my full agreement,' she emphasised. 'The man was a villain. No harm would be done in obscuring his identity. How I managed to get through I don't know.' Her voice trembled, and her hands were twisting and turning on her lap, Auguste noticed.

'She'll get off, of course,' Egbert said as they left after charging her. 'No jury would convict after that.' He sighed. 'That's something to tell the Tabors.'

'And Tatiana,' Auguste thought to himself, in this, at least, relieved.

She listened in appalled silence in the quiet of their room. Then, as he finished, she said quietly, 'How unhappy Rose would have been to learn that Tom descended to such behaviour, Auguste. She must have hoped for a better life for him, although her own life had turned out so tragic. Charles Tabor called her Rosa Mundi, the rose of the world, but she had little cause to bloom in her life. I tell you, Auguste, women are chained in marriage, victims of the men they are chosen by.'

'Or whom they choose.'

'Yes, but what choice did Rose really have? And Laura Tabor – did she have any choice? Her sweetheart put his own honour and stubborn pride before her, although he claimed to love *her*. Things must change, Auguste.'

291

'Are you my victim?' Auguste asked, somewhat alarmed.

She looked at him seriously. 'No, and I shall not be Society's either. Do you mind?'

'No.'

'Good. I have decided to be a motor engineer.'

'*What?*' He goggled at her.

Tatiana's eyes twinkled. 'You said the other day we could buy a motorcar.'

'I did *what?*'

'I asked if we could buy one, and you said nothing. That means you agreed.'

'Buying is one thing and working as an engineer is another,' her husband said logically.

'Would you buy an oven and not cook in it?'

'*Non,*' he conceded.

'So you may cook and detect, and I shall mend motorcars.'

'Where?' Were they to live in Yorkshire for ever?

'In London.'

Auguste's imagination ran riot: Queen Anne's Gate? Mayfair? Buckingham Palace? He put in a last plea. 'But you began life as a princess. What of your position in Society?'

'It is the same under a car as at the opera.'

'Perhaps.'

'So that's settled. I will obey the rules of Society, then push them aside.'

'And me? You promised to obey me. You will push me to one side also?'

'*Non.* For you would never order me to do what I do not wish.'

'*Ma mie,* you are as tactful a woman as you are perfect.'

'Like poor Rose. Like poor Laura. Neither had the chance to show their love. But I am lucky. I have been granted it. So let me show you . . .'

Ideas, faces, emotions . . . All began to come together, fighting for recognition, but Auguste would not let them in. The night was before him, and so was Tatiana.

Auguste woke up with a start. In fragmented dreams, a cottage track led to the churchyard, to Rose Griffin's epitaph. Breckles' hen crawed loudly throughout. Edith's sister's middle child danced up and down with a piece of string. Twitch stealthily pursued a green elf. Behind him marched two Tom Griffins: one to Clapham churchyard, the other to admire a nude lady bouncing on a bed. Now the jigsaw came together. There *were* two Tom Griffins. One was the Tom that Blackboots had known, the other the aggressive blackmailer described by the Tabors. Did they tally? No. There was only one Tom, but which was it?

At last he felt he understood Rose Griffin. He had to see Egbert immediately. Then he remembered Egbert had stayed overnight in Settle. Quickly he dressed, and descended to the breakfast room where he found George, who stared at him as if he had forgotten who he was. He shrugged when Auguste asked to be driven to Settle, as if events were out of his control.

As the carriage jolted over the fells, Auguste remembered what the Dowager had said: '*All Tabor women are good shots.*' Had the shot in the eye that killed Tom Griffin been such an accident on Laura's part after all?

Chapter Twelve

The Dowager Lady Tabor sat in her straight-backed chair looking out towards the fell called Willy's Brow, bright in the late afternoon sun. She did not move as they came in, her fragile hand still rested on the arm of her chair, and Savage still sat at her side. Miriam greeted them, as if she had been expecting their visit.

'You've released poor Laura?'

'No, ma'am.'

'I am so glad you have come too, Mr Didier.' Miriam smiled at him. 'It is pleasant to have friends to support one at such times.'

Auguste stumbled out a reply, but she did not wait to hear it.

'I really did have no idea that Charles had married that girl, Chief Inspector.'

'Then why did you murder her, ma'am?'

For a moment the impression of fragility vanished, jolted from her by the unexpectedness of the attack. The real emotions of Miriam Tabor flashed forth like venom. Auguste shuddered, even as they were speedily reinterred.

'Did I?' she asked vaguely. 'It was all so long ago.'

'Not *so* very long ago, ma'am. You were interested enough in the old times to go to check the parish register at Dent. If it hadn't been for that, I wouldn't have believed you didn't know about the marriage. As it is, I can't see why you needed to kill Rose Griffin.'

'Can't you?' Hardness entered her voice. *'Can't* you?' Savage half rose to her feet, but Miriam waved her impatiently aside.

'I am an old woman in body, Savage, but still young in my heart. I *can* remember why. I killed Rose Griffin because I hated her, Chief Inspector, and I hate her still. It was clever of you to realise she was murdered. Or is it Mr Didier I have to thank?' Her gaze rested almost in amusement on Auguste.

'Why did you hate her, Lady Tabor?' he asked gently. 'Where did you meet her?'

'The day I went to her cottage, believing her merely my husband's mistress. In fact, it seems, *I* was the mistress. What a quaint thought.' She laughed, the sound tinkling out over the still room. 'I had come to make friends, I said, and the foolish girl believed me. I said I wanted to meet her little son, and she called him in from the patch of garden outside. She must come to the Hall and bring him along, I said, to meet his new little brother George. *The boy looked like Charlie*. And you ask why I hated her!'

'But he had married *you*, or so you believed. You had nothing to fear, just because he once loved this girl,' said Auguste, puzzled.

'*Once* loved? I hated her because he went on loving her. I thought she was just a peasant girl he was amusing himself with, while I was waiting for my baby to arrive. I followed Charlie one day. He was very careful; he didn't go through the village but along the track leading to Ingleton, then up a footpath through the woods. But when I saw the boy, I realised that he'd known the slut for years.'

'Many men have had mistresses, ma'am, without their wives turning to murder,' Egbert said steadily.

'He still loved her, although he had *me*. I could not forgive that,' Miriam answered, as if in surprise that

296

they could not understand. 'I went home and that night I told him I knew. He broke down, the fool, and told me he'd make me a good husband, but he'd always loved this Rose person, and would have married her if he could. Even then he was betraying me. He *had* married her. Oh, he loved me in a fashion, no doubt, after the girl was dead. But even then she came between us. There was always the memory of that boy. I had meant to kill him too.'

Auguste shivered. The face that he had thought fragile, now displayed only the iron will of ruthlessness, any sensitivity merely for herself.

'I went to see her several times. Took her bonbons and sweetmeats – all quite innocent. And then I took some that weren't. They were full of hemlock. She'd share them with the child and they'd both die – that's what I wanted. But the child wasn't there. She said he'd gone to visit someone, and she looked so triumphant, I feared she guessed what I'd intended. But she died all the same. Charlie was mad with grief. He found out that she'd died when he slipped off to visit her one day. He came back sobbing. All he could discover about the boy was that someone had come to take him away before Rose died. He was never found.' Satisfaction oozed from the voice that had once seemed charming.

'Until the boy found *you*,' Egbert pointed out, 'over fifty years later. He came here asking for "her Ladyship", meaning you, though we took it to be your daughter-in-law.'

'He was as big a fool as his mother. Yes, he told me he was Charlie's bastard, but that he didn't want anything except to meet his family. He showed me a letter, though there was nothing about a marriage in it. Then George came bursting in with Priscilla, wanting to know what it was all about. He told them,

297

beaming all over his ugly face. They made this agreement to buy him off. But they didn't know I'd already planned to kill him. "Come along when the family party is on," I'd already told him. "His Majesty will be here. We'll give the family a big surprise and introduce you at midnight." The stupid fool wanted to know if he'd have to dress up and I told him not to worry about clothes as he'd have to climb over a wall because the gates would be guarded, so I would lend him some of Charlie's. I showed him from the window where the smokehouse was and told him to come there just before midnight and I'd escort him to the house and introduce him to the King. The idiot thought it a wonderful idea.'

'So you admit it was also you who killed Tom Tabor and not your daughter?'

There was a pause. Auguste felt sickened at the calculations clearly running through her mind, indecision shown on her face.

'Let me make it simple for you, ma'am,' Egbert continued. '*You* killed him. Your daughter was merely trying to protect you. Like your whole family has been doing ever since you returned to the house and no doubt told Savage what you'd done.'

Savage stared at him unblinking, unmoved.

Miriam said nothing, merely smiled.

'We know now your daughter is lying about what happened that night. Mr Didier was looking at a certain piece of art in the smokehouse earlier in the evening and is ready to swear there was no gun on the mantelpiece beneath.'

The Dowager gazed first in undisguised contempt, then with something like amusement. She shrugged those delicate shoulders.

'I had to kill him,' she said at last. 'He was *hers*, and after all he'd only escaped by chance all those years ago. I left the dance, and instead of going upstairs to where dear Savage would be waiting, I went to the gun room, took the Webley and hid it in the smokehouse until that terrible man arrived. I shot him at precisely twelve o'clock, dropped the gun and came back.'

'How did you get in again, ma'am? The doors were locked.'

'I was once the chatelaine of this house, Chief Inspector; I have a key. I told dear Savage what I had done of course,' she did not even glance at her, 'and she insisted on going straight to Priscilla. I was extremely annoyed. I daresay you meant it for the best,' she added kindly to Savage. 'I went to bed, and I understand Priscilla and Savage between them concocted some plan to obscure the truth. I believe Savage then woke poor Laura, and rooted out poor Victoria and Alfred. Didn't you, Savage?'

'If you say so, my lady.'

'So that's all. I couldn't let him live, could I?' Miriam was confident of their understanding. 'I think – if I might sleep here tonight, I shall be ready for you in the morning, Chief Inspector.'

Egbert looked at her steadily. 'Very well, ma'am. If that's the way you wish it.' As they left, the quiet was broken by a terrible sound. Not from Miriam. The harsh raucous sobs were Savage's.

Yet again Auguste was chilly and unable to sleep. He drew back the curtains, feeling the rush of cold air on his body, and hurriedly shut the window. Outside a cat howled, the trees were dark against the sky, bushes appeared as black indiscernible shapes. The cat yowled again. Auguste firmly drew the curtains, shutting out the menace of the outside world, and climbed back into bed, putting his arm round his sleeping wife. He dozed fitfully, dreaming of fleeing figures, one of which was himself, bounding across the limestone crags of the top of Malham Cave. Before him was Tatiana, arms outstretched, behind him . . .

He woke up with a jump. The curtains were drawn back, daylight streaming in, and Tatiana, dressed in a wrap, was standing over him.

'Wake up, Auguste. She's dead. Egbert wants to see you.'

No need to ask who. He had told Tatiana everything last night. No need to ask if Egbert had suspected this might happen. Some things were better unspoken. Once the ingredients had been added in their correct order, he had seen the truth. Not Tom, but Rose herself came first. And once that had been established, Miriam obviously became the catalyst of the whole tragic story. Moffat had given him the clue and he had not seen its significance: there had been no trace of the boy when Rose's body was found. He could not have run away on his own; he must have been sent away because Rose had feared for his life. Amos had mentioned an outcomer asking for her shortly before her death. Surely it must have been Scarface, come to take the boy? And as for poor Tom, who else would have invited him here and killed him the very night the King was dining? Only Miriam, with her casual disregard for detail in her overwhelming hate. Savage would cope with the detail. The servants would always cope with unpleasant details.

'How?' he asked Egbert, as soon as he had scrambled into his clothes, and burst into Rose's rooms.

Egbert shrugged. 'Sleeping powders. Suffocation,' and as Auguste looked puzzled, added impatiently, 'Do you think Savage would let her stand trial? Or maybe she just died of heart failure. It must have been a shock, after all, to be exposed as a double murderess. The doctor's with her now. *Her* doctor,' he emphasised.

300

'No need to have police doctors in unless we're forced to.'

The last unpleasant detail poor Savage had had to perform.

'Are you quite satisfied with your work, Chief Inspector?' Priscilla, grey-faced and subdued, came into the room.

'Yes, ma'am. We've found out the truth at last.'

'Truth,' retorted Priscilla bitterly. 'What is truth?'

'Facts. You all knew your mother-in-law murdered Thomas Tabor; you were all prepared to protect her even to the point of confessing to the crime yourselves.' Seeing her hesitate, 'This is between us. I haven't the evidence – now – to bring charges. Tom Griffin's death is officially recorded as that of an unknown man, and might stay that way. There's only one outside person who'd know otherwise, apart from Mr Didier and the police.'

'Who?'

'No one who need concern you, ma'am. A travelling showman by the name of Blackboots. And no doubt if he were told he could have Tom's galloper back, he wouldn't be too curious.'

Auguste, watching with interest, saw Blackboots instantly dismissed by Priscilla as a person not worthy of note.

'It'll not occur to him that folks like you could be capable of murder.'

The irony in his voice escaped Priscilla. 'Thank you, Chief Inspector.'

'And now maybe you'll tell me something; if you can, that is. Why didn't your father-in-law marry Rose again after he found out the marriage wasn't valid in '44?'

'He did not know where Rose was,' Priscilla said at last. 'Either she disappeared at her own wish, or his

301

father intervened and set Rose up in that cottage. By the time he tracked her down to Clapham he was married, or so he thought, to Miriam. He upbraided his father for his part in separating him from Rose, and there were terrible quarrels. His father told him nothing further about the validity of the marriage, but when his mother was dying in 1849, it was on her conscience and she told Charles the marriage had been valid, something he had never thought to check in the pain of losing Rose. It is, I suppose,' she sounded surprised, as if considering this for the first time, 'a sad story.'

'It is indeed, ma'am.'

'But that raises another point, Lady Tabor,' Auguste said, puzzled. 'If he knew his marriage to your mother-in-law was invalid, why didn't he marry her once Rose was dead?'

'George was born in March 1847 and the girl did not die until June of that year,' Priscilla told him unemotionally. 'So George would still have been illegitimate. It was not at all certain legally that a subsequent marriage could legitimise him. If my mother-in-law had failed to have another son, there would have been no heir.'

'Except poor Tom Griffin, if he could be found.'

'Charles Tabor made every effort to find him, and failed.'

'Even though he *knew* he was his legal heir?'

'There is more than banquets and balls to an estate and house such as this,' Priscilla replied stiffly after a moment. 'There are obligations which at times sit heavily on the heart. The boy could not be found, and beneath my father-in-law's roof was a child whom the world believed to be his legitimate heir. My father-in-law's will carefully bequeathed such goods as he could leave independently of the entail to George; as regards what passed under the entail he had to take the risk that one day a claimant might turn up.'

'And now the legitimate heir *has* turned up, Lady Tabor?'

'As you said, the body is officially that of an unknown man.' There might have been a note of appeal in her voice.

'Convince me,' said Rose grimly.

'Did Tom Griffin leave issue?'

'Not that we know of.'

'Then George is his nearest relative.'

'His illegitimate half-brother. He might be entitled to the chattels of the estate. And poor Tom's galloper. But the estate and title would never pass to him, isn't that so?'

Priscilla went white. 'Yes,' she whispered, her first sign of weakness.

'Then what are you going to do?'

'His Majesty the King—'

'Wouldn't touch it and you know it.'

Priscilla steadied herself. '*Cui bono*, Chief Inspector? Who profits by it if we are ruined? Charles' one brother left no sons. His father was an only son. Do we have to torture ourselves further?'

'Fortunately it's not my business, ma'am,' Rose told her. 'Murder is. Would you have let your sister-in-law stand trial?'

'She insisted, Chief Inspector. As a woman with such a story, she would have been acquitted, whereas George would have faced death.'

'All for the family name?'

'All for her mother, Chief Inspector.'

A mother who would cheerfully have allowed such a sacrifice, if she could have got away with it, Auguste reflected grimly.

'Why *did* you go to such lengths to protect your

mother-in-law?' Auguste asked her. 'Were you very fond of her?'

'No. I did not like her very much.'

'For the Tabor name?'

'In a way. It was for George. You could say, Chief Inspector, he is like Tom Griffin. Family is very important to him.'

'Of course, there's no proof the corpse is that of the son born to Rose and Charles Tabor,' Rose ruminated. 'No proof the High Court would accept. That's my opinion, of course. Lawyers might not agree.'

Priscilla's voice trembled as she stood up. 'Thank you, Chief Inspector, Mr Didier.'

'You're a formidable opponent, Lady Tabor.'

She inclined her head in acknowledgment. 'So I am told. It is not always easy. Chief Inspector,' she added as they rose to go, 'I think perhaps there might have been another reason my father-in-law did not marry my late mother-in-law again after Rose's death. It is just possible,' she paused, 'that he might not have wanted to.' Another pause. 'What did that girl die of, Chief Inspector?'

It was Auguste who answered. 'Of love.'

'It's a funny world, Auguste,' Rose grunted as they returned to his rooms. 'When I came here, Priscilla Tabor appeared to be like something out of a Bram Stoker novel, and Miriam Tabor the fair face of the aristocracy. I got it the wrong way round.'

Auguste made his way to the kitchens to bid farewell. Tomorrow they would be returning to London, to the world of haute cuisine, leaving far behind Yorkshire curd pies and puddings.

Breckles clapped him on the back. 'Did I nay say there was an evil eye upon the house? Mischief only needs a short summer to ripen, so my granny do say.'

'You were right, Mr Breckles,' agreed Auguste. 'And so was your crawing hen.'

'Maybe I'll come to London one day and see your kitchen. I'd like to meet that Mr Escoffier you told me about.'

'He is always honoured to meet true artists.'

'Artist?' Breckles guffawed. 'Nay, I'm a cook.'

'An artist. You take the best materials and you turn them into the highest perfection of which they are capable. That is art.'

'Mr Didier,' said Breckles, pumping his hand, 'I'll send thee a Yorkshire Christmas pie. 'Tis my granny's recipe. I'll give tha turkey, grouse, fowl, partridge, pigeons—' he spread his arms wide. 'And not that crawing hen, neither, but woodcocks, wild fowl.' His eyes were glazed with excitement. 'Nutmegs, cloves, mace. All loving one atop t'other in the pie together.'

'Thank you,' said Auguste sincerely, before remembering all too vividly his lack of breakfast. 'In the meantime, a muffin might suffice.'

Laura Tabor stepped out of the police carriage before the steps of Tabor Hall and hesitated. The family was not there to welcome her. Oliver Carstairs was.

'Laura!' He marched purposefully towards her.

'Yes, Oliver.' Her face was carefully composed. It was a struggle but she managed it.

'What's this nonsense I've been hearing about you?'

'They have dropped charges—'

'Not that. About you still being in love with Mariot.'

She hesitated. 'I am.'

'Nonsense.'

'It is the truth.'

'It is not, and you know it.'

'Perhaps.'

'Why then?'

Her head came up proudly. 'This family contained a murderer.'

'I don't intend to marry the family – I'm marrying you.'

'Oh.'

'Or I take that carriage and leave now,' he added, seeing signs of hesitation.

'It's the police carriage. You can't.'

'Then I marry you.'

'Very well, Oliver.'

'What did you say?' Oliver was taken aback. He had expected at least two more exchanges.

'I said *yes!*' she shouted in exasperation at the top of her voice.

Auguste Didier, glancing from the window to see the cause of the disturbance, smiled at the sight of Laura and Oliver kissing full on the lips. Priscilla Tabor, her attention similarly drawn, did not smile. Etiquette, after all, was etiquette. Private emotions were to be hidden, not indulged in outside the stately portico of Tabor Hall.

Oliver would marry Laura, and Victoria would marry Alexander, young Alfred would grow up, Gertie and Cyril return gratefully to their home, Priscilla and George would resume their roles in Society. The Gordale beck would bubble on by and all would be as before. He and Tatiana would return to London, there to begin again their married life. No more struggling as to whether he was acceptable to Society as a gentleman, no more expecting his wife to stay upon her royal pedestal.

Auguste slipped out of the room while Egbert was preoccupied with Cobbold, to escape, to be alone, without even Tatiana. He found himself upon the path to Janet's Foss. He also found Gertie.

'Oh, I am pleased to see you, Auguste. I haven't said goodbye. And I wanted to – like this.' Two hands stole round his neck, two lips were placed on his, as gently as the kiss of a salamander on cream. There was nothing a gentleman – and gentleman he was, he reminded himself proudly – could do but respond.

'There,' she said breathlessly a few minutes later. 'Now we can return to the house.'

'No,' he said hastily, just in case Tatiana should appear at the wrong moment. 'I am on my way to see Gordale Scar. Mr Wordsworth declared it was as "terrific as the lair – Where young lions crouch",' and he escaped, thanking the stars for Tatiana's guidebook and leaving Gertie staring perplexedly after him.

The woods by the beck leading to Janet's Foss reminded him of Rose Griffin's cottage, the Rose of the World, as Tabor had had written on her tombstone. Fair Rosamund, he recalled, who had been poisoned by the King's jealous wife in her labyrinth. A labyrinth like Clapham woods. Had Charles Tabor guessed that Miriam had killed his Rose? Perhaps he had suspected, but had lived with the knowledge. He was a weak man. But for Miriam, it must have been the last tragic irony to realise that the man she loved so much had chosen not to validate their marriage.

Ahead of him across a flat meadow through which the beck ambled its way, the vast limestone cliffs that flanked him to left and right were closing in to meet each other. A limestone mass to his right jutted out in front of him and the path wound around its foot. Round the corner must lie the chasm itself, and its waterfalls. He could hear the roaring water now over the sound of the beck beside him. He followed the path round and found himself in a vast cave, lacking only a roof. The fading light diminished further as the two cliffs met with a crashing waterfall at their junction, shutting out much of the sky. There was no way forward save to clamber up the rocks ahead of him by the side of those waters, tumbling in full spate. The ground under his foot was rocky, nothing green grew there. Where lions roar, indeed; he too felt caged here, glad that a few paces behind him lay easy retreat to the green world of the meadow.

Caged, just as George Tabor felt in London, according to his mother, just like the Shepherd Lord when he returned to claim his inheritance. In contrast Tom Griffin had only wanted a galloper on the open road, untempted by money and power. Like the Shepherd Lord, he had been sent away for his own safety by his mother, and had later returned to his family. But Tom had not been as lucky as the Lord. He had been murdered for a reason as old as man himself: jealousy.

The waterfall hurled itself down from a limestone shelf joining the two cliffs, with such force that it split in two around the huge slab of rock in the centre. Curious to see what was above the limestone, Auguste moved under the cliff face, craning his head upwards to see where the water came from. It was gushing through a hole in the rock, yet above it there was another fall, and above that the top of the scar. He felt dizzy, and suddenly very much alone in the gloom. An unreasoning panic seized him and he spun round. Blocking his path to the only way out was a man, not threatening, but solidly there. He was dressed in a suit so well cut he might have been walking down Jermyn Street. But even so Auguste recognised him.

It was Gregorin.

'*Bonsoir, monsieur.*' The Russian stood still, a cat ready to pounce, every muscle taut. A cat ready for its prey.

Now that the moment had come, adrenalin lent him strength. Auguste nodded coolly, and walked steadily

308

along the path towards him. Towards the only way out. If need be, he could run. Gregorin favoured the knife, not the bullet.

As if by sleight of hand, for surely no bulge had disturbed the pocket of that elegant suit, Gregorin's hand came up with a gun in it. So much for the stiletto – unless he had that too.

'Your ear is better, I trust, Monsieur Didier?'

'It is.' Auguste forced his voice to remain calm. He stopped. There was no way forward, no way back.

'So the time has come.' Gregorin's tone was pleasantly conversational.

He would walk on, call Gregorin's bluff. This charade was merely to frighten him. There were only a few feet left between them. He had taken three steps forward when the shot rang out, chipping the stone at his head, ricocheting past him.

'I think not this way. Back, Monsieur Didier. Please walk back. You need not fear: you may turn to do so. Walk towards the falls.'

He had no option. The sides of the scar closed in menacingly on either side as he approached the falls, the crashing water soaking him to the skin.

'Cross the beck to the other side. Do not be alarmed. It is wet, but not dangerous.'

Auguste obeyed and Gregorin nimbly leapt the stream lower down. 'And now I will kill you,' he called joyfully.

'Why?' Auguste's voice failed to obey him. The sound came out as a squeak.

'You have your job, I have mine, and like yours, mine is a pleasure.'

'I am a *chef*,' Auguste shouted indignantly, forced back against the rock, the water roaring on both sides of him.

'A chef who has married my niece. A Romanov. Most

presumptuous. Moreover, already you are unfaithful.'

Resentment filled Auguste with impotent rage. He had done nothing, *nothing*, to deserve to die thus in the gloom, surrounded by limestone cliffs and waterfalls with no one to hear or care. Even the sheep grazing at the top would not stop their munching, for the sound of the shot would be drowned in the noise of the falls. He had only married the woman he loved and who loved him. It wasn't his fault she was a Russian princess. He hadn't forced her to marry him. She had wanted to.

Such useless, ridiculous thoughts ran through his head. He remembered Tatiana at their wedding, Tatiana at the wheel of a motorcar, Tatiana at the opera in Paris, Tatiana in his arms – oh, never again would he make love to her. If only he could be spared, what a lover he would prove, what a husband he would be. The pistol was ready, pointing. He found himself shouting, then half singing, to make him understand. 'Gregorin, can you not understand how madly I love Tatiana?'

Fractionally the pistol was lowered. Then Gregorin laughed. It was a strange sound to echo round the walls of Auguste's prison chamber. 'I have two passions, Didier. No – stay where you are, if you please. One is for cheese, though, alas I have no cheese stall or Yorkshire wife. The other passion is for the music of Pyotr Tchaikovsky. I deduce that you have recently seen *Eugene Onegin*. It puts me in a tender mood, despite your execrable tenor voice.' He hummed in a surprisingly deep bass voice a few lines from the same aria.

The world is gone mad. Auguste's head spun. *What are we doing singing Grand Opera in the middle of Gordale Scar, when he intends to kill me? Or does he?*

'I cannot shoot a lover of Tchaikovsky in cold blood,

310

Didier, and these pistols are notoriously unreliable at a distance. So I will give you a chance. If you turn and can climb up high enough, while I count to ten, you may yet escape with your life.'

Auguste glanced upwards. He was almost directly underneath the waterfall. If he could make the corner of that crag somehow he might pull himself behind it, escape out of range. There was indeed a natural path of steps in the rock, he realised, but at this time of year could he climb them with all the rain and the water in spate?

Hardly knowing what he was doing, he sprang for a foothold up the rock behind him, then another, and another. He slipped, and scrabbled frantically for a foothold as Gregorin burst into an aria from *The Queen of Spades*, pausing only to count. Up and yet again. Where was the next foothold? There was none. He was lying against the rockface, fear fighting pain.

Down below, Gregorin laughed once more. The sound determined him: he, Auguste Didier, would not die thus.

'I won't do it,' he screamed down over the noise of the water. 'Shoot me facing you. I won't die like a frightened chicken.'

Gregorin shrugged. 'I am loth to kill one for whom I have now some small measure of respect, but I am afraid it really is necessary,' he said regretfully. Crouching down like a cat with his cat's eyes gleaming, he tantalised Auguste by first aiming then lowering the pistol. Then he raised it once more.

If he was going to die, he would die as a Frenchman should. 'I ask you, Gregorin, to tell Tatiana how I died and that I love her.'

The words sounded strange, like a play being acted out, despite the wind howling at one side and the water screaming at his other. If he let go now, the force of the water might kill him anyway, dashing him on to the rocks beneath.

Gregorin shouted, exhilarated, his finger on the trigger, 'Your widow, Didier.'

'Wife, Gregorin.' An almost chatty voice, and a well-aimed stone knocked Gregorin off-balance, sending the gun flying from his hand.

'Egbert!' Auguste croaked. His eyes had been so fixed on imminent death ten feet below, he had not been conscious of Rose's slow, stealthy approach. Nor of the four constables who now pounded round the corner in his support, as Egbert dived for the gun.

Gregorin recovered like a cat, whirling into action, clambering up past Auguste in a flash, knocking him viciously sideways so that he slipped off balance, slithering, then tumbling down the rockface. Gregorin's lithe figure seemed almost to dance with practised ease up by the side of the falls.

Auguste hit the ground, lying half on the stones, half in the beck, bruised and stunned. As he lay there he could see high above him, silhouetted against the patch of sky at the top of the falls, a man who paused briefly to wave to those below – and then was gone.

Egbert Rose was at Auguste's side, as he painfully eased himself up. There was a choke in his voice as he said, 'You damned fool, going off without telling me. We've had someone tailing Gregorin, but he lost him and ran back to tell me. You're lucky Mrs Gertie wanted to kiss you goodbye and knew where you were going.

'Only you, Sherlock,' he continued as he heaved him to his feet, 'only you could find a Moriarty who tries to push you *up* the blasted Reichenbach Falls.'

312